W9-BZP-044

ISBN: 9781075654985

Any references to historical events, real people, or real places are used fictitiously. Names, characters, and places are products of the author's imagination.

Cover by David I. Billingham

www.david-billingham.com

To my boys and girl.

The Life Inside Maggie Pincus

By David Billingham

Book 1: The Heart of the Matter

1

Ignoring the Itch

If you could live anywhere, and I do mean anywhere,
Breezy Lane would probably not spring to mind. In
fact, it probably wouldn't even make it onto your top
ten list. But for the one hundred and twenty-eight
residents who called it home, life didn't get any better.
It was a long, leafy lane with thirty-two perfect little
cottages; each with its own perfect little lawn and
perfect little family. Every morning fathers whistled on
their way to work, and returned home every evening to
smiling mothers and happy children; to spend their
evenings together by cozy fires in warm living rooms.

If you lived on Breezy Lane, you went to bed content and woke up feeling refreshed and ready for, yet, another perfect day.

Unless, of course, you were resident number one hundred and twenty-nine. She didn't think that life on Breezy Lane was all that great. In fact, she thought that just about anywhere else was preferable, for she was Breezy Lane's little secret. She was the one who didn't belong, the one who *wasn't* perfect.

Thud…thud…thud…BANG!

"Maggie…Pincus…get down here now, I'm hungry!" bellowed a deep voice.

Maggie pushed her feet out from under a pile of coats and forced herself to sit up, the noise of a ball bouncing against her door still pounding in her head.

"I'll be right there, Edward," she croaked, still half asleep.

"You've got two minutes!" he said, and then stomped away.

She rubbed her eyes and stared at the damp attic that she called home. Several missing roof tiles allowed dusty shafts of daylight to shine through the darkness, illuminating a room of bare wooden beams, stuffed with furry pink insulation. Several pots and pans balanced precariously across the empty spaces, each filled with graying rainwater that trembled with every vibration in the cottage. Various planks of old wood crisscrossed the bare beams to create a path from the bed to an old dresser that stood in the shadows.

Maggie sleepily balanced her way across the room. She knelt in front of a small mirror propped up against the dresser, as something small scurried away into the shadows. A large frying pan served as a sink. Maggie scooped up its contents, bending over to splash the freezing rainwater in her face to try and wake herself up. The attic had been unusually cold last night. Even with all of her father's old coats she struggled to stay warm. Several times she had been awoken by her own shivering, only to lie there watching her misty breath until she fell back to sleep. Again, she dipped her hands into the water, this time pulling back the dark hair that hung in front of her face. For a second, she hesitated. Staring into the pan's rippling contents, nervous of what she was about to do, and then, very slowly, she lifted her face and looked in the mirror.

"Hey you," she whispered.

Her eyes looked too tired to belong to a twelve-year-old. Her features were divided into two distinct halves, each separated by a river of tender pink skin that ran from the top of her head and down to her chin.

The right side of the face was Maggie, a pretty girl with a pale complexion, freckles, and a bright blue eye. To the left was a girl called by many names, most of which made her cry. This girl's face sagged noticeably and was patched with lines that gave her skin the look of an old greasy, brown paper bag that had been carelessly scrunched into a ball. Her lips bore deep cracks that flaked painfully downward, creating a permanent grimace that wilted loosely to the side. Only the blue of her eye showed that this girl was still Maggie, the drooping eyelid unable to hide its shine.

As she stared at her two halves, a small line of drool appeared from between her withered lips. She dabbed at it with the sleeve of an old work jacket, wincing as she felt her skin break under her touch. She took a deep breath, opened a drawer, and began to dress. It was time to make breakfast.

Of all Maggie's daily chores, making breakfast was the one she hated most. She had learned long ago that avoiding the company of her family was a good idea, and one that seemed to be equally popular with them. But breakfast was a different story. Having gone a whole eight hours without food, her three brothers always awoke in a ravenous mood, eager to aim their grumpiness at Maggie until breakfast was prepared.

"Is it ready yet? Is it ready yet? Is it ready yet? Is it ready yet?" repeated her brother Edward, as she struggled to juggle the four pans of food that were bubbling and spitting on top of the stove.

"Don't forget the mushrooms, and don't cook them too long. I like some soft and some crispy!" shouted her brother, Andrew, who sat two feet away from her.

"I'll have some mushrooms too, Pincus, but not the ones you grow on your face, save those for yourself! And get a move on, will you? We're starving here! We'll be nothing but bones in a minute!" said her eldest brother, Charles.

Maggie felt her frustration rising. She turned to stare at the three of them, fighting a deep urge to respond. There were many ways to describe her older brothers but starving was not one that immediately sprung to mind; their huge bodies made the kitchen table look like furniture from a nursery school.

Charles, Andrew, and Edward all had dirty blond hair with thick, ruddy faces; each of their broad jaws sported at least one cut or bruise. They were also all unusually large for their ages, with wide, muscular chests that strained their school uniforms as if they were grown men on their way to a fancy dress party.

Together, they were one of the most feared scrums in schoolboy rugby, they were predicted to, one day, play for England.

Unfortunately, years of training left little time for education. While their bodies were covered with large muscles, Maggie had long suspected that all the fat in their bodies had taken refuge in their empty minds.

"Breakfast is ready," said Maggie slowly, staring at her three brothers before deciding she was too tired to deal with them.

With three large plates of eggs, bacon, sausage, mushrooms, black pudding, beans, tomatoes, and fried bread finally in front of them, the brothers stopped trying to annoy Maggie and turned to the only other subject they seemed to know anything about.

"I can't wait 'til we play St. Henry's School tonight," said Edward through a mouthful of food, spraying particles of egg and sausage across the table. "I'm going to smash that McKenzie kid's face in. I'll show him how we play *real* rugby!"

"Yeah, give him one for me while you're there," replied Andrew, sending more food back in the opposite direction. "He scored against me last summer, then he had the nerve to go off injured when I fell on him. Total accident it was! I lost my balance while I was trying to hit him! I think he broke three ribs!"

All three guffawed loudly, sending a triple food spray across the table.

Having never been asked to go to one of their games, Maggie was unsure of the rules of rugby, but from listening to her brothers, it seemed to be a game where little people tried to get the ball away from big people who, then, tried to find ways to hurt the little people, without the referee finding out. From all the practice they got on her at home, she imagined they were very good at it, especially since here they didn't need a ball or referee.

"Hoi, Pincus!" said Charles, through a mouthful of sausage, "Mum said, last night, to tell you your list is on the fridge and to wake you up early so that you can get started on it before breakfast. You've got lots of extra jobs to do for her party."

"Oh, that's just great! Thank-you!" said Maggie, gritting her teeth, as she scoured the lists taped to the fridge.

"You're welcome, ugly!" said Charles.

Maggie's Jobs for Tuesday
Complete your daily list first.

*Do not forget that today is a Tuesday—so
clean all stair rails and door handles!*

*My boys shall be home at their usual time. They
have requested a pork dinner with roasted
potatoes, I will be joining them. Prepare my
usual.*

*Number of days to my Annual Garden Party: 12!
You have much to do, make haste!*

To-Do List

Laundry: wash, iron, starch, fold.

Lawn: trim hedges and remove all pebbles.

*Silverware: re-polish. Yesterday's work was not
good enough!*

Driveway: arrange gravel neatly.

Boys' Rooms: clean and remove smell.

Car: wash and wax.*

Light switches: check for fingerprints!

*Attic door: paint. It is covered with dirty round
marks.*

*Boys' game room: clean the food stains off their
TV.*

*Windows: re-wash. I can see fingerprints. Not up
to my standards!*

Smoke detectors: replace batteries, (not in attic).

Electric gates: broken.**

Boys' bathroom: the toilet is blocked again.
*Must be done after two o'clock, but before
three. I have an appointment that I will not be
late for.
** Visitors arriving at twelve o'clock. Be in the
bushes to operate manually at ten to twelve.
At midday, I shall be receiving the Major and his
good lady wife. Prepare a light lunch for three
and leave it in the sunroom at eleven fifty-five.
Do not let anyone *see you this time. I do not*
need your deformities upsetting anyone else!
-Victoria Linley-Eisenberg-Teddington-Pincus

Maggie's heart sank. It would be long after dark
before she could finish all the jobs. Suddenly her back
ached and her feet felt sore. She looked through the list
again but it was no use. It was going to be another long
day.

Ding went the clock on the wall. In an instant the
room was flooded with cold, brittle air.

Ding!

Maggie quickly harried a fresh pot of tea onto
the table, wiping away the food spray. The brothers fell
silent, beginning to preen themselves by tucking in
shirts and flattening their hair with eggy saliva. The

routine was a familiar one to them now, each knowing that at exactly eight o'clock their mother would join them for breakfast and their daily inspection.

As the eighth *ding* sounded, Victoria Linley-Eisenberg-Teddington-Pincus entered the room. She was a tall, dark-haired woman with a nose that pointed up and a mouth that hung down, as if she constantly smelled something unpleasant. As always, in case anybody dared to forget, she was dressed in all widow-black.

She paused for a moment to take in the kitchen, her eyes circling it as she surveyed for imperfections. Annoyed at being unable to find any, she strode over to the kitchen table glancing briefly at the first three photographs along the wall. Her deceased husbands smiled out from their golden frames, each standing next to an increasingly dour wife, until the fourth picture. A small passport photo of Maggie's father, which had been sticky-taped to the wall...sideways.

"Good morning, boys."

"Good morning, Mother," said the three boys in unison.

Maggie placed a single, boiled egg with toast in front of her stepmother and stood back to watch as her long fingers picked at the shell.

"Satisfactory, child, it shall do," said Victoria, coldly, squeezing the peeled egg before taking a bite and dabbing the corner of her mouth with a napkin.

The three brothers looked on with disappointment. Nothing amused them more than watching their mother pick on Maggie and having finished their breakfast, they were hoping for a show. Rarely did a morning go by without this entertainment and, by now, they counted on it to begin their day and distract their mother from asking them to do anything educational.

Each of them exchanged disappointed glances as they struggled to think of a way to get her into trouble…quickly.

"Maggie, did you clean my rugby boots?"

"Yes, Charles, I did."

"Maggie did you wash my school blazer?"

"Yes, Andrew, I did."

"Maggie, did you finish that homework for me?"

"Why yes, Edward, I did."

For a moment, there was silence as the brothers tried to think. Out the corner of her eye their mother flicked a look at them, ordering them to give her something she could use on the stepchild she despised.

"Is there any more bacon?" asked Andrew brightly, surprising himself that he had remembered Maggie throwing away an empty packet that morning.

"No, Andrew, but I can make you some more eggs if you'd like," said Maggie, forcing a smile.

"Maggie!" snapped her stepmother, pouncing on the opportunity. "We have previously addressed the need for the boys to be properly fed. They are, after all, one day going to represent England at our national sport. Their chances of success should not be lessened because you cannot do a few simple jobs. I have arranged for some very influential people to talk to them at my garden party and they should be looking their very best, not as though I starve them. This is a big day for us all! The fact that you were chosen to be one of life's…mistakes…does not mean that others should suffer."

Maggie stared at her stepmother. All the things she longed to say. Things she had rehearsed, many times, ran through her mind wanting, desperately, to come out.

"Yes, Mother, I'm sorry. It won't happen again," she whimpered.

"Be sure it doesn't!" barked her stepmother, annoyed at how easily Maggie had given in, yet again. "Now go and clean the kitchen...again!"

Silence fell over the room, once more, as Victoria sat motionless. Her three boys sat wondering who would pay the price for the poor ammunition she had been given to use on Maggie.

"It seems, boys, that we have a few minutes until you have to leave for school. I suggest we use this time to practice your French," said Victoria, "let us begin."

For the next twenty minutes, Maggie busied herself cleaning. Her mood steadily brightened, as she happily listened to the sounds of her brothers trying to pretend that they bothered to learn anything in French class, much to their mother's annoyance.

Maybe this isn't going to be such a bad day after all! Maggie thought to herself as her stepmother lost her temper, for the third time, squawking furiously at Andrew, who instead of asking in French for a double room with a shower, had asked to buy an airplane ticket for a policeman and his two sheep.

Finally, the sound of a car in the driveway signaled their release.

"Have a good day, boys! *Au revoir!*" said Maggie, brightly, as the three huge boys left for school, each growling as they stomped past her toward the hallway.

"Mother," said Charles, excitedly, suddenly appearing back at the table, "I thought you should know, I did tell Maggie that you wanted her to start early but she thought she'd ignore you and lay in bed instead."

Victoria glared at Maggie, unable to hide her delight at being given a reason to punish her.

"That's not true," said Maggie, "he didn't tell me until this morning!"

"Why, thank-you, Charles. That is most enlightening," said Victoria, ignoring Maggie's words as her eyes blazed into her stepdaughter. "I shall be sure to give her additional duties, if she has so much time to waste. Perhaps you can help by giving her your rugby boots to clean tonight? I have a feeling you'll be treading in something simply awful today after the game."

Charles smiled broadly at his mother.

"Yes, Mother," he said happily.

Maggie's heart sank. It was going to be another bad day.

2

Scratching the Surface

It was the day of the big garden party and Maggie had already been standing at the kitchen sink for four straight hours. Pruned skin covered her hands, and the front of her T-shirt and shorts were damp with dirty dishwater as yet another tray of dirty plates and glasses arrived through the hatch in the window. Maggie, dutifully, dumped everything into the soapy water, scrubbing at the greasy fingerprints and bright red lipstick marks. As she let out a deep yawn, she could feel the skin around the corner of her mouth crack under the strain. *Just great,* she thought to herself, wiping at the blood with her sleeve, *and only three more hours of this to go.*

The garden outside was a sea of perfect summer dresses and linen sports jackets, all spreading themselves across the manicured lawn, as they talked and laughed in the warm sun. A quartet of violins drifted classical music through the air. Waiters in high-necked jackets served the guests, who sat around tables decorated with large bouquets of flowers, as the waiters sweated and weaved their way between them with trays of colorful drinks and miniature sandwiches. In the middle of it all stood their proud hostess, dressed in all black, surveying her creation.

The Linley annual garden party had become *the* important date on the village's social calendar, a must-be-invite for anyone-who-was-someone-in-the-community, with local dignitaries coming from far and wide for an afternoon of knowing winks and meaningful handshakes. To miss it was social suicide, and anyone who wanted to belong was there.

For Victoria, it was her yearly chance to let them all know how important she was. It was a reminder that only *she* held the keys to social success in this village and they weren't to forget it. But, this year, she had a second agenda. Money was getting low and she needed a husband. If the guests knew how low her funds were, well, she shuddered to think.

Fortunately, there was no shortage of men willing to take on a wife who could further their careers quite like the good widow could. And while even she was willing to admit that she was not quite the beauty she once was, she knew it mattered little. When one had connections, like hers, one would always be attractive to any of the single businessmen of the town, and even some of the married ones.

Today's group of guests seemed to have provided her with a particularly good group of future husbands. True, they were a little younger than she would have liked, but all of them shared one wonderful trait. They were all rich and just stupid enough not to question the mountain of debts she would need them to pay for her once they were married—a mountain of debt she had amassed since her disastrous last marriage to Bert Pincus.

She met Maggie's father at a housewarming party for the new town Magistrate. She was the queen of the local society and he, unbeknown to her, was a lowly plumber. He'd been invited only because he'd hit it off with the kindly Magistrate during a conversation over the installation of a new toilet. While he had mistaken her for a kind and caring woman, who would be a good mother to his only child, she had mistaken him for being rich. So strong was their belief that each had been happy to pretend to be what the other thought they were for three weeks into their hastily arranged marriage. The truth only came out when he had died of a heart attack. In return, she had nearly suffered the same fate at the reading of his will, when he'd left her everything he had—a beaten-up old van, a book on how to sanitize sewerage pits, a dog with fleas, and Maggie.

A waiter slid another tray of glasses under the partition that had been built to hide Maggie from the guests, and banged on the board to let her know that more work had arrived. Someone had gone to the trouble of smearing these particular glasses with a tuna sandwich before dipping them in dirt. Maggie pictured her brothers giggling amongst themselves, as they thought of how to make her job harder.

She liked to think that she could handle anything they could throw at her by now. After all, she had scrubbed their boots, washed their underpants, and even cleaned their toilet. But, as she saw the graying pieces of tuna stuck to the glass, she was suddenly overcome with an overwhelming desire to vomit.

"She's backing up again, I told you that pump wouldn't hold," said a voice.

Maggie let out a huge burp, instantly recoiling at the smell under her nose.

"Alright, it's out. You can let control know, we got it," said the voice, "and while you're there send a nerve down to digestion. Tell them not to release anything into chamber three until I tell them. It's probably going to be at least an hour, hang on...make that two hours."

Maggie spun around to see who was behind her, only to be greeted by an empty kitchen.

"Hello?" she said, nervously.

"What do you say we have a quick cup of tea then go downstairs and have a look at that pump?" came the reply.

"Hello...Charles...Andrew...Phillip? Is that you?" said Maggie, searching the room.

Outside, her three step brothers had just finished telling a large group of men about their latest rugby game and were now challenging each of them to punch them as hard as they could in the stomach. In the kitchen Maggie heard a yell, and looked out through the small gap in the window, just in time, to see the mayor holding his fist in pain, as Charles stood proudly motionless.

Okay, stay calm, Maggie. You're just hearing the voices from outside, that's all, she thought, a cold tingle dancing up her spine.

"Oh thank-you, sweetheart. Any chance of a chocolate biscuit?"

Okay, that was definitely not from outside, thought Maggie.

"What do you mean she can hear me?" said the voice.

"Whoever that is, please stop now," said Maggie, backing into a corner, "this isn't funny!"

"Really? And you're sure she can hear me?"

"Please stop," said Maggie.

This time, there was no reply. Maggie stood there listening to the sounds of laughter and music drifting in from outside, waiting for the voice.

Only, there was no voice. There was only a scream. Maggie rushed to the window to see her brother, Edward, standing rigid at the end of the garden, pointing into the bushes as he unleashed a yell that caused several of the guests to cover their ears. Drinks were spilled and tiny sandwiches were dropped, as all of them watched the large muscular boy screaming like a young girl.

Confusion started to spread through the crowd. Everyone stood motionless, all of them unsure what to do. Only the widow seemed to be able to move.

"Stop doing that this instant!" she snarled at her eldest son, Charles.

Charles, who was enjoying the show, suddenly seemed annoyed. He walked over to his brother who, by now, had stopped screaming and stood frozen with one thick finger still pointing out into the bushes.

"I don't know what you're playing at but she'll get you good for this one," he whispered, before grabbing Edward by the neck and spinning him around to face the garden. The guests let out a gasp as they saw the large dark stain on the front of Edward's trousers, followed by several sniggers as everyone realized he had wet himself.

"DEAD PEOPLE!" shouted Edward, "DEAD PEOPLE...HERE...DEAD!"

The guests' confusion was growing, as the large boy kept screaming. Charles began to drag Edward toward his mother. She began to tap her knife against an empty glass before waving her two sons over, as they struggled between the guests.

"LADIES AND GENTLEMEN...LADIES AND GENTLEMEN," she announced, as Charles unceremoniously dumped his younger brother at her feet with a kick he hoped only his mother would see.

"Ladies and gentlemen, first let me thank you all for coming. I cannot tell you how wonderful it is to see so many of you here today and how much it means to share my annual garden party with you," she said, bowing her head.

Half of the guests understood her signal and managed polite applause. The rest of the crowd stood staring at Edward who, by now, was curled into a ball on the lawn sobbing the words, *dead people*, over and over.

"As you may or may not know," she continued, "I am a widow. It has been my burden that my husbands, Phillip, Henry, George, and Bernard, were all in poor health at the time of our marriages. I can only say that, despite how short my time was with each of them, I cherish every moment that we were able to share."

On cue, Victoria let loose a tear as Andrew scrambled forward with a fresh handkerchief in hand.

"I thought we weren't doing this until after the dessert?" he whispered as he placed a comforting arm around her.

"Well that was before your brother went crazy, wasn't it, stupid boy?" she whispered from behind the handkerchief while hugging her son with performed tenderness.

"I can only say that the stress of losing these wonderful men has been shared by my sons. My wonderful, caring sons, who are all predicted to, one day, play rugby for England. They, too, feel the pain of the great loss we have suffered, as a family, and I can only say that sometimes it becomes too much for us all," she said, placing a gentle hand atop Edward's head. Maggie could tell she was fighting the urge to scratch him with her nails.

The guests let out a group sigh, showing their sympathy. Victoria felt a surge of relief. Edward would pay later but, for now, she had a job to do, and had turned this embarrassing moment into a triumph. One of her potential husbands caught her eye and she smiled bravely at him. He raised a fist to her, as though willing her to be strong. He received a fluttering of wet eyelashes in return.

"But this is a day for celebration, for friendship, for…" Victoria suddenly found herself cut short by a moaning from the back of the garden.

Hhhuuurrrggghhh.

The guests turned to the look but Victoria was determined to keep their attention, "For friendship, for togetherness, for…"

"Hhhhhhuuuuurrrrrrgggggghhhhh," came the moan again, louder and deeper this time.

"For celebrating how much we all care about one another as a community, for..." But, nobody was listening now. All eyes were on the bushes and the terrible noise that was coming from within.

Hhhhhhhhuuuuuuurrrrrrrggggggghhhhhhh.

A wave of confused fear rushed over the group as the moan filled the garden. The bushes were shaking, sending leaves flying in all directions. Guests slowly started to back away toward the house. The noise of the brush moving under heavy feet became louder and angrier as glimpses of movement showed through the undergrowth. Something big was coming.

HHHHHHHHHHUUUUUUUUUURRRRRRRRR RRRRGGGGGGGGGHHHHHHHHHH.

The last of the guests was about to arrive.

3

A Break in the Skin

Maggie watched them burst out onto the lawn in a shower of broken branches and leaves, stumbling forward as their huge feet dug deep holes in the grass. For a second, they stood looking at the guests, surveying their new surroundings. Each of them was well over seven feet tall. Their bodies appeared to be made out of mismatched parts that hung awkwardly at their sides, forcing many of them to lean dramatically, to one side, as if they were turning an everlasting corner. Thick limbs, stitched together with old shoelaces, strained under their weight, revealing browning muscles behind the edges of dead skin. Flies crawled everywhere, darting in and out of their unblinking eyes, as they tickled the edges of large cuts that showed through the holes in their ripped and tattered clothing.

Then, as if by some unspoken signal, they surged forward as one, while creating a wave of screams as they ran at the group with surprising speed. Some of the guests tried to run but it was already too late. Six huge figures surrounded them, like watchtowers, staring at the prey caught in their trap.

A shocked silence fell upon the crowd, broken only by the gentle sobbing of Edward.

"Maggie Pincus. Bring here," breathed the largest one, through unmoving lips, with a rotting finger pointing at its feet.

Inside the kitchen, Maggie was open-mouthed. What was happening? First, the voices, and now this? She needed to find help. She needed the police, but how? There was no phone in the kitchen and Victoria had locked the only door. Her only escape would be to go out the window, towards the things—the things that were saying her name.

"Maggie Pincus…NOW," bellowed one of them, releasing a blast of rotten breath that sent several of the guests' hats flying.

In the middle of the crowd Victoria glared at them, as Edward and Charles cowered next to her.

"Whoever they are, they are ruining my party! Get them out of here now!" she growled, pushing her sons between herself and the things.

Standing in their visitor's shadow, the brothers looked up into his barren face. Edward sobbed, releasing a watery line of snot down his chin. They were far more used to being the biggest ones in the room and were not enjoying this game of role reversal. Fear filled them. They froze, before turning to one another to agree on an unspoken plan.

"Help..." they both whimpered.

"Oh, for goodness sake," snapped their mother, pushing between them to stride toward the largest of the invaders, "now look here, whoever you are, this is a private party for which you have no invite so I strongly suggest that you leave this instant! Obviously, we are civilized people here! We have no desire to have your kind, whatever you are inside those ridiculous outfits, here with us. So, I highly recommend that you do the decent thing, and leave now. Your little joke has gone quite far enough!"

Two pools of black stared down on her, as though examining a naughty child having a tantrum.

"You are Victoria Pincus?"

"That's Ms. Linley-Eisenburg-Teddington-Pincus," sniffed Victoria. "Was there something that I could help you with, before you leave?"

"Your husbands…we know what you did," he breathed.

The words seemed to hit her, like a train, snapping her calm exterior. She was left struggling for words.

"How…who…how dare you?" she forced, poking at his stomach, only to feel his skin tear like paper as her finger sank inward. Standing there, frozen in horror, she stared at her perfectly manicured finger that was now dipped deep inside him, like a stick stuck in the mud. A thick grey liquid was oozing out from either side.

"Get me Maggie," said the creature, bending over to draw his face to hers, "or should I tell everybody your dirty little secret?" he whispered, as Victoria's eyes widened.

Maggie still hadn't moved from the sink when she heard her mother unlock the door and step inside. Time seemed to have stopped since she had watched her stepmother leave to come and fetch her. All she could think of was how she was about to be taken outside, to the six huge things that looked like pieces of dead people sewn together. She didn't know why they wanted her or what they planned on doing. But, if there was one thing she did know, it was this—she was going to do everything possible to avoid finding out.

"Maggie, darling, I need you to come outside with me for a moment," said Victoria, brightly, clearly hoping that Maggie was unaware of what was happening.

Maggie stood frozen, with her back to her, as she scoured her mind for an escape.

"I don't feel very well…I'll stay here, if that's okay," said Maggie trying to sound calm.

"Come with me now, please," said Victoria, with all the niceness she could muster.

"I saw them…I can't go out there. I won't. I'm scared."

Victoria felt a surge of anger. She needed Maggie to go outside and she needed her to go willingly. She could always drag her. It wasn't an unpleasant option. But, how would the things that were holding her party hostage receive it? More importantly, how would it look to her guests?

"Maggie, please, this is very important. Now, I know you may be a little scared, but there is nothing to worry about. I'm sure they just want to talk to you."

"I can't do it," said Maggie, her voice cracking.

"You will do what I tell you to, you little—!" Victoria struggled to contain her anger.

Maggie turned, her own anger rising while she listened to her stepmother urging her to go outside, letting her know, once again, how unimportant she was. Suddenly, it was all too much for her to take. The voices, the things outside, the life of slavery, her constant tiredness, all of it came rushing upward, refusing to contain itself any longer.

"I'M NOT GOING OUT THERE!" she screamed.

Maggie had seen her stepmother angry before. She knew the signs and had long ago learned when to make a quick exit. But as she watched her eyes bulge and her top lip grizzle into a snarl, she knew that this time she wasn't going anywhere. For the first time, in a long time, she felt strong.

"Maggie, I will say this only once," said Victoria through gritted teeth, "You are going to walk out of this house with me and behave like the daughter that you should have been. Do not forget that it is I who took you in when nobody wanted you and I who will gladly put you out on the street if you do not do this. You owe me and now is the time for you to show me a little gratitude!"

Maggie stared in amazement. "I owe you? For what? Being your slave? Living in your attic? Not being allowed to go to school? Having you treat me like dirt? If my dad were here…"

"Your father," snapped Victoria, darting forward, "was a sniveling little man who lied to me. He was a worthless, penniless, pathetic excuse of a man who told me he had money. If I had known who he really was before I married him, then you and I wouldn't even be here. But he was a liar, and I'm stuck with you. So, you are going to do what I tell you!"

"He loved you," lashed Maggie, tears welling up in her eyes, "and he *wasn't* lying. He *was* rich and I know where his money is!"

Victoria stared at her with eyes that were, suddenly, shining.

"What do you mean he still is? Did that horrible little man have money after all?"

Maggie stood in silence, regret filling her face as her mind searched for what to do next.

"I knew it! I knew I smelled money on him the first time we met! I'm never wrong! Oh, this *is* good news, indeed!" said Victoria, who was now holding a conversation with herself. "No more fat, slobbering excuses for husbands! Tell me, Maggie, how much? How much money is there?"

Maggie stared up into her stepmother's face. "Do I still have to go outside if I tell you?" she said calmly.

"Of course you don't," said Victoria brightly, "you're far more important than any of those sniveling little idiots, that call themselves my friends, out there. And besides, what is the worst that those things could do? So, they tell a few stories about me. Nobody will believe them, not with my reputation, especially if I have money. You've seen them. As long as I'm rich, there's nothing I can't make those idiots out there do! I have to admit, I was starting to get a little worried. Just between you and me, if people knew how low my funds were…well, that doesn't really matter anymore —not if I have his money! So, tell me, where is the money?"

"I won't tell you," Maggie said. "I'll never tell you."

Victoria glared at her, the urge to charm her stepdaughter overwhelmed by hatred.

"Why, you, ungrateful freak!" she spat. "I've put up with four pathetic, little husbands for their money and if you think that an ugly little runt, like you, is going to stand in the way of what is rightfully mine, then you are sadly mistaken. You will tell me where that money is now or so help me, I shall make you!"

Victoria's mouth twitched as she stood face-to-face with Maggie, their eyes exchanging mutual hatred, as a warm breeze rushed between them. Over Maggie's shoulder a sudden gust of wind sent the net curtains billowing upward to reveal the faces of the guests outside. All of them were staring into the kitchen, through the open windows, at Victoria Linley-Eisenburg-Teddington-Pincus and her stepdaughter.

"I took down the partition while you were on your way in here. Just a suggestion, you might want to close the kitchen windows if you want to have a private conversation," said Maggie, "and I was just kidding… there isn't any money."

4

Signs of Infection

For the guests at 9 Breezy Lane, time seemed to stand still. Nobody had expected an afternoon quite like this. Being taken hostage by six large things, who looked more dead than alive, had been dramatic enough, but to then watch their host embarrass herself so badly...well, it was all quite unexpected and not at all appropriate for an English garden party. They would have all quite happily, and politely, excused themselves as a way to express their disgust, but as long as they were stuck here, they had to admit, it was enthralling to watch. Even their captors seemed to be enjoying the show playing out in the kitchen, their black eyes fixed on Victoria and the deformed girl.

Inside the pair stood motionless, Victoria's mind spinning with what had just happened. The creatures outside, suddenly, seemed irrelevant. Maggie had opened the windows so that everyone could hear their conversation. She had been tricked and would now be a social laughing stock. First the money, and now the power was gone. She had to fix this…but how? No one would marry her, not now that they knew she was poor. Everything was destroyed…because of Maggie.

As she watched her stepmother's face twisting inward, Maggie suddenly felt all of her newfound confidence drain away. It should have been the moment of triumph she had always wanted, the one she had dreamt of, when she finally showed the world who her stepmother truly was. But now that it was here, she realized that one thing was missing—an escape plan.

"I think maybe I will go outside after all," said Maggie, who had just decided that anything was preferable to staying in the kitchen with her stepmother.

Without reply, Victoria slowly crossed the kitchen to close the windows. Drawing shut the thick red curtains, she turned to face Maggie, her hands gripping the edges of the counter.

"Oh, you will go out there, young lady, but not before you and I have a moment alone. Do you realize what you just did? Do you have any idea how much you just humiliated me? Do you?" she hissed.

For a second, Maggie's newfound bravery returned, tempting her to answer, before Victoria's purple face made her think twice.

"You've embarrassed me for the last time! After all that I've done for you! Well I'll tell you this. You are going to fix this for me. We are going to march outside and you are going to tell everyone that you were lying…that it was just a sick little joke from your twisted imagination."

Maggie stared at the floor, despair flooding her, when a line of ants that were trickling out from under the fridge caught her eye. How she wished that she could swap places with any one of them. Even a life that small had to be better than being her right now.

"Are you listening to me?" spat Victoria.

But Maggie wasn't listening, she was still watching the ants who suddenly seemed to be rushing in all directions to form, what looked like, words.

H…e…l…p…h

Maggie squinted and looked again, sure that she must be seeing things.

H…e…l…p…h…e…r…e…m

"What?" said Maggie, under her breath.

"Is there no end to your insolence child?" Victoria said, her face turning from purple to red, "Do not push me any further!"

But Maggie didn't hear her. She was glued to the message that the ants seemed to be forming.

H…e…l…p…h…e…r…e…m…a…g…g…i…e

"Are you trying to talk…to me?" said Maggie.

"HOW DARE YOU?!" screamed Victoria, rushing across the room as she crushed Maggie's name beneath her foot.

Instinctively, Maggie snapped from her trance and threw her arms over her head, preparing for her stepmother's charge, only to be surrounded by a loud crash. The window exploded inward, showering them both with broken glass. Victoria screamed, as a black hooded figure emerged through the downpour, sending her flying in a circle over the top of the kitchen table. Shards of glass flew in every direction. Maggie watched, as though in slow motion, as the intruder slowly got to his feet and turned to face her. Pulling back his hood, he revealed a beaming smile beneath a mass of blond hair that spiked in all directions. For a second, she stared into his blue eyes. They burned into hers, making her feel as though he could see inside her.

"Maggie!" he said, excitedly, as if they were long lost friends, rushing over to wrap two thin arms around her, "Oh Maggie, it's so good to see you!"

Maggie didn't know what to say. She stood frozen in his embrace, trying desperately to think of who he might be. He wasn't family and she had no school friends. She had no friends at all, so who was he?

"We have so much to talk about!" he said, excitedly. "But there will be time for that, once we get you home."

"Do...do I know you?" stammered Maggie.

"A lot better than you think!" he replied. "But, there's plenty of time for that later. Right now, we need to get you away from those things outside. Oh, and also that rather angry woman behind me!"

Maggie peered over his shoulder to see her stepmother sprawled by the radiator, her face raging with anger, as she slowly got to her feet—a murderous look in her eyes.

"See," he said, without looking back, "don't you agree it's time we got out of here?"

Without waiting for an answer, he quickly scooped Maggie up into his arms, cradling her to his chest like a newborn baby, before turning to leave. The shards of glass crunched beneath his bare feet.

"You may want that. You won't be coming back," he said nodding at the small photograph on the wall.

Maggie took the picture of her father with a trembling hand, and buried it tight into her neck.

The next moment they were flying backwards through the broken window, as Victoria lunged at them, her fingers curling around empty space before crashing painfully into the kitchen cupboard. A rush of warm air filled Maggie's lungs as they emerged outside to land softly on the edge of the lawn. From inside her cradle she could hear screaming. Peeking out, she saw the guests running in every direction, as they found themselves suddenly free of the guards, who were now scrambling toward her with their grey hands outstretched.

"Hold tight," he said, spinning away, as one of the things dived at them with its face twisted in desperation.

Before she could think, they were sprinting down the garden, as more things closed in on them.

Maggie felt a huge weight grab her ankle. She looked down to see one of the things hanging from her leg, as it was dragged behind them, refusing to let go. Maggie began kicking, furiously, at its huge, rotten hand. Suddenly a loud *CRACK* filled the air, as its wrist snapped. The thing slid on without them while bouncing across the lawn to demolish several tables. Its separated grey hand hung loosely from her ankle before, finally, falling free into a flowerbed.

Instantly, they accelerated at an incredible speed. Maggie felt herself sucked into the man's chest, feeling as though they had just been shot out of a cannon. Everything became a blur. Only after rubbing her eyes, did she risk peeking out from under his arm, just in time to see her house fade rapidly into the distance. The things bellowed her name, as her stepmother's furious face quickly shrank away into nothing.

"Won't be long, Maggie. I just need to get out of fly range and I'll slow down. Don't worry, they can't catch us," he said, in the same casual voice he had used in the kitchen. Maggie tried to look up at his face, but nearly lost her grip so had to be satisfied with forcing her head back into his body. Beneath them, his feet were blurred into a storm of activity, propelling them forward faster than most cars could travel, let alone a man carrying a twelve-year-old girl.

For several minutes, they continued. Maggie's mind was a whirlwind of confusion, as she tried to make sense of everything that was happening to her. She was happy to have escaped the things back at the cottage. And, she was particularly pleased to be away from her, much scarier, stepmother. But, was she really safe now? This man had saved her, but from what? And how was he able to move so fast, without even losing any breath?

"I think we should be safe to stop now," he said, still sounding as if he was just out taking a stroll.

Maggie watched his feet slowly come back into focus. The world around them returned to normal as they slowed to a casual jog before, finally, coming to a stop on a dark, concrete floor. Looking around, she was surprised to find that the green trees and fields of Breezy Lane no longer surrounded them. Instead, she found they were in a red brick alley, next to a large dumpster, piled high with yellow trash bags. Windows spotted the dirty walls high above them, several of which were broken or boarded up. Oil-stained trickles of water ran between the brickwork. Shadows hung heavily around them. Through the dark, Maggie could just make out two lines of buckets that ran down either side of the alley's walls. Thin lines of heat rose from them, like the sun on hot tarmac, as they released an acid smell that stung Maggie's eyes.

"It's a vinegar mix. My own recipe," said the man, proudly, giving a nod to one of the buckets as he lowered her to the floor. "Flies can't stand it…stops their wings working…thought it might buy us some time until we can get you transported."

"What…transport…what's happening?" asked Maggie, as a line of drool ran from the corner of her mouth. In all of the excitement Maggie had forgotten about her face and she blushed, as she realized she was around someone who hadn't seen her before. Quickly she dabbed at her spit, embarrassment rushing over her. She looked down at her feet, trying desperately to hide her deformity. Then she felt it. A warm hand pressed itself against her withered cheek.

"Well, look at that," said the man, turning her face to get a better look. "Just when you think they don't have any more tricks! It looks as though they cut off all the power in the jaw and drained the fluid in the cheek. That must have shut down any eye muscles that were still working. I guess they thought that with all those levels removed, they would be able to access the mind's central chamber. They were wrong, but it's still very clever. Of course, it's a total waste of a body. I mean, it's completely irreversible."

Maggie, who was more used to people staring in shock at her, looked back at him, perplexed.

"The internals," he said, seeing her confusion. "They shut down part of your face to try to get to you."

Maggie continued to stare at him.

"You do understand what I'm talking about, don't you?" he continued, with a raised eyebrow.

"No," replied Maggie, "am I supposed to?"

His stare told her that he couldn't believe what he was hearing. "Well, considering who your father is, I presumed that you would have some sort of idea about all of this!" he shouted.

"ENOUGH!" bellowed a voice from the shadows, both of them turned toward the sound.

A tall man strode out of the dark toward them. His eyes were fixed on Maggie's rescuer, who stared angrily at his approach. For a second, one arm raised, as if he was about to attack them. He paused and, instead, pushed a long silver strand of hair behind his ear. He came to a halt next to them. Standing in his shadow, Maggie stared up, trying to see the face inside the hood of his long cloak. She watched his breath mist the air between them.

"Enough," he said, gently this time, placing his hand on the man's shoulder, "there will be plenty of time for her to learn who she is. Now is the time to celebrate her return to our family."

The man gave an almost undetectable shudder. His face still full of anger as he glared into the older man's eyes, only for them to ignore him—their gaze refused to leave Maggie. Slowly, he slipped back the hood with a bony hand, revealing another smile that seemed to say he knew her well. This man was older than the one who had rescued her, his grey hair framing a face lined with deep cracks, and cheeks that were beginning to smother the corners of his mouth.

"Forgive him," said the grey-haired man, keeping his attention on Maggie, "it is a pleasure to meet you. I am Terminus and this is Janus. We have met before, when you were just a baby, but I presume that you do not remember that. No? Of course not, how would you? Well, never mind, we have been awaiting your arrival for a very long time and we are overjoyed that the wait is finally over."

The man offered a boney hand to Maggie, surprising her with its coldness, as she shook it politely.

"What…who?" she fumbled.

Somewhere in the gloom, the slow dripping of water was becoming a steady trickle, as a dog began to bark restlessly.

"No!" gritted Janus at the noise. His eyes suddenly wide, as if an alarm bell had just sounded, "I never thought they'd use dogs! The buckets will be useless!"

The bark sounded again, closer this time, followed by the shrieking of a cat, as it scurried toward them.

"No time to explain," snapped Terminus, grabbing Maggie and pulling her to the side of the dumpster, "we'll have to transport you from here."

"But….what do you mean? It's just a dog chasing a cat!" blurted Maggie.

Terminus glanced over at Janus who was standing rigid, his hands balled into fists, as if ready for a fight to the death. Again, the dog barked, the sound echoing against the alley walls as it mingled with the sound of hundreds of animals scurrying toward them.

"Quickly!" hissed the younger man.

Terminus looked into Maggie's eyes, their blueness betraying his panic. "I need to get you to safety," he said softly, placing a hand on her shoulder.

Maggie tensed as she prepared for him to pick her up, expecting once again to be carried away, only to feel the press of his cold palm against her forehead. For a second, she froze against his touch, unsure of how to react, as the clawing sound of the animal seemed to close in around them.

"NOW!" shouted Janus.

Maggie turned to look at him, only to feel a blinding pain, as the cold palm suddenly became a circle of fiery red heat. Instinctively, she grabbed his wrist, but it was as though he was made of stone. Squirming wildly, she desperately tried to wrench herself free. The skin on her forehead began to bubble. Pain filled her head, burning through her, as it flooded every corner of her body. She felt tears on her cheeks and her voice cry out in pain. It was as though she was on fire. Her mind searched for an escape. Her feet began frantically kicking, with all her strength, against Terminus's legs, only to realize that they, too, were immune to being moved. It was all too much, the pain too great. Then, just as quickly as it had arrived, it was gone—the pain spinning into retreat, as though it was done with her. Now she was falling, leaving her pain-filled body behind, as she drifted backward into the dark. Down she fell, a distant voice calling for her to come back, to fight. But she quickly dismissed it, knowing that nothing could stop what was about happen. She was too tired, all she wanted to do now was sleep. She had to sleep, even if it was just for a few minutes...she had to sleep. The pain was far behind her now. She was safe and warm, she was in a good place. It was going to be okay. She had to sleep.

5

Cleaning the Wound

If you could live anywhere, and I do mean anywhere, Breezy Lane would definitely spring to mind; in fact, it would be on the very top of your top-ten list. For the two residents who called it home, life just couldn't get any better. It was a long, leafy lane with just one perfect little cottage. It sat behind its own perfect, little lawn and contained its own perfect, little family. Every morning, Maggie's father whistled on his way to work, and returned home every night to his smiling daughter, to spend the evening playing games. They would talk in front of a roaring fire until bedtime when he would read to her as she lay tucked up in a cozy bed in her own warm room.

If you were a twelve-year-old girl, who thought there could be no better life than living on Breezy Lane with your father, then you went to bed content and woke up feeling refreshed and ready for yet another perfect day—unless, of course, you were just dreaming. Then, you wouldn't think that life was all that great. Indeed, you might think that anywhere else was preferable. For each time you awoke, you would have to experience the same feeling of disappointment, as you realized that it was all just a dream and that you were still just someone's little secret—you still didn't belong.

Maggie slowly drifted back into the real world. Her head hurt and she'd had the bad dream again. A bright light was forcing its way through her eyes and her mouth felt as if she had eaten a bag of cotton balls. She scrunched her eyes tight to force away the memory of her dream, desperate for more sleep as she pulled on the thick blanket before curling herself inside the warm feathery cave.

Something felt strange against her skin and she sleepily reached down to discover she was wearing soft flannel pajamas that made her skin tingle as she brushed her hand over their fabric. She felt so warm and safe in her little secret den; maybe she should try to sleep for just a little longer.

Maggie's eyes snapped open.

I'm in a bed! she thought, *Where am I? How did I get here? Who dressed me?*

Confusion and fear chased her as everything that had happened began to push itself into her mind. The party, the things, her stepmother, Janus, Terminus, everything came rushing back as Maggie struggled to make sense of it.

Time began to stretch as she lay there searching desperately for answers. Then, very slowly, she pulled back the blanket.

Peeking out between her fingers she saw that she was in a room that was entirely pink. The walls were pink, the floor was pink, the ceiling was pink. It was as though she had woken up inside a huge pink marshmallow.

Wow, thought Maggie, looking around the room, *Who lives here?*

Then she saw the open pink door with the letters painted in even brighter pink paint across its front. M.A.G.G.I.E.

Presuming that she must be in another Maggie's room she stared around at its contents. Several large pictures of horses and kittens hung on either side of the open door while the floor beneath them was covered in every type of pink fluffy toy imaginable. Several pink teddy bears struggled under the weight of a large pink unicorn that leaned precariously against a pink lion that lay on its side as if embarrassed by its new fur color, while in the corner stood a pink armchair, its arm covered in neatly folded piles of pink clothes.

Whoever this Maggie is, thought Maggie, *she really likes pink.*

The dryness in her mouth felt suddenly unbearable and she reached for a bottle of water on the nightstand only to suddenly recoil in horror. Her hand…she didn't recognize it. She reached it out into the light again and once more she pulled back in horror. Her own hand had short fingers that were covered in hard skin, while this one was delicate and soft with perfect fingernails. This time she pushed both hands out from beneath the blanket only to find a second perfect twin. Lying there she stared at the strange objects, slowly turning each one over as if they were made of glass. In her mind, she ordered them to form two fists and watched in amazement as they responded. Then she placed the tip of one finger between her teeth and bit down hard as a rush of pain flooded through her. These hands were hers, but how?

As the pain faded away there was a new sensation, a feeling Maggie hadn't felt for a long time. The dry cracked skin was gone; her lips were soft again. With a trembling hand she reached up to touch her cheek. It too was soft. Where once there was hard leathery skin was now tender warm flesh. Running her hand over the side of her face she began searching for the dry dead surface she knew so well, only to find it missing. Then there was another new sensation—the warmth of happy tears running down her soft cheeks and settling between her delicate fingers.

Maggie didn't know how long she lay there under the blanket. If it was a dream she didn't want to wake up. She kept scrunching up her face, a flood of excitement filling her every time it returned to its new form, until she slowly dared to believe that this might just be permanent.

"Maggie, love," came a whisper from above. "Are you awake yet?"

Light rushed in as the corner of the blanket was gently pulled back and Maggie found herself looking into the face of a beautiful woman with long blonde hair and perfectly tanned skin. Just like Terminus and

Janus, she too had perfect blue eyes that seemed to go beyond just looking at her. Almost as if they could see everything inside her.

"Oh Maggie, you are awake!" came her excited voice, "Oh look at you, look at you! Oh you have no idea how good it is to have you here."

Maggie stared, wide-eyed, back at her trying to work out who this woman was and why she would be so excited to see her. Was she a nurse? She didn't look like a nurse, and that would make this the strangest hospital room ever. She looked more like the girls she was used to her brothers pointing at on TV, the sort of girl who seemed to only talk to other beautiful people, and definitely not the sort of girl who would be excited about talking to her.

"I'm Pethora," she said, sitting down on the bed and talking in rapid bursts, "I know, I know it's kind of a mouthful but it grows on you. Anyway, let's not worry about who I am, you're the important one now. You must have so many questions. So many things you need to know. Oh this is so exciting! Oh and Arac, you have no idea how excited he is, he's been bouncing around the house for days! It's been, 'Do you think Maggie will like this?' or 'Will Maggie want that?' It's been non-stop! If he asks, do tell him that you love your room. I did try to tell him that girls of your age aren't really interested in horses and kittens anymore but he looked so disappointed, he'd worked so hard on it. Anyway, tell him you love it, he'll be so happy and we can always make a few changes of our own later! Oh Maggie I know this must all seem so strange but please get dressed and come down stairs. We are all so excited to finally have you here and we have so much to tell you!" She was almost bouncing now, clapping her hands together as she let out tiny slight squeals of delight that left Maggie more confused than ever.

"Can I hug you?" she suddenly asked, leaning in to squeeze Maggie tightly before she could answer.

"My hands!" blurted out Maggie, lifting the unfamiliar items out from under the cover of the duvet as if in surrender, "My face!"

"I know! Aren't they all beautiful?" said Pethora, letting loose another clap, "Brand new! I am so jealous, you are so lucky!"

Maggie looked up without knowing what to say as Pethora stared at her behind a wide smile.

"Oh look at me," she suddenly chirped, "I'm just so excited! I'll see you downstairs!"

With a giggle she sprang off the bed and skipped out of the room.

Maggie lay there motionless, staring at the alien hands in front of her. A wave of panic spread through her as a cheer erupted downstairs. It seemed Pethora wasn't the only one excited by her arrival. Unfortunately for them going downstairs to a room of strangers was the last thing she wanted to do, especially before she had a chance to see what her new face looked like. But apparently this was where all the answers were, and unfortunately for her she needed answers more than anything right now.

Maggie changed quickly into some of the new clothes and headed toward the noise of the party, hoping to find a mirror on the way. Outside she found herself in a long corridor and with a skip she quickly moved toward its end, relieved to leave the bright pink bedroom behind her. She didn't know who Arac was, or why he had gone to so much trouble, but the thought of looking at the pink walls in the bedroom made her feel as though her eyes might fall out of her head.

Thankfully the rest of the house seemed to be much easier to look at with light brown walls decorated with an endless line of gold-framed photographs that hung neatly along its length. All of the pictures seemed to be of different people, each of them proudly showing off the tools of their profession for the camera. There were garbage men lifting trash cans, doctors holding up stethoscopes, farmers sitting on tractors, teachers reading from books. It was as if every job you ever could think of was there; each worker bearing a smile that suggested they were having the greatest day of their life. Even the man dressed as a chicken outside of a fast food restaurant seemed to be ecstatic, his feathery thumb raised beneath a happy wink as he handed out coupons with his other wing. Next to him Maggie recognized a famous actress from TV displaying a thick script, while next to her hung a large man she recognized from her brothers' posters as the England rugby captain, his toothless grin smiling proudly behind the ball he held up for the camera.

As she looked at each picture Maggie tried desperately to make out her reflection, but it was hopeless. The dullness of the glass only increased her frustration until the smiles within seemed to taunt her efforts to see herself. A large window stood in the middle of the wall and Maggie blinked in its bright light as she uselessly tried to polish it to a reflective shine with her sleeve. Beyond a sea of forest stretched for miles in front of her, its edges cut by tiny roads that ran away into the distance, while far off on the horizon a lazy grey smoke drifted upward from a stone cottage.

Towering next to it stood two large iron gates between thick walls that dwarfed the tiny house before weaving their way between the trees and disappearing out of sight.

The noise of the party was growing louder now and reluctantly Maggie forced herself down the stairs, nerves filling her stomach with butterflies. Downstairs she found a hallway with more photographs that led to a large wooden door standing ajar at the far end, the sounds of laughter and music drifting out. She knocked lightly. No one answered. Deciding to peek in she gently pushed against it, only to gape in horror as it swung wildly open before slamming against the wall. Instantly the laughter stopped and a sea of faces turned to stare at her. An eternity seemed to pass as everyone froze, their eyes on Maggie.

"Hello?" said Maggie nervously, "I…I don't know if I'm in the right place? Pethora said I should come down…and join you?"

Instantly the spell was broken and they rushed toward her, arms outstretched, each of them scrambling to embrace her in a sea of hugs. They were saying her name over and over, passing her down a line as they pulled her into the room, telling her again and again how good it was to have her home. Over and over they hugged her tight, Maggie thanking each of them as she looked at their faces trying desperately to recognize anyone. Many of them were crying as she was passed between them, their wet smiles sending a rush of embarrassment through her as she wondered what she had done to deserve such adoration. After what seemed an eternity she finally came to the end of the group and felt herself pop into the open as if she had been squeezed out thorough a straw. Looking back, not sure of what to say, she suddenly realized that they were no longer staring at her. Each of the smiling faces was fixed on someone behind her and she turned slowly, expecting the worst.

There was someone here she recognized after all, someone who shouldn't be here. For a second she didn't know what to do, they couldn't be real. Before she knew it she was running across the room, throwing herself into them and squeezing hard as she felt herself enveloped in the safety of their arms. Behind her there was the sound of more crying followed by clapping and the whooping of cheers. Maggie heard none of them. She was lost in the smell of grease and copper that only ever meant one thing to her. Her father was hugging her.

6
New Skin

Maggie watched her father from across the room surrounded by his adoring guests. It had taken a long time for her to finally release him, and even longer before she could be persuaded to leave his side, but after Pethora's constant begging she had agreed to meet some of the guests at the party. Everyone had apparently traveled great distances to meet her and while she was trying her best to be polite she was finding it hard to concentrate. An old lady was hugging her, squeezing the air out of her with surprising strength, as Maggie thanked her, her eyes fastened on her father, as if he might disappear again if she lost sight of him.

He looked exactly as Maggie remembered him —as if he had been plucked from the small photograph that had been taped to the kitchen wall. It had been three years since his funeral and seeing him now she realized just how much she had missed him. Even the changes to her hands and face no longer seemed important. Her father was alive and nothing else mattered, it could all wait. It was as if everything was back, back to how it had been before he left.

"You must excuse me but my husband and I have to leave a little early and we simply couldn't go without getting a little slice of the Maggie pie!"

Maggie turned to find herself looking at a short round couple who were dressed in identical yellow and black striped jumpers with large wings made of coat hangers and stockings hanging loosely on their backs. A smell of wine hung in the air around them and Maggie noticed that the man in particular was having trouble focusing his left eye, which kept spinning around in his head.

"Such a great pleasure to meet you, sincerely it is. Really, really great pleasure," slurred the man as his head drooped to one side. "I am Tally McKensie and this beauty next to me is my lovely wife Sally."

"Pleased to meet you…Tally and Sally," said Maggie, suppressing a smile.

"Exactly! You'll have to excuse the outfits. We got a little confused with the invite," continued Tally, turning his good eye to his wife, "thought it was fancy dress, didn't we? She was going to get on my back and we'd be a double decker bus! See it's funny, isn't it? Double decker bus, get it?"

Sally let loose a machine-gun burst of laughter that seemed to take everyone but her husband by surprise.

Maggie stared back at them in confusion. "I thought you were bees?" she said, hoping not to appear impolite.

"Yeah but they're buses, aren't they? You get it now? She's on me back and we're a double decker. Double decker bus. It's funny!"

Sally let loose another volley of laughter as Tally rested his head on her shoulder and sniggered.

"Oh," said Maggie, not wanting to offend them, "of course. Double decker bus. That is funny."

"I knew you'd think so," said Tally, swinging his head back toward Maggie, "I said it didn't I, Sally? I said it. You mark my words, she'll be a smart one. And you are! You are a smart one! So tell me, where do you go to school?"

Maggie leaned back slightly as Tally and Sally swayed toward her in anticipation of her answer.

"I don't actually go to school," she said apologetically.

Sally and Tally looked at one another as if she was speaking another language.

"No school? Arac's daughter doesn't go to school? Well that's a surprise! But I guess you don't need to go when you have your powers. Better than any education I'll wager!" said Tally with a knowing wink as he tapped his nose with a porky finger.

"I'm sorry?" questioned Maggie, "Powers? And who is Arac?"

"Thank-you, Tally and Sally. Maggie has lots of people to meet and you really should be going," interrupted Pethora as she guided Tally toward the door.

"Don't you touch my husband," said Sally, her kind round face suddenly full of rage, "we have as much right to be here as you do! You think you're better than everyone else just because Janus has a thing for you. Well listen to me, Pethora, don't think that everyone here doesn't know what you were before!

You may act all high and mighty but we both know that you were just a cheap little supermarket, and not even a very good one at that! I'll have you know my Tally was home to one of the finest schools in this country so it would do for you to show him a little respect."

"Is everything okay here?"

Maggie looked over to find Janus standing next to her, his eyes fixed on the couple before him. In a room full of people who seemed to be obsessed with meeting her he had been the only one happy not to take a turn, always seeming to be wherever she wasn't... until now. Now he was next to her, smothering them with his presence as Maggie saw fear in the McKensies' eyes.

"Janus," said Tally, turning suddenly sober, "You'll have to excuse my wife. She didn't mean anything by it. She's just had a few too many is all. Please don't tell Arac. We'll be off home now. Sorry, Maggie, very sorry."

"See that you do that" said Janus as Tally shuffled his wife away, her eyes still glaring angrily at Pethora.

Janus shot a frozen glance at Pethora before turning to Maggie.

"Ignore them," he said sharply, "Too much champagne. A good reason never to touch the stuff. Terrible for the body and terrible for you. Will you excuse me?"

In a snap he was gone leaving the air heavy behind him. Maggie watched as he strode across the room to whisper in her father's ear, making his smile fade momentarily. Then with the briefest exchange of nods he was gone, turning sharply to leave through the same door that two rather large bees had staggered through only moments before.

"I am sooo sorry," said Pethora, bending down to hug Maggie yet again. "We are so not usually like that. It's just with all of the excitement about your arrival and everything, I think some people are just a little bit too happy for their own good tonight."

"That's okay," said Maggie, not really understanding why she was being apologized to, "everyone's been really nice, but I don't know what I've done to deserve all of this."

Before she could finish she felt a familiar hand on her shoulder, its hard layers of skin prickling against her.

"You deserve it, my dear, because you are my one and only daughter and I have had to wait too long to spend time with you!" said her father, sweeping her up into another hug. "How about you and I sneak out of here and steal a little father and daughter time?"

"I'd like that," said Maggie, smiling up at him.

Returning her smile he grabbed her hand and led her through the groups of people toward a heavy oak door in the corner marked *OFFICE.*

Unlocking it, he pulled her inside and closed it behind them with a sigh, happy to have a moment away from the party.

"Well this has been a crazy evening, hasn't it?" he said, guiding her toward a red leather seat in front of a large wooden desk. Maggie looked up at the office's many bookcases, each of them straining under the mass of books and loose papers that were stuffed into them. Between them hung a black and white photograph that was larger than all the others in the house, its worn surface showing a picture of two old men in old-fashioned suits shaking hands. Unlike all the other photographs these men were definitely not in a good mood, each of them grasping each other's hands as they stared at each other with looks of barely suppressed hatred. Something about looking at them unsettled Maggie and as she stared at them she wondered why anyone would want to have this photo on their wall when there seemed to be so many others to choose from.

"You never did meet your grandfather, did you?" said her father, pointing at the picture.

"That's my grandfather?" said Maggie in surprise.

For a moment he didn't reply, seeming to be lost in thought as stared at the old man who loomed over him.

"So you must have questions?" he said, clapping his hands as he turned suddenly.

"Err, yes, I mean I guess so," stammered Maggie, unsure of where to begin. It was true that she had a long list of questions. Since seeing him for the first time her mind had been a storm of puzzles, and some answers would be nice.

"Same old Maggie, never wanting to cause a fuss," he replied, his blue eyes shining brightly at his daughter, "why don't I get the ball rolling by saying that we have time…plenty of time. I can't tell you how good it feels to say that, it was as if each day apart from you was a lifetime, but I promise you that I'm not going anywhere, and I hope that you'll be willing to live here with me so that I can start to make it up to you. I want to be your father again."

Maggie stared into his face as a warm glow ran through her spine. The answers didn't seem to matter anymore; it was as if he had taken all the bad feeling away. He had said just what she wanted to hear and now nothing mattered as long as she was close to him.

"And with that in mind, perhaps now is the time for a little welcome home gift," he continued, pulling out a bright silver mirror, " I hope you like it." He smiled, squeezing her hand around the mirror's handle.

With trembling hands Maggie slowly raised the mirror up. She knew all too well the face that greeted her every morning, and wanted nothing more than to look in the mirror and see it gone forever. But how could that be? Surely it was impossible. What if she wasn't different? What if it had all been her imagination?

Through watery eyes she slowly peeked at the reflection of her crying face before a hiccup of surprise jumped out from between her trembling lips.

"How?" she managed, running her fingers down her new face.

The bright blue eyes were still there but everything else was different. Gone was the withered dead skin, replaced by a pale face that shaped itself softly over high cheekbones framed by dark glossy hair that hung long over her shoulders. Two full red lips curled forward as a trembling hand instinctively came up to her mouth, the sensation of her warm soft skin once again taking her by surprise.

"I hope you like it? How could you not like it? Look at you!" said her father as he beamed proudly.

It was all too much for Maggie to take. Before she knew it her tears had become an overwhelming flood that sent her sobbing into her father's chest as he wrapped his arms tightly around her.

"It's okay…it's over…you're home now, you're home," he whispered over and over, holding her safely against him until both their tears finally subsided.

Then he gently lifted her head and wiped away the tears that lingered on her chin.

"Come with me," he said suddenly, grabbing her hand and pulling her up from the couch.

He pulled open the office door and stepped back into the party before moving Maggie in front of him. Then with a quick raise of one hand he began to speak as the guests instantly fell silent at his command.

"My dear guests, I would like to introduce you to my daughter, the most beautiful girl in the world!" he announced proudly as everyone broke into another rapturous applause.

For a second Maggie managed to suppress her smile, but as the clapping continued, a broad grin filled her new face. Yesterday she had been the ugly girl who had to be hidden away in the kitchen to avoid offending the guests, and now she was here, the guest of honor. Nothing mattered anymore. She was beautiful and loved, and she didn't have to feel ashamed any longer. Whatever was happening felt special and that was something she hadn't felt in a long time, not since before her father had died. But now he was here again, back to save her. Her dad had fixed everything.

7

Beneath the Surface

The next few weeks passed by in a cloud of happiness for Maggie. No longer were her days filled with chores. Now she spent time in a house filled with new friends, all of them eager to be with her. Each morning, after her father left for work, they would crowd around the kitchen table all competing with ideas to make her want to be with them. Maggie would try, politely, to find something they could all do together. Not that it was difficult, as every one of them seemed to be incredibly happy and she enjoyed spending time with them all. Only Janus kept his distance, rarely making an appearance until late in the day and excusing himself from any activity at the first opportunity. Not that Maggie cared, she was happy and was far too busy counting the minutes until five o'clock and the moment her father's old beaten van would pull into the driveway. This was the true highlight of Maggie's day, for it meant he was about to jump out and wrap her inside one of his huge hugs before insisting that she join him for a walk through the seemingly endless woods that surrounded the house. Here, they would easily talk with one another, laughing at silly jokes, and listening to eachother's stories from the day, until they would finally emerge into the small garden at the back of the house, where they would sit together and watch the sunset. Hunger would finally drive them to go back inside.

It didn't seem as though life could get any better. She had her father back and right now that was more than she could have ever wished for. She still didn't know why or how her father had come back from the dead, or how he had fixed her face, but she was happy to wait…for now.

It was a Tuesday evening and, for the first time since Maggie arrived, the sun had stayed away, leaving the house surrounded in a cold grey rain. Beads of water merged lazily into tiny streams on the living room window as Maggie looked for signs of life in the dark woods outside. Boredom seemed to be everywhere. Pethora and the others tried to think of things to entertain themselves but one by one they had all given up and retreated to their own quiet corners of the house, their spirits dampened by the rain outside.

Even her father didn't seem immune to the mood of the day and it was long after dark when his van finally splashed into the driveway, the broken headlights sweeping only a single shaft of light across the living room wall. Maggie jumped up from in front of the fire, leaving a sleeping Pethora curled on the couch, and ran to the window instinctively, feeling that something was wrong. His dark figure seemed tense as he made the short run to the porch. He dropped his hood and the small light above the door revealed a sad face, that seemed to be drowning in the shadows.

Maggie walked out into the hallway to receive her usual hug only for him to stop her in her tracks, turning his back before she could get near him.

"Where's Pethora?" he said, hanging his wet coat over the banister and removing his boots. A wet dog walked in behind him and gave a lazy shake before curling itself into a ball by her father's muddy shoes.

"She's asleep in the living room. Dad, is everything okay?" asked Maggie.

"I really don't know. Please come with me," he said, walking into the living room.

In the flickering light of the fire Pethora was unrecognizable from before; no longer asleep, she sat upright, looking as if she had been awake for hours.

"Good evening, Arac. How was your day?" she said brightly.

"We'll talk later, Pethora. Please see that we are not disturbed," he replied coldly, opening the door to his office and ushering Maggie inside.

Here was another roaring fireplace, larger than the one outside, its light stabbing at the shadows of darkness that filled the walls as it danced along the books before creating new scowls on the pictures of her grandfather. This was the first time she had been in the office since the day she found out her father was alive, and she realized now how little attention she paid it that day, her eyes becoming wide at how big it was. Everything seemed larger than she remembered with towering bookshelves that seemed to strain under a thousand books, many piled atop of each other, as though they were trying to force their way up through the ceiling. In each corner stood a large globe of the earth, their surfaces covered with tiny black nail heads, while all around the floor sat large crates that brimmed with crusted jars and test tubes, as others overflowed with old maps that were bound tightly by brown string. Only one wall remained untouched by boxes or books, this one providing a home for six glass frames that were filled with thousands of dead insects, each of their bodies pinned above a tiny handwritten sign.

As her father crossed the room to his large desk Maggie suddenly found herself wondering why he needed an office like this. He didn't have an office when they lived with Victoria and her stepbrothers, and when it was just the two of them, he'd managed with just a small box of files under his bed. Now he had an office that looked as though it belonged to a professor or a scientist, not a plumber.

"Maggie, please," he said, gesturing for her to sit on the couch opposite his desk. "I have something to tell you and I don't know where to begin…don't know how you'll feel about what I have to say. But I can't put it off any longer. I have to tell you the truth. It's killing me to keep it from you. There are answers you deserve and I have to give them to you—no matter what you think of me."

Maggie stared up at her father, her mind rushing with possibilities.

Slowly he crossed the room to sit next to her as his eyes danced with the flame reflected in the fire.

"Listen Maggie, what I'm about to tell you may at first sound ridiculous but I promise, I promise with all my heart, that it is the truth."

He leaned back and closed his eyes for a moment trying to prepare himself for what he was about to say. Slowly he angled forward onto his knees, two thick fingers rubbing his bristled chin, before he began to speak with a voice that betrayed his nerves. "So much of what you have been told about this world is not true, or rather you have only been told part of the truth. You see there are things in this world, in us, that are both simpler and far more complicated than anything you have been taught."

Maggie watched her father's nervous face, unsure of what to say.

"I know you saw them, Maggie. I see them too and they are real. I know it doesn't feel like it right now but trust me, you've been given a great gift that means that you stand a chance to be free." There was a long pause as Maggie realized that he was waiting for her to speak. "The internals…the voices that you heard…the insects that wrote your name…I know you saw them and it's okay. You did see them, didn't you?"

Maggie stared at her feet. Even though she was being told it was okay to admit, she still felt ridiculous saying it out loud. What if he thought that she was crazy? "There was some…I saw some…weird stuff," she mumbled.

"I knew it!" bellowed her father, bouncing across the couch to seize Maggie's hands. "This is such a gift! Maggie there's so few of us left!"

Maggie swallowed, unable to hide her confusion.

"You'll really have to slow down and explain," she said, relieved at her father's change in mood, "I don't know if I really understand what you're talking about."

"I'm sorry, I was just so nervous. Worried that you'd think I was crazy, that you might want to leave. I've wanted to tell you for so long but I didn't think I could go through the pain of losing you again. If you didn't see…if you didn't give me the chance to explain, to teach you…." he said, gently replacing Maggie's hands in her lap as he tried to calm himself.

"In this world you have been taught that humans are separate individuals, but this isn't true. Humans are merely a shell for another world, a world inhabited by beings known as souls and internals. You, my lovely daughter, are a soul, a living breathing soul. You are the life force of everything that happens in the body, its driving force. I'm getting ahead of myself, just remember, as your father, I swear I will never lie to you, and everything I am about to tell you is the truth."

Maggie sat staring at him, the flame in his eyes burning furiously.

"The body you live in, all bodies, are powered by internals. They are the ones who control the machines inside. They help the body to breathe…they work its muscles, grow its bones, make its skin, all of it is the work of the internals. If you think of your body as a car, then it is the engine that makes it work. But you, the wonderful soul that you are, you are the one that drives that car…and you live in here," he said, gently placing a finger against her forehead. "This is your home. And as long as you are in here you are one with the body, controlling all that it does in the outside world. Only a body's true soul can do this—and this is what you are—a true soul."

Maggie watched as her father dropped his finger and slowly crossed the room to stand in front of the fire, his frame silhouetted against the fiery backdrop.

"You see, Maggie, internals and souls, we both need the body. It gives them food, shelter, homes for their families, schools for their children, industry so they can thrive and grow. While, for us, it is life. It laughs or cries because we laugh or cry, and without it we can never be complete. But something went wrong. For as long as anybody could remember it was a perfect relationship, both of us working to help the body but always reliant on one another. No one ever thought that it could ever be any different. So we lived peacefully together, sharing in each others' lives without question. They were like our family and we theirs. Then, without warning, the bond was broken.

For a second he was silent as if the weight of his memories was too much for him to bear.

"So many lives were lost, Maggie, all for simple greed. You see, the internals were no longer happy to share. Some of their leaders decided to end our partnership and instead become our masters. With time more and more followed them, revolting against a partnership that had served us both so well, demanding that souls should do as they demanded. We responded by retreating to the safety of the mind and staying permanently connected to the body in the one place that the internals could not go. But it seems that even that was not enough for them and soon we were in a war like no other, a war that neither side could win. If they killed us the body would die and if we killed them the same would happen. The death of the very thing we both needed to keep us alive was the only way to win the war. And yet still we fought to find ways to hurt each other. They would shut down the machines depriving us of oxygen while we would refuse to bring food in, even going so far as to expose the body to disease, anything to push each other to the brink of death in the hope that it would be enough to make them abandon their demands."

Maggie stared at her father. Everything he was telling her seemed too incredible to be real, but then didn't everything that had happened to her? Something inside her seemed to say that it was true, and hadn't her father told her he would never lie to her? It had to be true.

"Why didn't the souls just leave?" said Maggie.

Slowly her father turned to face her, showing the tears, she had sensed, running down his face. "Where could we go? The body was our home and, unlike the internals, we share a link with it that can never be broken. Sometimes I think that's why they hated us so much."

"But you're here now," said Maggie, "so the war must have ended."

"It did, or so we thought," said her father, rubbing his tear-stained cheeks, "Finally the leaders of both sides sat down and accepted that neither side could win. Yet still nobody would yield. That's when they sent for your grandfather. He'd spent his life in the study of internals and was one of the few souls that they still trusted. His job was to negotiate a peace between them, but when he saw the internal leaders around the table arguing for their own selfish needs he realized one thing—that the bond between the two had been permanently broken. So when all their words finally ran dry he told them of a plan that allowed them to live together, then he made both sides see that it was the only way."

Maggie stared up at the aggressive old man in the picture on the wall, wishing that the news of his greatness would somehow make him look less angry, but it only seemed to make him look more sinister, his eyes suddenly blacker than ever.

"His plan was to give the world inside the body to the internals, while souls would permanently commit themselves to the mind and live only in the outside world. The link between us was to be broken forever and no longer would we spend time together. Each of us was to maintain the body but as people we were to grow apart and never communicate again. It seemed to solve everything. Even the internals appeared happy with the plan and overnight, there was peace once more. I was just a small boy but I remember how happy everyone was that the war was finally over. The mood just seemed to overwhelm everyone, even the sadness that we were severing ties with one another. Within days a date was set for the plan to be completed and as it drew nearer, word was sent out by both sides that every town was to select one body to host a great gathering for every soul and internal who lived there. It was a night like no other with souls and internals all over the world eating and drinking together for the last time, as they celebrated the end of the conflict. Then, at the end of the evening, souls everywhere returned home to their minds for the last time as the internals sealed the corridor to the mind behind them."

The wood in the fire popped sending out a shower of glowing ash onto the floor behind Maggie's father. Without looking, he lazily kicked the dying embers back into the fire with his bare foot before crossing the room to sit next to Maggie.

"So my grandfather was like a hero to the souls...our people?"

Her father seemed to tense at the question, flaring his nostrils as his fingers unwittingly curled into talons.

"He should have been, but he was deceived like we all were," he sighed, relaxing his fingers, "The celebrations were not as innocent as they had seemed. Everything happened so quickly and we just didn't have time to think it through like we should have. We were so happy for the war to be over that we let down our guard, just as they knew we would. The food, the drink, all of it was filled with poison. They knew that they couldn't kill us so they had created a new plan, one that would give them all that they wanted. Only weeks later when the poison started to work, attacking our memories, did some of us realize that something was wrong, but by then it was too late."

Maggie placed her palms against her temple as if she were guarding her thoughts. "But why attack our memories?"

"Without memories we had no knowledge that internals even existed. It's impossible to fight a war if you don't know there is an enemy. Souls everywhere were living in the mind without knowing that it was even possible for them to leave. All they knew was the outside world. After that, all the internals had to do was remove the bodies ability to see them. That was just a simple matter of putting a block on the signal from the eye and they were free to do whatever they wanted. If they couldn't become our masters they made sure to get the next best thing—a life without us and the freedom to go where they wanted. They had both worlds for their own. Sometimes I think it was their plan all along."

Maggie placed her hand on his and he took it gratefully, squeezing her soft fingers against his.

"So how do you know this?" she questioned, "why aren't you trapped?"

Again he was silent, the words refusing to come easily, before a deep breath seemed to return his strength.

"For some reason I've always been different from other souls. I was born with an ability that wasn't given to others, the ability to live without internals. As a young boy I found I could control any body I chose without them, I'd just have to be inside it and picture it doing what I wanted, and somehow it just seemed to listen. Now I don't even have to think about it, as long as I'm in a body all the machines just seem to work on their own."

"So that's what Janus meant when he said I didn't have any powers? He wanted to know if I could do what you can?" said Maggie.

"Yes," said her father, the word dropping heavily into his lap, "to the others it seems like a great gift but trust me when I tell you that most of the time it feels like a curse. While it has been useful in helping me to free souls, it has also been the reason that I lost my family—lost you. I have never wanted anything more than to live a simple life and be your father. No part of me is interested in ever hurting anyone, least of all the internals. If it were left to me, we would still be living peacefully today. But it seems that I represent something that the internals despise and so they will not rest until I am gone. Before the war it was easy to hide my abilities but when the others lost their memories, and I didn't, my differences quickly became obvious. And so they came looking for me. It was all I could do to run and hide. For years I was constantly on the move, going from town to town, living in any body where I could find shelter, all the time looking over my shoulder for the day they would come. Then, when I least expected it, I met your mother. Falling in love with her and having you was the happiest time of my life. We made a home in the country where no one knew us and even though I was never able to tell your mother my secret, she showed me only love. We had each other and for the first time I was truly happy, but it was too good to be true. It seemed my curse was not the only thing intent on finding ways to torture me. When your mother became sick and died I felt as though the world had come to an end. The pain was worse than anything I could ever have imagined. If it hadn't been for you, well I hate to think of how I would have carried on. You were the only good thing in my life and I promised myself that I would do everything I could to make you happy. I think that's why I was so eager to marry Victoria. I just wanted you to have a mother and she seemed to be so kind. I knew that she could never be as good as your real mother but in the early days she seemed to want to really love you. Then, just days after we were married, I discovered that the internals were closing in on me. That's when I realized that the only way to keep you safe was to leave. So I faked my death and went back on the run. I had no other choice."

He hung his head and scrubbed at his rough cheeks as if he could rub away his guilt.

"I never stopped working. Everyday has been about creating a small corner of the world where we could be a family again. So many times I wanted to come and get you but I knew I had to wait. Being apart from you has been a living hell, especially since I discovered what sort of woman Victoria truly was, but all I could do was wait. You were safe there and I knew that they would never suspect who you were as long as you were living on Breezy Lane. What internal would ever believe that a free soul would willingly choose to live with that woman and her three idiot sons? As long as you didn't know that you were a free soul then there was no way for them to discover who you truly were. You were safe. Even when the internals became suspicious and destroyed your face with one of their clumsy inspections, I resisted coming to get you. Only years later when I received word that they were coming after you, that they knew who you were, did I know it was time. That was the day Janus came to get you."

"So, do I have the same powers as you?" asked Maggie nervously.

"Only time will tell but I hope with all my heart that you do not. You're already able to see things that no other soul can when you are inside your body, but you are also much older than I was when I discovered my abilities, and trust me when I say your life will be far better without them. I honestly doubt that you will ever be able to do what I can, but I think you should easily be able to live as a free soul. Sadly, there are others who are already expecting great things from you, but give it time. Let them get to know you, even Janus will learn to accept you for who you are, with or without powers. It is my fate to be a part of this war, not yours. I hope that your path lies elsewhere."

The air in the room suddenly seemed to soften and Maggie's father sighed with relief as the last of his story fell from his lips.

"But now I have talked more than enough," he said as a small smile appeared beneath his moustache, "Now, I think it's time to show you what you've been missing; the world outside. We can go now if you are ready. I'll be with you every step of the way."

"But how?" said Maggie nervously. It was all happening so fast but she wanted to believe; she wanted to make her father happy.

"It's simple," he said, returning his finger to her forehead, "right now you are in here, when you should be…"

A sharp tingle surged out of her father's touch and raced down her spine, his words becoming a distant noise as her skin began to feel like she was inside a can of pins that was being shaken vigorously. From above her head there was a crack and abruptly the room was flooded with blackness. Then, just as quickly, a warm sensation wrapped itself around her, overwhelming her with a desire to sleep.

"Open your eyes," whispered her father from above her as a soft hand stroked her hair, "open your eyes, Maggie."

Fighting her annoyance at being woken, Maggie looked up into the face of a man she didn't recognize, a man with the same startling blue eyes as her father, only he was older, his bald head and moustache both flecked with grey.

"It's me, Maggie, your father…the real me, the soul form of me. In this world I am known as Arac, but I am still your father," he said in a soft voice. "Look up, Maggie, see the real world for the first time. You're free now."

Maggie rubbed at her eyes with balled hands, trying to focus. Looking up over his shoulder two figures towered over her, their size beyond belief, the length of their bodies stretching endlessly upward to reveal two giant statues. Each was as tall as a skyscraper with hands as big as houses and feet the size of large trucks. Her eyes slowly drifted up the colossal figures before settling on their two faces—she gasped. Towering above her in the sky was a girl's face resting gently against the shoulder of a sleeping man.

She sat staring at the two sleeping giants, trying to make sense of what she was seeing. High above her sat the tear-stained man she knew as her father, and curled into his chest was the face she had only recently come to accept as her own. It was her, sleeping next to her father, their bodies dwarfing her into insignificance.

"You're free now, Maggie," said the man again, still stroking her hair, "you're a free soul."

8

The Deepest Cut

The life of someone smaller than a pinhead was not, as Maggie was finding out, so bad at all. In fact, she was quickly discovering that being tiny was actually quite a lot of fun! For a start everything seemed to be a playground. Piles of old wires became the world's longest slide, an old greasy frying pan transformed into a giant skating rink, and the couch in her father's office was now the worlds largest private trampoline. And then there was the food, which certainly wasn't in short supply when you were this small. Every meal seemed to be the size of a car and required you to climb on top of it, or in it, to eat it, and invariably left Maggie stuffed and in need of a bath.

Not that it wasn't also without its dangers. She had discovered that in this world Pethora's dainty feet quickly became huge wrecking balls. And the heights…well there were lots of them…everywhere! Ever since she had fallen off the roof in the middle of a hurricane while trying to fix the satellite dish for her brothers' TV she had hated heights. Now everything she looked at seemed to have its own cliff edge with deadly drops below. Not that this seemed to bother any of the other free souls in the house.

"You'll get used to it," assured Terminus as he stood on the edge of the kitchen sink one afternoon, looking down at the red tiled canyon beneath them.

All of them were spending the day washing up, throwing themselves one by one down the shiny wet plates and cups to disappear into a mountain of soapy wet bubbles before splash landing in the deep lake of warm water below.

Maggie's father slid over to sit next to Maggie just as Terminus disappeared down the butter dish. Since that day in the office he had rarely left her side, no longer going to work, instead spending his days teaching her how this new world worked. Together the days seemed to fly by as they jumped in and out of their bodies, her father's gentle touch on her forehead signaling the change between the two.

"When will I be able to move in and out of my body on my own? And when will I get to look around inside my body? Everyone else does it," she said, popping a giant bubble with her foot.

With a laugh, he playfully hugged her before slipping down the shiny metal side and into the cloud of bubbles, his soapy face emerging in a clear pool beneath her.

"Give it time." He laughed, wiping at his eyes. "There's no rush. It's only been a few weeks and already you've learned so much. Besides, if we never stop working how could we do this?"

Maggie heard the fizz of the bubbles, as Terminus pushed her down the slide and into the warm water, before she re-surfaced to see her father swimming away chuckling.

Above them an enormous hand reached across the sky to turn a huge handle, sending down a thick warm waterfall into their gigantic pool.

"More hot water," boomed Pethora from above as she turned on the faucet.

Moments before she had sat on the edge of a giant teaspoon only inches away and Maggie was still impressed at how quickly and easily they jumped in and out of their bodies. Everywhere they went a row of parked giants, their faces half asleep, seemed to watch over them as their owners played in the tiny land below, jumping between the two like an old pair of slippers.

Get-togethers like these had become commonplace since the day her father had told her about the internals. And each adventure seemed only to bring them all closer together as Maggie quickly began to think of everyone in the house as family. In a small room, on the ground floor, lived Frederick and Epona; the oldest souls in the house, who were married to each other longer than either of them could remember. Even after all this time they were rarely apart, liking nothing more than to sit hand in hand while they told Maggie stories of their lives before the war. In the outside world they were both farmers but on the inside her body had housed a large library while he had been a home to a shopping center and several small offices. As teenagers they had fallen in love, sneaking out each night to meet in secrecy between his toes, while they avoided her disapproving mother's eyes and the security internals that patrolled her skin.

In the attic apartment lived the McCurdy family
—McCrae, Freya, and their son Morris, a six-year-old
who was the first soul to be born free since the war
began.

Unfortunately, he had also been born with a
tendency to run away, and more than once they had
found him half frozen in the icebox of the fridge with
his tongue stuck to the side of a truck-sized ice lolly.

Sharing the first floor with Maggie and her
father, were Terminus, Pethora, and Janus; the first
three to be released by her father and his closest
friends. Terminus and Pethora had both become close
to Maggie, doing all that she could to make her feel at
home. While Janus was still distant, often disappearing
for days on end.

Leaning against a gigantic sponge, Maggie
stared up at the large version of herself, motionless by
the stove, a droopy tongue hanging to one side. As she
watched Terminus jump into the open hand of his body,
his face calm as the giant hand clenched into a tight
ball around him. No matter how many times she saw
this, Maggie still felt herself wince, fully expecting the
hand to open and reveal a tiny crushed body.

"Why doesn't Dad want me to transport myself in and out of my body like all of you?" Maggie asked Pethora, who had reappeared back at the sink.

"Give it time. You don't want to get that one wrong," said Pethora with a smile, as Terminus's hand opened to reveal a clean palm, his two large eyes suddenly bright with life.

"Besides, it's much safer out here. Remember, when you're in the body we share everything that happens to it," she said, jamming a tiny thumb at the gigantic body behind her, "We're connected and if it gets hurt we get hurt. You may not think you like it out here but if you're in there when it dies then it's all over, for both of you."

"See you later," said Terminus from above, "I'm just off to the shop, won't be long."

Maggie watched him go as a trickle of envy filled her stomach. She didn't care if it was as dangerous as Pethora said it was. She wanted to learn everything there was to this new life but so far her father had limited her to what she could learn from books. But in truth it was the freedom to move in and out of her body, like all the others, that she wanted more than anything. Everyday her frustration grew as her father sat with her and they studied another book from the library in his office, all the while longing to try something for herself. Not having her father's powers was bad enough, but being unable to do the same as the others only made it worse.

"But why won't he let me do more?"

Pethora looked up from checking her reflection in the potato peeler and smiled.

"He's your father and he's protective of his little girl, but he knows what he's doing. Even if we all had his powers I don't know how many of us would have also been clever enough to find a cure for the poison. Then to discover a way for those of us without powers to be able to run our own bodies without internals… he's a great man, Maggie, and you just have to trust him."

Maggie hung her head. She had heard the stories of his achievements many times, and Pethora's gentle reminder made her feel guilty for doubting him.

"Will you look at the weather out there!" said her father, standing on top of a bar of soap, looking up at the brilliant sunlight that was flooding through the kitchen window, "It's far too nice to be indoors. What do you say we take a trip outside? Get ourselves a little fresh air before Terminus comes back with lunch?"

A happy ripple of agreement ran through the group and soon they were headed for the line of bodies, as Maggie turned to him to await his help.

"Wait," said Maggie's father. "Let's make this a family trip and travel together. All aboard!"

In a flash he was inside his body, his huge hand laid flat for them all to climb aboard, before gently depositing them on his shoulder. This was the first time Maggie had traveled this way and she found herself smiling broadly as the wind rushed by her face, she tucked her legs under the threads of her father's shirt for support. Outside was awash with summer as the group crossed over to a small cluster of trees that sat on the edge of the garden, all of them enjoying the hot sun as it dried their wet skin. Gently her father deposited them all on a branch filled with huge bundles of soft green leaves and oversized pink flowers before making his own appearance, leaving his body standing lifeless in the shade.

"Now this is what life is about!" he said as the group spread out amongst the leaves, each finding their own soft green sun-bed to stretch out on.

Below the green lawn seemed to stretch for miles, circling the house's stone walls that seemed to be glowing in the sunlight. Flower boxes edged the home's windows with bright petals that seemed to sparkle in the light like a rainbow of confetti, and as Maggie lay on the soft green leaf looking out at their beautiful little oasis of freedom her guilt returned. Her father had done so much for her...there was so much to be grateful about. He had given her a family, friends, a home, and everyday she was learning more and more. She could wait to learn how to transport like the others. She was living in paradise, a place her father had created just for her, she shouldn't be complaining.

"Morris!" shouted Freya from a small leaf on the other side of the branch, "Morris, love, where are you?"

By now, everyone was used to hearing the young mother call for her son and, at first, none of them moved from the comfort of their soft, warm leaves.

"Morris...MORRIS...MORRIS!" Freya was shouting louder now, panic grew in her voice with each cry.

Maggie rolled over to see her father and Pethora already at Freya's side, trying to calm her down, as McCrae began to search frantically between the leaves for signs of his son.

"Are you sure he was with you when we came out here?" said Pethora, her hands on Freya's shoulders.

"Yes…I mean, I think so. It was all so rushed, I'm not sure," said Freya, her eyes full of panic.

"I'll check the house," said Maggie's father, jumping from stem to stem to get to his body, "Frederick, Epona, you check the grass below, make sure he didn't fall. Janus, you, Freya, and McCrae come with me to search the house. Pethora, stay here, with Maggie."

As she watched them climb back onto his shoulder, Maggie felt her frustration at her father's protective ways return. Why should she have to stay here when everyone else was allowed to help search? Worse still, why did she need a babysitter?

"Don't take it so personally," said Pethora, sensing Maggie's mood, "he lost you for a long time. It's only natural that he wants to protect you. He will get there."

Together they stood at the edge of the leaf and watched as he bent to drop the old couple in the grass below before striding up the lawn and disappearing inside the house.

For what seemed like an eternity, there was nothing; just the sound of the gentle breeze, rocking the leaves around them as they watched the open door, waiting for him to return. Then came a noise that chilled Maggie's heart, filling her with dread. A sound she had hoped she would never again hear. Quickly she ran to the back of the leaf to look out into the woods behind her as Pethora chased after her, following the sound that was ringing in Maggie's thoughts.

"What is it, what's wrong?" said Pethora, squeezing Maggie's arm.

"Quiet…listen," urged Maggie.

This time it came louder, filling the air around their tiny leaf as it pulled their eyes deep into the woods.

"Hhhhuuuuuuuuuurrrrrrrrrgggghhhhhhhhh," came the moan.

Branches crackled, then it was out of the woods before they had a second to think, its large frame bearing down on them as it blocked out the sun with a shadow that instantly turned day to night.

"QUICK, GRAB ONTO SOMETHING!" screamed Pethora as its large feet shook the ground, driving the decaying body toward them.

Maggie stood frozen on the leaf's edge as memories of the last time she had seen the things flooded her mind. The day the giant mismatched beings had come to her stepmother's garden party demanding that she be given to them. Then she felt Pethora grab her shirt and pull her down onto the soft surface before landing on top of her with a thud, her two tiny hands digging themselves into the green flesh of the leaf.

Before they could think, the shoulder of the thing slammed into the tiny bundle of leaves, folding them into a ball that crushed in on top of Maggie and Pethora. Green juice squirted out all around them, filling their eyes and mouths as their bodies began to slide violently from side to side like windscreen wipers. Pethora dug her hands deeper into the leaf. Then they were flying backwards as the branch freed itself from the thing's path to spring back and forth as Pethora pinned Maggie beneath her. Finally the branch steadied itself as the two of them fell to one side and began to cough violently, trying desperately to free themselves of the sticky green substance that filled their throats. Maggie wiped at her eyes and watched the huge grey body lumber itself up the garden, its moan suddenly silent.

"What is that thing?" spat Maggie, a thick line of green drool running between her lips.

"It's a deathwalker," heaved Pethora, between frantic breathes, "the internals make them out of dead body parts. They don't last long, but while they do the internals can control them without a soul."

Maggie stared at the torn skin that crossed the thing's bare back. A thick liquid that looked like cold gravy oozed from a large gash at the top of its neck.

"No, please, no!" cried Pethora from the edge of the leaf.

Maggie crawled over, the sickly juice still burning her throat. Far below she saw a large footprint in the grass, the two tiny crushed figures of Frederick and Epona in its center, his lifeless shape still uselessly trying to shield her dead body.

"NO!" screamed Pethora as she looked down on her two dead friends in disbelief.

Instinctively Maggie scrambled over the top of the leaves to get a better view of the house. Her mind searched for ways to raise the alarm. But all she saw was the thing begin to slow as it moved silently toward the back door...and her father.

"Dad...Dad!" croaked Maggie as she fought to breathe, "DAD!"

It stopped for a second when it reached the door. Its large gray arms swung loosely at its side like decomposing pendulums. Then it turned and pressed itself against the wall of the house, peeling fingers gently pulling back the open door to hide its huge frame. Seconds later Maggie's father stepped into the garden, oblivious to the unwelcome visitor concealed behind him.

"DAD...DAD...LOOK OUT!" screamed Maggie through burning lungs.

"It's okay, we found Morris," shouted Maggie's father, unable to hear his daughter's tiny voice, "the others are inside. We'll be back with you in a minute."

Behind him the door swung silently back into its frame as the thing took a step toward it. Maggie looked at its dead black eyes, coldly focused on her father, its face expressionless as it raised two giant rotting hands over its head.

"Oh and after lunch it's time to study, young lady. Don't worry, it's time for us to get out of that library and take a walk around inside your body!" called her father with a broad smile.

The fists came down upon him without warning, driving him into the grass like a hammer on a nail. Before she could see any more, Pethora seized Maggie, her tiny friend pulling her into her chest as she wrapped her arms around her face.

"Don't look," she whimpered, "Don't look."

But Maggie couldn't help herself. Grabbing at Pethora's arm, she pulled it away as if it might save him. Instead she saw only his lifeless body lying on the floor, his neck inextricably bent to one side as his attacker's arms swung carelessly at its side. Slowly the thing turned from the body below, its eyes wide like black saucers as it stared at the small tree where Maggie and Pethora sat. Again Maggie felt Pethora's grip pulling her behind a curl in the leaf's edge to hide their two tiny shapes.

"Don't move," she hissed, "they'll have extra internals working in the eyes and ears. They can probably see and hear for miles."

The two of them lay there for what seemed an eternity until finally Pethora relented, slowly peeking up above the leaf's edge as Maggie ignored her demands to stay down. At the other end of the garden the thing was slowly emerging from the house, Maggie's body pulled damply behind, as it casually dragged her by the ankle. Her head bumped heavily out of the doorway and her arms banged clumsily against the walls as the thing dragged her body over to her father's, her free leg twisting awkwardly to one side. Without looking, it reached down and grabbed her father's foot before dragging the two bodies across the lawn as sticks and leaves were raked between them. Lazily the two figures flopped limply against each other, Maggie's perfect hands flapping against her father's dead face as the thing and its two trophies disappeared into the woods.

Maggie stared blankly at the empty space between the trees as a numb confusion overwhelmed her. Of all the pains that existed in the world there were few greater than the agony of a child losing a parent. Today, as Pethora's warm tears flooded down on top of her head, Maggie experienced it for the second time in her young life. Her father had been inside his body when it was killed. He was dead. She had lost him again.

9

Swelling Sets In

"SHE'S USLESS TO US. WHY SHOULD WE HAVE TO TAKE CARE OF HER?"

Maggie sat on the coffee table, the heat from a giant mug of tea warming her back as she listened to the argument leaking out from the kitchen. Two weeks had passed since her father's death but time had done little to alter the sense of despair that had descended on the house since that day.

It had been dark when Terminus finally found them. Through their shock they had listened to his shouts as he returned home and tried in vain to find anyone in the house, his panic escalating until he had finally found the others huddled next to the trash can, unable to reach their bodies.

When he finally reached his giant hand up to bring Maggie and Pethora back into the house, he had been unable to look at them, the weight of their two tiny shivering bodies almost more than he could bear. Without a word he had put them both in the palm of Pethora's hand before walking upstairs, and barely uttered a word since.

Janus had become the overwhelming voice in the house now, demanding everyone take turns keeping watch in case the deathwalkers returned. It had only taken three days before the McCurdy family packed their bags and left in the middle of the night, leaving only a note that they felt too guilty to stay after what happened. Maggie, meanwhile, had been desperate to help, anything to take her mind off her father's death, but without her body there was little that she could do and so she had taken up home on the small coffee table to spend her days feeling invisible. As more shouting emerged from the kitchen she realized how successful she had been. They no longer seemed to care if she heard them by the way they screamed.

"YOU WOULDN'T BE TALKING LIKE THAT IF ARAC WAS STILL HERE," roared Pethora, her voice filling the house.

"DO YOU SEE HIM HERE, PETHORA? IF WE HADN'T SAVED HER, THEY WOULD NEVER HAVE KNOW WHERE TO LOOK FOR US. HE GOT HIMSELF KILLED FOR THAT USLESS DAUGHTER OF HIS AND NOW IT'S JUST US, ON OUR OWN, WITHOUT HIM TO PROTECT US! WHAT HELP CAN SHE BE?"

Maggie heard footsteps as Pethora crossed the kitchen to confront Janus.

"ARAC ASKED US TO TAKE CARE OF HER AND THAT'S WHAT WE ARE GOING TO DO. HAVE YOU FORGOTTEN WHO IT WAS WHO FREED US IN THE FIRST PLACE, JANUS? DON'T YOU THINK WE OWE HIM AT LEAST THAT MUCH?"

"I'LL TELL YOU WHAT WE OWE HIM, NOTHING! IT WAS IRRESPONSIBLE OF HIM TO PUT HIMSELF AT RISK, WITH HIS POWERS HE COULD HAVE FREED THOUSANDS OF SOULS. IF HE HADN'T TOLD US THAT SHE HAD HIS POWERS WE WOULD NEVER HAVE AGREED TO FETCH HER. IT WAS A STUPID, SELFISH RISK

AND SHE'S NOTHING BUT A BURDEN. I SAY WE
GIVE HER TO THE INTERNALS SO THEY DON'T
COME LOOKING FOR US. THAT'S THE ONLY
WAY SHE CAN HELP US NOW!"

The air in the house seemed to freeze. Maggie
searched her mind for the words she wanted Pethora to
say, only to find her mind blank. The silent closing of
the kitchen door quickly followed a scuffling of chairs
as the voices inside became muted. Maggie strained to
hear what they were saying but soon realized it was
useless. If her fate was to be decided it seemed that she
was not to be included, and feeling more worthless
then she ever thought possible, she walked over to a
piece of paper that covered the table like a huge
runway, feeling it crunch beneath her feet.

Two days earlier Janus had discovered four
letters in a drawer in the office, one for each them in
the house, and ever since, the arguments had raged
over what to do next. Maggie's letter lay curled open
beneath her, the words covered in tiny footprints from
the many times she had walked amongst his writing,
the touch of his pen lines beneath her bare feet making
her feel as if he was still close:

Dearest Maggie,

If you are reading this I can only presume that I am no longer with you. While I do not know the manner of my death, I can only presume that the internals were able to find me and consequently we are no longer able to be a family. For this I am truly sorry. You have been through so much at such a young age and I cannot help but think that I must have somehow failed you. I only hope that you can, once again, find it in your heart to forgive me for leaving you.

While I am gone I do have one last thing that I must ask of you. The expectations on you as my daughter have always been great and consequently I have always wanted to protect you from the war. But now that I am gone I need to ask that you play your part in helping free the souls who are trapped by the internals. I had hoped that I would never have to ask this of you but now my hand has been forced. There are so many still trapped and, with or without powers, I am sure that you will want to help them.

I have left instructions for the others to let you join them, if you choose, and become apart of the war. They have all chosen to make this their life and I know that you will be able to help them. Even if you decided not to I know that as my dearest and closest friends they will continue to take care of you until you are old enough to do so yourself.

In the meantime, I have left them the fruits of my knowledge so that they may continue to free souls. If you choose to help them they shall share my secrets with you. Until then I can only urge you to be cautious. The internal leaders continue to hunt us and none of them are to be trusted. Their hatred of all souls is strong. They killed your mother and now they have killed me, I am sure they want nothing more than to make you their next victim.

The only thing left for me to do is to remind you of how much I love you. Being your father has been my greatest honor and I am prouder of you than you will ever know.

I promise I will always find a way to be here for you.

I love you,
Dad.

Maggie stood beneath the words, 'they killed your mother and now they have killed me,' as if they were deadly quicksand, sucking her in. There was no explanation, just cold words, and no matter how many times she read them they only made her feel more and more pathetic. Just when life seemed to be good everything had turned upside down. Now, to make things even worse, she had lost her body. How could she help anyone when she could barely help herself?

The kitchen door banged open as Janus stormed across the living room, glaring at Maggie's tabletop as he heaved up the hood on his jacket, before leaving the house. Maggie sat down and ran her finger down the groove in the paper left by the word 'Dad.' Then, feeling more alone and useless than she ever thought possible, she began to cry.

After what seemed an eternity, Terminus came out of the kitchen and sat on the couch next to Maggie's temporary home, he slowly opened his balled fist as he jumped down onto the tabletop.

"I guess you heard most of that?" he said, placing a comforting arm around Maggie.

Maggie hung her head. "I'm sorry, it was hard not to," she said quietly. Despite her guilt it was good to hear him talking again. After weeks of silence it was as though a piece of the good days had returned, as though it might just be possible for everything to be okay again.

"Don't take it personally. We're all trying to find ways to deal with Arac's death. Janus loved your father very much, we all did, he just wants him back."

"Is it true, that you only came to get me because he thought I had powers?"

Terminus hesitated for a second, reluctant to reply. "I think deep down we all knew that you probably didn't. Arac was exceptional and all of us had taken turns watching over you and there was never any sign that you were like him. Janus just doesn't want to admit that he only did it because it was the right thing to do. He needs to be angry at someone, and right now he's chosen you. Give him time, he'll remember that we are still a family."

Maggie wiped away her tears and took a deep breath. "I want to help. My dad said it was my decision. I want to help in the war with the internals."

Terminus looked into Maggie's eyes with a sad smile. "I'm sure you want to help. Even before you arrived here it was as if every conversation, with your father, centered around you and how amazing you were. But,…but without your body, it's difficult to know what you can do."

Maggie hung her head as a surge of regret flooded through her.

"Couldn't I use another body?" pleaded Maggie, "I want to help!"

"It's impossible, you don't have your father's powers. He was the only soul who could control different bodies. You'll only ever be able to control the body you were born in and right now we don't know where that is," he said, pulling her face up to look at his, "But, Maggie, I want you to know that we will search for your body and while we are searching we will take care of you, even if you can't help us in the war, we will always be here for you."

"Great," said Maggie angrily, "just what you need, another burden."

Terminus stood up and pulled back his long grey hair, "I'm sorry, Maggie, but I don't know what to say, there's nothing you can do to help," he said, stepping back onto his open hand, "I'll talk to the others and decide how to keep you safe. I'm sorry, that's all that can happen right now."

Four fingers closed tightly around him, and without another word he got up and walked outside into the fading light.

A tiny hand touched Maggie's shoulder, as a small whisper tickled her ear. "Wake up, wake up, Maggie."

Maggie slowly lifted her head from the strip of cloth she was using for a bed, and began to search through the darkness for the owner of the voice. It had been hours since Terminus had left and after many hours of being alone she had finally fallen asleep. Now it was dark outside and Maggie squinted into the gloom just making out the soul of Pethora standing over her.

"Please be quiet, Maggie, I don't know how long we have."

Maggie sat up on one elbow and rubbed at her eyes. "What's going on?" she croaked.

"I have to get you out of here," she replied. "We received word that the internals are on their way here. Janus wants us to leave you for them. I've never seen him so angry. Terminus and I have somewhere for you to go until all of this calms down. Somewhere safe."

"What...where?" said Maggie, struggling to think.

"There's no time, I'll explain on the way," said Pethora, pulling Maggie up on to her feet.

Without knowing why, Maggie dressed as quickly as she could while Pethora busied herself, randomly throwing Maggie's few possessions into small suitcases that she carried with increasing difficulty. Soon she was ready, and Pethora moved inside her body before gently placing Maggie, and her bags, onto her shoulder.

In the gloom of the hallway several of the crates from her father's office, still tightly packed with small glass jars filled with a swirling blue liquid, greeted them. Through the doorway to the office Maggie could just make out the sleeping body of Janus draped across her father's desk, his eyes black slits that seemed as though they might open any second.

"We have to hurry," whispered Pethora, "he'll be back soon."

"But what will he do to you when he finds out that I'm gone?" said Maggie.

Pethora kept walking and pretended not to hear the question until a flicker of fear in her eyes betrayed her, letting Maggie know that it was not going to be good.

Soon they were outside on the path that ran through the heart of the woods, the darkness surrounding them as Maggie began to feel even smaller against its smothering weight as they headed ever deeper inside. The walks with her father through the forest held treasured memories, but now the thick trees seemed to be whispering to one another, as if planning their attack, as the darkness grew ever thicker around them. Soon the light of the house disappeared behind them as the sky opened up with a cold downpour of rain that quickly turned the dirt path into a wide puddle of mud. Pethora pushed on through the shadows, jumping from one side of the path to the other as she tried to avoid the growing stream, sending them ever farther into the darkness. Maggie wrapped herself under a fold in Pethora's shirt as she felt the bottom of her small trousers begin to soak up the rain. Thick strands of Pethora's wet hair started to weigh down on her from above, only adding to the feeling that they would never find a way out. Then, just when it seemed as though it would never end, there was a light ahead, and the end of the path broke through the gloom to reveal the first light of dawn. Pethora surged ahead, the last few drops of rain falling behind them as they left the forest and entered a large green clearing next to a road. In the dawn light, Maggie recognized the village spreading out in front of them. She had only seen it before on the horizon through the window by her bedroom but now the houses loomed large before her, towering like skyscrapers over the road that split them down the middle like a black river. Next to them stood a gigantic neglected red telephone booth while on the other side of the road stood a large grey sign:

WELCOME TO QUIGGLESBROOK
-population 47-

Beneath it, in a strange bright greenish yellow, someone had written the words:

Welcome to Quigglesbrook Adventure Park
Fun for all the family! Over 47 Rides!
Summer Hours: 9am-7pm
Insect parking in the mailbox
Buses- 3rd trashcan on the left

"Well, this is us," said Pethora, opening the phone booth and picking up the receiver. In seconds the tiny Pethora was standing next to Maggie, her vacant body looking as if it was in the middle of a particularly boring phone call.

"What does that writing mean?" asked Maggie, pointing at the sign.

Pethora glanced up at the bright writing. "That's brellow," she said, fumbling with the bags, "The internals use it to communicate with each other. You won't have seen it before. Souls can only see it when they are outside the body, and it's not as if there's a lot of brellow at the house!"

Maggie stared at the writing as if aliens wrote it.

"Everything you need is in here," said Pethora, patting the suitcases, "There's food, money, clothes. Take the cat to the end of the pink line and then you'll want to take the number 10 beetle to Mildred Potts 79. There'll be someone there to meet you."

"Cat…beetle…what?" stammered Maggie.

"Quick, or you'll miss it," ordered Pethora, grabbing Maggie's hand before sliding their tiny bodies down the folds of her shirtsleeve.

Below, a large ginger cat had emerged from the undergrowth and was beginning to slide its body against the edge of the phone booth, curving its head back with a deep yawn as it enjoyed its scratching post. As Maggie and Pethora reached the end of the sleeve, the cat looked up, the hairs on its back standing on end as if it had just seen its prey.

"Up here," shouted Pethora, "Wait for us!"

With an easy leap, the ginger cat joined them on the shelf, crouching down next to the woman on the telephone, its huge eyes staring widely at the dangling hand as its tail flicked back and forth in the space between them. Maggie looked at her frozen reflection in the huge black eyes, and waited for the giant creature to snap out with its sharp teeth and swallow her whole, when she felt a hand on her back. Before she could resist, Pethora had pushed her forward, sending her flying through the air toward the back of the giant ginger cat beneath them. They landed with a thud on a patch of soft pink skin surrounded by thick ginger hairs that protruded like small trees all around them. Maggie stood up and looked across the hairy landscape nervously. Pushing his way through the ginger locks, a man dressed in a black uniform, a belt with three small bags and a roll of tickets hanging from his waist, appeared.

"I don't know what you think you're playing at jumping onboard like that. This isn't an official stop you know," huffed the man angrily, his eyes settling on Pethora, his belly rising up into his chest.

"Oh dear. I'm so sorry, you are so kind to have stopped." Pethora giggled innocently as she dropped two small coins into his hand. "I won't be travelling, but would you mind awfully if I just took a minute to say goodbye to my friend?"

"Yes, well, its highly unusual but I guess we can stop for a minute," said the ticket collector, and handed Maggie a bright red ticket, "always happy to help a lovely young lady such as yourself!"

Placing the coins in his pouch, he headed back toward the cat's head, quickly disappearing amongst the thousands of ginger hairs. Pethora's eyes were suddenly full of tears as she looked at Maggie before pulling her in for a hug. Maggie didn't know how many times they had shared these hugs since she arrived at the house, but as she felt her warm embrace she realized just how much she would miss these moments. Only now did she appreciate how close she felt to Pethora, as though she were the big sister she had always wanted.

"You take care of yourself, Maggie. As soon as we have somewhere safe I'll come to get you. Just promise me you'll be careful. We're sending you to the safest place we can think of but there's no telling how far the internals will go to get to you. Whatever happens do not tell anyone that you're a soul...no matter what! You have to pretend to be an internal.

They have to think that you're one of them. We'll come for you as soon as we can."

Beneath them the cat let out a purr as its skin began to ripple beneath their feet.

"I'm going to miss you, Maggie Pincus," said Pethora, giving her an extra squeeze, "Just keep a low profile and we'll have you back with us before you know it. It will all be okay. I promise."

Before she could answer, Maggie felt another shudder beneath them, and Pethora pushed her away. She disappeared down the cat's tail as a deep sob hung in the air behind her.

"ALL ABOARD!" barked the conductor from up between the cat's ears, "HOLD ON TIGHT BECAUSE I AIN'T COMING BACK FOR YOU!"

Instinctively, Maggie searched for something to grab onto before anxiously lodging herself between two spiny bumps and gripping her bags. The cat gave another shudder and a second later they were moving, darting across the road and into the woods. Maggie looked behind her and saw the woman in the phone booth suddenly come to life, as Pethora looked sadly out at the ginger cat disappearing amongst the wet green bushes.

For a second, Maggie was lost in sadness until the wind rushed hard against her, pulling her back and threatening to throw her free, as the cat leapt silently over the wet tree trunks and thick bushes that surrounded them. Jamming herself deeper between the bumps Maggie felt her small frame bouncing violently from side to side, strands of thick ginger hair whipping against her curled legs, as the floor of the forest flew by in a blur of green. On and on they went, going ever deeper. Steadily the flashes of sunlight between the leafy roof became fewer, plunging them into a green jungle as the cat seemed to do all it could to shake itself free of any passengers. Then, just when she thought she could hold on no longer, Maggie felt the cat finally slow as the remains of an old stone building appeared up ahead, between a thick circle of trees. The walls had long ago collapsed, leaving only the chimney standing against the thick layers of scrub that grew up its length, determined to finish the demolition on their own. The ginger cat skipped up amongst the fallen gray stones and easily padded its way between the slippery moss, before coming to rest atop an old metal table that had been placed in the corner of the ruins, thick vines grew up its legs.

"Russell Farm North, last connection for the pink line," shouted the conductor from up between the ears of the cat, "All change here for blue lines and central lines."

Several small flies were buzzing around one corner, while beneath them a group of large black beetles sat huddled together in a tight circle. Maggie watched one particularly large beetle break from the group and scurry toward the edge of the table, the number '10' written along the side of its body in the same brellow letters she had seen on the sign by the village. In the shadows, Maggie could just make out a small line of people standing behind a line that had been scratched into the table top, the number '10' written next to it.

The cat crouched slowly down as if it was going to pounce on the circling flies, before lowering its large green eyes and curling its tail toward the middle of the table. Suddenly Maggie was surrounded as hundreds of passengers appeared around her, zigzagging their way from their hiding place between the thick shafts of hair as they rushed past the disheveled girl squatting on the floor, grimly holding her suitcases. Soon the crowd thinned and finally Maggie heaved herself up from the cat's spine and followed after them, muttering a promise to herself never to ride on a cat again. The heavy bags were clumsy to carry between the thick hairs, and several times Maggie drew annoyed looks from her fellow passengers as she banged into them, before she was finally able to emerge onto the rusted table top.

An incredible sight met her—hundreds of tiny figures were rushed in every direction as they fought to stand behind lines marked by large brellow numbers. For the first time Maggie was seeing the people her father had warned her about, and she pictured them fighting their war with the souls, their hearts full of hate. Instantly she wanted only to turn back, to tell Janus that she was ready to fight now, whatever it took to win the war against this evil. But it was no good. Behind her was a forest that didn't care about helping her find her way home. She could only move forward, Pethora's words ringing in her ears, "You have to pretend to be an internal. They have to think that you're one of them…"

Another beetle broke from the circle, the number '12' painted on its side, and let out a shrill hiss as it crossed in front of the large ginger cat.

"I'LL MOVE WHEN I'M READY ALRIGHT!" shouted the conductor from between the cat's ears.

The hissing and shouting continued as Maggie remembered Pethora's instructions. She dragged her two bags over to join the line that had formed next to the number ten beetle. A large woman in a flowery dress shuffled in, and Maggie trained her eyes downward. Suddenly it felt as though everyone was staring at her, as if they knew she wasn't one of them. But every time she dared to look up all she saw were faces staring blankly off into the distance, or reading from newspapers, as they waited patiently in the line— oblivious to the soul in their midst.

Maggie gasped. Up ahead, the beetle let out a steady hum as one of its shiny black wings lifted deliberately upward to reveal a small door in the side of its body. A thick black leg gave a twitch and smoothly laid itself flat, providing a small bridge. The line shuffled its way into the opening. Maggie's mouth hung open. Riding on top of a cat was one thing, but inside a beetle?

"Line is moving, miss," said a man behind her.

Maggie nodded to him—a thank-you—and gulped back her fear. This is what Pethora had told her to do. She had to go.

More and more people seemed to be disappearing inside as Maggie finally dragged her bags up to the door, hoping that there would be no room for her.

"She's the last one," said a man in a black uniform, pointing at Maggie as she finally bumped her way inside the beetle. Behind her the line gave a disgruntled grumble as they headed back down onto the table top to resume their wait.

"It looks like your lucky day, girly," said the man, holding open a wet hand as the door slowly eased its way back into place, "You got the last seat and it's right behind me. Where are you wanting to go today?"

Maggie smiled awkwardly back at him. Right now she didn't feel lucky at all.

"Errmm, Mildred Potts 79, please," she mumbled, feeling more than a little ridiculous.

"Oh," said the man in surprise, "well…good for you. That's a long trip though, and not cheap either."

Maggie reached inside her bag and found a fistful of coins, which she slowly counted out until he withdrew his hand, seemingly satisfied.

"Welcome aboard!" He smiled before sitting down and unbuttoning his jacket.

Two huge round windows in front looked out into the woods, as the beetle's thick black antennas danced in and out of view from above.

"Throw those bags over there," said the man, nodding toward an empty corner.

Maggie looked back to see a long pink cabin filled with internals, each sat upon red seats that looked out on small blue windows that sunk deep into the puffy walls. Above them thin red and blue plastic pipes formed tight bundles that ran up and down the walls, releasing a soft pink glow. Dropping herself into the last of the seats, she watched the man in uniform press his fingers together and bend them back with a loud cracking sound, before pushing his hands deep into the fleshy wall as if it were soft pink dough.

"Name is Reg, by the way," he said over his shoulder to Maggie.

Behind her the internals were making themselves comfortable, slipping off shoes and opening books. Maggie stared at the man in front of her, half of his arm was stuck inside the wall of the beetle.

"Erm...nice to meet you, Reg...I'm Maggie."

"Well, Maggie, get yourself comfy," he said, wiggling his shoulders, "we've got plenty of time to get to know each other."

Outside, the giant ginger cat turned and vaulted off the edge of the table. Inside the beetle a buzzing began to vibrate up through the seats. Soon there was a slow hiss like steam escaping from a boiling pot as the beetle's gigantic wings started to shake before disappearing into a blur of activity. They rose slowly into the air, Maggie's stomach flipping over and up into her chest as the deep green forest gave way to a bright sky. Up and up they went, everything below them shrinking, as Maggie began to search the thick forest below, before catching sight of her father's house far on the horizon.

Maggie watched as the red brick building slowly dissolved into a sea of green trees, realizing that she was leaving behind the only happy home that she could remember. Turning back, she stared at the internals around her as her sadness began to give way to anger. She didn't know where she was going, or what was to come, but as she felt herself being taken away she thought of the words in her father's letter. He had wanted her to join in his battle to free the souls. These internals were the enemy and she was going to find a way to stop them. She would make them regret what they had done to her parents.

10

A Successful Transplant

Maggie felt her head drop as a line of drool ran from the corner of her mouth. Instinctively wiping at it, she propped herself up and looked around, before rubbing her eyes. She didn't know how long she had been asleep but most of the passengers looked different to the ones that had been onboard when they took off from the table in the woods.

"Afternoon, sleepy head," said Reg, looking back over his shoulder, "you've been out of it for quite a while."

Maggie rubbed her face as she tried to remind herself that this wasn't a dream and she really was inside of a giant flying beetle.

"How long have I been asleep?" she asked.

"Long enough to sleep through lunch," he joked.

Maggie's stomach growled, confirming he was telling the truth. With a stretch she got to her feet and dragged the bags over to her chair, remembering the food that Pethora had told her was inside. The first bag contained only clothes, but the second provided two thick cheese sandwiches and a chocolate slice that was as big as her head. After quickly devouring the first sandwich, she leaned over and offered the second to Reg who had been hungrily eyeing it over his shoulder.

"Don't mind if I do," he said, plucking one hand from inside the wet pink wall, and a line of clear goo ran between his fingers.

Maggie watched him slurp at it hungrily as the wide blue sky outside gradually turned upward sending them toward a tall grey building. Hundreds of windows lined the outside walls, reflecting the afternoon sun as the beetle drifted closer and closer to the top floor and the one window that sat slightly ajar to the outside.

Maggie wasn't sure what made her stomach flip again. Perhaps it was the food, or the sudden lurch that the beetle took as it entered the open window, or maybe it was watching Reg lick the last of the cheese sandwich from his goo covered fingers, but as the beetle finally slowed to a stop on the window ledge she allowed herself a grateful sigh as her desire to throw up finally eased.

Sprawling out before them was a huge office that glowed in bright neon light, its size dwarfing their own tiny transport. Long lines of brown carpet ran up and down the length of the room like huge runways, each split by a low gray fabric wall that divided the hundreds of small entryways, revealing the top of a giant's head at work inside. To the left a large glass office looked out over the cubicles, its space consumed by a huge desk and a round headed man in a blue suit, who sat staring coldly out at the workers.

"That's our stop," announced Reg, drawing a finger across the room to the man behind the glass walls, "Hold on, folks, Simon Shepard 52 is coming up."

Maggie's stomach lurched again as they scooped upward to the ceiling. Beneath them the cubicles began to open up like a giant chessboard, as the tops of huge heads drifted in and out of view, moving the beetle closer to the corner office. Out of her window, Maggie noticed large brellow writing that covered the ceiling tiles like huge billboards:

Tiredness Kills…Take A Break!

Rest Area Ahead-Photocopier 2nd level
Clean bathrooms and snacks available

Tiny Chef
Home of the all-day breakfast!
Mary Jackson, 26, Receptionist
Parking in ear

Circling widely across the room, Reg slowed the beetle to a gentle hum as more and more heads below glanced up at the insect that had entered their office. Thankfully all of them seemed too bored to do anything to stop it, and as they drew closer to the glass office nobody noticed as Reg swung the beetle slowly from side to side, looking for a way in as he watched the closed door like his prey. A woman in a bright green dress approached, and Reg became suddenly tense, rolling his shoulders as though he was preparing to do something big. The woman knocked on the office window and, with a wave from the man inside, opened the door to enter. Instantly Maggie felt Reg throw the beetle down toward the opening, zooming in at the ever-decreasing gap, as the door started to swing shut. It seemed as though he was going to be too late, the side of the door swinging across their view, but at the last minute Reg swung the beetle hard to the left and snipped inside as the door sucked closed behind them with a slurp.

Maggie stared wide-eyed at the passengers behind her, expecting to see faces full of fear. But she only saw them sitting calmly, as if this was an everyday occurrence.

"You okay there, Maggie?" asked Reg.

"Errr, yeah…absolutely," she replied, trying not to reveal her fear.

The beetle continued downward, drifting toward the floor and sweeping between the desk legs before coming to rest on the arm of a chair. Out her window Maggie could see the folds in the man's trousers sweep past them like a sea of grey fabric circling a large cavernous pocket as the beetle scampered up toward the large hand hanging off the end of the armrest, its fingers dangling loosely against the cold metal frame. As they got closer Maggie saw that the skin under the fingernail had been peeled back to create a small pink doorway. Inside it stood two internals, both dressed in bright orange jackets. Reg swung around to face them as the black wing lifted and the door to the beetle swept inside itself, leaving a small gap between them and the end of the gigantic finger.

"SIMON SHEPHARD, 52. THIS IS THE SIMON SHEPARD, 52 STOP, FOLKS!" he shouted, before looking at the men who stood in the doorway under the giant fingernail. "Alright, Stan. Alright, Kev. How's life treating you?"

"No complaints, how's tricks?" asked one of the men.

Reg and the two men talked as Maggie watched the passengers leave the beetle, one by one, retrieving their bags before jumping over the gap and into the doorway beneath Simon Shepard's fingernail. High above them the giant woman in the bright green dress handed the man in the suit a thick folder of papers before turning to leave. As the last passenger disembarked, Reg said his goodbyes to the two internals inside and swung the beetle away from the finger just as the woman made her exit from the office. Later they found themselves leaving the office behind, the wide blue sky once again warming the inside of the beetle as Reg chatted about his wife and kids with Maggie.

Over and over the process was repeated with stops in giant coffee shops, colossal gift stores, mammoth car dealers, and titanic fast food restaurants. Time and again they would swoop in to deposit passengers under giant fingernails or beneath thick toes as Reg shouted out the names and numbers of their enormous owners, letting the passengers know where they were.

Soon the light outside faded, while inside more empty seats appeared as passengers stopped getting on. Maggie looked over Reg's shoulder at the disappearing daylight and began to worry. How many stops could be left?

Time was starting to drag, but still the beetle kept going. Even an attack by a waitress, armed with a magazine, failed to stop their progress. An exhausted Maggie slumped down into her chair and looked back, realizing that there were two other passengers left.

"TRACEY REYNOLDS 29," shouted Reg, as they landed on a tired looking hairdresser, "NEXT STOP IS THE LAST STOP."

The two men at the back got up and wrapped thick blue and white striped scarves around their necks as they headed for the door.

"Enjoy the match, lads," said Reg, as they stepped under Tracey's large red fingernail.

Maggie saw a line of ants below steadily making their way through piles of hair as they headed for Tracey's rather large big red toenail.

"That's a lot of traffic down there," said Reg, "don't know why they bother. Rovers will never win the cup, not with their keeper."

"I'm sorry," said Maggie, "Is there some sort of game happening...in her?"

Reg looked back at Maggie as the beetle gave a small shudder. "Is there a game on? Whose pocket have you been living in? Tracey Reynolds 29 is only the home ground of Kidney City and tonight is only the quarter finals of the Inter Cup!"

Maggie gazed at him, unsure of what to say. She had sat through enough of her stepbrothers' rugby conversations to fake some knowledge of the sport but she guessed that any attempt to pretend she knew who, or what, Kidney City was would be a bad idea.

"Never mind!" said Reg, shaking his head as they headed for the door.

In the shop window a large bluebottle fly was repeatedly banging into the clear glass before falling helplessly onto the shelf. It scrambled back up onto its feet to start the process all over again.

"Learner drivers," said Reg as the beetle darted out into the open.

The sun was starting to fall into the horizon as the beetle left the hairdressers behind and headed out over a large yellow field. Gradually the houses disappeared behind them as the roads below became thinner and thinner, leaving little space for the cars that struggled to pass each other. On and on they went, the dusky light revealing only more fields, until Reg swung the beetle slowly to the right, and a large bundle of trees drifted into view. As they drew closer, small red rooftops appeared between the treetops, and Maggie sensed the smell of a log fire burning. The beetle gave a small tremble and began to slowly descend through the leaves as flashes of green streaked past Maggie's small window before disappearing to reveal a long street lined with red brick houses and a neatly painted sign on its corner that read 'Green Lanes.'

The evening light had all but left them and yet still they flew on, Maggie watching the day come to a close for the giant bodies around her as the beetle went farther and farther into the darkness. Then, just when it seemed that they were about to leave the town behind them, the beetle swung on its side and headed down a cracked pathway toward a house that looked badly in need of repair. Neatly trimmed bushes or clean white walls fronted the rest of the homes on the street, but this house was fighting a losing battle against its front garden. Bushes and vines climbed high up its front, circling its grey windows or creeping inside its drains.

"Nearly there," said Reg, "Mildred Potts 79 coming right up."

The beetle flew into the shadowy porch of the house and circled up and down as they looked for a way in. Unlike all the other stops they had made, there appeared to be little chance of any help to get them inside. One look at the pile of leaves and trash at the base of the door told Maggie that it had been a long time since anyone had visited here.

"That'll do us," said Reg excitedly, circling the beetle toward a dark corner of the porch. Built into the wall sat a rusted mailbox, overflowing with old magazines and letters offering a 'Once In A Lifetime Opportunity!' or declaring 'YOU'RE A WINNER!' Maggie noticed a small shaft of light shining out from between the old mail as they flew closer. She felt the beetle shoot down inside a rolled up flyer, as a giant offer for an unbeatable credit card shot past her window. Emerging out of the paper tunnel they found themselves in a narrow hallway lit only by an old lamp that sat amongst a pile of browning junk mail. A staircase ran up into the darkness while opposite a photograph of a man in a soldier uniform stood guard between two doorways. Reg circled over the light before taking them down under the cold radiator that leaned against the peeling wall.

"Well...it's been a while since I had any passengers for this stop," he said with a yawn, as the beetle turned in through the open doorway, "but at least I can always count on Mildred to stay in the same place."

Maggie found herself looking out of the beetle at the figure of a large old woman nestled deep into an oversized armchair in the middle of a small sitting room. A TV stood in one corner, silently flickering an old black and white movie across the room, its light revealing a wrinkled face, her eyes fixed on the mantelpiece and more photographs of the soldier Maggie had seen in the hallway. Everything about the room seemed to be old and grey, just like its tired looking occupant who sat motionless.

"Here we go. Mildred Potts 79. Last stop."

Maggie looked up at the old woman. The ones she had seen on TV always had snowy hair and friendly smiles, and spent their time thanking people for helping them on buses or giving their grandchildren boiled sweets. This old woman was large, and looked in need of a bath, with a dour face that suggested she would punch anyone who tried to help her or take her candy. They had stopped at many bodies that day, and while she would rather not have to get off at any of them, this was definitely her last choice.

"Can't use the fingers stop for Mildred," said Reg, pulling the beetle upward, "there will be no one there to meet us at this time of night. Good thing Mildred's deaf because I'm going to have to drop you off in her ear."

Unsure if this was a good thing or not Maggie watched as the beetle homed in on the old woman's head, flying casually past her face and in through her grey hair. There was a familiar slowing of the buzzing as the beetle landed softly on the edge of her unmoving cheek, before scuttling down into the opening of her ear.

"Your stop, Maggie," said Reg, smiling back at his young passenger.

Nervously Maggie got to her feet and picked up her bags as the door on the beetle slid open to the darkness outside.

"You take care, Maggie," said Reg, plucking a sticky hand from the wall of the beetle to offer a handshake, "It's been a pleasure."

Maggie took the hand and shook it, cold slime slid between her fingers. "Are you sure this is my stop?" she said anxiously.

"It's got to be," replied Reg, "Last stop of the day."

Maggie slowly turned and stepped cautiously out onto the beetle's outstretched leg, squinting into the cavernous darkness around her.

"You're sure?" she questioned, turning back to Reg.

"This is you. Wherever you're supposed to be going, this is it," replied Reg.

Maggie looked up into the warm door of the beetle and then down into the cold darkness below. Earlier that day it had filled her with dread, but right now she would have done anything to stay inside with Reg. She took a small step and felt her foot sink into the soft ground of the old lady's ear. Then the beetle's leg slid backward, and behind her the small square of light narrowed between the closing doors as Reg waved goodbye.

"Take care, Maggie Pincus," he shouted, "and thanks for the sandwich!"

Then he was gone, the black body of the beetle disappearing into the darkness as it flew quickly away leaving Maggie standing alone in the chill of the cavernous ear. A small light from the TV outside fought its way through the thick strands of hair, and Maggie dragged her bags over to sit next to it, feeling as though she sat behind a giant grey waterfall.

Pethora had said that there would be someone there to meet her, but as she waited in the cold her hopes quickly started to fade. What if there had been a mistake? What if she couldn't reach the person who was supposed to meet her, or even worse, what if they'd refused to meet her and she was wanted by the internals after all? Then, just as she was about to give up all hope, a small light appeared at the end of the tunnel as a tiny yellow candle flame drifted slowly toward her from inside the darkness.

"Hello?" said Maggie nervously, her voice echoing around her, "Is someone there?"

Without a word the candlelight came closer, slowly revealing a head hovering above it in the shadows. A woman with a long thin face approached, her hooked nose casting a shadow over the top of her unsmiling mouth. Strands of curled blonde hair fell sporadically onto her forehead.

"Maggie?" she asked coldly.

"Yes, I'm Maggie," she replied, unable to hide the fear in her voice.

The woman looked down at her as the light from the candle contorted her face into a furious expression. "Well it's about time! I've been all over Mildred looking for you! Why they dropped you off up here I'll never know."

"I'm sorry?" said Maggie timidly.

"So you should be. I'm Miss Devlin and I'm your house matron. Now hurry up, you're late and I'm tired," she snapped.

Maggie scrambled to her feet and dragged the two bags over the soft floor as Miss Devlin strode ahead.

"Excuse me," said Maggie, struggling to keep up, "but what's a house matron?"

Miss Devlin stopped in her tracks and turned to face Maggie, who only just managed to stop herself from crashing into the boney woman in her path. "Don't be ridiculous, child, you can't tell me you don't know what a house matron is! I'm the head of the orphanage...surely you're not that stupid?"

Maggie stared back at her blankly.

"Oh no...you are stupid, aren't you?" she said, pulling a thick file of papers from under her arm.

"Let's see...Maggie...Maggie," she mumbled as she picked between the thick piles of pages, "Aha! Maggie Pincus! So let's see...twelve years old...good eyesight...no allergies...no medications...parents killed in a bumble bee crash...normal height...your last home was, oh wonderful!"

"What, what is it?" asked Maggie apprehensively.

"Says here you're a nobo and I can tell you right now I don't have the time to deal with that!" she snapped.

"I'm sorry," said Maggie, "but what's a nobo?"

"A nobo? A no-body? An internal who has never lived in a body. You probably had some freethinking parents who thought they were better than the rest of us and spent their lives living in a dandelion! I knew you were going to be trouble the moment I heard you were coming. I don't get anyone for years and now you? How dare they send me a nobo with everything else that's going on!" she ranted, turning her back on Maggie before striding away.

Maggie stood there for a second trying to understand. Is this what Pethora had meant when she said they had a safe place for her—that she was supposed to go and live in an orphanage? Surely this was wrong.

"Come along, child!" said Miss Devlin, marching over to snatch up Maggie's bags with surprising ease. "I haven't time for you to dawdle. As long as I'm going to do all the work then the least you can do is help, here take this hair slice."

Miss Devlin produced a thick grey string and gave it to Maggie who stared at it in her open hand, hoping that it would know what to do without her.

"Oh good grief," snapped Miss Devlin, snatching it back and walking over to one of the black walls.

She scooped her thin hand deep into the dark surface, producing what looked like a thick pile of mud in her palm.

"Here," she said, dropping it into Maggie's hand, before stabbing the hair into its center and lighting it from her own small flame, "Earwax candle. Don't think I have time to be teaching you everything, nobo. You can thank me for this lesson later. You'll need it with all the power cutbacks around here."

Maggie looked down in disgust at the slimy candle as she chased after Miss Devlin, who was once again striding off into the dark. Deeper and deeper into the ear they went, leaving the entrance far behind them as the earwax in Maggie's hands became steadily softer, threatening to run between her fingers as it released a smell that reminded her of warm trash.

"Come along, whatever your name is," said Miss Devlin as they came to a fork in the passage, "this way!"

Maggie watched her drop the small candle on the floor and descend a steep flight of stairs that led down into a bright circle of light far below. She already had a suspicion that Miss Devlin disliked her enough to say no to every question Maggie could ever ask, and so without permission she decided to drop her own muddy candle before chasing after her. At first it seemed like a good plan, but as she tried to catch up to the surprisingly fast house matron she realized that she was going too fast for the ever-steepening stairs. In a panic she reached out to grab the handrail. Only then did she feel the layer of slimy earwax take its revenge, greasing her grasp as her hands slipped away from the rail, leaving her flailing as though she were trying to juggle wet soap. Before she knew it she was bouncing,

one, two, three steps at a time until finally she thudded
to a stop.

A blur of feet slowly appeared all around her.
With an aching heave, she pushed herself up onto her
feet as figures rushed busily around her, oblivious to
her pain. Unlike most of the internals she had seen that
day these were definitely not a group she could blend
into easily. A huge man with incredibly large muscles
brushed by, his tiny head narrowly avoiding the ceiling
as he talked happily with a misty grey form drifting
next to him, his transparent body shaped like an
upturned raindrop with two long arms and a single pink
eye. While behind them slid, what looked like, a close
relative of the candle Maggie had been holding, its
long brown fingers stretching out one at a time to pull
its bulky wet body along. A thick soggy trail formed
behind it.

"Excuse me, sorry, in a hurry here," said an
urgent voice behind Maggie.

She turned to see a tiny old man standing behind
her, occasional bursts of flame dancing over his body
as bursts of electricity sporadically crackled around his
head. In a world where everything was small, this man
was definitely not the exception, his bald white head
hovering just below Maggie's waist.

She moved to one side, and the small man continued on his way, repeating his words as he tried to negotiate the crowd who were all moving much faster than him.

Everywhere she looked more and more of the strange creatures appeared, each seemingly more fantastic than the next, walking happily amongst internals who dotted the crowded pink corridor. Above them, swollen plastic pipes crisscrossed the ceiling. The walls rippled against the pumping of their thick red contents, before disappearing behind large white plates that glowed bright with the pipe's warm contents.

"Come on," snapped Miss Devlin, grabbing Maggie's shoulder with her boney hand, "This is no playground, nobo!"

Several strange pairs of eyes turned to stare at Maggie as the word 'nobo' hung in the air, slowing the group rushing past her. Then she was being pulled against the traffic as Miss Devlin navigated their way up the hallway to one of the large openings that branched outward from the pink walls. The crowd disappeared behind them as they stepped inside, and Maggie felt the hand on her shoulder release.

"MISS DEVLIN, MISS DEVLIN," wheezed a breathless voice. Around the corner a large man wearing a policeman's uniform with a large white badge that read 'Antibody PC' jogged toward them. Beneath the uniform, a large belly was draped precariously over the top of a black belt that looked so overworked that it might willingly snap any second. He bent over in front of them trying to catch his breath as he raised a hand, asking them to wait.

Miss Devlin, who was certainly in no mood for waiting, leaned forward and tapped him on the top of his helmet. "What do you want, Officer Tilly? I'm in something of a hurry here. They sent me a child that is, quite frankly, unacceptable and I have an urgent letter of complaint to write."

The policeman remained bent over, but looked up to give Maggie a friendly smile.

"Sorry, Miss Devlin." He grimaced as he struggled upright. "It's just that we've been tracking a cold virus all day, and now Buddy's gone missing. Have you seen him?"

"You mean him?" She pointed.

A strange shape waited patiently behind for its master to turn around, but unlike any other police dog that Maggie had ever seen this one was completely transparent. Its jelly-like body squirmed as it crouched on four clear legs, its long tongue dripping a thick yellow slime. Inside its belly a small blue creature was twisting in fury.

"BUDDY!" shouted Officer Tilly in delight as the lumpy animal jumped up against his chest and licked his face, "And you got him! Good boy, Buddy! Who's a good boy? Who's a good boy? You are, yes you are!"

Maggie watched Buddy slobber over the policeman, who seemed oblivious to the thick lines of slime that were dripping down his uniform, much to the disgust of Miss Devlin.

"Goodnight, Officer Tilly," she snipped, pulling Maggie away as the reunion continued behind them.

They descended, through stairwells and narrow corridors, leaving everyone far behind them until they emerged into the middle of a dark hallway that ended at a brown doorway buried deep in the shadows. The sign on the door read 'The Tibia Home for Children.' Miss Devlin pulled a large key from her pocket and opened it to reveal a circular room filled with several couches that circled around a low table covered with old magazines. Trash seemed to be everywhere— empty food wrappers stuffed between the cushions and old plates lying on every surface as if they were relaxing after a long day. More red pipes pumped their way across the ceiling, disappearing behind light panels or weaving themselves under pink circles that glowed with a warm heat filling the room. In one corner was a large glass window that revealed another small room dominated by a desk and walls of files, while across from it was another wooden door that was labeled 'Dormitory.'

"This is the living room, bathroom is in the middle of the dorm, which is over there. Go on then, child. Do try not to wake the others up, I have work to do," said Miss Devlin, gesturing for Maggie to continue on alone.

Nervously, Maggie took her bags and stepped toward the dormitory door, presuming that she was supposed to go to bed. After the long beetle trip all she really wanted was more to eat but the look on Miss Devlin's face told her that this wasn't part of the plan and so she continued on as her stomach grumbled its disappointment.

Maggie gently opened the heavy door and peeked in as the light behind her swept outward to reveal one half of a seemingly endless room that was filled with hundreds of empty beds. Each of them was neatly made with thick red blankets and greying pillowcases that were split by dusty nightstands.

"Hey, shut the door, I'm trying to sleep here!" came an angry voice from deep in the darkness. Maggie stepped inside and quickly closed the door, only to instantly regret it as the light disappeared, leaving her standing helpless in the dark. As her eyes slowly adjusted she tried to remember where the first bed had been, and dragged her bags in its general direction until her shin banged hard into something, letting her know she had found it. She sat down and opened her suitcase, looking through the murky darkness for something to wear to bed. She found the chocolate slice that remained forgotten in her bag, which she devoured hungrily. She felt the thick spongy chocolate slide warmly down her throat as her stomach gave up its grumble. As she took another large bite, she noticed something out of the corner of her eye and looked down to see that a small white envelope had fallen out of her bag and was now lying next to her. She tucked away the chocolate slice and picked up the envelope, and felt along its length as something hard rolled between her fingers. Reaching inside, she found a silver necklace with a shiny round pendant hanging in its middle. Tied to it was a small piece of paper marked with blue letters that even in the dark Maggie recognized as Pethora's handwriting.

Your dad wanted you to have this.

Maggie ran her fingers across the words before lying down and curling into a ball, the silver pendant tight in her hand. The mattress was cold and lumpy but at that moment she didn't feel a thing; her mind was anywhere but here. She was lost in the darkness still trying to make sense of everything that had happened to her since the day they had come for her on Breezy Lane, and all the turns her life had taken since then. All of them bringing her here…to a new life…alone in an orphanage inside an old woman…pretending to be someone she wasn't.

She scrunched her eyes against the flow of tears that were trying to escape, and forced herself to remember walks through the woods with her father. The necklace began to warm between her fingers. The air was hot and in the distance birds were singing. They stepped into the clearing and sat down on their bench and watched the sun set on another perfect day before he leaned over to hug her and he kissed the top of her head.

"It's going to be okay," he said, "I promise it will be okay."

Maggie sat there with him for a long time, clinging to his memory until tiredness finally overtook her. The necklace slipped from between her fingers and hung against her sleeping chest. For now, he had made it okay.

Malcolm...The fly is back again...If you were here you'd chase it around the room for me and hit it with your newspaper...but all I can do is watch it circling me as if I'm some sort of tourist attraction...I must remember to tell the nurse next time she's here. Maybe she'll kill it for me.

11

Icing the Area

"This one will do!"

Maggie was pulled upright; her sleeping head flopped heavily behind.

"Wh…what…why is…what's going on?" she managed, as someone padded her face with a sponge.

"Richie," said a voice behind her, "I think this is the one. Yep, Jackie's doing her makeup right now. I'll see how she looks on the memorizer."

Maggie turned to see a man talking into a large headset. His face was long and the heavy black speakers that covered his ears only added to his tired expression.

"Hey, pretty girl," he said to Maggie without any sincerity, "Today is your lucky day. You're being interviewed for Good Morning Green Village. All your little friends will get to see you. How's that for a treat? Basically, it's just a quick Q and A. The minister comes on, talks to Julie, asks you a couple of nice questions, you smile and answer, we're all happy. Okay?"

"Minister? What? I just got here," stammered Maggie as someone flashed a bright red light in her face.

"YEP, SHE'LL DO. BRING THE CHILD IN!" shouted someone from the other room.

Maggie felt the man grab her hand and pull her up as she tried to straighten the clothes she was still wearing from yesterday, unsure of where she was going. Through the bodies surrounding her she caught sight of three children sitting around a bed, all smiling intently at her as if they knew something she didn't. She tried to raise her hand to wave hello, only to feel herself pulled roughly away and out into the living room. The room she entered was very different from the one she had left the night before. Gone were the piles of trash and plates, replaced by a clean room that was now swarming with people all busy at work. Suddenly Miss Devlin burst out of the group, her mouth falling open at the sight of Maggie, before quickly twisting back up into a rigid smile.

"Oh good!" she said loudly through gritted teeth, "It's Maggie! Come here, child, did you sleep okay? I was so worried about you, what with it being your first night and all. Fear not, Miss Devlin is here to take care of you now."

Miss Devlin locked her in a vice-like hug with her two boney arms. Maggie looked up at the bright red lips smiling down at her and wondered what had happened to the mean woman who had met her last night.

"There, there, child," she said, finally releasing her, "come and meet the minister. He's a wonderful man."

Miss Devlin looked around the room, hoping to catch someone listening in on her conversation, only to be disappointed as everyone continued to work busily around her. With a snort of annoyance she spun around and grabbed Maggie's wrist before pushing her way into a small circle of people who stood drinking from steaming yellow cups.

"Excuse me!" she spat, as if they had been in the wrong, "We are needed by the minister."

Maggie looked up apologetically at the group as they were quickly divided by the housemistress, only to forget to watch where she was going and trip over a bundle of wires that lay on the floor. Miss Devlin barely noticed and continued to drag her, as if she were made of rags, before coming to a stop in front of a man and a rather bored looking woman who was applying his makeup.

"Ira, this is the new child I was telling you about," said Miss Devlin, tapping him on the shoulder.

A middle-aged man in a white suit turned around. His sleeves were rolled up past his elbows, exposing a hairy chest that looked as though it might jump out and attack them any second.

"Pleased to meet you. Minister for Waste, Ira Marsh…that's right, THE Ira Marsh!" he said, offering her a soft hand. "Sorry about the whole 'you being an orphan thing.' Had a very similar experience myself once when my parents lost me in a department store. Worst two hours of my life I can tell you. It totally ruined my seventeenth birthday. Still at least I overcame it. And as you can see, I went on to do great things with my life…and you can too."

The minister winked at her and gave two thumbs up. From across the room Maggie heard sniggers and turned to see the three children from the dormitory watching as they huddled in the doorway, their faces red as they tried not to laugh.

"Minister Marsh, two minutes until we go live. Can we get you and Julie together so we can work on your lighting?" The man from the dorm pushed into the group and pulled the minister away as Miss Devlin dragged a confused Maggie behind her.

More people filled the room, making the crowd impossible to navigate and Maggie gratefully felt Miss Devlin release her grip as she pushed forward alone. Looking around, she found herself on the edge of a circle of bright light that shone onto a small area of floor that was surrounded by yellow tape. Pink cables squirmed all around her feet, looping themselves away toward a large circular panel that seemed to have grown up from the floor like an oversized pink mushroom. Behind it two men stood arguing loudly as they poked at its surface, sending sparks flying up from under their fingers. Next to them stood a tall man holding what looked like an oversized white tube on his shoulder and Maggie watched in amazement as he pressed the side of his face against it, only for it to sink deep inside, absorbing his eye, before he pulled himself free with a wet 'POP!'

"Can I get you something, Miss Pincus?" said a small voice from below.

Maggie looked down to see a young man looking up at her with wide green eyes, his body covered in the same flashes of fire and electricity that she had seen on the old man in the hallway the day before. Unlike the older man this one could barely stay still, jumping from foot to foot with incredible speed, powered by thick legs that bulged against his shorts as he waited impatiently for an answer.

"Well, can I?"

Maggie fumbled. "Errmm, some water would be nice?" she said apologetically.

There was a crack of bright light and he was gone, followed instantly by a second crack as he reappeared holding a small glass of water in his outstretched hand, as if he had just produced it from his pocket.

"Thank-you," said Maggie, slightly taken aback, "Can I ask how you know my name?"

The young man looked up at her as if she had lost her mind. "I saw you standing over there, I went upstairs to the central registry, I checked the listing for the Tibia Orphanage, I cross referenced that with the Mildred Potts resident listing and found your file—

164

Maggie Pincus, age 12, likes chocolate shakes and pasta, no sauce."

"But…how did you do all that so fast?" questioned Maggie.

"I'm a nerve!" he replied indignantly, "My purpose in life is to deliver things fast!"

"Sorry," said Maggie, sensing that it had been a bad question to ask, "but thank-you again," she said, taking a drink.

As she put the glass to her lips there was another crack and he was gone again. Maggie looked down at her glass of water and the thick line of makeup where her mouth had just been. Suddenly she was glad that there were no mirrors around, this morning was turning out be hard enough and having to see what she looked like under all the makeup they had put on her was more than she thought she could handle right now.

"Julie? Minister Marsh? Can you come on over?" said a man, wearing a hat marked 'DIRECTOR,' pulling Maggie to one side, "You… Magdy, is it? Okay Magdy, you stand there for a minute and wait for my cue. Julie will ask you some questions. Be honest…and entertaining…and funny… entertaining and funny is always good. You look wonderful! Be great!"

The group parted as the minister entered the circle, followed by a rather orange woman in a sparkling white suit. The man with the giant white tube stepped forward and sunk his head back into its side as it suddenly dawned on Maggie that it was a camera. Instantly she felt a rush of fear sting her spine as she realized what was happening. They were about to film something, and that something was her.

"QUIET ON SET EVERYONE!" shouted the director, "And we're live in four, three…" He stepped back stabbing his fingers into the numbers two and one as all eyes in the room fell on Julie and the minister.

"Good morning, residents of Green Village!" said the woman, flashing a perfect white smile into the red light, "I'm here this morning in Mildred Potts, 79 with the Minister for Waste, Ira Marsh. And today we're visiting the Tibia Orphanage for Children. The minister is a big supporter of those in need and we are here today to meet some of the special children he helps. Minister, why don't you tell us a little bit about what it is you do here?"

"Thank-you, Julie," said the minister with yet another wink as he leaned over to talk into the white ball in Julie's hand, "As you so wonderfully said, I am the Minister for Waste, and while that is a very…very demanding job, I don't like to forget that there are many less fortunate than myself out there who need my help. So when I'm not being Minister for Waste, which is a very...very demanding job, I like to come here and spend time with the kids…kids who don't have parents…to let them know I care."

"He only comes here late at night and even then we have to go straight to bed," said a small voice in Maggie's ear.

One of the children from the dormitory was standing close behind her, whispering in her ear as the minister continued to tell Julie how great he was.

"It's not as if he's any good at being Minister for Waste either," continued the boy in hushed tones, "Mildred hasn't been able to go regularly since he took the job. Used to be she was as regular, like clockwork, but since he was put in charge we're lucky if she goes once a week. You can't even go up Sacrum Street anymore, the smell will kill you."

Maggie let out an involuntary snort of laughter as the director shot her a silencing glare.

"Oh, pleased to meet you by the way, the name's Stick."

Maggie glanced over at Stick, who looked like his name suggested, with a wiry body that supported a messy mop of brown hair that spiked randomly in every direction.

"Please to meet you, too. I'm Maggie," she whispered.

Behind them, the minister was still talking as Julie patiently waited, her painted smile showing no signs of fading.

"You see, good people of Green Village, the thing about me is that I really care. As I said to Thaddeus Miles last night, 'you may be the regional minister in charge of Mildred Potts, 79 but you don't have to thank me for all the advice that I give you, I don't do it for the credit, I do it because I want to make all of Green Village…and lots of other towns…or even cities…a better place.'"

"He's not very subtle is he?" whispered Stick, "You'd never guess he wants a promotion to a new body, would you? Well not unless you'd never seen him, heard him, or talked to him."

Maggie allowed a smile, only to freeze as she suddenly realized that everyone in the room was looking at her. Julie and the minister stood like statues smiling expectantly in her direction as the director waved furiously for her to walk toward them. Hurriedly, Maggie went to take a step forward only to feel her foot stop in midair as if she had kicked a large rock. Forward she went as her feet failed to follow her commands, sending her down toward the mass of wires on the floor. In mid-fall she caught sight of her shoelaces tied tightly together, and Stick and the two girls from the doorway shuffling backward, their faces threatening to burst with laughter. Maggie reached out to stop herself only to send the glass spinning upward. At first it managed to keep its contents, as it arched high over the ministers head, but as it slowly started downward toward the wide-eyed Julie, the water made its escape. Julie let out a scream as she felt the cold liquid hit her in the face, blinding her to the glass that was following rapidly behind it, bouncing against her head with a heavy, 'THUNK.' From atop of her nest of wires, Maggie watched as she fell to the floor, her layers of makeup already beginning to wash damply down onto her white suit. A silent panic filled the room as Julie lay there motionless. It was as if every second lasted an hour. Everyone stood in silence, staring at the two bodies on the floor as the minister stood frozen over them, smiling blankly into the camera. Then, out of nowhere, he seemed to come back to life. Calmly he picked up the white ball and stepped over the unconscious Julie, as if she were invisible, before talking into the camera as though nothing unusual had happened.

"I'm sure she'll be just fine, folks. Now where were we?" he said, walking out of the circle, "Well, as long as Julie is taking a little snooze, why don't we take a detour?"

For a second the camera operator froze, unsure of what to do, as the director snapped at him, angrily mouthing the silent words, 'WE'RE LIVE! KEEP HIM ON MEMORIZER, GO WITH IT!"

The crowd parted as the minister walked over to Miss Devlin, who was leaning against a small box by her office, her confused face fighting a battle to look good for the camera. The memorizer swung in her direction and she snapped upright, forcing a smile that only succeeded in making her look like she had just been caught doing something she shouldn't.

"Now, this lovely lady is Miss Devlin and she is the one who takes care of the orphans when I can't be here to help. Miss Devlin and I practically run this place together. Isn't that right?" he asked with a curled smile.

Miss Devlin leaned into the white ball, but before she could speak the minister started talking again, leaving her to suck back her words as if she had never planned to say anything in the first place.

"Well, that's good to know. Now then, why don't we do something a little different?" said the minister, patting the small box on the wall. "As you know, the government ministers gave these suggestion boxes to all the organizations throughout Green Village and while I'm not saying that it was my idea, even though it was, I think we should have a little look and see what a great job the orphans think myself and Miss Devlin are doing here."

A look of panic appeared in Miss Devlin's eyes, and she gripped the lid of the box as the three children gasped.

"Here we are," said the minister, peeling back Miss Devlin's fingers to pull out a piece of paper, "suggestion number one: 'Miss Devlin should stop selling our schoolbooks and using the money to get her hair done.'"

Everyone stared in horror at the housemistress, who instantly flushed bright red.

"Well, that was obviously a joke! You little scamps you!" said the minister, waving a hairy finger at the three children who suddenly looked as though they would rather be anywhere but here.

"Let's try again, shall we? Suggestion number two: 'If there's no pets allowed in the dorm, why is Minister Marsh allowed to bring in his chest hair?'"

The minister's voice trailed off and he shot a cold look over at the children before turning his gaze onto Miss Devlin. Tension filled the air like thick syrup as everyone waited to see what the minister would say. He paused for just a moment too long. A woman silently broke from the watching crowd, skipping over to whisper in the director's ear, prompting him to swirl his finger in a circle as he mouthed the words, 'WRAP IT UP, NOW!"

"Perhaps one more. A real one perhaps this time!" said the minister with a fake laugh, as he ignored the director and pulled out another piece of paper from the box, "Miss Devlin should learn my name. She thinks I'm called…stupid brat!"

Ira Marsh stood and stared at the small bead of sweat that was running down Miss Devlin's face as time stood still around them.

"WE'RE OFF AIR!" shouted the director finally, "We are no longer memorizing. Pack it all up. Oh what a disaster!"

The minister stood, glaring at Miss Devlin, his face twisted in fury as she tried to avoid his eyes.

172

"Will you excuse me for a second?" she said through a gritted smile, walking quickly toward the three children who stood like statues. A steady hum returned to the room as everyone pretended to work, all the while keeping one eye on the housemistress who was bearing down on the three children with a look of fury. Their faces hung heavy as she approached and they scrunched their mouths up tight as if they knew what was about to happen.

"SORRY ABOUT THAT MINISTER," said Maggie as she got to her feet, "I THOUGHT IT WOULD BE FUNNY!"

Everyone stopped. Miss Devlin turned around. Ira Marsh walked over to look at Maggie, his face looking like it was about to burst.

"The suggestions…they were supposed to be a joke. I didn't know you were going to read them out. They were just a joke to make you and Miss Devlin laugh. I'm new here and I just wanted to make you both laugh. It was just a joke." Maggie didn't know why she was speaking, all she knew was that something in Miss Devlin's eyes had reminded her of her stepmother, and before she could think the words had come out of her, leaving her fumbling for what to say next.

"Do you have any idea what you just did?" snarled the minister, "Do you know how much I paid to have this memorizer crew interview me this morning? A small fortune! This was supposed to be my moment to shine and you ruined it! I made sure that every minister, for as far as Mildred can see, was watching and now I'll be a laughing stock. This wasn't about you and your silly little joke, this was about me getting out of this lousy old woman and into a place I belong!"

His bad breath rushed at Maggie like a hairdryer filled with rotting onions.

"I'm sorry," she repeated, "It was just a joke."

Miss Devlin's tight grip fell on Maggie's shoulders.

"Don't you worry, minister. I'll see that she's punished," she said, squeezing her nails into Maggie's shoulders.

Ira Marsh stood red-faced before her with hands that were balled into tight fists.

"I shall expect a full report on how you chose to deal with her as soon as possible," he growled, his eyes still boring into Maggie.

Flush with anger, he turned and slammed the front door, sending the suggestion box crashing to the floor. The silence returned as everyone looked amongst themselves, the only sound a wet 'pop' from the cameraman as he freed his head from inside the memorizer and stretched his eye against the bright light.

"Right, that's enough," announced the director, "back to work. We've got a traffic report over at Shirley Talbot 52, and then we've got an interview with a man who works in Mary Reed 24. She just had eight babies. We've got a long day, people."

A groan filled the room as cases were clicked open and equipment was packed away. The mushroom sank into the floor and someone helped a rather damp looking Linda to her feet. Miss Devlin gave Maggie a push and guided her through the crowd and into the dormitory, before spinning her around to sit on a bed, the old springs creaking their disapproval.

Maggie searched the room frantically for a way to escape. Small pink windows lined the walls but they were all too small for her to climb out of, and the only other door led to the bathroom. Deep in the shadows at the end of the long room someone was balled up in bed sleeping peacefully through all of the commotion. Maggie wondered if she should try to wake them up to be a witness for what was about to happen.

"I don't know what you think you're playing at," said Miss Devlin under her breath, her face returning to its previous day's shape, "but you and I both know that little suggestion box trick wasn't you. Why you want to take the blame for those brats I do not know, but I do know this! The minister was my ticket out of here and someone just ruined it for me so now there's a price to be paid. And as long as you're so keen on volunteering it's going to be you! Now, I'm going to walk out of here, but I'll be back as soon as everyone leaves. Then I'm going to ask you who is to blame. If you want to tell the truth this time, then you'll save yourself a lot of trouble. But if you insist that it was you then I'm going to give you a punishment so bad that it will make those three think twice before doing any more of their little pranks ever again!"

Maggie watched her leave, fear running through her body. She felt cold and alone. It was as if everything had gone backwards and she was once again in Breezy Lane where everyone hated her.

"Pssssssssstttttttttttttttttttttttttttt!" came a noise, "Psssssssssttttttttttt!"

Maggie looked over at the bed opposite her. In the shadows below, a set of eyes stared urgently up. "Quick, before she gets back," they hissed.

Hesitantly Maggie walked over to lift the skirt of the bed. Beneath it she found a square just big enough for a child dug into the floor, its dark entrance circling the boy who had introduced himself as Stick.

"Come on! Do you want to stay with Devlin or get out of here?" he urged.

In the next room the front door slammed shut and a set of feet clicked toward them. Miss Devlin was coming back, but which was worse? Going with the boy who had tricked her or taking her chances with a very angry housemistress?

"Move over!" she urged, sliding herself under the bed.

The edges of the hole were wet under her hands and she slipped clumsily down to land inside a low tunnel, just as a pair of bright red shoes clicked angrily past the bed.

"Wherever you are, come here now. You have two seconds, nobo!" hissed Miss Devlin's voice from above.

For a second Maggie thought about shouting out. Maybe she could explain what had happened. But before she could change her mind everything went black as Stick pulled the flap closed, sealing them in. It was too late to go back now—it seemed she had made her choice. Whoever this boy was, even if he was an internal, she needed him.

Malcolm...I'm starting to hear voices. It's a girl's voice...it seems far away, but she's definitely there. Maybe it's just one of the neighborhood kids...or maybe she isn't there at all...maybe I'm just going crazy.

12

The Infection Inside

'CRACK!'

A bright light filled the tunnel, illuminating walls lined with thick yellow goop that hung in drips all around them like exploded jelly. Maggie pushed one of the large gooey drops away from her face, only for it to spring back like a rubber ball and hit her in the side of the head.

"Owwwww!" she said, rubbing at the red mark on the side of her face.

For a second, Stick struggled to suppress a laugh before regaining his smile and holding up his hand to Maggie. There, dancing in his palm, was a small bolt of electricity that was glowing a brilliant white as it lit up his face and shone bright in his blue eyes. His messy brown hair still crowded his thin face but in the glow Maggie could see a kindness that made her nervousness disappear. Realizing she was staring at him, Stick scratched at his chin with a dirty fingernail until the bolt released a sharp spark that made Maggie blink wildly in surprise.

"I stole this off that nerve that showed up with the memory crew. All the ones who work in Mildred are too old but that one still had lots of crackles. Do you want to hold it?" he said proudly offering it to her.

Maggie stared suspiciously at him, expecting another trick. The light certainly was beautiful to look at but trusting him seemed foolish.

"It's safe, I promise," he said, sensing her trepidation.

Cautiously Maggie wrapped her hand around it, only to feel the tiny bolt stab into her skin with a powerful shock.

"Owww!" she snapped, dropping it back into his hand.

"Just be gentle with it. You can't grab it like that," he said, coaxing it back toward her.

As Maggie watched, it hopped gently onto her hand and continued its dance, sending a warm tickle up her arm.

"Sorry…about all of that up there," he continued, thankful that Maggie wasn't looking at him, "It wasn't meant to be…we just thought…the shoelaces thing was just supposed to be funny. I mean, thanks for taking the blame for everything because we were done for. We've been in enough trouble lately, and between Devlin and the minister we'd have been packing our bags to go and live in an Eskimo somewhere if you hadn't done what you did."

There was an awkward silence that filled the tunnel as Stick waited nervously for Maggie to speak.

"It's okay," she finally said, "I suppose you did come back and save me after all."

Stick gave a grateful smile before crawling past her, "I promise it won't happen again…well, unless you turn out to be a total loser!" he replied cheekily.

Maggie sat back to let him pass but as he drew next to her a thought jumped into her head, and she quickly dropped the lightning bolt into his open pocket before driving her hand hard against his leg. Stick flew forward with a scream and flipped himself over onto his back as he fumbled for the lightning bolt. It was shocking him over and over in the tight confines of his pocket.

"OWW…OWW…OWW! What'd you do that for?" he shouted as he finally managed to throw the lightning bolt free of his trousers.

"Sorry," said Maggie calmly picking up the light, "Now we're even. Well, unless you turn out to be a total loser!"

Stick sat there for a moment rubbing his injured thigh as Maggie crawled ahead of him. Then, his smile returned and he followed her.

After several minutes of slipping and sliding along the tunnel Maggie was starting to run out of energy. It was like crawling atop a balloon that was half filled with syrup. Her hands and feet sunk into the wet floor with every move while her limbs groaned against the effort. To make things worse, the lightning bolt kept sliding out of her hand and into the wet corners forcing her to dig blindly into the slimy edges as Stick teased her in the darkness. Maggie pressed on, ignoring him, until the tunnel finally ended and she flopped out onto the floor with a thankful moan.

She found herself inside a large room with yellow walls and a high ceiling that loomed over her like the inside of an egg. Several red pipes stuck awkwardly through the dimpled surface with light panels hanging loosely from them, illuminating thick yellow drips that hung everywhere like rubber teardrops, threatening to weep any second. Below them, three oversized couches had been molded up out of the floor, all of them circling a large white disk. It was showing an old movie of a soldier sitting motionless on a train, staring out at the green blur of fields outside.

"What do you think?" said Stick proudly spreading his arms wide.

Maggie's eyes did another turn of the room. "What is it?" she asked.

"Well, it's fat, isn't it?" said Stick as if it were the most obvious thing in the world, "Lucky for us Mildred has lots of it. I found an air pocket and then just scooped some out to make us a base! And best of all, Miss Devlin doesn't know about it!"

Revulsion filled Maggie as she realized what she had just crawled through.

"Isn't it great?" said Stick.

Maggie looked at the proud expression on his face. "Its…very nice," she said half-heartedly, not wanting to hurt his feelings.

"It's not great, or nice, it's disgusting," said a voice. An arm appeared over the back of the couch. A pretty blonde girl lazily propped her head into view as her eyes stayed fixed on the solider in the movie.

Stick gritted his teeth. "Maggie this is my sister, Taylor, and that over there is Pritch."

A small head of brown hair rose up from the other couch, followed by a pale face with two bright blue eyes that stared nervously at her.

"Hi," said Maggie cautiously, recognizing the two girls from the dormitory. They hadn't exactly made the best first impression and she still wasn't sure if she was quite ready to forgive them.

Pritch walked guiltily over, her eyes never leaving her feet. She seemed to be about the same age as Maggie but with small, pretty features that she looked happy to hide behind her long dark hair.

"Hi…sorry…about the trick we played on you, I think we got a little carried away. We never meant for those things in the suggestion box to be read out. We did them months ago when we were bored. We never thought anyone would ever bother to read them," she said meekly.

"Yeah, me too," said Taylor casually waving a hand over her head as if it was no big deal, "We went too far, sorry. Oh, quick, Pritch. It's the best bit."

On the screen the train was pulling into the station as thick clouds of steam billowed up all around it. The soldier stepped down onto the platform as a woman in a flowery dress emerged through the mist and started to run toward him. He dropped his backpack to the floor and stepped toward her with tears in his eyes, catching her mid-run as she threw herself into his arms and kissed him passionately.

Taylor and Pritch both took a sharp breath and gulped.

"Isn't that just the most beautiful thing you've ever seen?" said Taylor to no one in particular.

Stick put a finger into his mouth and pretended to gag, drawing an angry look from his sister.

"Why do you have to be such an insensitive idiot?" she snapped.

"Why do you have to watch this for the hundredth time?" he snapped back, "There's lots of other stuff in Mildred's memory banks you know!"

Pritch stepped out of the way as the brother and sister argued back and forth.

"It's our favorite," she whispered in Maggie's ear, as if the fight was nothing unusual. "It's when Mildred's husband Malcolm came home from the war. See how pretty she was? She was supposed to have been a really nice place to live back then. There were five orphanages in her with over a thousand kids. Now there's just the four of us…oh, and now you of course."

Maggie watched the young, happy version of Mildred walking hand in hand with Malcolm down the platform, and wondered if she could really be the same old woman that she had landed in yesterday. This one was much thinner with shiny blonde curls, held back by a red flower behind her ear, and a smile that seemed contagious

"What happened to her?" asked Maggie.

Taylor flicked Stick repeatedly in the head while he countered by swinging his arms around in wide circles, daring her to move. Pritch tilted her head to see the screen as Stick's hands windmilled in and out of view.

"Malcolm died," she said casually, "six years ago. They say she's never been the same since. I've only been here four years, Stick and Taylor have been here their whole lives so they know more about it, but everything was supposed to have changed the day he died. She stopped going out. Stopped taking care of herself. She just stayed home and lay in bed all day. After that a lot of people just decided they didn't want to live in her anymore. So they opened a new orphanage and sent all the kids there...well, all except for us. Nowadays she just sits in her chair all day watching TV or staring at Malcolm's picture. They never had children of their own so no one comes to see her. There's a woman who delivers her meals, and a nurse who stops by once a week to check on her, but that's it. No wonder they want to close her down."

"Right, that's it!" shouted Stick as Taylor sucked her finger before twisting it hard into his ear.

There was a great clattering as he threw himself wildly at his sister, only for her to quickly sidestep, sending him toppling forward to crash over the couch and into the wall. The force was too much for one of the thick drips of fat and it burst against his back in a shower of thick yellow goo.

"Eeeeeuuuuuuuuwwwwwwwww!" he moaned as the fat slowly slimed its way down over his head and dripped onto his face.

"Serves you right," said Taylor, "you should know better than to fight with a girl!"

Grabbing Pritch's hand, she pulled her toward an opening on the far side of the room.

"Come on, Pritch, let's go up top and see what Mildred's watching on TV," she demanded.

As Taylor dragged her away, Pritch looked back and waved a hand in Maggie's direction.

"Nice to meet you. Sorry again about earlier," she said, "See you later."

"Nice to meet you too," replied Maggie as they disappeared behind a large yellow flap.

Maggie stared down at the limp figure of Stick who sat embarrassed on the floor.

"She's no girl, she's a monster," he mumbled.

Maggie sat down next to him. Ten minutes ago she was furious at him but now, as he sat here covered in yellow goo, she could only feel sorry for him.

"I used to fight with my brothers too," she said.

For the next few minutes they sat there, Stick picking large yellow lumps out of his hair while Maggie told him about some of the things her stepbrothers had done to her.

"Lucky for me I saw what they put in it," she said, finishing her story, "the best bit was that I pretended to be sick and when my stepmother got home they had to eat it instead!"

Stick laughed as he peeled a large piece of fat from the back of his neck.

"Thanks, Maggie," he said warmly.

"That's alright." She smiled.

There was silence as both of them thought of what to say next. Finally Stick got up and started to shake out his shirt as Maggie pretended to watch Malcolm and Mildred on the memory screen.

"So what happened to your brothers?" asked Stick as the final globs of fat fell to the floor.

Panic filled her stomach. Maggie realized what she had just done. She was supposed to be an orphan, so what had happened to all her family?

"Gone…in a bumblebee accident," she replied, remembering what Ms. Devlin had said was in her file.

Every word sounded ridiculous, even to her, and she waited for Stick to catch her lie.

"Sorry about that, they can be dangerous things, bumblebees. My mum and dad died when we were babies. Some hunters shot down the goose they were travelling on. After that, we went to live with my grandma, but we were too much for her. She tried her best but she was old and it wasn't long before she died too. That's when they brought us here."

Beneath her shirt, Maggie's heart flipped. Part of her was relieved that he had accepted her story while another part of her hesitated, unsure of just how she should respond to the news of someone's parents being killed inside a giant bird.

"Er…so you've lived here since you were little?" she asked, trying to change the conversation.

"Yeah, for as long as I can remember. She may not be much to look at anymore but Mildred is home, you know? What about you? Where did you used to live?"

Maggie's heart sank again; was there no getting away from who she was supposed to be?

"I don't know…I mean, Ms. Devlin said I was something called a nobo," she mumbled.

"Really, you're a nobo? Wow!" said Stick, breaking into a broad grin, you must have seen some weird stuff out there. You know…not living in a body?"

Maggie gave a relieved smile. She was beginning to really like Stick.

"I lived in a dandelion for a while but I don't remember much about it, to tell you the truth," she said, deciding to push her luck.

"So this is your first time in a body?" he asked.

Maggie sniffed, happy that she could finally tell the truth again. "Afraid so."

"Well, what are we waiting for?" he said, striding toward the door, "if this is the first body you've ever been in then you need the full tour!"

Soon, they were standing in a bright white corridor that ended at two large grey doors. A peeling sign hung overhead, the words 'Main Cavity' barely visible, as several large muscular creatures with tiny heads stood below, boasting loudly about who was the strongest. Maggie sucked in a deep breath. She would never have guessed that the body had so many steps inside it. She'd been fine the night before when it had been all downhill, but when, as Stick explained, you live in an orphanage in the bottom half of an old woman's right leg, you spend a lot of your time going up stairs, not down. To make it worse, all of the steps in this area seemed to be filled with more soft yellow fat, making her feel as if she were trying to trudge through wet sand. She'd never thought of herself as unfit, but life inside Mildred was proving much harder than she thought.

"Any chance of getting a drink of water? Maybe some food?" gasped Maggie, hoping for an opportunity to stop for a while.

"Sure," said Stick, who looked as though he could keep climbing steps all day.

They pushed through the doors, and Stick nodded hello to one of the large men.

"Muscles," he whispered to Maggie, "nice, but not exactly geniuses if you know what I mean."

But Maggie wasn't listening. She was staring at a room unlike anything she had ever seen before. The whole area was huge with a ceiling that was split in two halves, each of them swelling up and down as they released a bright light that seemed to make the whole area glow. Thick pipes of blue and red ran everywhere, jumping over and under one another as they weaved their way around the pink walls, before circling upward to surround a line of spiny white bumps that ran up the back of the wall. Hanging over the room was another of the screens Maggie had seen in the kids' den, only this was a hundred times its size, filling the air with a picture of the living room mantelpiece and its photographs of Mildred's husband as thick green letters flashed the words 'Live' in one corner. Beneath it, the large grey floor seemed to be alive, sending ripples across its surface as hundreds of creatures stepped, easily, over each wave as if this was perfectly normal; their thoughts consumed with getting to one of the twelve doors that lined the walls.

Fading signs hung over each door, the words 'Integumentary,' 'Respiratory,' and 'Nervous' painted in peeling black letters on each one. Yet one doorway seemed to dwarf the rest, its shining white archway carved deep into the base of the spiny bumps making it look twice the size of the other entrances. Nerves flashed in and out of the doorway as two large men in blue uniforms stood motionless against the pull of leashes that were attached to two transparent dogs who crouched at their feet, their bodies revealing lumps of meat squirming inside their bellies. A large white sign hung overhead, the words 'Spine; L3, restricted area' written in bright gold letters.

"You don't want to mess with them," said Stick, nodding at the guards, "those are Antibody Police and the ugly things next to them are Lymphs. The only ones they'll listen to are their owners; everyone else is just something for them to chew on."

A pale man in white dungarees left the door marked 'Skeletal,' struggling under the weight of several white rods that were balanced on his shoulder, as an older man chased after him shouting orders for him to be careful. A long slender creature that appeared to be made out of grey mist drifted by, and the younger man turned to avoid her, only to misjudge one of the waves in the floor and stagger sideways toward the Lymphs, who immediately sprang to life. There was a large crash as the rods went flying in every direction, and several sets of sharp glassy teeth snapped at the man who lay frozen with fear on the floor. The older man shouted at him to get up. The Antibody Police stared coldly out and loosened the leashes on the Lymphs just enough for one of them to take a bite out of the younger man's back pocket, springing him miraculously upward, as he ran blindly away clutching his behind.

"I'm afraid I can't show you the spine. Nerves and government officials only. Unless you want to feed yourself to the Lymphs! Come on, I'll tell you more about it over breakfast," said Stick, leading Maggie down onto the rippling floor below.

As soon as her foot touched the floor Maggie knew she was in trouble. Each wave took a personal dislike to her, making her scramble awkwardly behind Stick, who glided over the rippling floor with ease. He reached the door marked 'Digestive.' With a clumsy leap, Maggie stumbled in behind him just as one last grey wave clipped her heels, sending her toppling forward through the door and into a long table.

She was thankful to have made it in one piece, but she was suddenly attacked by a powerful odor that reminded her of her stepbrothers' old bags of laundry.

Stick held out a tray, raising his eyebrow. "Nice entry," he said with a smile.

Maggie shot him an angry look that fit in perfectly with her nose, which was curled upward against the smell.

The room was long and dirty with tables that showed their age, even in the gloomy light that filled the air. One wall opened up into a drab kitchen covered in dirty pots, and a sink piled high with long-unwashed plates. In the shadows Maggie could just make out a spiky black animal crouched over something, while small bones flew over its shoulder. As they headed toward the counter the stench became stronger, filling the air with a green smoke that drifted over their heads. It emerged from between two large women who stood facing a stove of bubbling pots.

"Morning, Rita. Morning, Rita," said Stick brightly, "What wonderful things do you have for us this morning?"

195

As the two women turned around Maggie gave an involuntary jump of surprise. Each wore dirty blue uniforms, the name tag 'Rita' hanging from both of their lapels, and each had a perfectly round face that seemed to be struggling under the weight of a single huge eye that was pressed into the middle of their foreheads like an egg sinking into a bowl of pink slime. Nestled below was a thin mouth that protruded forward like a long pink straw with two bright red lips at its end; lips that drooped precariously over the steaming bowls that they carried over to the counter.

"Mornin' Stick," squeaked Rita on the left.

"Mornin' Stick," squeaked Rita on the right.

"Sorry, Stick, not much to choose from again," said Rita on the left in a squeaky voice, "Mildred only 'ad cereal for breakfast. We tried to make it a little interestin' by mixing it with some of that fish she had on Tuesday but I'll be honest with you, I wouldn't eat it. Tastes like Rita's armpits after one of her hair-obics lessons."

Both the women laughed, releasing high-pitched squeals that made Maggie wince. Rita on the right's lips fluttered lower into the bowl of green liquid, before dipping down to kiss its surface as her eye rolled up her head in delight. "Now this one on the other hand is good stuff," she exclaimed, "I always say you can't go wrong with booger bangers."

Maggie looked at the objects floating up and down in the green concoction and waited for Rita to laugh at her own joke, but nothing came. It seemed that they really were made of boogers.

"Booger bangers it is then," said Stick cheerfully, "I don't think I'll ever get bored of those! Oh and this is Maggie by the way, she's new here."

Rita and Rita wiped their hands down their fronts, adding to the thick layers of food stains, before both shaking Maggie's hand at the same time.

"Pleased to meet you," said Maggie, trying not to stare.

"Pleased to meet you too," said the Rita's in unison.

"Where you from, love?" said Rita on the right.

"Oh you know…here and there," she stumbled, making a personal note to get her story organized at the earliest opportunity.

Rita on the left scooped out a large sausage from the pot and dropped it onto a plate before dribbling it in the green mixture.

"Well, love, wherever you're from, you're in good hands here. Mildred might not give us much good ingredients to work with anymore but we find a way, don't we, Rita?" she said, winking her single eye.

Rita on the right plopped down another thick sausage and handed the two plates to the children.

"We do indeed, Rita, we do indeed. Shall I put hers on the orphan bill too, Stick?"

"Absolutely, Rita, she's one of us now," said Stick brightly.

They walked over to sit at a table at the far end of the room as Rita and Rita chattered happily away behind them. Maggie stared down at the thick green sausage in front of her. A long black hair was lying across it as though asleep.

"See, now isn't this better than living as a nobo?" Stick bit down hard on the pudgy sausage sending a greasy green dribble down his chin, "Once you get used to them these are great. It's pretty much all I eat. You are going to love them!"

A picture of a giant green booger filled Maggie's mind.

"Sounds great," she lied, poking at the green sausage with her fork.

"If you're ever hungry, you just come here," said Stick proudly, "All the food is free for us orphans."

There was a loud crunch as he bit down on something hard, and winced. He dug a boney finger into his cheek and pulled out what looked like a small shell. He wiped it on his sleeve before continuing to chew his sausage, as if this was completely normal.

"Not that anyone else really eats here anymore. Most of the people who work here get take out up the street from Mr. Singh 64, or go next door to Mrs. Talbot 52. On Sundays she has these roast dinners that everyone raves about. I think they're overpriced," he said through a mouthful of green mush.

A nerve appeared at the counter and looked, in horror, at the green bowl of sausages before instantly disappearing amidst a look of disgust and several rude words. Maggie picked up her fork and tried to pick the black hair off her sausage, only to find it firmly attached.

"I have some money," she said brightly, "perhaps we can go to Mrs. Talbot 52 today? My treat?"

Stick looked up with a hurt expression. "Nah… thanks, but I kinda like to stay here. I know she's old and they're probably going to close her down, but Mildred's home, you know? I feel bad deserting her, even if everyone else does. I can take you over there if you'd prefer it though? There's a flea that leaves from Mildred's foot every half hour."

Slowly it dawned on Maggie what she had just done. She could kick herself for not realizing it sooner. Today wasn't about showing her around just any old body; Mildred was his home and he was proud of her.

The sausage let loose a squirt of green juice as she stabbed it with her fork, before biting down on its rubbery end.

"You're right, these are kind of good." She chomped. "I feel better already. So where's next on the tour?"

As Maggie collapsed into bed that night she regretted eating the booger banger for the thousandth time that day. Stick had shown her so many amazing things that afternoon and yet she had been unable to enjoy any of it. All she'd been able to think about was that sausage and how to stop herself from vomiting…again.

Looking back, the ride on the blood stream had not been the best place to start. The tiny raft had rocked far too easily from side to side and despite the best efforts of the old man in charge, they had hit lots of large lumps as they sailed around its dark trenches. By the time Maggie set foot back on Mildred's elbow, she felt as though she had been through a washing machine filled with hammers.

Next there had been a visit to one of the muscle departments where teams of large men with small heads pulled on thick ropes, like a giant game of tug of war. Somebody called an ion man banged on a pink drum and screamed at them to pull and release, as nerves flashed in and out delivering orders. Many of the muscles looked old and struggled to keep up with the demands as their large bodies poured out a thick sweat that filled the air with an acidic smell. It made Maggie's head spin as she tried to keep down the contents of her stomach.

Thinking some fresh air might help, Stick had taken her up to the surface where hundreds of small mustached men were repairing a cut in Mildred's finger, as another group busied themselves by planting new hair seeds in one of her moles. Unfortunately the fresh air had only served to bring up a string of green sausage burps from Maggie that caused a twenty-minute delay in work while someone from the waste department checked for gas leaks.

The day had finally ended with a visit to the lungs where teams of women sorted through a conveyor belt of old blue balloons before pressing them, one by one, against the wall where they grew and swelled into bright red balls that were rolled down a chute to land, unseen, with a splash. Unable to hold back any longer, Maggie had thrown up on the conveyor belt before being dragged out by Stick, who told her that he thought it best if they called it a day. A series of screams erupted behind them.

Now, as her face sank into the satisfyingly cold pillow, Maggie closed her eyes and found, to her relief, that her stomach wasn't churning anymore. She rolled the pendant on her father's necklace between her fingers and looked up at the pink ceiling. After all the times she had asked him to show her the inside of the body she had finally done it. She pictured herself sitting with him in his office telling him everything that had happened but no matter how hard she tried, one thought kept interrupting her thoughts: Ms. Devlin.

The dorm had been dark as they'd crawled out of the secret tunnel, Stick assuring her that she would have long since gone to bed. But as she lay on top of her blanket she found her worries were still there—tomorrow she had to face Ms. Devlin.

Perhaps Stick will be right and she'll have calmed down, she thought to herself, *besides, nothing could be worse than spending your whole day trying not to vomit on everyone.*

From across the room there was a rippling sound as Stick slid into bed, the shapes of Taylor and Pritch snoring peacefully in the beds next to him.

Slowly she felt herself beginning to join them as the pendant fell from between her fingers.

"Goodnight, nobo," whispered Stick.

"Goodnight, dork," said Maggie, her eyes heavy.

Despite everything, she'd had fun today. Maybe it wasn't going to be so bad here after all.

Malcom...I look at my body sometimes and wonder what happened to me? I used to be so young, and now...nothing really works anymore...I'm just old...and alone.

13

A Quickening Pulse

Stick had been right, there was no need to worry about Miss Devlin. On the contrary, she had started the day in what could only be described as a good mood. As they awoke that morning the four of them had emerged from under their blankets, squinting into the bright pink light, as Miss Devlin sang loudly over their heads and skipped from bed to bed, throwing open the flaps on the small windows. A confused Pritch pulled the covers up under her chin as Miss Devlin drew next to her, only to feel an affectionate hand rub the top of her head playfully.

"I think she's finally lost it," said Taylor as soon as she was gone.

"While I hate to agree with her, I think she might be right," said Stick to the others, who sat huddled at the end of Pritch's bed, discussing this unexpected development. "Maybe it's a trap. Maybe she just wants us to think she's not mad so she can get us when we're not expecting it."

The four of them looked at each other and came to an unspoken decision. In the next room, Miss Devlin's singing was only getting louder as they ran to the bathroom and dressed quickly, over their pajamas. They prepared to leave as soon as they could.

"Children?" said Miss Devlin in a tone that could only be described as happy.

They scrambled for the secret entrance but it was too late, a mop of blonde hair appeared around the door, freezing them in their tracks.

"I have to go out, you don't mind, do you? Important business I'm afraid, but I'll be back later. Maybe we could do something? I hear that teenage body next door is going to the movies tonight. Maybe we could get a ride on him? We could see that movie you've been talking about then get some dinner, you know, together? Great! See you all back here at six!"

Like broken statues, four mouths dropped open as Miss Devlin slipped back into the living room and returned to her singing.

"Oh, we are in big trouble," said Taylor as the front door clicked closed behind their housemistress.

After watching Stick eat a quick breakfast of booger bangers and cereal with gravy, they all headed down to the lake to discuss what to do next. A stale smell hung heavy in the air while the high grey roof swept ominously overhead, only adding to their strange moods as they walked down to the water's edge.

"Maybe we should run away?" said Taylor, skimming a stone over the yellow pool of water, "We know they are going to close Mildred soon anyway and we could be gone before Devlin has time to do anything to us. I mean, what if it's really bad?"

Maggie watched the stone skip several times, before diving under the surface. Stick picked up his own stone and tried to beat his sister's throw. A beaten metal sign that read 'No Stone Throwing- by order of the Kidney Dept.' was stuck in the soft ground, a tired looking Pritch leaning heavily against it.

"I'm not leaving Mildred," said Stick. His stone skipped twice, before diving under the water. "And besides, what if she's actually changed?"

"And what if she's planning to kill us while we are asleep!" said Taylor.

"This is silly," said Pritch, "We don't have anywhere else to go. We have to go back sometime and if we're not there when she returns then we're only going to make it worse for ourselves. And besides, what if Stick's right? Maybe yesterday did make her think about being nicer?"

Three heads hung in thought—Maggie looked out over the lake. Being the newest one in the group she didn't want to contradict them, but as she thought back to the housemistress growling at her in the bunk, and pictured that look in her eyes, something inside told her that her instinct was right; Miss Devlin wasn't ready to forgive and forget just yet. She wanted revenge.

Across the lake, a man walked out to the water's edge as a small grey ball of fur yapped excitedly at his feet. A ball was produced and thrown out into the water, prompting the furry dog to scurry after it, before disappearing with a large splash. As it trotted back onto the shore, ball in mouth, its hair hung like a wet tent on either side of its body, revealing a head covered with hundreds of tiny eyes, all bundled together in an unblinking mass. The man knelt down and took the ball with a smile before rubbing the thing's head. Its small black tail began to wag, then with a quick look at his watch he walked over to a small door in the grey wall behind him. He unlocked it and began to turn the large wheel that was inside, releasing a rusty squeak. Instantly the middle of the yellow lake seemed to drop downward, swirling inside itself as if someone had just stirred it with a giant teaspoon. The edges of the water started to bleed away from the shore, leaving behind a grey slime that oozed downward as the whirlwind of water began to spin faster and faster. Then, as quickly as it had begun, a loud croak signaled that it was all over and the last of the water fell inside itself, leaving behind an empty basin dotted with slimy lumps and a large black hole in its middle.

"I need the bathroom," said Pritch suddenly.

"Me too," followed Taylor, squeezing her knees together.

"Me three," said Stick urgently.

"Right behind you," said Maggie.

The four children jumped up and ran desperately for the exit, all of them too busy to notice the cloaked figure that had appeared across the empty lake. The furry black creature growled at the approach as his master turned back the wheel, sliding a large grey flap over the hole in the middle of the lake's bed. A new river of water began to run steadily down the grey walls. After re-locking the door he turned to find himself suddenly face to face with a visitor in a long brown cloak, a dark hood hiding the stranger's face in a thick shadow. They spoke briefly, nodding politely to one another before a question was exchanged and the man pointed toward the place where the children had just been with the words 'no, four.' Without waiting to thank him the cloaked figure walked quickly away, kicking the small wet creature that jumped at his ankles, and he began to cross the empty basin toward the children's wet footprints.

Mildred closed her eyes and counted to ten before throwing it as high as she could. The bouquet of flowers flipped over and over in the air, spinning in tight circles as its yellow petals held tight for their big moment. It couldn't fall fast enough for the army of hands that were desperate to make it their own. They jumped as one, as though they were catching a falling baby. For a second the bouquet seemed to disappear inside the group, before a hand emerged victorious from the rabble of dresses, holding the flowers tightly over the group in triumph. Mildred looked at her best friend, holding her wedding bouquet, and flushed with happiness. Malcolm came over to slip an arm around his new bride as they watched the swarm of women leave the dance floor to the sound of familiar music filling the air. Their song was playing. The room went dark and a single spotlight fell on them. It was time for their first dance together as man and wife.

"Will you turn that off already!" moaned Stick, throwing his sock across the room at the memory player.

The two girls sniffed back tears as Maggie swallowed down the lump that had formed in her throat, all of them barely noticing the old sock that bounced off the memory player, before settling itself precariously on top of Pritch's bed.

Much of the day had been spent trying to take their minds off Miss Devlin but it was no good, nothing seemed to work. They'd been hair climbing on Mildred's head, watched a game of football between the muscles and the skin builders, they'd even gone to see the baby fungus that was growing in the foot department, but nothing had helped. All of it was smothered in worry about what was going to happen at six o'clock. And so they had finally given up and trudged slowly back to the bunk where they had brought the memory player in from the living room. They awaited their fate to be sealed while they watched old movies and ate the last of the sweets from Maggie's suitcase.

Stick popped a chocolate into his mouth and turned up Mildred's favorite song on the small memory box next to him, before rolling onto his side to pick up the rather withered looking electric bolt. There was a 'zap' as he aimed a weak flash of lightning down onto a piece of cold fish and green bean pizza. The bolt jumped sideways and hit him on the arm.

"Owwwwwwwwwwww," he moaned, trying to get someone's attention.

Maggie looked up with a sympathetic smile as the other two girls ignored him, their eyes fixed on Malcolm and Mildred, who were dancing in perfect union together.

"What is that?" said Maggie, suddenly noticing something.

Deep in the shadows of the far end of the bunk something had just moved in one of the beds. With all the excitement of exploring Mildred she had failed to notice that here, at the end of a long row of beds, was one more resident of The Tibia Home for Children.

Thinking back, she remembered seeing the same sleeping figure there yesterday, the one who had snored peacefully as Miss Devlin had issued her threat to give her the world's worst punishment. Stick peeled a wet fish scale off his pillow and dropped it into his mouth before looking up to follow Maggie's gaze.

"Oh, that's just Roosela," he said. "Best leave her alone if I was you."

The shape curled into a tight ball, pulling the covers tightly around herself to reveal a boney back that molded itself against the grey blanket.

"Who is she?" whispered Maggie.

"Don't know exactly. She got here two days after Taylor and me, but she's not much for talking. They tried to get her to leave with all the other kids but she refused, and whenever we tried to make friends with her she told us to go away. I think she prefers to be alone in the library. I see her sleeping back there but that's it. Don't worry, you get used to her after a while. Pritch and Taylor are scared of her, they think she's some sort of creature that's going to attack them in their sleep!"

A pillow came flying across the room, hitting Stick in the side of his head.

"What did you do that for?" he said innocently.

"First, we are not scared of her," said Taylor, "and second if you're so brave, why don't you go and talk to her?

"Yeah, well, if one of you two scared little girls wanted to come with me maybe I would," snapped Stick.

"I'll come with you," said Maggie brightly.

Stick spun around to stare at her.

"There you go, brave big brother. You have a volunteer, and no excuses, now go make friends!" Taylor smiled.

"Well maybe I'll do that," he replied dryly.

"Off you go then."

"Maybe I will," said Stick.

"Oh, come on," said Maggie, pulling at Stick's boney arm, "How bad can it be?"

As they walked down the bunk, it looked pretty bad. Sitting in the bright lights at their end of the dorm it had all seemed so easy, but now, as the darkness of the far end of the room began to consume them, it felt as though they were about to jump into a black hole. A thick layer of dust covered everything and the air felt thicker, as if it were sucking all of the excitement out of her. Slowly Maggie walked toward the sleeping figure—her feet left a trail of dusty white footprints behind her.

"This is a bad idea," whispered Stick, "You only ever hear weird noises from this end of the bunk. I bumped into her in the liver one time and she bit me, for no reason. Look I've still got the scar."

He held up his hand to Maggie who squinted at a tiny white mark on the back of his hand.

"Are there any girls that don't beat you up?" she said without thinking.

Stick stared at her angrily.

"Even Miss Devlin leaves her alone, you know!"

"Oh, come on," said Maggie, pulling him forward as she rediscovered her courage.

Something about the bed hidden in the shadows reminded her of her own old mattress in the attic. Whoever Roosela was, perhaps she just needed someone to be nice to her.

Drawing nearer they could just make out the light from a small ear wax candle glowing up from the space next to the bed. It revealed an awkward drawing on the wall of six figures surrounded by tiny brellow writing, all of it too small to read in the faint light.

"Hello?" said Maggie, taking a slow step forward to knock against the bedpost.

Instantly a shadow flashed across the wall, the sleeping figure slipping nimbly from under the sheets and onto the floor. The two children waited in silence.

"Hello. My name's Maggie. I'm here with Stick, we just wanted to say hello."

"Speak for yourself," mumbled Stick before Maggie could pinch him to be quiet.

Across the bed there was a rustling of paper as another large shadow swept onto the wall.

"Go away," said a cold voice.

Maggie leaned forward and peered around the edge of the bed, pulling Stick closely behind her. "We just wanted to say hello. I'm new here and I wanted to introduce myself."

A skinny girl with long, greasy black hair that fell in clumps around her thick glasses sat hunched on the floor. She was dressed in black and read from one of the hundreds of books that were piled messily behind her, their torn pages covering the floor beneath her, their words hidden behind thick blue lines that cut through them like a knife. Refusing to look up at her two visitors she continued to stroke something unseen in her lap.

"Hello...I'm Maggie."

The girl sat unmoving, ignoring them.

"I'm Roosela, now go away," she finally said dryly.

"Oh that's just charming, isn't it?" replied Stick.

The girl glared up at him from behind her book.

"You want to be careful, Stick, remember what happened last time we talked?"

Stick started to flush a bright red, instinctively rubbing the scar on the back of his hand, when he suddenly saw something lying on the floor.

"Hey, that's my football," he said, pointing to the corner, "You stole it!"

Roosela turned her gaze back to her book as if she was suddenly bored. "I don't think that's your ball. Its Fluffy's ball."

"Look, I don't know who Fluffy is but that ball has got my name written on it. Here, I'll show you," he said, striding forward to reach out for it.

His hand was hovering just above it when the teeth sank deep into his skin. The thing in Roosela's lap had leapt forward in a blur of blue hair, revealing two sets of sharp teeth, which were now embedded in Stick. With a scream, he stumbled backward, clenching his hand as the creature stood frozen by the ball, its blue hair spiking everywhere in rigid spines like an exploded bottle of ink.

"Are you crazy?" shouted Stick, shaking his hand against the pain, "that's a germ! You can't keep a germ for a pet! They're full of disease!"

Roosela sat motionless, her face never leaving her book. Only the slight curl of a smile revealed that anything had just happened. The spiny blue germ relaxed its spines and waddled over to lie next to her, as she gently stroked it again it released a soft purring noise. In the shadows behind her something brown moved forward, only to shrink backward as the light hit its wet nose.

"And that's a baby sludgie!" exclaimed Stick, pointing into the darkness, "Are you mental? Those things can kill you! Do you know how much trouble you'll be in if the antibodies find out?"

"Well, they aren't going to find out, are they?" said Roosela, her eyes firmly fixed on her book. "Unless you want me to share a few secrets of my own? I can always update Miss Devlin on some of your…little adventures. I'm sure she'd love to know who put those hair growth seeds in her face cream. Or how that foot fungus found its way into her pillowcase. Maybe we should just keep it simple and tell her where that secret little room of yours is. After all, there's lots of things down there she might find interesting. Like where that extra set of keys went…or where her memory player is. Don't forget that I see everything back here, and you have all been very busy!"

Stick glared at her, trying not to show the pain he was in, when suddenly he stopped and gulped, his eyes bulging.

"Oh, that's right," sniggered Roosela, "Did I forget to mention that Fluffy here is a diarrhea germ? Why don't you go take a seat and think about what I said before you run off and tell anybody about my pets."

From between Fluffy's shafts of blue hair, a small chin protruded forward as Roosela scratched its back. In the shadows there was more movement as a grizzled meow came from deep under the bed.

"Got to go," Stick said, before turning to sprint up the dorm toward the bathroom.

Maggie stood there, unsure of what to say. It seemed like a good time to leave.

"Nice to meet you, Roosela," she said, making her own quick exit.

As Maggie strode quickly away, Roosela put down her book and pushed Fluffy to one side. Taking a pen from her pocket she leaned forward and quickly wrote under one of the figures drawn on the wall.

"Nice to meet you, too, Maggie Pincus," she whispered.

Hearing that Roosela had a pet sludgie made them think twice about staying in the dorm, at least until she had calmed down. So while Stick was busy in the bathroom, the three girls decided to take a trip up onto Mildred's shoulder to see what was happening outside.

They stepped out onto her black cardigan and saw that they were not alone in their idea. At least twenty other internals were scattered across the dark landscape, all of them enjoying the late afternoon sun that was flooding through the living room window and onto the old sleeping giant. Some had obviously planned ahead, bringing blankets and picnics, while the rest satisfied themselves with scrunching up the black wool floor to make sunken chairs. Mildred's soft snoring drifted through the air around them like waves crashing on the beach.

They had been there for nearly an hour before a pale faced Stick finally walked slowly over to join them, gently lowering himself down, with a sigh of relief, as he slid down into the soft floor like a deflated balloon. Taylor and Pritch caught each other's gaze with barely suppressed sniggers.

"Are you okay?" said Taylor with an over-the-top smile.

"Leave me alone," moaned Stick.

"I'm sorry," said Pritch, "You're right of course, it would be wrong to tease you while you're not feeling so good. We just wanted *toilet* you know that we're here for you."

His sister spat out a laugh, before covering her mouth with her hand. Stick groaned.

"That's right," croaked Taylor, "It's just that I'm a little worried that diarrhea is hereditary. What if it *runs* in our family?"

Pritch rolled over and buried her face in a strand of wool as her body heaved with laughter. Even Maggie, who was filled with guilt for making him go and meet Roosela in the first place, had to bite down on her lip to stop herself from laughing. Stick shot an angry look at the three of them.

"Oh, come on, don't be a party pooper!" said Maggie.

The three girls collapsed in laughter—even Stick managed a small smile.

"Alright, very funny. You win," he said with a submittal wave of his bandaged hand, "From now on I promise to admit that I'm scared of Roosela."

From up above there was a sudden snort as Mildred's head bobbed awake and stared around the room, oblivious to the tiny invisible people that covered both her shoulders. She picked up the newspaper from her lap and opened the large white front page, instantly blocking the sun and sending a large shadow over the internals below. For a second, everyone waited and watched the giant sleeping head droop slowly back to sleep, willing her to drop the newspaper and give them back their afternoon in the sun. But it was no good. As the steady snoring returned, her hands remained locked in place, holding open the pages that none of them wanted to see. Soon, one by one, they began to drift away making the climb back up the long grey hairs to the cavernous ear as they complained to one another about how much they disliked living in Mildred.

"You coming?" asked Taylor.

Maggie glanced down at Stick who looked as though moving was the last thing he wanted to do.

"I think I'll stay here," she said.

"Suit yourself, how about you?"

Pritch gave a halfhearted shrug, and jumped to her feet.

With the two of them gone, Maggie scrunched up the soft cardigan floor into a large ball and settled inside it. The thick strands of wool felt good against her face, and as she curled into them the sensation of feeling relaxed for the first time that day overtook her.

Looking out across the living room, she saw Malcolm, still smiling out from his picture on the mantelpiece, as he watched his wife sleep peacefully in his old chair. So much had happened since she got here that it felt good to finally relax for a while. She closed her eyes and felt ready to take a nap as her body sunk farther into the soft floor. Something tickled her nose and she swatted at it uselessly. Again she flapped at the offending object, but once again it refused to stop, forcing her to delay her nap. She opened her eyes to see a loose strand of fabric curling itself into her face. Annoyed, she pulled at it when something in the newspaper suddenly caught her eye, instantly pulling her awake. She sat upright, her eyes wide in surprise. Unlike any newspaper she had seen before, this one was covered in thousands of brellow words. At the top of the page a green line ran through the middle of the newspaper's title, and beneath it the words 'Internal

National Daily News' had been written in thick brellow letters. Below that the green and yellow letters were everywhere, weaving themselves in and out of the black newsprint, creating a whole new newspaper that only internals could see.

"Don't tell me. You've never seen a newspaper before?" said Stick, watching her reaction.

"That's a newspaper?" replied Maggie, staring at the jumble of words that filled every inch of the page.

The floor trembled beneath them as Mildred let out a sleeping snort that rippled through their tiny bodies.

"Ha, will you look at that?" said Stick. Some of the color seemed to have returned to his face and he seemed to be feeling better. "Down there, bottom of page two."

Maggie looked down at the large black letters at the bottom of the newspaper.

Dead Husband comes back for dinner!

Yesterday morning, two police officers were called to a disturbance outside the 'Wish You Wash Here' launderette on Summerville High Street. Upon arrival at the scene, Officers Hatch and Piper found one Mrs. Tibbs in a state of obvious distress, grabbing

*bystanders and mumbling that she had just bumped
into her dead husband coming out of 'The Cod Father'
fish and chip shop next door. Upon questioning, it was
determined that Mr. Tibbs had passed away two weeks
prior to the incident after choking on a pickled egg
from the fish and chip shop and was consequently
buried earlier that week. The officers took Mrs. Tibbs
home and said that no charges would be pressed. This
is the third reported sighting of a deceased loved one
this month. Police said that their inquiries were
ongoing.*

The story continued in a mass of scribbled
brellow writing that swarmed beneath it like graffiti:

*Anti-body police working inside Officers Hatch 29 and
Piper 36 interviewed residents of Mrs. Tibbs 70, and
received several confirmed sightings of Mr. Tibbs 72,
leaving the fish and chip shop eating a steak and
kidney pie.*

*In an official statement, police said, 'we can
neither confirm nor deny that this is the third sighting
of a dead body apparently coming back to life. Our
investigations are ongoing.'*

Our research did tell us that Mrs. Tibbs, 70 is home to one of the towns largest breweries, although police declined to comment if the two are connected.

"Ha! Some people are crazy." Stick laughed.

Maggie gave him a halfhearted laugh of agreement and pushed her fingers into the sides of her head, plowing at her hair. She was suddenly tense. Halfway through reading the story, she had found herself drawn to an article on the opposite page. Two huge photographs stared out at her, the words **FOUND AT LAST!** printed above them in thick black letters.

The black and white faces were smiling brightly, oblivious to the trouble they were causing. Both were faces that Maggie knew well; on the right was her father, and on the left was her own face, staring out at her like a huge billboard. The memory of the day her father died filled her again, his body being dragged away, her hands flapping uselessly against him.

"Hey, look," said Stick, "that body looks just like you."

Maggie froze in panic, her mind still swirling from the shock of seeing the photos of her and her father in the newspaper. She opened her mouth to speak, hoping that an excuse would come to her, but nothing came. How could she explain this? She couldn't. Surely he'd realize. He was an internal and she was a soul. This was it. She was about to be caught. It was all over.

"Go figure," he continued, "Do you know there's a boy at our school who looks just like that body off the TV, that one from that show that Mildred watches? About all those people who live on the same street and spend all their time shouting at each other?"

Maggie stared back at him, still unable to speak.

"Oh well," he said, rolling onto his side and molding the floor into a pillow. "I'm going to take a nap. Wake me up if she turns the page to the football scores, will you?"

Maggie turned back to the newspaper as her heart thumped heavily against her chest like a basketball on a steel drum. It was definitely her picture and there was no mistaking her father's next to it. Even the grey ink couldn't hide the light in those familiar blue eyes. Suddenly it was as though she was back in his office, staring at the two giants for the first time.

Something clicked in the back of her mind. Her body had been found. She needed to tell Pethora! She would get her body for her. Maggie would be able to help in the war! Surely now they would come and take her back to her father's house.

Her heart dropped. Only two days ago she wanted nothing more than to leave Mildred, but now… she pushed the thought to the back of her mind and started to read:

FOUND AT LAST!

Mr. Jamie Scott and his daughter, Elsie were found alive and well yesterday after missing for two months. Father and daughter had been subject to a nationwide manhunt, but in recent weeks police had downsized the search, presuming they were no longer in the country. The two were finally discovered nearly 300 miles away from their home after entering the Quigglesbrook village post office, apparently unaware that they were missing and with no recollection of the past two months.

Police drove father and daughter home to Mrs. Scott who broke down in tears at their return. In a later interview Mrs. Scott said, "I'm glad to have them home but my husband certainly has a few questions to answer. I don't know where they've been but I've never seen them looking so well. They've both got lovely tans and I think he's even had a manicure. If I find out they've been off on holiday all this time without me they're in big trouble!"

An anonymous police source later told us, "It's true. I've never seen healthier looking missing people. It's like they were kidnapped and taken away to a spa for two months. If that's the case I hope someone kidnaps me soon!"

Squeezed tightly underneath it, in brellow writing, the story continued:

Upon boarding Jamie Scott 33, and Elsie 12, anti-body police found that all the internals aboard were in various states of exhaustion and distress. All 245 workers were taken to the local hospital for evaluation while emergency crews took over at the two bodies.

Medical staff reports that all of the internals involved in the disappearance show signs of extreme amnesia, with some even no longer able to remember their names.

An internal affairs spokesman said, 'Bodies going missing is nothing unusual, but we usually get a message from everyone inside letting us know where they are. This time we heard nothing, and to see memory loss on this scale is unprecedented. We are taking this matter very seriously and hope to have some answers for the internal community as soon as possible.

The two pictures were still smiling as though they found Maggie's confusion funny. Mildred's head bounced up one more time, to release another loud snort, before slowly drifting forward once again. Maggie tried to make sense of what she had read. Stick rolled over, accidentally kicking her hard in the leg, but Maggie barely noticed. At that moment a fly could have landed on her and she wouldn't have felt a thing. She was completely numb. How could her body have been missing only a few weeks? It was her body, wasn't it? She had lived in it for twelve years. There had been some changes made to it when she got to her father's house, but it was still her body. How could it not be?

"Excuse me, Miss Pincus."

Maggie felt the voice enter her thoughts.

"Maggie Pincus?"

She slowly turned, realizing that someone was behind her.

"Miss Pincus, Miss Devlin is ready for you now," said the tired voice.

Maggie turned to see a rather sad looking nerve standing breathless at her side, waiting for a reply. Maggie looked at the clock above the fireplace. "Oh no!" she exclaimed, shaking Stick awake, "Come on, it's six, we're late."

Stick staggered blearily to his feet and pushed past the nerve as he chased after Maggie, who was already starting to grapple her way up a strand of Mildred's hair.

"Tell Miss Devlin we'll be right there," he shouted over his shoulder.

The nerve looked sympathetically up at the two children as they swung over into the large ear, and disappeared down the dark tunnel.

"With the message I just gave her I think you might want to take your time," he mumbled, before disappearing with a loud crackle.

Malcolm...I know you're there. Even when I'm on my own I know you're with me. I feel your presence. I know you're here. I know I'm not alone...I just wish I could see you.

14

A Worsening Headache

Two angry eyes glared down a long nose at the four
children. In the tiny confines of her office it felt as
though Miss Devlin was only inches away from them,
her hot breath burning their cheeks. When Maggie and
Stick arrived, breathless and sweating, they found
Taylor and Pritch standing in silence, as their
housemistress stared at them blankly from her chair.
Several large maps of bodies were spread in front of
her, their edges curling over one another as they
clamored for space on the tiny desktop. Forgetting
where she was for a second, Maggie tipped her head to
one side to try to see the maps in more detail, but

before she had a chance to see anything a bony hand slammed down on them to sweep them away.

"Those are not for you to look at!" snarled Miss Devlin as the maps crumpled to the floor around her, "Do not forget where you are, nobo!"

Maggie looked down, trying desperately to avoid Miss Devlin's fierce glare, but it was useless. Looking at her shoes was no cure for those burning eyes, and she felt her face flush bright pink.

"Right, where were we?" she sniffed, leaning calmly back in her chair, "As I was just telling your two little friends here, yesterday was what you might call a bad day for me. Not only did you make me the laughing stock for everybody in this village, but I was also embarrassed in front of the minister—the very man I was counting on to get me a new job before they close this old junk heap, Mildred, down!"

Unable to help himself, Stick shot an angry look up at her only to force his eyes back down before she could notice.

"Yesterday was supposed to be about me getting a new life, one that didn't include little brats like you. Unfortunately you decided to ruin it for me, but rather than give up, like your parents did on you, I've decided to do something about it. You see, I am, and always will be, cleverer than all of you. That's why I've kept a few little tricks up my sleeve…just in case. And that's why I went to see the minister today with a proposition that will make everything better. A proposition that includes the four of you!"

They all looked up to see her smiling broadly at them, with a delight she could barely restrain. The thought that she might really have become nice had quickly vanished. Something big was coming, something that she wanted to unleash slowly, something that would make them suffer.

"What! Did you think I would let you off that easily? After all that you did? No! Sacrifices have to be made and you are the ones who are going to make them for me!"

A black box on the shelf behind her suddenly fizzed into life, pulling their attention away as it filled the room with an impatient voice.

"Miss Devlin, this is Ira Marsh's secretary speaking. The minister asked me to let you know that it has all been arranged. There's a nerve on its way over now with the letter, and transportation will be left on the window ledge tomorrow morning. They just have to be ready to depart Mildred at exit RH3 when she goes to get her breakfast. The minister also asked me to warn you about the…"

In a flash, Miss Devlin flipped a dial on the box silencing the voice mid-sentence as she slipped on a pair of headphones.

"What is that thing?" whispered Maggie through gritted teeth, as Miss Devlin mumbled silently into the small headset.

"It's a sub-conscious radio. You use them to communicate between bodies," muttered Stick, still looking furious, "That one's mine. She confiscated it last year. She said there was some new rule about no use of SBC radios in Mildred."

Miss Devlin slipped off the headphones and turned around to reveal a proud smile.

"Good news." She smirked. "It seems as though you are going to be able to make it up to me sooner than I thought!"

The next morning, the four of them awoke early and dressed under their blankets. Through the small windows that lined their bunks they could see the fabric of Mildred's nightdress forming a dark, thick curtain, letting them know that it was still early outside.

"How long have we got?" sniffed Pritch, releasing a misty cold breath.

"Not long," Stick shivered, rubbing his hands up and down his skinny arms in a useless attempt to get warm.

On the ceiling above them, pipes that usually pumped red with warm blood hung limp against two large clamps, closed tightly over each end shutting off the heat. This had been another 'gift' from Miss Devlin last night. Something, she'd said, 'to help make sure they didn't oversleep.'

All of them stopped to glare at Miss Devlin's door as they left the dorm, warm red veins pumping their way inside, as they pushed through the cold and out of the orphanage. Heading upward, they found Mildred deserted, except for the few internals arriving early for work as the nightshift groggily counted the minutes until their bedtime. Passing the entry to the lungs, they noticed large cotton flowers at the window as Mildred began to dress for the day. Time was passing quickly, and all four of them began to walk faster. Being late today of all days was not an option, and soon they arrived at the end of a long pink corridor marked 'RH3,' a large square fingernail overhead flooding its end in light.

They found a shadowy corner that matched their moods and sat next to a large panel of skin. Pritch reached into her pocket to retrieve a piece of paper as the others looked away. Since Miss Devlin had given it to them in her office, they'd all looked at it so many times, that now just the thought of it made them feel miserable. Only Pritch could bear to read it anymore:

The Department for Lost and Orphaned Children:
Taking care of tomorrow's children, despite yesterday.
Reginald Jefferies, 52. 14th Floor
Manager of the Black Swan Bank,
Coldmouth, London, LC90 RJ52
Sbc number: 002 354-761
Brellow Fax: 0021 345-935 att: R Jefferies

Dear Miss Devlin,
It is with deep regret that I am writing to inform you that the Mildred Potts 79, home for orphans is to be closed.
Recent developments make it no longer possible to keep the body open, and consequently we will cease operation at the end of next month. I can

only say that we have not taken this decision lightly. I also assure you that your many years of devotion to all the children who have passed through the doors of Mildred Potts 79 will not be forgotten. The recommendation from Minister Marsh will not be forgotten, especially when the time comes to review your application for a transfer to our head office in Alan White 57.

In the meantime, we do have the pressing task of re-locating the young orphans presently in your care. While we are always reluctant to split up any group of children, particularly siblings that have been together for a long time, it has been brought to my attention that an exception may need to be made in this instance. Consequently, we are leaving the decision in your caring hands. I am assured that you love each of these children as if they were your own and I can think of no one more suited to decide their future.

Please find below a list of five orphanages that have spaces available. While this must be a very difficult time for you I do request that you submit the completed list by the end of the week. If you wish to discuss this matter further, please do not hesitate to contact me.

Samantha Jewel 32. (Chef, Thornbury) – *5 spaces available.

Thomas Jenkins 46. (Homeless, London) – 2 spaces available.

Capt. Boris 65. (Sailor, whereabouts vary/ unknown) - 1 space available

Frank Pritchard 53. (Dog food tester, Cornwall) – 2 spaces available

*Commutable distance to children's current school.

Sincerely,

T Smith

Regional Director of Orphan Services

"Do you really think she'd do it?" said Pritch, jamming the letter back into her pocket, "I mean, we've played a few jokes on her but do you really think she'd split us all up?"

"Of course she would," said Taylor, "She only cares about herself. She wouldn't care if we never saw each other again. That's why she's making us do this."

Maggie listened, too tired to say anything. All night they'd tried to think of ways to escape their housemistress' demands, but it had been useless. There was no escaping it. Miss Devlin had the power to separate them forever, and she was happy to use it.

Not that it should matter to Maggie. She was new here, and now that her body had been found it would surely only be a matter of time before Pethora came to get her. But why did she still care what happened to the others? And why, when Miss Devlin threatened to split them up, had she felt so sad? Everything was happening so fast, but something deep inside her told her that leaving was wrong, that this was where she should be. Even the others seemed to agree. Only last night they'd told her how much better life seemed in Mildred since she had arrived. And then this morning Taylor, who Maggie was quickly learning was not used to being emotional, had given her a hug for seemingly no reason at all. Maggie found herself wanting to stay…at least until she knew they were going to be okay.

"Can we just stop talking about this already?" snapped Stick, "I mean, if we go and pick up this parcel for Miss Devlin then we're off the hook, right? She gets her recommendation from Ira Marsh and then she gets her job in the big fancy body. Then we'll all get to go and live together in the Samantha Jewel 32 and never have to see her again. It'll be fine."

All of them looked over at him sympathetically. Even his sister seemed to feel bad for him. The orphanage being closed could only mean one thing. That Mildred, too, was being closed. Stick had taken the news hardest of them all.

"Stick's right. I mean how hard can it be to fetch some silly parcel? We've certainly done errands for her before. Remember when she made us take that dragonfly into town for her Christmas shopping? Or when we queued overnight in the armpit of that department store body so she could get the spider-skin coat that was on sale? This'll be easy. And if anything goes wrong then I think we all know which one of us will be happy living at the dog food tester!" said Taylor, nodding at her brother.

Stick looked at his sister while Maggie and Pritch sat like statues. All of them wanted to believe that this was going to be simple, but something told them this was a long way from anything they had done before. All the other jobs had been things that Miss Devlin was too lazy to do herself, but the look in her eyes had told them that this one was different. This was something that scared her.

The light from above suddenly swung in a wide arc across the room, stealing the shadows away as the floor hardened beneath them. Realizing that Mildred must be leaning on something, Taylor peeled back the slit in the skin and held it open for the others to step out onto the wide window ledge below. They looked up and saw a second giant at the open window, wearing a 'Meals for the Elderly' T-shirt.

"Hello, Mrs. Potts," boomed the friendly voice from above, "It's porridge for breakfast, a cheese sandwich for lunch, and a lovely Mushroom pie for dinner, just pop it in the oven for twenty minutes when you're ready."

Mildred thanked her and took the tray into the kitchen, unknowingly leaving the four tiny children on the window ledge behind her. Quickly they walked over to the curtain and slipped inside its folds, all of them searching for the thing that Miss Devlin had told them would be here. They hadn't been hunting long when Stick let them know he had found what they were looking for.

"You have got to be kidding me!"

The other three rushed around the curtain, only to be greeted by a look of horror on his face.

In front of them a giant fly was lying frozen on its side like a statue, its legs pointing rigidly outward beneath two huge watery eyes.

"What a piece of junk!" exclaimed Stick, kicking one of the fly's rigid legs, "There's no way this thing is going to fly. I mean, look at it. It must be at least six months old!"

"Well, we don't really have much choice right now, do we?" said Taylor, climbing onto one of the bristly limbs and rooting her hand inside the carpet of black hairs that covered its belly.

"Here we go!" she said triumphantly.

There was a small click as a door in the fly's chest slowly creaked open to reveal a dark grey cabin containing four red chairs. One by one they all climbed inside, Maggie and Pritch taking the seats in the back, as Stick and Taylor began rummaging beneath the two grey windows in front.

"Don't worry, she's really good," whispered Pritch to Maggie in a voice full of pride. "We started our flying lessons last year at school. It's supposed to take two years to get your license but Taylor makes it look easy. I could barely get the wings to move but she was buzzing around in seconds. Our teacher said she was the most natural flyer she'd ever seen. Stick's not bad either. I think one of their parents must have been a pilot."

Maggie looked at the 'natural' pilot upfront, arguing with her brother as they both wiggled their hands inside the wall of greying flesh.

"There, that's the starter," said Stick, feeling blindly at the fly's soft insides.

"No, that's the wipers!" said Taylor as if he was stupid.

Two black rods on the grey windows swept upward, revealing Mildred returning to her chair, porridge in hand.

"I meant to do that," muttered Stick, without looking up.

The fly gave a sudden lurch, heaving the compartment forward with a violent thud as though they had just been kicked. Taylor smiled. There was another lurch, even worse than the first, throwing Maggie and Pritch forward into the seats in front, quickly followed by another and another. The fly was out from behind the curtains now, the window ledge jumping alarmingly closer and closer.

"What are you doing?" shouted Stick as they took another huge leap toward the drop below.

"The wings are stuck. I've got to get the weight off them before I can start it."

"You are not going to...." said Stick in horror.

The fly bucked up into the air and took a giant hop before crashing back down to teeter on the window ledge. The next leap would surely take them over the rim and crashing down onto the old carpet far below. They all tried to shout for her to stop but it was too late, and with one last jolt Taylor sent the old fly plunging down into the canyon. In the back, Maggie and Pritch closed their eyes tight; someone screamed. Strands on the old carpet grew larger as they hurtled rapidly toward them.

"Come on!" muttered Taylor through gritted teeth, "Come on!"

At the last instant the fly's wings spluttered to life, filling the cabin with a loud buzzing that felt like it might shake them apart. Taylor pulled hard against the inside of the wall, swinging them upward as the fly's legs whipped against the floor.

"There we go," she said, "I knew that would work."

Three terrified faces stared at her in shock.

"What?" she exclaimed, "Oh please, you are all such babies sometimes!"

After several minutes, and fourteen practice laps around the living room, they found themselves finally outside, the sun shining brightly through the fly's eyes, as Taylor turned the insect out over Green Lanes. Cutting between two houses on the other side of the street, they emerged through a red brick alley to reveal a sea of green fields that stretched out endlessly before them. Rows of huge gardens drifted below, many of them already dotted with young bodies playing games in the early morning sun; the neatly trimmed hedges that contained them began to give way to a horizon of endless farmland.

Onward they went, flying out over farms that seemed impossibly far away. While none of them would say it out loud, it felt good to leave Mildred for a little while. The past few days had been far too stressful for their liking, and even though they would soon have to return, it lifted their spirits to leave their troubles behind them for a while.

As the morning gradually drifted toward midday, they stopped to buy some breakfast at an old scarecrow with a large brellow *café* sign on its hat. Several drivers stared at the young children sitting next to the parked fly, its tiny old body pathetically small in comparison to the line of beetles and moths that were next to it, but as the children happily ate cheese and jelly sandwiches they soon found themselves laughing together for the first time that day. Their bad moods were gone; this was just the four of them, together.

Soon they were underway again, their bellies full, as they headed back out over the open fields of green and yellow. Gradually small roads began to appear beneath them, splitting the land into large squares as they squirmed their way toward a town that lay far on the horizon. All of them watched it approach, as the wall of trees that surrounded it grew larger, before splitting to reveal rows of cottages that spread outward, forming a web of homes below. For a moment, Maggie thought she recognized one of the shops. She blinked her eyes wide before slowly sitting back in her seat, convinced she must be seeing things. It was impossible; this simply couldn't be the place she was thinking of. A row of smaller houses gave way to two lines of leafy trees that split a long lane of houses, sixteen on each side, each with its own neat green lawn. Maggie sat upright in horror.

"Why are we here?" she said, poking Stick in the back.

"Ow!" he said, turning back to look at her, "What do you mean, why are we here? We're here because this is where Miss Devlin told us to pick up the parcel. Here, look at the map yourself if you don't believe me."

Maggie grabbed the large sheet of paper in Stick's hand. Slowly she examined it, regretting not looking at it earlier. A long red line was drawn across its length like an arrow, taking her from the home of Mildred 79 to a small town she knew very well. Upon arrival, the line danced over the roads before leading her eyes down a long lane with thirty-two homes—all of them bearing the tiny names of their inhabitants in letters that Maggie could barely read. Then as the bright red line finally reached its destination, four names jumped out at her, each one hitting her like a slap to the face.

32 Breezy Lane
Edward Linley Esienberg Teddington Pincus 14
Andrew Linley Esienberg Teddington Pincus 16
Charles Linley Esienberg Teddington Pincus 17
Victoria Linley Esienberg Teddington Pincus 52

Maggie sat, staring in horror, as the names of her old family danced in front of her. Slowly she dropped the paper, only to have her worst fears confirmed as the fly made the turn into Breezy Lane, and to the last house on the left. A row of perfect lawns gaped open beneath them, drawing them down a row of perfect little cottages toward one she knew all too well. One she had hoped never to return to.

She was going home.

Malcolm. How do the flies keep getting in here? And why do they just keep circling around my living room like they have nothing better to do?

15
The Fever Sets In

The fly swung lazily from side to side as 32 Breezy Lane drew closer. Inside, Maggie sat in silence watching its approach. She wanted to shout out for them to stop and turn around. Coming here couldn't possibly be a coincidence, it had to be a trap, but how could she tell them without letting them know who she truly was? Even if they did believe her, it would ruin everything. She'd be their enemy. They might even leave her here. It was useless. She had to go through with this…whatever it was.

Below them, the white gravel driveway swept away like a wide river drawing them to the house, as Maggie sat with her head in her hands. Next to her,

Pritch stared out the window at the giant world outside, as Stick and Taylor started a new argument about the best way into the house. Without thinking, Maggie opened her mouth to tell them to use the open window in the attic, before catching herself at the last second. She couldn't let them know that she had been here before, not unless she had to.

"Alright, go that way if you want to," moaned Stick, as the fly swooped downward, "It's not as if you haven't got lots of broken windows to choose from."

Maggie slowly lifted her head, thinking she had misheard. It was impossible that her stepmother's house would have broken windows. Victoria would simply never have allowed it. But looking up she saw, to her surprise, that Stick was telling the truth. There were broken windows everywhere. Most looked smashed, while those that weren't hung loosely in their frames, as if it was only a matter of time before they joined the others. Even more surprising was the front entrance. Victoria had always been sure to keep it pristine, insisting that Maggie clean several times a day, polishing the door handle and sweeping the step. But, no longer. Envelopes scarred with the words 'Final Notice' were everywhere, while the perfect front door stood broken—a wide crack splitting the greasy fingerprints that covered it.

Maggie looked up for the familiar number '32' hoping that they were at the wrong house, only to see that one of the numbers was now missing, a metal '3' sitting next to a patch of perfect pink brickwork that revealed the outline of a missing number two. This was her old home, but not as she had left it. Something had changed.

The fly took a wide arch over the top of the overgrown lawn, and ducked in through a large hole in the front window to find a room consumed by old food wrappers and empty drink cans. Trash was everywhere, pushing itself up against the edges of the walls and covering a food splattered dining table. When she had been living there, Maggie had vacuumed the room twice a day, but now only a small patch of carpet was still visible, a tiny island in the sea of trash with three golf clubs and a small bucket of balls at its edge.

"Well, I guess we know how the windows were broken. Who'd be stupid enough to play golf indoors?" said Stick.

Maggie pictured her three stepbrothers. It was just the sort of thing that only they would think was a good idea. Only, where was her stepmother? She would never have allowed it and they weren't brave enough to do anything that might upset her. Something was wrong. Buzzing their way down the hallway they found more trash, all of it sharing space with large tumbleweeds of dog hair. In front, Taylor struggled with the directions in her lap.

"Where is she?" she mumbled to no one in particular.

"Who are you looking for?" asked Maggie.

"A female body. Her name's Victoria, and she's supposed to live here somewhere. It says she's a factory for cleaning hospital blankets and sheets, but I don't see any signs yet."

Maggie snorted a snigger that surprised even her. Her stepmother, the queen of the local society, the woman who thought she was better than everyone else, was just a regular old launderette.

"What's so funny?" asked Taylor.

"Oh, nothing," lied Maggie, feeling a sudden rush of guilt.

Turning into the living room they found a similar story of destruction. More trash was spread everywhere, consuming the previously perfect couch and coffee table with old tea stains and empty pizza boxes, before growing upward into huge piles of food wrappers that threatened to overtake the room's large TV. The whole place was so dirty that for a second they failed to notice the three bodies below that were lying amongst the piles of trash like logs floating in a lake. On the TV's oversized screen, three angry soldiers were attacking a jungle village while below, the three brothers lay motionless, their thumbs stabbing at the buttons on their game controllers as though their lives depended on it. Maggie looked down at them, trying to imagine what could have happened here for them to have changed so much in such a short time. No longer did they look like the fearsome trio of schoolboy rugby, now they looked as though tackling a short walk was beyond them. Each of them was flabby and pale, and while outside the sun was just starting to touch down on the horizon, all of them were still in their pajamas. Andrew and Edward both wore T-shirts that sported huge circles of dried sweat, while Charles wore a dirty dressing gown that hung open to reveal a pair of yellowing underpants beneath a bloated belly.

"Are those bodies dead?" Pritch pointed, failing to notice the moving of their fingers.

"I don't think so. Looks like someone still lives there," replied Stick.

There on Charles's large stomach, they could clearly see hundreds of tiny figures all spread across his pale skin like freckles. Taylor took the fly down lower, only to see that most of them were muscles, their small heads consumed by blank looks. A few bothered to wave at the fly swooping overhead, raising their chiseled arms to say hello, but most just lay there seemingly too annoyed to do anything.

"Why aren't they inside?" asked Maggie.

"I think they're bored," replied Stick, "That's the trouble with muscles—too moody. If they're busy they're fine, but when there's no work to do they cause trouble. By the looks of it I can't imagine it'll be long before those ones look for a new job."

It seemed that the boredom was already becoming too much for them and as they watched from above, several of them beckoned for the fly to land, while another group wrote the words 'Work Wanted' in brellow on Charles's pale skin. Avoiding them, Taylor swung the fly upward leaving the living room behind. Charles reached for a half-eaten cheeseburger off the floor, inadvertently sweeping the invisible muscles off his belly and into an old bag of chips.

Once back in the hallway, the fly headed for the stairs, taking great care not to wake the creature that lay snoring far below, a half eaten burrito lying securely under its paw as if it had fallen asleep in the middle of its meal. Maggie stared down at the huge old dog. When her father had been alive, Bailey had gone to work with him everyday, standing at the front door each morning full of excitement for the day ahead. Now he just looked withered and ancient. His soft brown fur was a brittle grey, and several bald patches revealed islands of blotched skin that hung loosely over his yellow teeth. Of all the changes she had seen in the house this was the first one to make her sad, a wave of regret filling her for leaving him behind. The house being a mess, her stepbrothers getting fat, none of it bothered her…but Bailey didn't deserve this. Even if beneath it all he was probably a supermarket or garage, there was a soul in there who missed her father as much as she did. And if anyone could understand what it would have meant to see him again it was Bailey.

Upstairs they found a similar story, only here the trash seemed to be losing its battle for domination to the piles of old clothes that covered every inch of the floor. A sea of dirty rugby shirts and school uniforms leaked across the landing before meeting up with a black tide of dresses that flooded out through a darkened doorway at the end of the hall, forming a wall that warned against entering. Maggie sat silently and watched as the fly buzzed in and out of a mold-filled bathroom, before turning toward the shadowy entrance and the bedroom that she knew belonged to Victoria Linley Eisenburg Teddington Pincus 52; their final destination.

As they approached, Taylor read out the large brellow words that were written on the door.

Victoria Linley Eisenburg Teddington Pincus 52
~~**As Good As New Commercial Launderette - 24 hour service**~~
~~**Large insect deliveries at nighttime only please.**~~
CLOSED UNTIL FURTHER NOTICE

"I think that's us," she said, nodding toward the darkened doorway.

The heavy wooden door to the bedroom hung loosely on its hinges, the words 'NO ENTRY' written on its handle in brellow. The fly hovered silently in front of it. Inside the dark interior, they could just see an old broken mirror leaning casually against the wall, the floor around it surrounded by scrunched balls of used tissues.

"We are not going in there!" exclaimed Stick.

"Sadly, little brother, we don't have a choice," replied Taylor, "Unless you want to live on your own of course?"

Stick stared at her as though he'd like a minute to think about it, only to watch as his sister steered the fly down through the doorway, plunging them into darkness.

"I'll get the headlights!" said Stick enthusiastically, rummaging deep into the wall.

A second later, a blast of hot air filled the cabin, drawing in a stale smell from the room outside.

"That's the heater!" snapped Taylor, "It's this one!"

With a shrug of her shoulder, a wall of tiny green squares flickered into life on the two large eyes in front. Instantly Maggie felt as though she was back watching her brothers play their favorite computer game, the one with soldiers in night goggles attacking each other. Some of the shapes remained cold and black while others quickly warmed into a soft green picture, making them feel like they were looking at the outside world through a chess board.

"Told you this fly was a piece of rubbish," mumbled Stick, looking at the black squares liberally spread across their view.

Even after everything downstairs, Maggie struggled to believe what she was now seeing. She had never been allowed to leave so much as a speck of dust in her stepmother's bedroom, but now it was everywhere, smothering every surface like an old woolen blanket. Beneath it, the room's furniture lay broken and awkward, as though someone had tipped it all over in a fit of rage, while the door to the bathroom hung limply on one hinge, revealing a toilet that had been ripped from the wall. It now lay on its side, leaking a thick slime onto the white rug.

"This is so nasty," said Pritch in disgust, as Taylor circled the fly around the room.

The smell inside the cabin was growing steadily stronger, and even with the green night vision the darkness seemed to be squeezing in around them. All of them were eager to get out of there as soon as possible. Taylor was just about to turn the fly around to leave when something caught Stick's eye.

"Is that a foot?" he asked, pointing to the bed at the far end of the room.

Taylor swung the fly back into the room, as everyone peered into the darkness at the large bed that stood in the shadows. Newspapers were everywhere, covering the top of the mattress with loose pages that were pulled apart to form a moat, surrounding the heaped blanket in its center. As soon as she saw the foot, Maggie knew instinctively it was her stepmother. Even if she hadn't seen the name Victoria Linley Eisenberg Teddington Pincus 52, written in thick brellow letters on the huge heel, there was no mistaking the curled toes and rough skin that Maggie had been made to rub at the end of every day. Even at this distance she thought she could still smell the mix of lavender and foot sweat.

"Well, that's her," said Pritch, "Is it supposed to be dead?"

Maggie felt her heart skip a guilty beat.

"Nah, she's not dead, look at the blanket. See it's going up and down? Someone's breathing in there, and listen, it's crying!" said Stick.

All of them fell silent as the sounds of gentle sobbing seeped into the cabin, leaving them to nervously watch the heaving mountain approach. As they crossed the edge of the bed, Maggie looked down on the sea of newspapers below, the headlines jumping out through the dim light from the hallway.

THE WITCH NEXT DOOR!
Local socialite raised the dead for party from hell!

SHE DID IT!
Police charge local woman with planning to kidnap her guests to pay off her debts!

HOW THE MIGHTY HAVE FALLEN!
Police drop charges but now she's bankrupt!

Suddenly it all made sense. The house, the mess, her brothers, even Victoria herself. Maggie had tricked her into revealing that she had no money, and with no income or reputation everything would have fallen apart. And if there was one person who couldn't cope with having less in her life it was her stepmother. Being rich and respected was all that mattered. Without that it seemed she had simply given up. And with no mother to watch over them, the three brothers would have had to take care of themselves, a disastrous idea at anytime.

Taylor took the fly in several sharp circles above the swelling mound, before swooping down toward a thick fold in the blanket. They shot inside and were suddenly consumed by a new, deeper darkness, as a smell of body odor swamped the air around them. The heat was incredible, as if they were flying into a volcano, making every gulp of air feel like chewing on a thick toffee.

Taylor reached forward, increasing the strength of the green glow on the fly's eyes, only to find it useless against the blackness outside. It was as though they were trapped in a small cave with invisible walls. The small compartment felt cramped and, after several near misses of the blanket wall, Taylor turned the fly downward.

"What now?" asked Maggie, as they landed with a dull thump on the bed. She considered herself used to being in dark spaces, the attic she once called home had only one small lamp, and Maggie often found herself sitting in darkness, the only light bulb confiscated by her stepmother. But, even that couldn't compare to the blackness that surrounded them now. Taylor squinted and leaned back, pulling her arms free from the walls with a wet pop.

"The instructions say that we have to find Victoria Linley Eisenberg Teddington Pincus 52 and go to her Eastern Elbow entrance.

"How are we supposed to find her Eastern Elbow?" said Stick, "I'm not going out there, I mean look at it. I can barely see my own elbow!"

Taylor propped herself up and began rummaging in her backpack.

"Here you go, we'll use these," she said, passing everyone a small white cylinder.

Maggie turned the white tube over in her hands, trying to work out what to do with it.

"Toothies!" said Pritch, "brilliant!"

There was a loud crack, and suddenly a bright light shot out from inside Pritch's hand, quickly followed by two others as Taylor and Stick snapped theirs to life. Maggie fumbled at it again before finally realizing that she needed to bend it in half, shooting its bright light directly into her eyes as the others erupted in laughter.

"Careful," said Taylor, turning the white tube around, "these are pretty strong. I bought them from a bone builder who's working in a pregnant body down the street. He said they are made of new baby teeth so they should be really good."

Maggie blinked against the burst of white light that had blinded her, before slowly being able to see the faces of the others again. None of them looked like they wanted to leave the safety of the fly, but the heat was quickly becoming unbearable and finally Taylor snapped open the cabin's lock, swinging open the hatch for the four of them to step down onto the soft cotton floor below. The light from the toothies glowed like a shield around them, but as they squinted into the darkness for signs of life, their fear only grew. Moving quickly as one, they left the fly behind and began to search the area around them, eager to finish the task as quickly as possible. After what seemed an eternity, the light from the toothies finally began to reveal something ahead. They soon found themselves standing next to a huge pale wall that heaved with an echoing sob.

"Well this is her stomach," said Taylor, pointing up at the huge mound of a belly button that protruded forward like half a pink planet over their heads, "but which way is her elbow?"

Before they had time to think, a gigantic hand came sweeping toward them and scratched at the soft pink wall. The kids threw themselves wildly away into balls of tumbling light.

"I guess we go that way," said Stick, pointing toward the disappearing hand as the others slowly got to their feet.

They walked cautiously along the wall of skin, ready for the hand to return, as a layer of silk pajamas appeared next to them. Following it in and out of Victoria's huge armpit, they soon found themselves at a section of rounded wall that strained against the black silk, shimmering the light from their toothies along its length.

"Well, we're here," said Taylor.

The four of them stood staring at each other, unsure of what to do next. Miss Devlin had told them that there would be someone there to meet them, that all they'd have to do was deliver the package and leave. But there was no one to be seen. Waiting in the silence, their eyes circled the darkness for anything that would tell them what to do next. Seconds dragged into minutes and slowly the sense that something was wrong began to grow stronger and stronger. Miss Devlin, the only one who knew they were here, the same woman who hated them, had sent them all alone into the dark. Slowly their fears started to multiply as the sense that something bad was going to happen overwhelmed them.

"I say we go," whispered Pritch, as though the darkness was listening to them, "this feels wrong."

"We can't go back without giving them the package," replied Stick, "We have to wait!"

All of them looked uneasily at one another. Their toothies suddenly didn't seem so bright and the smell in the air felt stronger than before, as if it was burning inside them. None of them wanted to leave, but the fear was becoming too much for any of them to stand.

Maggie stared at the others. She knew how hard it would be for them to be split up but she couldn't take much more; coming back to Breezy Lane had to be more than just a coincidence. She opened her mouth to say they should leave but before the words could come out, the light from her toothie suddenly disappeared.

She turned for help. A sudden rush of air passed between their frozen bodies, leaving them no time to react as it pulled the precious lights from each of their hands. Pritch managed a small squeak of surprise, but everything was happening too quickly. They could only watch as their lights shot away into the night like a disappearing train plunging them into darkness.

For a moment they stood motionless, engulfed in fear as their minds searched frantically for answers. One by one they began to press themselves into one another, desperate not to be alone as their eyes strained to see anything in the blackness around them. Something creaked as a rush of cold air flashed past Maggie's ear, flicking her hair up off her neck. She reached out, desperate to grab onto the others, but felt only a cold empty space. A second rush of air flew by, this one chasing a sudden scream that spun into the distance as if it was being sucked into the gloom.

"Stick?" She trembled. "Are you there?"

She heard him start to speak, but before he had a chance there was another rush, and his voice was gone —leaving only Maggie's half spoken name behind him. Spinning desperately around she looked pleadingly into the pitch darkness, overwhelmed with helplessness. Again she opened her mouth, the urge to scream too strong, only to feel two cold hands fix themselves tightly over her mouth, before pulling her backwards like a bundle of rags. She looked for someone, anyone, to help but there was nothing. Just darkness. It was too late; the trap had been sprung.

Malcolm, It's been quieter today. I think that neighbor with the noisy girl has moved out…I hope she doesn't come back.

16

Bruised to the Bone

Two luminous green eyes stared deeply into Maggie's face as if they were trying to burn their way into her mind. Above the cold stare a shiny black shell of a head scooped backward to form two black horns. They rested on either side of a thin mouth; its skin the color of burnt mud. Slowly the lips parted, releasing a voice that surrounded Maggie, encircling her in a cold chill as it crackled against her.

"Hello, child. It's been a long time."

Maggie stared up into the black face, looking at the skin patched with squares of broken flesh, as the stench from its hot breath pulled at the contents of her stomach.

"Do I know you?" She trembled, turning her head against the smell.

For a second, the green eyes seemed surprised. Then a crooked smile slowly curled itself upward revealing several rows of sharp, yellow teeth.

"Of course! You don't know who I am, do you? How fascinating! So much at risk and yet it doesn't even trust its own offspring? What a sad little species you are."

Maggie watched as the creature raised a skinny black finger, its end long and sharp like a knife, before trailing it down the side of her face, resisting the urge to break her skin.

"LEAVE HER ALONE! I HAVE WHAT YOU WANT!" screamed Taylor's voice from somewhere in the darkness.

For a second, the thing hesitated, trying to decide which was more important. Then, it quickly turned, a long tail flicking itself against Maggie's legs as it disappeared into the blackness.

"Give me some light here, I need to see it for myself," said the voice after a few moments.

There was a loud brush of nails on fabric as Victoria's giant hand suddenly returned, sweeping up the blanket that surrounded them, and throwing it back to allow in a faint light from the hallway. Maggie quickly searched through the welcome gloom to see that they had been pulled all the way to the opposite end of Victoria, far away from the fly, which now sat in the murky shadows of her huge knee like a forgotten relic in a museum. One by one she searched for her friends, finding each of their scared faces inside thick green arms that were bound tightly around them.

"Get off me you big ugly parasite," shouted Stick, as the creature slid a heavy two-fingered hand over his mouth to silence him.

Their captors stood with excited smiles, their small heads covered with long stalks that leaned forward to reveal a sea of tiny red eyes, dancing excitedly up and down the children's bodies like a bucket of worms hungrily grasping for their next meal. All of them were large with thick, muscular bodies that easily dwarfed the slender black creature that walked before them, and yet as he came close they all hesitated, their small red eyes showing obvious fear.

The thick black tail turned smoothly behind as it circled in front of the four children, examining the contents of the package grasped tightly in its long fingers. Taylor's ripped backpack fell to the floor, as it peeled back the lid on a small box. A bright red glow was released; it bounced off its black face to reveal a broad grin of teeth that protruded forward like rows of sharp knives sunken into a marsh of pink flesh. Then, with a slow turn of his head, he crossed back to Maggie. Once again the long black finger returned to her cheek, and his voice whispered in her ear, instantly sending a surge of fear through her.

With wide eyes, she watched as he slipped slowly backward, his eyes never leaving hers, before turning sharply to disappear into the shadows, leaving only his words behind him.

"Kill them."

For a second, the creatures that held them hesitated, and then slowly they began to squeeze, their thick arms forcing the air out of the four children with their incredible strength. Maggie looked pleadingly up into the red eyes that danced around her head, only to see them looking down on her with delight. Pritch let loose a muffled scream, as Stick kicked wildly against the legs of the creature that stood motionless despite his attack. The pressure was incredible now, leaving Maggie feeling as though her insides were about to burst out through her ears, thumping the inside of her head—she felt herself slowly losing consciousness. The blackness pulled her in, as a slow growl filled the air around her. Something inside her told her to fight, to not let go, and she flailed wildly with the last of her strength, only to feel the arms squeeze even tighter. Everything began to get darker and darker.

The paw crashed down from above without warning, bouncing all of them high into the air. Through the dark, Maggie felt the sudden release of the arms around her. Air filled her lungs, and she looked back to see the thing that had been holding her spun wildly across the bed, before slamming hard into Victoria's elbow with a loud crunch. She watched him fall into a heap on the mattress below, when the sudden realization that she too was falling came to her. She felt her shoulder pound into the floor as her body slapped down hard behind it. Closing her eyes against the pain, she rolled onto her back and began to cough, sucking in precious breaths. Everything was shaking, as though she was lying in the middle of a giant earthquake. Maggie looked up to see that someone had replaced the ceiling with soft brown fur that was patched with flecks of grey hair and islands of pink skin.

"Bailey!" she groaned gratefully at the huge dog standing overhead, his front paws sinking into the mattress on either side of her, like the legs of a bridge. He released a deep growl.

A hand pulled her upright as the floor took a new lurch.

"RUN!" yelled Stick

Struggling to stand, she fought for balance, and through blurry eyes she tried to find an escape. Only then did she see the black creature deep in the shadows, its arms raised high against the wall of Victoria's hand. It silently mouthed orders to something unseen in her giant palm.

For a second, everything seemed to stop as a foreboding silence surrounded all of them. Then it fell away, a heavy shadow sweeping over them as the large hand of Victoria swung in a wide circle, hitting Bailey hard against the side of his head, and toppling the old dog from the bed.

"COME ON!" screamed Stick.

The floor began to ripple violently beneath them but Maggie didn't feel a thing. She was standing motionless, transfixed at the sight of her stepmother jumping out of bed to attack the old dog that lay tangled on the floor, trying desperately to scramble back onto his feet as the woman in black closed in. With a speed that seemed impossible, Victoria lunged at Bailey who twisted backward, barely avoiding the giant fist that tore through the carpet and splintered the floorboard below. She tried to stand, ready to attack again, only to feel her hand trapped in the large hole in the floor. Instantly Bailey recognized his chance and threw himself hard into her stomach, snapping her hand free as she toppled backward onto the bed, landing just inches away from the tiny Maggie, who was still shocked at the fight before her.

"MAGGIE…WE HAVE TO GO…NOW!"

Maggie turned to see Pritch screaming at her. An angry Stick stood next to her, glaring at the three muscular creatures that were closing in, all of them ready to finish the job they had started, as the fight between the two giants crashed loudly above them. Bailey clung bravely to the wriggling body of Victoria and pawed at her wrists, as though he was trying to hold her down, when her huge hand once again broke free and drove itself hard into his neck, sending him flying across the room to slam into the wardrobe where he slumped into a heap.

"COME ON!"

Pritch grabbed Maggie by the wrist and pulled at her with a force that she couldn't ignore, moving her backward just as the thick fist of one of the red-eyed creatures swiped uselessly behind her. She turned and began to run, suddenly realizing just how much danger they were in. Up ahead, Taylor was already at the fly, while behind them the three creatures gave lumbering chase, the floor shaking beneath their feet. Wildly the children ran, fear driving them forward until, with bursting lungs they threw themselves inside the fly's entry hatch. Taylor slammed it closed. Outside, the creatures beat furiously against the fly's body with angry fists, shaking the small compartment as Taylor struggled into the driver's seat and plunged her hands into the wall.

"HANG ON!" she screamed to the others, pulling hard against the fly's soft flesh. Maggie felt herself once again thrown through the air as the whole cabin flipped to one side, before spinning onto its back. Over and over it went, swirling Maggie, Pritch, and Stick around the cabin, as it rolled faster across the surface of the bed. Through flashing windows, Maggie caught sight of one of the creatures shaking its fists angrily at the rolling fly as they spiraled away from his reach.

Again and again they turned, all the while getting closer to the edge of the bed, and freedom, when suddenly everything stopped. Maggie felt something soft beneath her and realized she was lying on top of Pritch, who was now lying on top of Stick.

Above them, Taylor, who was still strapped into her chair, was furiously trying to get the fly to start.

"I think I'm going to be sick!" moaned Stick from the bottom of the pile of children. Maggie pulled herself up into the seat next to Taylor, as Pritch followed her lead, strapping in behind.

"OH NO!" shouted Taylor.

The fly trembled to life as, up ahead, its eyes began to glow bright. It revealed an angry Victoria charging at them, a thick roll of newspaper in her hand, ready to strike.

Taylor threw herself backward, shooting the fly upward, as the newspaper flashed in front of them before slapping hard against the bed. Below Maggie caught sight of Bailey lying motionless on the floor, his body bent awkwardly beneath an unmoving chest. Still upwards they went, only for Victoria to come at them again, swinging the paper in wide circles, as Taylor slammed them from side to side desperately trying to avoid the blows that would surely crush their tiny fly.

Fsssh! Fssssh! Fssssh!

The attacks from the newspaper were coming faster and faster, filling the cabin with panic, as each swing came closer and closer. A sudden crash shook the floor beneath them and Maggie looked out to see four of the fly's legs fall away behind them as the newspaper just missed the fly's cabin. Yellowing teeth flashed past the window, sending a shiver through Maggie as she realized that Victoria was now smiling; as though she knew she was finally about to take her revenge on the stepdaughter she hated.

"She's too fast!" gritted Taylor.

The light from outside was growing brighter, and Taylor swung them hard to the left, diving beneath Victoria's latest onslaught, trying desperately to steer them toward the open doorway.

Fsssh! Fssssh! Fsssssh!

More swings beat down around them, coming closer and closer with each strike, as though they were being toyed with. Another swing, then another, and another rained down around them. A loud crack sent them shuddering sideways as the newspaper clipped the edge of one wing. Up ahead a giant hand appeared, reaching for the doorway that was their only escape, before slowly starting to close it.

Fsssh! Fssssh! Fsssssh!

Maggie had seen Reg make some dramatic maneuvers to get to his destination, but as the air around them filled with the ripples of Victoria's laughter, every one of them knew that they would never make it in time. The rectangle of light was slimming fast and they were still too far away. They were about to be trapped. Once alone in a room with Victoria they would be lucky to last more than a few seconds.

BANG!

The door suddenly stopped moving. The giant hand pushed again with all its strength, but still the door refused to close, leaving the light from the hallway hanging there like a golden road beckoning the children toward it.

Fsssh! Fssssh! Fsssssh! Went the newspaper, slashing at them with a new urgency. Taylor flipped them over as she threw the fly forward, desperate to take their second chance. Again the hand tried to force the door closed, but it was useless, something was refusing to let it close. Screams filled the air as Victoria slammed it over and over, frustration pouring out of her.

Then, light filled the cabin as the fly darted through the open gap and out into the hallway, as one last swing of the newspaper threw itself uselessly behind them.

Free of Victoria's bedroom, they listened as her screams faded behind them, the door slamming over and over into whatever was blocking it, as she vented her anger.

"YES!" shouted Stick.

Overwhelmed with excitement, each of them bounced in their seats, celebrating their escape as they patted Taylor on the back and told her what an amazing pilot she was. Even Stick reached over to hug his sister, before slumping back into his seat with a slightly embarrassed look as he realized what he had just done. Moments before, they had been only seconds away from death, but now, as they flew to freedom, they were filled with pride. They were so excited that they failed to notice one amongst them who wasn't quite as happy. That one of them was sitting motionless; her face pressed against one of the fly's small windows as she looked back at the unmoving grey dog that had jammed himself in the doorway to let them escape. Bailey, her father's dog, was lying dead at her stepmother's feet.

"What was that about?" asked Stick as they darted outside through a broken pane of glass.

"That was weird. I have never seen a body act like that before. It's usually really easy to avoid them when you're flying. Did you see how strong and quick she was?" asked Pritch.

Back and forth they went, analyzing everything that had just happened, each of them paying no attention to the unmoving shapes of Maggie and Taylor, sitting silently in front. Outside, the last of the light was falling behind the horizon as Maggie opened the map once more, hoping to hide behind it as she tried to stop thinking of Bailey.

"What did he say to you?" whispered Taylor coldly.

Maggie stared up at Taylor. She had never seen her like this before, and for a second Maggie thought there was anger in her new friend's eyes. Behind them, Stick and Pritch carried on talking, oblivious to the conversation in front.

"What did he say?" she repeated.

"Who?" asked Maggie innocently.

Taylor suddenly plucked a wet hand from the wall and grabbed Maggie's wrist.

"The virus! He whispered something to you. What did he say?"

"What virus? What are you talking about?" stammered Maggie.

"That creature back there, the one who ordered them to kill us, that was a virus, a deadly virus, and it whispered something to you. What was it?" she demanded again.

"Oh, he said to say thank-you to Miss Devlin," said Maggie, looking down at her lap.

For a second, Taylor's eyes narrowed as if she knew Maggie was lying.

"As long as that's all it said…." she replied, relaxing her grip.

"So, what do you two think?" shouted Stick behind them.

There was silence, and for a second Maggie thought he must have heard them talking.

"About what?" asked Taylor grumpily.

"About what we were just talking about. When we move, who gets first choice of beds?"

"You're an idiot," said Taylor.

"What? What did I say?" said Stick, resuming their normal relationship.

Maggie looked back at her two friends, wishing she could share in their joy as she told herself to be happy. Not only had they escaped but they had also completed Miss Devlin's job. The package had been delivered and now they could pick where they wanted to live. But Maggie was far from happy. Something deep inside told her that there was more to today than she knew. Bailey fighting back was no accident; he had done it to save her. Victoria too had known who she was. Everything felt wrong. She had put them all in danger, all because she was lying about who she really was. And now she had done it again. Taylor had been right. The virus had whispered something in her ear. But it hadn't been a message of thanks. It had whispered what no one in this world was supposed to know; that she was not an internal, but rather the daughter of the great Bert Pincus…a free soul.

'Let the prophecy come true and let the war be won!' he had finally hissed, his thin mouth curling up into what Maggie supposed was a smile.

As the others laughed loudly, recounting their escape to one another, Maggie sat quietly in the corner, her mind a blur of questions. What did he mean, let the prophecy come true? And what did he know about the war?

Her cheek still felt hot from its touch, and the memory of those green eyes still filled her with fear, and yet she wanted to scream out for them to go back. She needed to know what he meant, she needed answers. But it was no good; how could she go back without letting the others know who she was? There was only one thing she could do… she had to hope that

Pethora would come for her soon. The desire to stay here with the others could not be listened to. She needed to leave. To stay would only put them in danger.

Back at 32 Breezy Lane everything was silent. Victoria stood motionless, every part of her frozen since the children had escaped. At her feet Bailey gave a shake and rolled onto his paws with a sprightly leap that pushed open the door. Several loud clicks were released as he arched his back, cracking his bent spine back into place, before jumping up to place his paws on Victoria's shoulder. Then gently he rested his nose against her neck with an ease that defied his age.

Stepping down onto Victoria's shoulder, a hooded figure walked slowly over to meet the virus, its long black fingers still playing with the box the children had delivered.

"Is it the right one?"

"Yes indeed," said the virus, "this will do perfectly."

"Good. This is where and when I want you to use it," said the hooded figure, pulling out a piece of yellow paper and handing it to the virus.

A long black finger slipped it open, as two rows of knives slowly formed a wide smile on its black face.

"Well, this will be even more fun than I had thought!" it snarled, unable to hide his delight.

"I'm glad you are so happy about it," came the cold reply, "Tell your men they did a good job today... very believable."

"That will mean a lot to them. I shall tell them myself now," said the virus, turning to leave.

"Oh Marburg...." said the hooded figure, casually stopping the black creature in his tracks, "When I tell you not to talk to Maggie without my permission again you will listen, do you understand? Unless, of course, you need a little reminder of what I'm capable of?"

The virus spun around angrily, his full dislike at following orders was suddenly apparent. His black tail twitched and his green eyes burned brighter than ever.

"I understand," it replied, forcing the lines of teeth into a submissive smile, "It will not happen again. I am...sorry."

The cloak stood motionless as the virus turned and walked away. The light from the hallway rippled across the silky floor of Victoria's pajamas like shimmering air bubbles trapped beneath a sheet of black glass. Within the dark hood, two eyes stared down the hallway towards where the fly had made its escape.

"Very well, Maggie Pincus," came a low voice from within the hood, "Let's see who you truly are."

Malcolm…There's bits of you I remember, like your smell, or how it felt when you held me. Then sometimes I forget the simple things, like how you looked when you were older. I just remember you in your uniform. You were so handsome and strong. My husband.

17

The Poison Within

After everything that had happened that evening, a quiet trip back to Mildred was a welcome relief for the exhausted foursome. Yet despite her tiredness, Maggie found herself unable to sleep, her mind filling her with jealousy at the sound of heavy snoring emerging from Pritch and Stick in the back seat. But no matter how hard she tried it was no good, there was too much for her to think about.

Next to her, Taylor fought to stay awake, her heavy eyes resting on dark circles, until eventually she gave in and punched Stick awake, demanding he take a turn at flying.

Within minutes it was Taylor who was snoring loudly in the back, as Maggie found herself sitting next to a blurry eyed Stick, his thin arms embedded in the pink fleshy wall of the fly.

"Can I ask you a question?" said Maggie after a while.

Stick stretched his eyes open, sending a line of wrinkles up his forehead.

"Sure, go for it," he replied, happy for the conversation.

"The war…the one between the internals and the souls…can you tell me about it?"

Stick looked over at her, his wrinkles returning as a confused expression filled his face.

"What war would that be?" he asked.

For a moment Maggie was unsure what to say. What did he mean 'what war?' Since she had arrived in Mildred he had become her teacher on how bodies worked. Surely he knew about the war?

"The war between the internals and the souls," she said hesitating, "you know, when the internals tricked all the souls into going into the mind and then

287

stole all of their memories so that they could do what they wanted."

Stick's eyes formed two thin slits, looking at her as though she was crazy.

"What are you on about?" he said.

Maggie looked down sheepishly, regretting ever starting the conversation.

"It doesn't matter," she muttered.

"If you're talking about the great divide, well that's something else. But there was never any war," continued Stick, rolling his arm as he gradually turned the fly, "The great divide was when all the souls went into the mind and never came out. No internal knows why. But there wasn't any war. Souls are the ones who won't come out; it's nothing to do with us. I guess they just like it better up there without us."

Maggie turned to look at him sharply, surprising even herself. After all that she had seen: the books that documented the struggle of souls everywhere, the awful lumbering deatheaters, the murder of her father. How dare he pretend that it had nothing to do with the internals?

"How can they be happy up there? That's so unfair. They were tricked!" she demanded.

Behind them Taylor let out a sudden snort as Pritch sleepily pulled her coat around her.

"Slow down, Maggie!" said Stick, not wanting to fight, "I'm just telling you what I know. If someone told you something different then feel free to ask the professors when we start back to school next week. But I promise you this, no one is stopping the souls from coming out of the mind. We don't know why they won't come out and we don't know why they ignore us, but until they decide the time is right there's nothing we can do to help them. What are we supposed to do, go in after them? That would be suicide. No internal can enter any mind without being burned to a crisp!"

Maggie looked at his tired face. Part of her wanted to fight with him, but something inside told her he was telling the truth. At least he believed what he was saying. Silence returned to the front seat as both of them sat there pretending to stare out of the fly's eyes. Outside, the first signs of morning started to appear, pushing back the night. Maggie watched it gradually make its way upward until, at last, the sun appeared on the horizon.

"Wait a minute," she said suddenly, "What do you mean we start school next week?"

Drawing closer to Mildred's house, a grumpy Stick pulled back on the fly, slowing the wings to a dull hum as they lazily made their way home. After spending the last hour explaining that yes, they would all be going to school next week, he was in no mood to land the fly himself. Instead he reached back and jammed a finger into his sleeping sister's mouth, demanding that she finish the job, as she choked herself awake.

"I can't believe I'm related to you!" she moaned, sliding in next to him.

Soon they were inside the house, Taylor bringing them deftly in through the unused cat flap before swooping them up into the living room. The familiar smell of Mildred's home filled the air around them, padding the cabin with warmth that seemed to welcome them back. Then, with a wide sweep to the right, there was Mildred Potts 79, sitting exactly where she could be found everyday—in her favorite chair staring blankly past the newspaper at the photographs of Malcolm on the fireplace.

Maggie stared up at the giant old woman. The first time she had seen her she had looked miserable, with a face that sent chills through her, but now something was different. Perhaps it was seeing the young Mildred in all the old movies on the memory player, or maybe it was because she knew that she was going to be closed soon, but seeing her now was like seeing a whole different body. Her face seemed softer, as though she was full of longing, not anger. And while her body looked tired it also seemed strangely beautiful, like an old house that just needed someone to realize how great it could be.

Taylor pulled them high overhead, circling Mildred as she searched for the safest place to land. In the back, Pritch gave a sleepy stretch and peeled back a pink flap of skin from the floor, revealing another small hole that looked out over the top of Mildred's head, her thinning white hairs split down the middle to create a pink path.

"What about the runway?" she asked, looking up toward the front of the fly.

Taylor peeked over the front of the fly's bulbous eyes at the pink strip of skin below.

"Not a chance," she replied, "Look at it. It's been closed for years. It's like a jungle down there. You'd have to be mad to land on that."

"Errrrrr…new problem," said Pritch nervously, "we only have two legs left."

Taylor turned her head slowly, as if Pritch would change her mind before she looked at her.

"What?"

"Two legs? Our landing gear? The fly only has two legs left," repeated Pritch nervously.

All four of them squirmed to look down through the hole where two thick legs dangled into view behind four stubs, each one pink and raw with dripping blood.

"Is that bad?" asked Maggie. She suddenly regretted not having mentioned the missing legs earlier; it seemed obvious now that they would need them to land.

"Yes, it's bad!" said Stick, leaping into the seat next to his sister as if an alarm had just sounded, "If we're lucky we'll just have to crash land, if we're not then those legs have been leaking for a long time and…."

"We're out of fuel!" interrupted Taylor.

In the fly's skin, a small blister was blinking red as Taylor and Stick both shot angry looks back and forth, each blaming the other for not having noticed it earlier.

As if it was listening, the fly's wings gave a sudden shudder and began spluttering, signaling that that they were ready to stop any second.

"Okay, nobody panic!" said Stick, his face filled with panic.

The fly gave another shudder and dropped suddenly, flipping the children's stomachs up into their mouths, before leveling out as it started drifting slowly downward. Outside, the sounds of Mildred's snoring rippled heavily through the air as strands of her hair whipped perilously close to the windows.

"Hang on everyone," Taylor said between gritted teeth, "I'm going to have to use the runway!"

"I thought you said you had to be mad to do that?" asked Maggie.

Taylor shrugged her shoulders, too busy to answer. Through the front windows, thick masses of Mildred's hair were starting to form a dark forest, clouding the light as the fly fought against Taylor's demands. A thick trunk of hair came perilously close before another made contact with the remaining legs, forcing the wings to shudder to a halt.

Taylor pushed down hard on the controls but it was useless. More strands of hair banged mercilessly against the fly as the runway below disappeared, and the fly plummeted downward. Screams surrounded them as they bounced against Mildred's top lip, the thought that they were about to die overwhelming them.

'PPPPPPPHHHHHHHIIIIIIIIIIIIIIPPPPPPPPPP
PP'

The world seemed to freeze.

Maggie felt herself thrown forward as the fly suddenly swung upward, plunging them into darkness before coming to a sudden stop.

Slowly opening one eye, Maggie saw one of Stick's legs hanging loosely over the back of the chair. Pritch threw up an arm and tried to pull herself upright.

"Ooooohhhhhhhhhhhhhhh!" said Taylor from the driver's seat, "I think we're in the booger fields."

Maggie looked around in confusion as Stick bolted upright.

"Quick, let's get out of here!" he said.

"Why?" said Maggie innocently, unsure of what the panic was.

"The booger fields," he said, "we're in Mildred's nose. She must have breathed us in. We have to get out of here before she blows!"

Maggie looked back at him, still confused, until Taylor swung open the hatch revealing the wide canyon and the danger they were in below.

"Follow me!" said Taylor, jumping blindly out of the fly and into the abyss below.

Maggie stared after her, unmoving, when a hand pushed hard against her back. Instantly she felt herself falling, wind rushing past her as she left the safety of the fly behind. Thick wet branches of hair slapped hard against her body, spinning her sideways as they whipped against her. Maggie threw up her arms, just as her fall was stopped by something warm and wet. Pritch and Stick followed quickly after her, their faces covered in a thick green goo.

Maggie reached up a hand as she watched the slime stretch and drop between her fingers.

"Boogers," said Stick with a laugh. "Saved by boogers!"

"Eeeeewwwwww," said Pritch and Taylor, jumping up from the wet ball before furiously wiping at the green that covered them.

"What?" said Stick, "We're lucky Mildred sucked us up here…you should really be happy, I mean at least they were wet ones…it could have been far worse!"

"Get out of there now!" snapped Taylor, "Do you have any idea of how much trouble we'll be in if we're caught up here? It's a forbidden area you know!"

Maggie looked over at Stick who was spreading his arms and legs to make booger angels beneath him.

Something inside her told her to listen to Taylor, but after everything that had happened to them she couldn't help but release a laugh.

"NOW!" snarled Taylor.

"Slow down," replied Stick, "don't pick on me…get it? Pick on me…PICK…boogers!"

"Young lady," said a cold voice.

Stick's face dropped as his sister turned to see a nerve staring coldly at her. "You and your friends are in a restricted area and are automatically ordered to appear before the regional minister. I have warned him of your imminent arrival and given him details on how you came to be in here. He is waiting for you in his office."

Taylor stared coldly at Stick as the nerve left with a crack.

They were back…and they were in trouble.

Maggie and Pritch walked in silence as Stick and Taylor argued their way down twelve flights of stairs to the regional minister's office. A large muscle stepped aside as they approached, showing them inside. Above them, several large red pipes were pumping their warmth into the small room that was empty except for a desk pressed against one wall, a man sat with his back to them, seated lazily behind it.

"Just our luck," whispered Pritch, "He's usually not here. For someone who is supposed to be in charge of Mildred he's always finding excuses to leave. But the one time he's here we go and crash a fly into Mildred's face...we're done for!"

"I think I shall make that decision," came a tired voice from the man at the desk.

Pritch began to blush, and Maggie shot her a sympathetic look.

"But I do agree, it doesn't look good for you right now...stealing an unlicensed fly...underage flying...leaving Mildred without a guardian's permission. Oh, and there's the small matter of crashing into an illegal entrance. I think saying you're done for is the only thing you've gotten right today! Would you like to explain just what you were thinking?"

Thaddeus Miles spun slowly backward from the desk, revealing a thin man with a broad bald head. Specks of grey beard covered his face, and he rubbed at the sleepless eyes above his spectacles, trying to focus on the four children before him.

"Well?" he said to the four individuals staring at their feet. "Rest assured your housematron is on her way as we speak, and I really don't have time for all this, so why doesn't the one whose idea it was just hand themselves over so that I can have someone to blame and we can move this along quickly?"

Silence filled the air. Maggie went to take a step forward, but before she could move she felt Stick brush against her.

"It was me," he said loudly, "It was all my idea and I made them do it."

Without wanting it, Maggie felt a rush of relief overtake her.

"No…it was me!" said Pritch, stepping forward.

For a second the room was silent.

"Actually, it was me," said Maggie, moving toward the minister.

Silence returned as everyone waited.

"What?" said Taylor, staring at the other three, "alright, it was me, not them, happy now!"

Thaddeus looked down and started to rub at his temples as if all this made his brain hurt.

"Look, this is all very admirable, but I really am busy and this is…."

Looking up he suddenly stopped, his eyes staring at Maggie with disbelief.

"How…you…but…."

The three children looked at Maggie in confusion. Thaddeus slowly rose from his chair and stepped toward Maggie, his face filled with confusion.

"But you're supposed to be…."

"MINISTER!" said a breathless Miss Devlin, suddenly bursting in through the door, "I came…as soon…as I heard."

But Thaddeus heard nothing. He was lost, staring only at Maggie.

"I don't even know where to begin," she continued, pushing the children behind her, "I know how busy you are, what with the closing and everything, so I'll take this from here. Rest assured, they will be punished most severely!"

Maggie felt the familiar grip of Miss Devlin's claw like hands pulling her backward and out into the hall, as she did the same with the other three.

"Don't you worry minister. I'll deal with them," she said, closing the door, leaving a speechless Thaddeus behind.

Outside, Miss Devlin pushed the four children past the guard and down the hallway, herding them down thin stairwells with soft gray walls. Nerves flashed past them at varying speeds with hurried looks on their faces that only matched the children's desire to stop. Then, Miss Devlin's arms surrounded them once more as she forced them into a small opening of fat that had been scooped into one wall.

The four of them stood there, backs pressed against the yellow warmth, waiting for the punishment that was surely about to come.

"Did you do it?" said Miss Devlin angrily, "Did you?!"

With everything that had happened they had almost forgotten about why they had left Mildred in the first place. They shot confused looks at each other. Finally, it was Taylor who spoke.

"I gave it the package," she said shamefully.

A broad grin spread across Miss Devlin's face.

"Good…better than good," she said, turning swiftly and striding away to leave the children standing in confusion.

"Is that it?" said Pritch eventually, "Is she coming back? Are we still in trouble?"

"I think she's too happy to care right now, look," said Stick, pointing at a bright yellow paper pinned to opposite wall.

OFFICIAL NOTICE
CLOSURE OF MILDRED POTTS, 79

Dear Residents,

I am hereby ordered to notify you that by order of the Internal National Government, Mildred Potts, 79 is to be closed. All residents of Mildred Potts, 79 are hereby served notice that their tenancy will end and that they will need to find alternate places to live and work.

The official closure will take place on the date listed below. There will be a formal gathering held that day to commemorate this event in the main cavity from 7pm to 10pm. All residents are requested to attend.

Official closure shall commence at 11pm. Please be aware that all life sustaining machines will cease to operate at this time and, for their own safety, all internals are ordered to leave within 30 minutes.

By order of:

Thaddeus Miles

Regional Minister

Closure Date: Mildred Potts, 79. November 30th.

"I guess that's it," said Stick, staring sadly into space, "Mildred's going to die on her birthday."

Malcolm...I felt a tickle all day and the nurse said I might be coming down with something. Then she said she wasn't going to be able to visit me so often. Something about cutbacks. Then she said I was getting too weak to keep using the stairs, and two men came in and moved my bed down to the living room. It's going to be strange sleeping down here. At least now I'll be able to see your photo all the time.

18

A Pocket of Pus

"Great…just great," fumed a wet Taylor, stomping across the dorm.

Large clumps of soapy bubbles fell from her hair and onto the bed, as she began furiously rubbing at her head with a ragged red cloth that was wrapped around her.

"It was bad enough when we just used to run out of hot water, now it seems we've run out of water all together! Is there anything in Mildred that isn't in short supply nowadays?"

On the bed opposite her, Pritch, Stick, and Maggie sat playing a game of cards made out of flakes of dandruff, as they tried their hardest to ignore her.

Next to them the memorizer was glowing warm as it played the latest live traffic news from the mosquito that hovered above Mildred's bed. On screen, a cockroach had turned upside down and was wriggling its legs frantically as ants swarmed over it, their drivers shouting furiously as they tried to get to work.

"This is ridiculous! First day of school and I've got to go looking like this!" ranted Taylor, pulling at the white clumps that had formed in her hair.

"Why is he always here now?" said Stick, continuing to ignore her.

On the memorizer the camera zoomed in on the bald head of Thaddeus Miles, as he emerged from the body of a very shiny green fly, before disappearing into the shadow of Mildred's toe nail.

"What do you mean? Isn't it his job to be here?" asked Maggie.

"Well yeah, but it's not as though he was ever here before. Everyone called him 'Missing Miles' because he was always off on some mysterious business trip or other. He never seemed to care about what was happening here. Even old Devlin used to complain about how much he was gone, and she doesn't care about anything! But now he's here all the time. You'd think he'd be off finding a new job like everyone else, but he's always here. Everyday this week I've passed him at least once in the hallway, and each time he's given me this look like I knew something he didn't. It's weird."

Maggie remembered how he had looked at her that day in his office, his eyes cold with surprise.

"Well I for one don't care if he's here or not," said Taylor, "soon we'll have a new place to live, and hopefully there I'll be able to take a shower that doesn't run out of water before I have time to get my feet wet!"

Stick shot her a look, but Taylor glared back at him, refusing to feel bad. It had been a week since Mildred's closing had been announced, and all the areas in the body had slowly begun to prepare to shut themselves down, leaving everyone full of frustration. Some of those who worked in Mildred had already left, taking new jobs in the triplet babies that had just opened up down the street. But for those who still lived in Mildred, each day seemed to only bring more sadness as the hallways became emptier and emptier, as if they too knew that the end was near.

With everything going on, the first day of school seemed like a welcome relief to the children. Even Stick was ready to go that morning, his mind eager for a distraction that would stop him from thinking about Mildred's closure. Only Maggie walked slowly that day. As the R5 bus stop at the end of Mildred's little toe drew closer, nerves filled her stomach as she thought about what was ahead. Her stepmother had always said that school was a waste of time for her, insisting that the only things she needed to learn were 'how to be useful, invisible, and someone else!'

Now she was about to go to a strange new school. One filled with kids who knew more about this tiny world than she could ever hope to. The whole idea was terrifying, and for a second she wished she were everything her stepmother wanted her to be.

"Come on, Maggie, don't worry, I'll take care of you," said Pritch, seeming to sense her nerves. "You're going to be fine. You're one of us now."

Maggie smiled at Pritch, who looped her arm inside hers and pulled her forward. The idea of being one of them made her feel happy, and for a second her anxiety disappeared, only to quickly return as a large bumble bee squeezed itself up against the new opening at the end of the hallway. There was a small fizzing as the stripy wall of the bee peeled open to make a small ramp up into its pink insides.

"Cheese sandwich girl. Maggie Pincus, how are you?"

Maggie blinked into the driver's seat as a goo-covered hand reached toward her.

"Reg?" she said, shaking his wet fingers politely.

"Absolutely, nice to see you again." Reg smiled, popping his hand back into the wall. "Fancy us bumping into each other. I don't usually do the school run but the wife's got her eye on a new fancy grasshopper for her birthday, so I need the money."

Maggie felt the others squeeze into her from behind, as the wall of the bee slowly slid back into place.

"Reg, these are my friends. Stick, Pritch, and Taylor."

"Any friends of Maggie's are friends of mine... pleased to meet you!" said Reg, freeing his hand once more. A fresh line of goo dripped heavily from his palm as Stick and Pritch each reluctantly shook it. Taylor ignored it and made her way to an empty seat. Thick wads of hair were still clumped together around her unsmiling face, and she slumped into her seat where she returned to picking at them furiously.

"Sorry about her," said Stick, nodding at his sister, "she's a little upset about her hair. I keep telling her that her face is a much, much larger problem, but she won't listen."

Reg gave a confused smile, "Okay, nice to see you've made some friends," he said to Maggie as Pritch and Stick joined Taylor, "Let's get you to school, shall we? Good to see you, Maggie."

"Nice to see you, too," said Maggie, taking a seat.

Soon they were flying once again, as the bee soared away from Mildred Potts, 79, before spinning out through the mailbox and onto Green Lanes. Ahead of them, huge bodies were just beginning their day, as giants in suits walked past the old house, all of them too distracted to pay any attention to the small insect that zipped between them with ease. Once across the street, the bee flew high between the houses before turning a sharp left where it buzzed its way slowly forward. Huge bedroom windows passed by, filling their view outside. Several minutes passed, and Maggie tried not to look at all the naked giants that drifted by, each of them oblivious to tiny residents of the bee that stared at them as they dressed for the day.

"That one's got an extra entrance…oh wait, it's just a mole," said Stick as they made their first stop at Anne Smith, 28, a rather tired looking mother who was trying to persuade a crying Tommy Smith, 4 that, 'yes, he did have to brush his teeth and no, chocolate was not a vegetable.'

After stops at both bodies the seats on the bus filled, and soon none remained. They flew high over a shopping center before swooping down toward a small playground that had been built next to a fast food restaurant. Ahead of them, a huge teenage boy sat on a swing staring blankly ahead, a single headphone thumping in his ear, as its twin hung loosely by his neck. Pulling slowly upward, Reg mumbled to himself in frustration as he looked for a place to land. Beneath them, insects swarmed everywhere, flies and midges forming a thick cloud that circled the oblivious teenage boy. Bees seemed to stand no chance amongst the fast moving swarm, and twice Reg sent everyone inside sliding sideways as he dodged the shiny bluebottles that seemed to dominate all the other insects.

"Who buys their kids a sports insect for a first vehicle?" he growled, as yet another fly narrowly missed them, "Bad enough they have learner permits without putting them in something as fast as that!"

Beneath them, insects were beginning to land on the shoulders of the teenage boy. Seeing his chance, Reg threw the bee downward, sending two midges bouncing off one another as he swooped in to land softly next to an oversized label.

"CHARLIE COMP, 17! TIME FOR SCHOOL!" he yelled, far too brightly for the occupants of the bee, who groaned as they begrudgingly made their way down onto Charlie Comp 17's shoulder.

Bad breath and old sweat filled the air as Maggie said goodbye to Reg, before following after them. Ahead of her, hundreds of flies and midges dotted the landscape of Charlie's neck as parents dropped off their children who steadily snaked their way up into an ear that stood over them like a gigantic archway summoning them inside. Looking for the others, Maggie caught a glimpse of Pritch and Taylor, only to see them disappear into the crowd as they expertly weaved their way amongst the other students, leaving her suddenly alone. Instantly her panic returned, and she desperately scanned the heads of the crowd, trying in vain to find a familiar face, until finally she heard Stick shout out from inside a circle of internals that had formed up ahead.

"Get off me, you big idiot!"

Maggie pushed forward through the students and stood on tiptoe as she tried to see what was happening inside the ever-growing circle that surrounded Stick's voice.

"I said get off me, Ridge!"

Ahead, a large boy turned his head finally allowing Maggie to glimpse Stick's face, wrapped tightly inside a thick arm as an oversized knuckle rubbed furiously against his head. A look of delight filled the large boy who squeezed Stick tightly, as an unpleasant smile spread across his face.

"No need to be so mean, Sticky boy," said Ridge, squeezing him even tighter, "I just want to welcome you back to school. I haven't seen you all summer. I missed this."

Maggie ducked under a large backpack and squeezed past a small blonde girl, to find herself standing inside the circle, just as Stick caught her gaze.

"I SAID GET OFF ME…NOW!"

Instantly, Stick's wriggling became wilder and he kicked out catching the bully hard on the knee. Stumbling backward, Ridge released his prey as his face screwed up into a ball of pain, and he slammed hard against the shiny black fly that was behind him. For a second, everything seemed to freeze as the large boy rubbed at his knee with one hand, the other curling into a fist as he glared at Stick.

'Crrrreeeeekkkkkkk'

All pain forgotten, Ridge spun around as one of the flies' legs slowly began to bend downward.

'Ccccrrrrrreeeeeeeeeekkkkkkkkkkkkkkkk'

"NO, NO, NO!" bellowed Ridge, his arms raised as if he could stop what was about to happen.

The other legs began to screech as they followed their leader, bending slowly until with a loud 'BOOF!' the fly smashed down hard onto its side. Several children scattered as the fly continued to roll over, before stopping with a shudder on its back, its shiny sides now revealing several new large scratches.

"MY FLY!" yelled Ridge, staring at the bright pink scars, "I JUST GOT THIS LAST WEEK!"

Nobody moved, as with stifled smiles, they watched Ridge pull at his short black hair in frustration. Only Stick moved, the sight of Ridge swelling in size, both his fists curled so tight it looked as though they could break rocks, telling him that now was a good time to slowly back away.

"Backus, Belvin…grab him…NOW!" growled Ridge from between gritted teeth.

Instantly, two even larger boys emerged from the circle's edge, their faces full of excitement as though they had been waiting all their lives for this order. Like

Ridge, their bodies were thick and muscular, both topped by gritty faces that smiled eagerly as they walked toward Stick. Before he knew what was happening they were upon him, their large hands pulling at his arms, leaving him helpless as they dragged him with ease over to Ridge. Staring up into Ridge's furious face, a wave of panic filled Stick as he prepared for the worst.

"It wasn't my fault!"

But Ridge wasn't listening. He was pulling back a large curled hand, ready to bring it down hard.

Maggie turned away at the sight of the familiar raised fist not wanting to see what was about to happen next. She scrunched up her eyes against the sour taste in her mouth, as the memory of her father's death came rushing in. The look in the Deathwalker's eyes, the sense that she was helpless to stop it, knowing with certainty that someone she cared about was about to be hurt, all of it flowed over her once more, bringing her back to that day. Suddenly the muscles in her body began to tighten, and an electric tingle flooded her spine as she waited for the thud and the scream that would surely come next.

'BOOM!'

The ground began to shake as Charlie Comps, 17's, skin began to shudder beneath their feet. Everyone stood frozen, their faces full of confusion. Maggie opened her eyes wide, trying to take in what was happening. Puzzled faces surrounded her, telling her that this was not normal, and she went to move when her foot struck something hard. Looking down, she saw that the floor was changing as Charlie Comps, 17's, skin glowed red, its surface swelling as it began to expand. Quickly it grew, pulsing as it filled the circle, looming over them with a whiteness that seemed to be stretching the thin layer of skin that held it back. Maggie caught a glimpse of Stick as he wriggled free of the bemused Backus and Belvin, who stood open-mouthed at the new mountain in front of them. Time seemed to freeze. Everyone just stared. Then one lone voice slowly realized what it was; shouting as though all their lives depended on it.

"ZZZZIIIIIIIITTTTTTTTT...ZIT...ZIT...IT'S GOING TO BLOW!"

As if following orders, the side of the zit suddenly burst open as the pressure inside began to send thick globs of white rocketing high into the air. Maggie stared in amazement as they soared above her, before separating into smaller balls, leaving her open-mouthed at their beauty as if she was at the world's best fireworks show. Then the globs were no longer rising, their wet shapes seeming to hover high above, before suddenly they formed grasping hands and yellow eyes that stared hungrily as they fell toward the watching crowd below. Instinctively, the children ran in every direction as the yellow globs of puss began to splash down around them, grabbing eagerly at the ankles that skipped and jumped to avoid them. Bags were thrown over heads, as the children ran for safety, trying desperately to shield themselves from the slimy creatures that were flying everywhere.

Only Maggie remained motionless, staring at a large ball of the puss that was bearing down upon her, its long fingers ready to pounce.

"What are you waiting for, Maggie? RUN!" shouted Stick, grabbing Maggie.

Flipping around, Maggie felt herself being pushed past a blonde girl, just as the yellow mass splashed behind her, its hands instantly snapping at her feet. Children were everywhere, all running wildly toward the huge ear as they tried to force their way inside, and away from the slimy wet rain around them.

"What are those things?" said a breathless Maggie, as another white creature splash landed between her and Stick.

"Zit bacteria!" he replied, "Nasty little things. They like to bite. They won't kill you…but it hurts for a while…a lot!"

Up ahead, a girl was spinning around and around, beating at a large ball of puss with her schoolbag as it clenched her arm between two rows of slimy wet teeth.

"Bit of luck for me really," continued Stick, ignoring her, "Charlie Comp gets zits all the time but they usually grow really slowly. I've never seen one happen that quickly. Usually the janitors have plenty of time to drain them before they blow up."

Up ahead, bright flashes emerged from the ear as Maggie glimpsed several nerves blazing back and forth from the large mountain, carrying news of what was happening back inside. The rain of puss began to slow, revealing a large red hole in the top of the zit, which now lay open like an old firework surrounded by a pool of wet clawing hands. Behind it, Ridge was kicking furiously at four bacteria that were chewing on his legs, as Backus and Belvin uselessly tried to thump them.

"Serves him right," said Stick, slowing to a walk, "He's been picking on me for years. Thinks he's better than me just because his dad works in the government and he lives in a big fancy body and he's dating Julia. I can't stand him."

Maggie stopped next to him, leaning on her knees to gulp for air as she watched Backus and Belvin begin their own fight with the bacteria. It had now latched onto their fists before pulling their way up their arms. Men in brown overalls ran toward them, beating at the bacteria with large brooms, as they tried to circle the tiny pools of white hands all around them.

"Who's Julia?" heaved Maggie.

Stick nodded at a group of girls up ahead, and the blonde girl that Maggie recognized from the circle. Sensing them looking at her, she glanced back, her gaze fixing on Stick for a second before she turned back to her friends.

"That is Julia," said Taylor, appearing out of nowhere to point at the blonde girl, "Stick's in love with her...but she doesn't know he's alive. It's pretty pathetic really."

Stick looked angrily at Taylor's back as she walked away, leaving only an embarrassed silence between him and Maggie.

317

Up ahead, the large ear started to ring loudly, drawing in the last few children outside.

"Come on, we're going to be late," said Stick, trudging ahead.

School was about to start.

Malcolm...I sleep so much now that I've moved downstairs...I just feel so tired all the time...like I have no energy left in me. It's been a while since I saw the nurse. I keep forgetting to tell her about all the flies. They're getting worse.

19

The Infection Takes Hold

If Maggie had been nervous about school, it only took one step inside Charlie Comp, 17, for her to quickly become distracted from her worries. In the months since she had discovered the world of souls and internals she had only ever been inside Mildred, her hallways dripping with fat beneath red bloodlines that pumped and glowed weakly. Now as she entered this new body all she could do was stare in amazement. Here the hallways were smooth and white with ceilings that were lit by firm red pipes that radiated warmth as they pulled the children inside and down a long shining staircase. Following closely behind Stick, Maggie ran her fingers along the wall, feeling their pulsing warmth until she emerged into a large circular room below. Two antibody security guards stared hard at her as she approached before a nerve flashed by, whispering in one of their ears that she was a new student. Maggie stared obliviously open-mouthed at her surroundings. Here the pipes seemed to have multiplied, all of them arching high overhead like a bowl of red spaghetti that was spread across the ceiling, before wrapping themselves around a large screen that was embedded beneath tight white skin, playing Charlie Comps, 17's, view of the world inside. Far below it, children were everywhere, most of them standing casually in groups while others stood eagerly in line for food at one of the many holes that had been carved into the side of the bright pink walls.

"Here, have some of these," said Pritch brightly, shoving a crisp brown bag under her nose. Maggie reached inside, the smell drawing her in, as she pulled out a sugary ball that was warm against her fingers. Biting into it, she felt her insides begin to glow as the taste of fresh donut filled her senses, making her moan happily.

"You should go get some," said Taylor, pointing at one of the holes. "It's all free and soooooo good."

Maggie sniffed the air, which was filled with the smells pouring from each of the lines of children. Bacon sandwiches mixed into French fries, then transformed into pizza, before morphing into fresh brownies, with a final serving of cheeseburgers. After what seemed a lifetime of eating booger bangers and strange cereal mixes, it was almost too much for her and she let out another moan as the donut fell into her empty belly.

"So the food is better here than back home in Mildred, it's not her fault...she's old, you know," said Stick, looking annoyed.

Maggie tried to feel guilty, but the taste of the donuts made her unable to think.

"Come on," said Pritch, "Ignore him. We have classes together today. Here, I grabbed your schedule for you from the office."

Maggie stared at the bright pink paper as she followed Pritch onto a line of stairs that rippled its way downward, as Stick followed closely behind.

1st Immunology - Thymus Room 4
2nd Skeletal Class - L Trapezium Level 3
3rd Digestive Class - Pancreas Level 2
Lunch

4th Nerve Class - Sacral Level 5
5th Excretion Class - Rectum Top Level
*Breathing mask optional
6th Respiration Class - R Lung Middle Level
Beetles Depart 15, 30, and 60 minutes after 6th

Maggie squinted her eyes, trying to make sense of it, when suddenly Pritch pulled her sideways through a door that read 'Immunology.'

Dragging her into an empty row of seats, Maggie continued to stare at the paper as Stick forced himself into the chair next to his sister.

"Budge up will you!" he said, elbowing her in the side.

But Maggie wasn't listening. She was suddenly locked in fear as she stared up at the creatures surrounding her. Faces full of rage stared down as though ready to devour her. A large ball of slime smiled at her, its single eye unblinking, as a line of green spit dribbled from its mouth. Next to it stood a bony figure, its long fingers dragging on the floor against their sharpened ends, while on the other side of that stood a lizard-like creature with bright pink scales that bent upward against its sharp yellow teeth.

"Don't worry," said Pritch, oblivious, pulling a seat up next to Maggie, "Immunology is a good way to start the day. It's with Professor Morrigan, he likes to talk...a lot, so just be quiet and smile. Don't say anything dumb, and he'll leave you alone."

Maggie didn't reply, her mind consumed by the monsters surrounding her.

"Oh," said Pritch, realizing what was happening, "Don't worry, they aren't real diseases. Those are just memory bank screens...the ones here are just more realistic than in Mildred."

Maggie stared at Pritch, unsure of what to say. Knowing they were just moving pictures on a screen didn't seem to help at all.

"The real ones would never just sit there on a wall like that. They're far more likely to try to attack you when you least expect it, not that they are all bad," said Pritch, pointing at one of the screens that lined the walls, "I knew a girl whose sister's best friend's cousin dated a pneumonia bacteria and she said he was actually really nice."

Maggie looked up at the picture of an overweight, grey man, his arms crossed above the large naked belly that flopped down to his knees. Staring into his dark eyes, Maggie could feel hundreds of tiny red dots staring back at her as if they were reaching out through the screen.

"He looks scary to me," said Maggie, still staring up at the bacteria.

"And you would be right to be scared!" said a voice behind her, "Fear is our greatest weapon against the diseases that destroy our homes! Without fear we do not act, and if we do not act they…."

Suddenly a hand shot up from the front row, its fingers waving inside a thick black sleeve.

"Yes, Roosela?" said the professor wearily.

For a second Maggie couldn't place her name, then she realized that she was looking at the girl who lived at the other end of their empty dormitory.

"If we do not act they will take over," she said eagerly, "the pneumonia bacteria you are talking about likes to eat the walls of the lungs, gorging itself until it's just holes everywhere making the lungs leak. Then it likes to sleep until it becomes hungry enough to look for a new set of lungs to eat. It's really quite clever when you think about it."

The professor gave a sigh and walked to the front of the full classroom, rubbing at his bald head as he went. "Thank-you for that, Roosela. Good to see that the summer vacation has made you an even bigger fan of all the evil diseases out there!" he said dryly.

Roosela stared back at him with a half smile as though she had secretly enjoyed the compliment.

"Right, let's get started, shall we?" he said, turning away from her, "Good Morning, class. I see that we have some new faces amongst you, so I shall introduce myself. I am Professor Morrigan, and this is Immunology. Immunology is of course the study of how we stop all those nasty things that take over and destroy the body."

Amongst the sea of blank faces Maggie stared intently, eager to learn, while Taylor picked at her fingernails.

"So, let's see how much you remember after the holidays, shall we? Can anyone tell me what this is?" he said, pointing to the large screen over his desk.

Maggie took in a sharp breath as the screen flickered to life. High above her stood another familiar face. The shiny black head scooping backward to rest on either side of a thin mouth, skin the color of burnt mud, two luminous green eyes that burned into her. Fear tickled her spine like bubbles in a shaken bottle of soda, as once again the lone hand of Roosela shot into the air. Glancing at her, the professor continued as though he hadn't seen her.

"No ideas? Well, this up here, ladies and gentlemen, is one of the most terrifying viruses known to internals. This is Marburg, and he and his kind are responsible for the destruction of hundreds of thousands of bodies…maybe even millions if you go back through history."

Roosela was now glaring at Professor Morrigan, who continued to ignore her.

"If you ever see this virus you must alert the authorities immediately. Marburg has been known to wipe out whole towns of bodies in hours, killing thousands of internals as a consequence. All Marburgs are immune to most of our defenses and can only be stopped by…."

There was a screech of shoes as Ridge ran into the room, his breath heavy from running. He opened his mouth to speak but before he had a chance, Backus and Belvin followed behind, plowing into him so hard that all three of them went head first into a bookshelf that quickly toppled on them.

"Gerroofff me, you big dummies," snarled Ridge, trying to push the two boys and the bookshelf off him. Wet yellow slime from the puss was still stuck to his trousers, and he brushed at it angrily as he got to his feet.

"Sorry we're late, Professor. I had some…fly trouble." He gritted, staring at Stick.

Behind him, Backus and Belvin hurriedly returned the bookshelf to its upright position as Professor Morrigan waved them toward an empty row of desks at the front of the room.

"Yes, yes, hurry up, boys. You haven't missed anything. It seems nobody remembers anything from last year anyway!" he said with a look of frustration. "How about we try something a little simpler, shall we? Can anyone tell me how we stop pneumonia from doing its worst? Class?"

"If it's a bacterial pneumonia you have to call the Anti-Bio-Techs," said Roosela without waiting for Professor Morrigan to call on her this time. "If it's a virus, then they are useless. A lot of viruses aren't very clever but the pneumonia virus is way too intelligent to get stopped by them."

"Correct," said Professor Morrigan reluctantly, "There are many things out there that love to destroy the bodies that we live in. What you always have to ask yourself is, are you dealing with a virus or bacteria? If it's a bacteria, call for the Anti-Bio-Techs. They're the experts at getting rid of them. Unfortunately, they can do little about viruses."

Roosela opened her mouth to speak, but before she had a chance Professor Morrigan cut her off.

"This does not mean that we are powerless, however. Viruses and bacteria need to live inside the body, and most do not live for long, at all, outside. So if we are vigilant and stop them from getting in, or make them leave if they are inside, then they will be able to do no harm. Put quite simply, inside they are deadly, and outside they are dead."

He walked over to his desk and reached down to reveal a large container covered in red cloth.

"We must keep them outside…but if we can't keep them outside, then we must contain them!" he said dramatically, pulling off the covering.

The room gasped as they saw what he had unveiled. Beneath a glass dome shone brightly revealing a large white bird that blinked against the light as it shuffled from side to side on yellow feet.

"Now," said Professor Morrigan seemingly pleased to finally have everyone's attention, "What is this?"

Instantly Roosela's arm shot in the air, only for Professor Morrigan to raise his hand just as quickly, letting her know that he would be calling on someone else. Silence greeted him.

"Come on now, don't be shy," he said hopefully to the room, "You, new girl, what do you think it is?"

Maggie felt her face turning red as her mind spun in circles. After seeing her schedule she'd decided to try and be invisible for at least the next few months as she tried to catch up with the rest of her class. But, it seemed that her plan had failed already. Suddenly every eye in the room was looking at her, including the bird that stared blackly in her direction. Maggie focused hard on it, trying to picture what it might be called, but it was useless. Even the bird seemed to know that she was an imposter, stepping angrily from side to side as it slapped its feathers against the glass.

The yellow beak, the red skin on its head, something about it looked very familiar to Maggie but her mind seemed to be blank.

The bird suddenly began throwing itself hard against the inside of the dome as though desperate to escape.

"Errrr, Professor," said Roosela, noticing that the glass case began to slide toward the edge of the desk.

"Not now, Roosela, let others have a chance!" he said, turning his back to her.

Inside the dome the sight of Maggie, only, seemed to be creating more panic as its flapping wings began to make a feathery snow globe. But Maggie saw none of it. Her eyes were screwed up tight. Something inside told her that she knew the answer. She just needed to think.

More hands were springing up now, but Professor Morrigan ignored them all, insisting that Maggie be allowed to answer. Behind him the bird became wilder and wilder as the dome moved closer and closer to the edge of the desk.

"CHICKEN! It looks like a chicken!" exclaimed Maggie suddenly.

As if this were the last push it needed, the bird gave one last surge into the glass sending it tottering on the edge of the desk.

"YES!" said Professor Morrigan triumphantly, "It's a chicken, a chicken pox! And what does it...."

But no one heard him finish. Only the sound of the dome shattering on the floor could be heard, as the white bird escaped its trap. Flapping wildly, it flew around the room, shrieking as it showered the children with feathers.

Diving under their desks for cover, the children covered their heads with books as the bird continued to rampage through the air before slamming hard again and again into the pink ceiling. Behind it large red welts instantly formed, swelling themselves up into huge red circles.

"GET IT!" shouted the professor, realizing what was happening. "QUICK, BEFORE IT INFECTS ANYTHING ELSE!"

But nobody cared. They wanted nothing to do with the chicken pox that was terrorizing the air above them, and as Maggie opened her eyes she saw that she was the only one still sitting at her desk. In a trance, she watched as the more and more red welts formed on the ceiling. Stick's hand fumbled for hers.

"Get down here, will you?" he shouted as he pulled at her, "If that thing pecks you, you'll be in the hospital for weeks!"

Maggie shook her head, unable to move. Feathers were falling everywhere but she could barely hear him. Her mind was frozen as she stared at Roosela, who was walking calmly across the room, her eyes never leaving Maggie. Then, with a whistle, she tapped the edge of a box that sat empty on the desk. Seeming to understand her command the panic in the chicken pox suddenly disappeared, and it glided down to perch on the box edge, before hopping inside.

"Oh thank goodness!" said Professor Morrigan, throwing his jacket over the top of the box.

Around him, the floor was covered in feathers and discarded bags, but Roosela stepped calmly between them, returning to her desk as though nothing unusual had just happened. Behind her, the professor stared up in disbelief at the ceiling that was beginning to sag under the weight of the large red circles. They were still swelling over the children's heads.

"It seems as though we won't be able to have the lesson today, class. Grab your things and make your way to your next class. Dismissed!" he said sheepishly, looking from the box to the ceiling.

Relieved, the students slowly came out from under their desks and walked to the door, happy to be as far away from the chicken pox as possible. Maggie followed them, but as she reached the exit a sudden feeling of guilt overwhelmed her.

"Professor Morrigan, would you like some help cleaning up in here?"

Professor Morrigan scratched his head as he surveyed the upturned desks and drooping ceiling.

"That would be most welcome. Err, I don't know your name."

"It's Maggie," she replied.

Maggie busied herself with picking up the feathers, both of them working in silence, while Professor Morrigan stood on a chair to rub at the large red circles with a white paste. Shuffling the last desk back into place, Maggie carefully avoided the box containing the chicken pox as she began replacing the fallen books that had been left behind by Backus and Belvin. Sliding them carefully back into their homes, she barely noticed their names until one suddenly caught her attention.

The Internals: A History, Volume III- Souls: Why Did They Leave Us?

For a second she stared at its faded gold letters— a rush of thoughts filling her mind.

"Professor?" said Maggie, holding out the book, "Can I ask you a question?"

Dabbing the last of the paste over the final red spot, Professor Morrigan jumped down from his chair and surveyed the room.

"Yes, Maggie, you certainly may," he said happily.

"What started the war between the Souls and the Internals?"

Tipping his head to one side, the professor gave her a look as though she was speaking another language.

"You know? When the internals...I mean us... tricked the souls?"

The professor stared back, his eyebrows raised so high that for a second it seemed as though they might disappear altogether over the top of his bald head.

"When we told them they were going to share everything, then we trapped them in the mind. Then, we erased their memories and removed their ability to see us. You know...the war?"

Maggie wanted to continue, but the look on Professor Morrigan's face told her it was pointless.

"Maggie, there has never been a war between the internals and the souls," he said gently. "The souls went into the mind one day and never came out. We don't know why. At this point we don't think we'll ever know why. All we know is that they chose to leave."

"But, the Deathwalkers...the war...the internals," stammered Maggie, sure he was lying.

"Maggie, I don't know where you are getting all this from but none of that is true. There are lots of theories about why they left, but the only truth is that we don't know the truth. We can only guess, and many of our guesses aren't even based in reality anymore. I was once told a story about a bacteria army that poisoned souls so that they would follow their orders. Then there's the old myth about the three brothers with the power to control all bodies. And Deathwalkers? Dead bodies that work without internals? Well those are just things someone made up to scare children at bedtime."

Maggie stared at him, forcing back the tears of confusion that were forcing their way out. She wanted to say something. That he was wrong. That he was a liar. That her father had told her the truth and he had been killed for it. She opened her mouth to speak but the bell was too quick, filling the room with its ringing as it told her that it was time to go. Outside, the noise of children crowding the hallways pushed its way in through the open door, reminding her that soon more students would be here.

"Look, if you don't believe me, why don't you read it for yourself?" he said, nodding at the book, "take it with you, give it back next week. I think you'll find it really interesting."

Maggie stared down at the cover of the book, wanting to push it away, as though just touching it made the lie worse.

"Trust me, it will give you answers to your questions," said the professor kindly.

Maggie crammed the book in her bag as she mumbled a begrudging thank you and headed for the door. Walking quickly past Professor Morrigan's desk she failed to notice that the box containing the chicken pox began to shake as she passed by. If she had paid any attention to what was happening she would have seen the box fly open as the bird escaped once more, before beginning a second attack on the ceiling as the professor chased wildly after it. But she didn't hear or see a thing. Her mind was lost in the professor's words...words that kept refusing to go away.

There was no war.

Malcolm...Remember when we were young and you took me on that camping holiday? When we walked for miles and miles, and you made me a necklace out of daisies, and then we finally found the perfect place to camp? Then we sat up all night looking at the stars, and the next morning you took me home and kissed me on the cheek. My father saw you and chased you down the street. I miss you.

20

Hormonal Imbalance

Back at the staircase, Maggie was relieved to see Pritch
and Stick waiting for her. Without speaking, Pritch led
the way upward as Stick began teasing Maggie for
staying to help Professor Morrigan clean up after the
chicken pox incident.

"First ever day at school and you're already
sucking up to the teachers? Is that who my best friend
is? A teacher's pet!"

Maggie smiled. He didn't realize he had called
her his best friend. Until recently, she had no friends at
all and now she had three more than she ever thought
possible. She even had a best friend.

"What?" said Stick, "Oh come on, let's get to class!"

Back in the large main entry hall, Maggie followed Pritch between the bobbing heads of internals trying to get to class, nerves flashing between their legs, as everyone flooded toward one of several large entrances that dwarfed the food stands.

Following a line that led toward a large pink entry marked 'Cardiology' Maggie felt the sea of bodies around her start to thin out. She had no clue what her next class was and even less clue what 'Cardiology' was, but at that moment she didn't care. As long as it was a quiet class with no drama, no questions, and definitely no killer chicken pox, she'd be fine.

"OY…YOU!"

Ridge's large hand narrowly missed her as it surged past her face. The sea of bodies around her instantly froze, sensing something interesting. Stick stopped walking as a hand spun him around.

Ridge's face was still twisted in anger as he leaned in close to Stick. "You owe me a new fly!"

An instant circle formed around the boys as silence fell upon them. Feeling everyone's eyes upon him, Stick looked for an escape, only to see Julia peeking at him over the top of Ridge's rather large shoulder.

"I don't think so!" he said, feeling suddenly brave.

"What did you say to me?" growled Ridge, leaning in more so that Stick could feel his breath on his cheeks.

"I said no! I'm not scared of you, or your meathead bodyguards!"

The circle let out a gasp of shock. Nobody stood up to Ridge. He was rich, big, and the captain of every sports team in Charlie Comps 17. When he spoke, you listened, especially if you were a skinny little poor kid from an orphanage.

"Really!" said Ridge half smiling, half grimacing.

Out of the corner of his eye he saw one of the anti-body security men trying to push his way inside the circle.

"Right…" said Ridge just loud enough for everyone to hear, "Seeing as you've suddenly found yourself some guts how about you, me, a hormone battle. After school…today!"

The circle gasped again as Stick seemed to shrivel like a deflated balloon.

"Don't be late," he said, taking Julia's hand before pushing past Stick. The breathless anti-body security guard finally reached the middle of the circle, just as it disappeared, leaving him to loop his large fingers into his belt. He pretended to know what had been going on.

"Come on!" said Pritch, pulling Maggie and a shocked looking Stick toward the Cardiology entry.

"Err…what just happened?" said Maggie.

Around them, children were whispering as they stared at Stick.

"What just happened is Stick just did something dumb…really, really dumb," replied Pritch.

If Maggie had thought that the rest of the day would be quieter, it seemed that she was wrong…just as wrong as everything she seemed to do that day. For a brief moment she even found herself missing Breezy Lane and the watchful stare of her stepmother. At least there only one person stared at her mistakes, unlike here where there was an entire school to watch her clumsiness.

If the chicken incident had made her feel guilty, then sneezing during the demonstration in Skeleton class made her feel even worse. Especially as it had caused the bone builder to jump in surprise; his hammer forming a large crack in the knuckle he'd been working on. To follow that, she had burned a hole in the floor after spilling a bowl of acid in Digestion, sent several messages to the wrong end of the body in Nerve class, and her Excretion class experiment couldn't have gone any worse. Mostly because it had caused the closure of the Charlie Comps 17 right foot for a whole hour while several janitors fought to capture the sludgie, whose cage she had inadvertently left open.

By the time she accidentally leaned on the emergency shut off switch in Respiration class, she'd decided that school might not be for her after all. Even the other students seemed to be avoiding her, and several times she'd even noticed them sneaking furtive glances at their pink sheets of paper. They were trying to work out how many classes they were unlucky enough to share with what seemed to be the clumsiest internal in any body anywhere.

As they walked to their last class of the day, Maggie prepared herself for more of their looks but as they reached the end of Charlie Comp 17's giant little finger she realized that everyone had suddenly forgotten about her. Now it was Stick who drew their stares, their whispering faces filled with pity and excitement for the upcoming hormone battle. Trudging forward, he stared at his feet as he tried to ignore the murmur that floated around him. Maggie wasn't sure if in the internal world bad meant good, but as she listened to the whispers of how much trouble he was in she guessed that it was just as bad as it sounded.

"Why don't you just say sorry and tell him you don't want to fight him?" whispered Maggie to Stick as she tried to pick pieces of kidney that were stuck in her hair from her last disastrous class. Standing on top of a giant fingernail, the class waited eagerly for the bell as they pretended to watch the professor show them how to layer pieces of skin around the edges of Charlie Comps 17's huge thumb. Stick looked at her with a face that had been getting steadily greyer as the day went on.

"I can't do that. What if Juli—I mean, I don't want everyone to think I'm scared of that idiot. Besides, it's not a fight, it's a hormone battle."

"What's a hormone battle?" said Maggie.

Stick rubbed at his eyes as if just the thought of it hurt.

"It's where you fight using the body's moods," whispered Pritch, "hormones are these things that the body makes, and if they touch you then you become whatever they are. It's just for a little while but you never know which one's coming next, they just pop out and float around until they find their way up to the mind. They can be really scary, and this body makes loads of them, especially the angry depressed ones. That's the trouble with going to school in a teenager… too many hormones…."

The professor was just stamping the last piece of skin into place when the bell sounded from high above, sending the class running eagerly for what was next.

"Come on. It's time," sighed Stick, oblivious to the crowd of kids rushing behind him, "I just hope there's no one there to see it."

Unfortunately it seemed that Stick's wish wasn't about to come true. As they walked beneath a large sign that read 'Pituitary' it quickly became apparent that this was something that no one in the school wanted to miss. Every student in school seemed to be there, lining the edges of a long dark hallway that rippled down its length, before encircling a dark hole at its end. Even several muscles stared out, their blank smiles suggesting they had just followed the crowd without knowing why. Stick stopped in his tracks.

343

Scanning the hallway, Maggie caught sight of the pretty blonde girl Stick had been looking at earlier and realized that he had just seen her too.

"Right," he said nervously, "let's get this over with."

A hush fell over the horde as Stick strode forward with as much confidence as he could manage. Maggie and Pritch squeezed in next to Taylor, who seemed a little bored by her brother's imminent destruction.

"If this makes us late for the last bus I'll be really annoyed," she said with a huff.

Maggie stared at her wide-eyed. She didn't particularly like any of her stepbrothers, but she still cared about what happened to them. Most of the time anyway.

"What?" said Taylor, staring back at her. "It's not like he's going to win!"

The silence seemed to thicken as Stick strode forward. As he drew closer to the hole, Ridge stepped from inside a circle of even taller children to block his path.

"You ready to lose?"

Stick looked up before leaning past him to stare into the hole. A sudden rush of air came out of the darkness, pressing the two lines of students back into the wall, as though what was emerging was about to hurt them.

"Hhhhuuurrrggghhhh," said the hole, a small glow emerging.

The silence was overwhelming now and everyone seemed to have stopped breathing as they stared at the shimmering light that was coming toward them. Then, out of the darkness, the hazy shape of a man drifted forward into the light. Ignoring the crowds on either side, the man stared blankly ahead, his face thin and gaunt beneath the ragged cloak that was wrapped around him. It revealed bony legs that dragged uselessly behind his floating body, as every eye in the room stared.

"That's depression…that would have been a good one," whispered someone in the crowd. The shape continued onward without caring, before disappearing through the wall.

"Right," said Ridge loud enough for everyone to hear. "Three rules. We take it in turns standing in front of the hole with our backs turned. If you run away from the hormone when it comes out…you lose. If you're not standing in front of the hole when it's your turn for the hormone…you lose. If you react to whatever the hormone does to you…you lose."

Stick gulped as he looked at Ridge's snarling face. Out of the corner of his eye, he caught a flash of Julia's blonde hair as she turned to whisper to her friend, before smiling shyly in his direction.

"Fine," said Stick weakly, "Do I go first?"

"No, I'm first!" said Ridge, striding over to the hole. Turning his back, he shuffled his feet from side to side and spread them wide as though he was about to try to stop a train.

Maggie stared at him, trying to work out exactly what was going on when the rush of air spread through them once again and the light in the tunnel began to glow brightly as another shape emerged. This time the misty form was a large muscular man, his face red with a wide jaw that was clenched so tightly it seemed as though every one of his teeth must be about to crack. Ridge barely flinched as he hit him directly from behind, the man drifting into him like a ghost walking through a closed door, before two red eyes emerged from the other side of him, forcing him to ball his hands into tight fists. As the hormone moved away, Ridge looked as though he might explode. Large veins throbbed up the length of his arms while the sides of his neck pulled tight, as though invisible weights were pulling hard on each end. Ridge slowly turned his head to stare at Stick. The whites of his eyes seemed to fill his face as thousands of tiny red veins danced toward their green center.

He went to speak, but no words came. There was just a tremble as Ridge closed his eyes and let out several deep breaths. Slowly, the pulsing veins disappeared as his hands unfurled, leaving several red marks where his nails had dug into his own skin.

"HA!" he snorted proudly, waving his arm for Stick to go next.

"Great, he gets an angry hormone," mumbled Stick, taking his place. "How hard was that? He's like that most of the time anyway!"

Spreading his feet wide in a way that only seemed to make him look smaller than ever, Stick waited. Then the light was back. This time it spread slowly as though it was in no rush to be anywhere until finally the shape of a woman emerged, her small face peeking out at the children around her, as though she wanted nothing more than to disappear back inside the hole. Slowly she stepped forward, trying desperately to be invisible in the woolen shawl that was pulled tightly around her. Stick's face seemed to melt as she slipped inside him, before appearing on the other side to scurry away as quickly as she could from the eyes of the crowd. Instantly his eyes welled as he desperately forced back the large globs of tears that began to fill them. Suddenly he looked as though he wanted nothing more than for the ground beneath him to swallow him whole, and he began to sniff meekly before crouching downward like an un-watered flower.

Behind him, Ridge began laughed loudly, infuriating Maggie who glared at him before turning her gaze to Stick as she willed him to not embarrass himself in front of everyone. Two tiny hands covered his face now as though he couldn't hold back the tears any longer. The lines of kids leaned forward, sensing his defeat as Maggie felt a tingle run down her spine. She stared desperately at Stick, trying to give him the strength to resist.

Stick lowered his hands as gasps emerged around him. There were no tears, only a smile. The shyness hormone had passed through him and he had not reacted. Slowly he drew himself up to his full height and stepped to one side.

"All yours!" he said brightly. Ridge stared at him with a face that suggested there was still more than a little anger left inside him.

Back and forth the two competitors went for the next ten minutes. What was supposed to be Ridge's quick destruction of Stick had suddenly become anything but. Sensing that they were watching something exceptional, the children soon began hooping their congratulations for Stick, their excitement growing all the time, as he seemingly took every hormone with increasing ease; Maggie willed him on. Ridge, meanwhile, was soon beginning to look worse for wear. Fighting back against every shape that emerged from the hole seemed to be stripping him of his strength, and soon his group of supporters dwindled into silence against the noisy crowd. They realized that this might not go as they expected after all.

Stick rubbed his hands in delight and stepped away from the hole as a terror hormone drifted away in the distance with seemingly no effect at all. Around him everyone broke into applause as Ridge leaned, panting on his knees, before finally pushing himself upright to take his position in front of the hole. Maggie smiled as she watched Stick walk back to stand by her side, looking bigger and less Stick-like than she had ever seen him. Behind him, Linda tried to suppress a smile from Backus and Belvin as she sneaked glimpses at Stick, who seemed invincible.

Once again the light returned, Ridge trying desperately to summon up a last drop of energy, as the hazy figure emerged. She was smiling as she drifted forward, her arms spread wide as though she couldn't be happier. Everything about her seemed to radiate joy, but as she drifted inside Ridge he grimaced, as though her happiness was too much for him to take.

"Ooooh, love, that's an easy one," said Pritch in Maggie's ear.

But Ridge was finding it anything but easy. He tried to stiffen against the rush of emotion that was taking over him, but it was no good, he was too weak. As she emerged in front of him he seemed to realize what was coming and he turned his head, desperately seeking the face of Julia, only to lock eyes on Backus and Belvin, who stood blocking her. His shoulders relaxed and a broad smile appeared on his face. Suddenly it was as though there was no competition. He was a new version of Ridge, one who didn't know what anger was...one filled with love. Ignoring the staring crowd, he walked over to Backus and Belvin and knelt down before them, taking one hand from each as they looked at him with embarrassment.

"Backus, Belvin...I don't tell you this enough... but I love you both."

There was a silence. Then it was instantly gone, the hallway ringing with laughter as the kids howled at his words. Realizing what was happening, Backus and Belvin tried to pull their hands away, but it was no use. Ridge had them locked in his grip, his eyes never leaving them as he repeated the words 'I love you' over and over. A thick hand pressed against Ridge's head as Belvin tried to push him away, the laughter making him want to punch someone, but he quickly realized he was off balance, and instead found himself falling as Ridge refused to let go of his hand. Backus quickly followed, plunging down behind them to form a large heap that squirmed. Ridge repositioned himself into a large bear hug as he shouted the words over and over, 'I LOVE YOU BOTH SO MUCH!'

The sight of the three large boys squirming helplessly raised the laughter to a new volume that was matched only by Ridge. He was now shouting his love for his two friends as loud as he could, desperate for them to know how much they meant to him. Stick took a step forward to avoid their jumble of bodies as his own face filled with a large smile of victory. Even Julia seemed unable to suppress a laugh, peeking out between her fingers as she forced back a giggle. Only Maggie seemed to not be enjoying the show. Moments ago she wanted nothing more than for Ridge to get what he deserved, but now, as she watched him embarrass himself in front of the whole school, something had changed. She knew what it was to be laughed at, and as much as Ridge seemed to deserve it, she wanted it to stop.

Filled with confidence, Stick seized the moment, stepping back from the crowd as he tried to position himself where Julia could see him. Before he knew it she was staring at him, lowering her hand to give him a smile. Stick swelled as he felt himself locked inside her blue eyes, knowing that this was the time to tell her just how he felt. A warm breeze rushed over him, sweeping everyone but him and her away as time seemed to stop. He couldn't stop looking at her smile, a smile he had dreamed of so many times, a smile that was rapidly disappearing as it formed into a wide circle of shock. Suddenly the spell was broken as her blue eyes left his and fixed on something behind him. Stick turned to see what she was looking at, but it was too late. The hormone was out of the hole and filling his body before he knew what was happening, instantly overcoming him. Unprepared, he felt his insides twist as he turned back to see a long red dress beneath flowing white hair emerge from inside him as the air filled with perfume.

Helpless against it he closed his eyes and breathed deeply, filling his lungs with the sweet smell as warmth filled his insides, before spreading across his chest. For a second he was lost again, the intoxicating smell making him oblivious to the silence as everyone turned to stare at him. Slowly a murmur spread amongst the crowd, a murmur that quickly became a giggle. Now, Stick felt their eyes staring at him as fingers pointed, the giggles growing into laughter as he reached up to feel the heat that seemed to be growing inside him. Instantly he froze, realizing what was happening as he crossed his arms over his increasingly large chest, trying desperately to hide the growths that were sprouting beneath.

"Oooh." Pritch winced. "Feminine hormone. You don't see those too often around here. That's going to make him into a girl."

Laughter crowded around him. Once again his eyes returned to Julia, who stared back at him, desperate not to join in; a guilty snigger replaced her shock. Even Ridge seemed more interested in what was happening to Stick, and he released Backus and Belvin, his eyes fixed on his competition.

Howls of merriment swirled everywhere, becoming more than Stick could take. Then, without thinking, he began to run, hunching his shoulders forward as he bolted down the hallway. Maggie watched him pass, his T-shirt pulled tight against the new additions to his body.

"THAT'S RIGHT! RUN AWAY!" shouted Ridge, getting to his feet. He stabbed at the air with a triumphant fist, as the laughter in the crowd broke the hormone's spell upon him.

"DON'T FORGET WHO WON! ME! I WON!" he shouted, secretly fighting the urge to hug Backus and Belvin.

Maggie watched Stick turn the corner as the laughter rose to a new level. She knew what it was to feel ashamed, and watching him suffer the same fate was almost too much to take.

"Come on," said Taylor as if bored by what had just happened, "Let's go home."

Malcolm...Why did you leave me? I know I shouldn't be angry with you, but sometimes I can't stop myself. You said you'd never leave. This isn't how I thought life would be. I don't want to be alone. It was supposed to be the two of us. That's how you said it would always be. But you left me, and I'm angry about that. You lied to me...you said you'd never lie to me.

21

The Brain Stems

Maggie collapsed gratefully onto her bed. The trip back to Mildred had been a quiet one. After finally persuading Stick to come out of the bathroom, they had taken the late beetle home, which was empty except for the four of them, and a welcome silence.

Back in the dormitory, they had quickly gone their separate ways. Pritch and Taylor buried themselves in movies on the memorizer, while Stick found a new bathroom to lock himself in as he waited for the hormone to wear off.

The clips on the red bloodlines, that were supposed to heat their bunk, looked tighter than ever. Maggie curled under her bed covers and reached for her school bag, looking for a distraction against the cold. Pulling out the last of the bag of donut balls, she munched happily before she found the book Professor Morrigan had given her. The urge to throw it into Mildred's waste disposal system called to her, before curiosity won the battle and she opened the book to a page that had been marked by a thick sliver of eyebrow hair.

CHAPTER 16: THE DAY THE SOULS LEFT: The Beginning of the End

The annual holiday feast had been an annual event for as long as anyone could remember. A time when the body would be well-fed and tired, allowing most of the internal world to stop work and come together in celebration of everything that internals and souls had achieved together. That year was to be the biggest ever. Stories about the size of the feasts, whole body cavities filled with food piled so high that they touched the ceiling, are still legendary today. It was undoubtedly an occasion that no one would forget.

Yet as the evening wore on, reports suggest that the mood changed from celebration to a much more serious tone. Many of the internals who were there later stated that something seemed to be wrong with the souls, almost as if they were troubled by something. Yet these, and other warning signs were not heeded. A fact much discussed later when the internal community tried to think what they could have done to stop the great soul exodus.

As the feasts were drawing to a close, the souls made a toast. This in itself was not unusual, except that every speech they gave seemed to happen at exactly the same time. All of our records denote that the souls gave speeches at 10pm, exactly, in every body. Internal scientists have debated this fact for many years, arguing that such a coordinated worldwide event would have required such organization it would be impossible. Others feel that only mind control on a scale that is beyond anyone's comprehension could have made this possible. We may never know who is right.

What is known is that every soul gave a near identical speech, with all of them making reference to the fabled children's story of the Three Brothers. *Again, looking back, many internals see this as a signal that something was wrong and yet, in that moment, no one paid it much notice. They were in the midst of a celebration after all.*

As the festivities drew to a close, reports of the mood amongst the souls varied. Some state that they were happy, while others feel that they were subdued as they went their separate ways. Only the next morning did it become apparent that this was the last time they would see their soul 'family.' At first it seemed no more than an oversight. When their body's soul failed to emerge from the mind, many presumed that tiredness was to blame, a complaint many of the internals shared. But soon bodies everywhere began to report that they were unable to communicate with their souls, and that they could not gain access to many of the body's external functions. Only when reports of a high number of accidents involving internals outside the body emerged did government officials order an inspection of every body's visual system. This was when they discovered that the body's eyes had been reprogrammed to no longer recognize internals. Worse still, the mechanisms needed to correct this had been removed and, presumably, taken inside the mind. Internals everywhere could no longer feel safe outside the body.

The only solution was to go inside the mind and retrieve the body's visual system controls. But this was, and still is, impossible. Years of internal research has failed to find a way for any internal to make it past the mind's brain wave, a circle of heated electricity that only souls may pass through. In the early days of the great soul exodus, many internals died trying to cross this barrier. Not just to retrieve the visual control, but also in the hope that they might persuade the soul within to come out into the world again. But all attempts to-date have failed.

Will souls ever come out from their self-appointed exile within the mind? Only time will tell. The great internal minds of our time guess that they may not. Indeed, many of them think that, after all these years, most of the souls have forgotten that internals exist, and that they actually believe that they alone control their body. Why would they draw this conclusion? Locked inside the mind, they know only the outside world that they see. And with the visual controls permanently altered, they no longer see internals anymore. A whole new generation has been born inside the mind, a generation that has never had any contact with any internal. We can only guess that, unless something monumental happens, our two worlds are destined to run on different tracks, and that the internals will forever be invisible to souls.

Since the day of the great soul exodus, the annual feast has no longer been a feature of internal society. This unanimous decision, taken by the leaders of the internal society worldwide, is a commitment to never forgetting our soul brothers and sisters. And while many still mark the day on their calendars, it is now done only with sadness at the memory of all that we lost, and as a promise that we all made after that day—to forgo the celebration until the souls come out of the mind and join us once more.

Maggie slammed the book closed. How dare they lie! How dare they say that this is how it happened!

Anger filled her and she rubbed hard at the silver necklace her father had given, forming red welts on her fingertips. She thought back to that day in front of the fireplace when he had told her the truth about this world. How her grandfather had tried to stop the war and how he had been tricked by the internals and their hatred of us. How dare they deny what they had done! As if they could just wipe out the war and all their evil intentions.

Unable to contain herself any longer, Maggie threw the book down drawing a stare from Taylor.

Glaring back at her, Maggie pulled herself out from under the covers and headed for the back stairway, eager to be alone. Stomping by, she barely noticed the heartbroken faces on the internals as they headed home. They were amongst the bright yellow pieces of paper pinned to Mildred's insides declaring her closure. The air around her was thick with sadness, but Maggie kept climbing upward, caring only about her own bad mood. With every step, she pictured herself stomping on the book and crushing the lies inside. How dare they believe that they were the innocent ones? They were guilty! Guilty of trapping the souls and taking her father away from her!

Ahead of her, a group of nerves sat blocking the stairs as they lazily shared a drink from a small grey bottle, their sense of urgency long gone. For a moment Maggie kept going, her mind made up to push past them, when she realized that there was only a dead end behind them. She had reached the top of Mildred. She turned back and started downward, determined to find a new place to be lost in her thoughts, when she saw a slender gap in the pink fleshy wall next to her. Presuming she had failed to notice it on the way up, she slipped inside to find just what she had hoped for, a long lonely hallway with no end and no internals in sight. Striding forward, she continued upward barely noticing the narrowing of the walls and ceiling as they closed inward, making it impossible for anyone to pass her. Only when her hair brushed against the soft pink roof did she snap from her thoughts and realize that she had no idea where she was. Up ahead, the hallway curved sharply to the right and she thought about turning back when she heard the sound of distant footsteps behind her. Heading back now would mean having to talk to whoever it was in the small confines of the hallway, and instead she allowed her bad mood to make her decision, continuing onward to whatever lay ahead.

She turned the corner and was surprised to find her way blocked by a small door that seemed like it was squeezed into the wall, forming familiar pillows of pink flesh around its edges. Unlike all the other doors in Mildred, this one was hard and grey, as though it was made of metal, and upon inspection Maggie noticed a small plaque of writing pressed into its front, revealing tiny letters that were almost too small to read:

The Brain
No Entry.
Private.
Souls Only.
No Trespassers.
Extreme Danger.
By Order of Mildred Potts.

Maggie didn't want to break the rules, so she instinctively turned to leave when again she heard the sound of footsteps down the hallway. Something inside her whispered that this was a bad idea, urging her to go back, only for the bad mood to take control again once more. She reached for the door handle.

Surprised at how easily it opened, she ducked inside as a sudden wave of heat hit her like a hot blanket, instinctively turning her away from its bright glare. With hands raised, she squinted through her fingers, slowly allowing her eyes to adjust as she saw that she was standing inside a room that looped high overhead. Its center was filled by a large white ball that rippled with heat. Behind her, she heard the door close and she took a step forward, unable to stop herself, as she marveled at the glowing ball that hung in front of her like a huge moon. With each step she felt the heat increase, but something seemed to be drawing her in, hypnotizing her as she continued forward, ignoring the urge to resist as its light burned away her anger, leaving her overwhelmed with a sudden peace. Pausing, she went to move but something inside screamed at her to resist, telling her that even one more step would be enough to burn her. Instead she stood, stranded, wanting nothing more than to keep moving, but her feet refused to obey. Her lips were dry and she licked at them, feeling them instantly shrivel back into ridges against the heat before her. It was so beautiful but the heat was too much for her to take, and the voice inside her was growing louder now, demanding that she leave this place. Desperate to ignore it, she stood there, trying to enjoy the beauty of the globe for as long as she could. It was so elegant but she couldn't fight the heat any longer. She had to go.

She turned to leave, feeling a pang of regret, when suddenly she felt something stop her in her tracks. A hand was pushing on her back with incredible strength, sending her surging forward into the fiery heat. Only seconds before she wanted nothing more than to go into the fire, but now her panic was everywhere as its heat scorched her bare skin. She couldn't stop herself from falling; the hand was too strong. She turned desperately, trying to shield herself from the heat, only to catch a glimpse of a hooded figure flash past as the fire overwhelmed her and her cheek began to burn. The image of her old face filled her mind as she felt her skin wrinkling back into its old leathery shape. Instinctively, she flailed at the wall of light, desperate to stop herself from hitting the burning wall, her hands grasping at the empty space that pulled her closer and closer to the heat. Finally she could take it no more and she screwed up her eyes and waited for the pain to eat her whole.

She fell hard, landing with a dull thud against a cold floor. Her eyes were still closed, and confusion filled her as she slowly opened one eye, expecting to be blinded by the heat once more. Yet there was nothing. The light and heat were gone. Instead she was lying in the center of a large circular room, the air cool against her skin. Rolling onto her back, she frantically checked her body for burns as her eyes took in the high ceiling and the glowing cord that drifted lazily from its center. Realizing that she was unharmed, she followed the cord downward, finding that it ended on top of the head of a grey haired old woman who sat with her back to the center of the floor. Maggie coughed, hoping not to scare her, but there was no movement. The woman just sat there, only the rising and falling of her breath telling Maggie that she was alive.

Slowly Maggie got to her feet and placed a gentle hand on her shoulder as the old woman suddenly spun around. There was a loud 'POP' as the glowing cord awkwardly disconnected itself from her head, and she groped her way backward before forming a terrified ball on the floor. For what seemed an eternity the woman lay there unmoving until finally, slowly, a trembling hand came up to pull back her grey hair, revealing a face Maggie knew well. It was a face she had seen many times before. A face that was sometimes young, sometimes smiling, sometimes old...sometimes sad. It was the face of Mildred Potts, 79.

Crouching, Maggie took a step forward, wanting to comfort the woman she felt she knew so well, when the room suddenly lurched upwards sending them crashing into one another as the wall became their floor. For a second they lay next to each other, both of them trying to work out what had just happened, when Mildred began kicking out against the tangle of their bodies. There was fear in her eyes, and instinctively Maggie began to apologize as she sought to untangle herself.

"I'm sorry, I'm sorry. Mildred I'm sorry!"

At the sound of her name, Mildred froze as though the wildness had been stripped from her.

"How do you know my name? Where am I? Am I dead?" said Mildred.

Maggie smiled, unable to stop herself. This was the first time that she had heard her speak and she bit her lip, trying to think of what to say.

"You're in the mind…I live here…not here, but in this body. I'm a soul…just like you," she finally stammered.

Mildred stared at her as though she were speaking another language.

"Don't you remember? This is where you came after the Feast? The one to celebrate the end of the war? You just never came out. You've been in here a really long time."

Mildred looked down, trying to understand, when she saw a wrinkled pair of hands and raised them in front of her face.

"I'm so old. When did I get so old?"

Maggie looked at her, unsure of what to say. "You didn't come out. The internals tricked you. The food at the annual feast…I think it had something in it. It made you think you couldn't leave here."

Mildred paused for a second, trying to understand. "No...no...." she said, her face slowly losing its confusion. "No. The internals are my friends. They didn't do anything to me. I'm so old. How did I get so old?"

Maggie stepped forward, the fire inside her returning. Finally she was talking to another soul, someone who would understand the lies, yet even Mildred was denying her.

"They aren't your friends, Mildred. They are the reason you've been in here all this time. They poisoned you...they messed with your thoughts...they're the reason you're stuck in here."

"No...I don't understand...no...." stammered Mildred, "Where's my husband? He'll tell me what's going on...where's Malcolm?"

Maggie looked down at her feet, unsure of what to say. Shuffling from side to side, she kicked at a handle that was pressed deep into the floor, hoping that Mildred would remember on her own. Finally, she found the courage to speak.

"He's dead, Mildred. He died a long time ago... and you're supposed to die soon, too. I don't understand everything yet, but you're being shut down. They think you don't want to live anymore. You don't do anything…you need to fight back. Show them you want to live. I know people who can help. They'll come and save us…both of us!"

Mildred stared at her. "I want to see Malcolm!"

Maggie nodded sympathetically, wishing that she could make it happen, when Mildred suddenly turned and reached for the glowing cord.

"What are you doing?" said Maggie, "You can't go back. You need to come with me. We need to get you out of here."

Mildred ignored her. Maggie instinctively tried to grab the glowing cord, only to feel it snapped away from her.

"NO!" shouted Mildred, "I'm going back. If I go back, I can see him. I need to see him. I don't know what you've been told, but it's not true. The internals didn't poison me. I didn't even eat at the feast. I just want to be with Malcolm, so that's where I'm going. I need to see him. Now leave me alone. Don't come here again."

Maggie stood frozen, not knowing what to say. As Mildred went to place the end of the glowing cord back on her head, Maggie moved her hand once more, drawing a scolding look from Mildred.

"They're just pictures," said Maggie meekly, "If you go back, all you will have is pictures of Malcolm and then in a few weeks they'll shut you down."

"I don't care!" replied Mildred, the glowing end of the cord hovering just above her head. "It's better than this. Being here without him. Don't you see? I don't belong here. I'm better off out there with him. I don't care if they are only pictures. This used to be my home...a good home. I don't know who has been telling you lies. There have always been souls who think they're better than internals. They think they should be above us, but it's not true! They've only ever helped us. Remember that. I have to go back now. This is what I want. Use the hatch to leave, it'll take you down the spinal column, no one will know. Just don't come back."

Slowly, Mildred pressed the end of the glowing cord back onto her head. It released a slow hiss before forming its edges tight around her face. Her eyes closed as, once again, the room tipped upright, sliding her old body back into its center.

Maggie shook her head, wanting only to pull her away, but something told her that it was useless. Mildred had told her what she wanted, and anything less would not be tolerated. Slumping down, Maggie felt herself deflate as she tried to work out what she had done wrong. Mildred had refused to listen to her and, even worse, she believed the internals' lies. Angrily, she tried to push the thought aside, wanting only to feel the comfort of her rage at being right, but doubt kept leaking in. Finally she found the image of her father's face, and pressed the thoughts away. There were lies everywhere. Her father had warned her that they would stop at nothing, and this was just another one of their tricks. She looked at Mildred, wishing that she could help her. If only she had her father's powers. He would know what to do. Her father.

Suddenly, it was all too much for Maggie, she just wanted her father, but he wasn't there. There was only confusion…and tears.

Later, when her tears had finally dried, Maggie found the hatch and climbed out of Mildred's mind. Soon, the puffy pink walls on either side of the ladder rubbed at her shoulders as she climbed down into the unknown, grateful to avoid the hooded figure that might be waiting above. On and on she climbed until her arms grew tired, begging her to stop next to a cool breeze that was being released from a small vent in the wall. Resting there, feeling the air crisp the last of her tears, she heard a door slam. Leaning forward, she realized that there was a room on the other side of the vent. A room she recognized.

Below, Thaddeus Miles's bald head shined up at her, reminding her of the day they had been sent to his office after crashing the fly. He sat behind his large desk staring at something out of view. Leaning back into his chair, he sighed as a nerve flashed inside to deliver a letter, adding to the large pile that already crowded his desktop. Looking up at the ceiling, he let out another snort. Maggie saw his tired eyes, their edges marked with lines of worry. A loud buzzing noise pulled him back, as the shiny black SBC radio that sat next to him suddenly buzzed to life.

"Yes, this is Minister Miles," he said, pressing the button on its front.

There was an angry tingle of noise, as if mice were scurrying across the room, before a voice sprang from the box, filling the room with its anger.

"This is the prime minister. I just got a report that Mildred Potts, 79 shut down without authorization? What the hell is going on over there?"

"Yes, Prime Minister, she did. It was totally unexpected, but everyone's okay here. It was only for a few minutes," said Thaddeus, grimacing as though he knew what was coming next.

"That's all well and good," said the prime minister, unsatisfied, "but bodies don't just shut down unexpectedly! They only shut down when a soul disconnects, and that hasn't happened...well, since before the exodus! I need to know what happened and why. I need answers. This sort of thing can easily spread panic amongst the bodies you know!"

"I know, I will work on it, but it only just happened. I'll get you answers, but you have to give me some time," said Thaddeus, his voice betraying his tiredness.

Silence filled the air until, finally, the prime minister spoke again, his voice softer than before.

"Good...good...well, let's not delay on this one. I'll need to give a report to the ministry as soon as possible. We should think of something to make them feel at ease in the meantime. Maybe we should move up the closing of this Mildred Potts 79. Get it out of the way sooner so that there are no more problems."

"NO!" shouted Thaddeus, surprising even himself, "I need more time. You promised me I had until November 30th!"

"Oh really, not this again!" sighed the prime minister, "Look, Thaddeus, you and I go a long way back, all the way to our days in the army together, and I will always be grateful to you for all that you did to help me. We both know I wouldn't have made it without your help. But this obsession has to stop. It has cost you everything. You had such a bright future, but ever since you went missing on that silly mission you've been possessed with tales of deatheaters and souls with magical powers! And what do you have to show for it? You have no life, no family, just a job in a crumbling old body that you've allowed to fall to pieces by pursuing this silly fantasy of yours. And now you're even about to lose that! I can't keep protecting you, Thaddeus. You have to let this go!"

Thaddeus Miles stared at the SBC radio as though fighting the urge to throw it against the wall.

"You don't know," he said through gritted teeth, "you weren't there. That mission opened my eyes to the real world, a world that even you, Prime Minister, don't know about! There are internals who are hiding things from us, who know what's coming. I send you reports but you ignore all of them. I was in one of those bodies that was taken over by one of those 'souls with magical powers' and you don't know what we went through. What happened when the hallways filled with that blue smoke. You don't know what it was like to have your every move controlled so that you could only watch as your hands moved without you. Your feet taking you to places you didn't want to go. You couldn't control anything. And all the time there was pain—burning through you!"

"Alright!" said the prime minister, "You know as well as I do that you had some sort of stress induced attack that made you hallucinate. Every doctor has said just as much. As for your reports, well we both know why I ignore them. I do it so that we can both keep our jobs! Do you know what would happen if I told the world that your fairy stories were true? We'd both be on the first dragonfly to the crazy hospital. They are madness, Thaddeus, madness!"

"It's not madness, Peter! Bodies have been going missing for a long time and we both know what happens to the internals inside! If they're lucky they just lose their memory, and if they're unlucky, they die! They die! We both know it's true, but for some reason, someone in the ministry is keeping it a secret. But it's only going to get worse. Someone is developing something that controls internals, and we both know who that is! There are things out there that you don't want to see, but they are coming for all of us. Unless we find them and stop them—now!"

"Oh come on, Thaddeus! When will you let this stupid theory of yours go already? It's ridiculous to think that there are three souls out there who can control bodies without internals. It's simply not true, Thaddeus! Surely even you hear how absurd it sounds? It's just an old story made up to scare children at bedtime. There are no such things as free souls. They live in their world, and we live in ours. End of story. The idea that these three brothers could take over everything is just preposterous. And now I see that you're sending me messages that you think you've found someone who can prove their existence, and she just happens to be living right under your nose in Mildred Potts 79? Your mind is destroying you, Thaddeus, and I cannot keep covering for you. Do you know what the ministry thinks of you? Do you know how many favors I've already had to pull to keep you in a job?"

"I don't need your favors. I just need you to take me seriously! She is here and I'll prove it to you! And if you try to cover it up, Peter, then so help me…."

"ENOUGH! THAT IS ENOUGH,
THADDEUS! DO NOT FORGET WHO YOU ARE
TALKING TO!"

Thaddeus stared at the SBC radio, the air
becoming thick as something inside him screamed that
he had gone too far. Slowly, the quiet grew thinner and
it evaporated, waiting for either man to speak.

"Look, I know you don't believe me, but don't
shut this body down early, I just need more time, I can
prove it, I know I can," said Thaddeus softly.

There was a cough on the other end, and the
prime minister seemed to be thinking about it.

"Alright," he said reluctantly, "but this is it,
Thaddeus. Mildred Potts 79 is being closed on
November 30th. I'll make sure that I'm there, and I'll
bring all the other ministers too. We'll give her a good
send off. But after it's done, you have to promise me
that this will stop. That you'll finally let go of this silly
fantasy and try to live a normal life."

"Okay," said Thaddeus too quickly to be
believable, "agreed."

"Good. Well, let's talk no more of this. Let me
know if you find out any more information about that
body of yours closing down, and I'll see you on the
30th."

377

"Sure," said Thaddeus coldly.

The SBC released a scurry of noise before its lights dimmed and it glowed sleepily off.

"Just as soon as I find her," mumbled Thaddeus to himself, sliding the file open that had just been delivered to his desk.

Maggie leaned in close and pressed her face against the bony slits in the vent to see what he was looking at. Beneath her was another face she recognized. A face she hoped never to see again. Staring up at her from between Thaddeus Miles's, thick fingers was a blue eye surrounded by dark crinkled skin that drooped loosely around the cheek and sad mouth. It was her old face. A face she wanted to forget. A face that seemed to refuse to let go of her.

"You're somewhere close, aren't you?" said Thaddeus, sliding his finger down the side of the photo, "And you know the truth, don't you?"

Mildred shifted in her bed as she tried to get a better view of Malcom's pictures. The TV in the corner was trying to get her attention but she ignored its chatter and stared at the photos on the mantle piece. His face was so warm, almost as though she could feel him filling her insides with happy memories.

Suddenly, a fly shot past pulling her thoughts toward the open window. A generous breeze was stealing inside, while outside the light from the day was just dipping over the distant rooftops. Lying there, she watched the yellow light burn into redness before fading to black as a lone star took its place in her top windowpane. She stared at it, as she had many times before, feeling as though she was seeing it for the first time. Something inside told her that things were changing. Soon she would no longer be able to look out and see this beautiful scene play out every night, and for a second she felt sad. Then, just as it did every night, her old frame released a shivering ache to let her know how tired it was. Looking down, she stared at her unmoving toes peeking out from the end of the blanket. A sudden urge filled her and she willed them to move, only to watch as they refused her command, remaining lifeless. Sleep was calling her, but something told her to keep trying. Again she stared hard at the toes…her toes…demanding that this time they move. A tickle filled her spine as they stirred creakily into life, before wiggling like a bucket of worms.

Look at that, she thought, with a smile, as she watched them dance.

Rolling onto one side, she allowed herself one more wiggle. As the sensation ran through her again, she once more looked up at the star. It seemed brighter tonight.

Malcolm...I had a dream tonight that a girl told me I was going to die. She had the same voice as that neighbor's child. Now it's the middle of the night and I'm sitting here staring at your photo. I don't feel like I'm about to die, but I'll be honest, I don't really care if it's true. I do know that something feels different. Something has changed. In other news, I wiggled my toes tonight! Silly, isn't it? The small things. I haven't been able to wiggle my toes for a long time. Doesn't sound like the sort of thing that happens to someone who's about to die, does it!

22

Transplant Rejection

Maggie stared out the beetle's window. Outside, a large head of greasy hair was bobbing past, the neck below covered in oversized brellow letters:

Muscles Wanted.
Must start immediately.
John Gledhill, 15.
Has recently become interested in girls and joined a gym.
Needs lots of muscles as soon as possible.
Excellent salary.
Positions available in legs, arms, chest, back, shoulders, and stomach.

Maggie watched as the giant letters slowly disappeared behind her. It had been weeks since she overheard the conversation between Thaddeus Miles and the prime minister, and she had struggled to think of anything else, yet still she had no answers to what it all meant. Who were these three brothers and why was he looking at her picture as though she was a prize? And why did she feel like she was being watched all the time? Was it just her imagination?

The beetle lurched to the left as Reg pulled back hard on the beetle's fleshy insides. Up ahead, a toad sat atop a large brick wall, its face full of boredom. Slowly, the corner of its lip bent downward as a large bulbous tongue slipped over its edge. Suddenly, it snapped out with incredible speed, blurring into a flash of pink as it stretched forward to wrap itself around a fly that was zipping past. Holding tight to its prey, the long tongue shrank back inside the toad's mouth. Maggie caught a glimpse of the fly's driver staring angrily out of the large eyeball.

"Speed traps," said Reg with a sigh of annoyance, "They get you every time."

Back at home, Maggie and the others trudged silently over Mildred's kneecap as they headed to the dormitory. Inside, the hallways were quiet and empty and the children had taken to asking Reg to drop them off at the end of the bed. They wanted to avoid the air of sadness that seemed to have consumed Mildred and her impending closure.

A ripple of movement spread beneath their feet as the now familiar wiggling of Mildred's toes disturbed their walk home. Stick looked back and smiled as he watched her giant digits move as though they were waving at him.

"Give it up," said Taylor without stopping, "All these wiggles and stretches don't mean a thing. She's not trying to start living again. The nerves are just sending messages to the wrong places again. She's ready to be shut down. Besides, even if she was trying to show everyone she's worth keeping alive, it's too late. They aren't about to stop the closing ceremony now. Not with only two days to go."

Maggie watched Stick's face drop. She wanted to tell him that maybe it wasn't too late, that Mildred would surprise them all and decide to get out of bed. But she couldn't. If there was one thing her meeting with Mildred had taught her, it was that Taylor was right. Mildred was going to be shut down and she didn't care.

Up ahead, two large black spiders crawled over the bed carrying a web-covered crate of chairs that was strung between them like a hammock. Maggie noticed Stick shrink further as he read the words 'M Potts, 79. Closing Ceremony' painted on their sides. In front of them, a large peel of skin was pulled back from the side of Mildred's leg, allowing the spiders to deposit the crates inside, before quickly scurrying away.

"Look, I know Mildred is home," said Pritch, nudging him. "But we'll still be together. That's the main thing."

Up ahead, a nerve was sitting lazily against an old bristly hair stump and scratching himself as he snoozed peacefully in the late day sun. He leaned on one elbow and gave a lazy yawn as he heard them approach.

"Do I know you? Yeah, you all live in the orphanage, don't you?" he said happily.

"Yes," said Stick grumpily, "why?"

"Do me a favor, will you? Give this to Miss Devlin for me?" he said wearily, waving a crumpled piece of paper in their direction. "I was supposed to deliver it last week. I forgot."

"How could you forget? You're a nerve, it's your job!" said Taylor sharply.

The nerve rolled his eyes. "Unless you haven't noticed there's not too many jobs left around here anymore. Go on, take it for me, please? I'm tired!"

Taylor glared at him until Pritch stepped forward and took the paper from his hand.

"I'll take it for you. I'd be happy to," she said sympathetically.

"Thank-you, Miss. Care to give an old nerve some money? I'm going to be out of work soon and I don't know when I'll find some more?" he said, uncurling his hand flat.

Taylor mumbled something about him not looking very hard when Pritch dropped a coin into his hand with a friendly smile.

"What did you do that for?" whispered Stick as they walked away. "You didn't have to pay him. You're doing *him* the favor!"

Without answering, Pritch crouched down and held out the paper just far enough for them all to see.

"See that gold stamp?" she said, "The one on the back corner? I've seen it before. On the letter from the Department for Lost and Orphaned Children. The one about Mildred closing, and where Miss Devlin could choose for us to live."

Three sets of eyes grew wide as Pritch led them inside Mildred, before gently unfolding the letter.

The Department for Lost and Orphaned Children:
Taking care of tomorrow's children, despite yesterday.
Reginald Jefferies, 52. 14th Floor
Manager of the Black Swan Bank,
Coldmouth, London, LC90 RJ52
Sbc number: 002 354-761
Brellow Fax: 0021 345-935 att: R Jefferies

Dear Miss Devlin,

I am writing to confirm the new homes for the five children in your care. In line with your recommendations, we have decided to place the children in five separate orphanages. While it is highly unusual to separate siblings, in this instance the minister has read your report and agrees that the negative behaviors they exhibit will best be solved by extensive time apart.
As outlined in your report, the children currently exhibit many inappropriate behaviors. It is his

opinion that we must act quickly to stop these and, subsequently, the five listings below are new from those I previously listed. This list is made up only of high security orphanages where the children will learn to curb their negative behaviors through hard work and sacrifice. He is sure that this will be good for their futures. On a side note, may I take this opportunity to congratulate you on your new position as assistant to the National Minister of Orphan Services. Minister Ira Marsh's recent promotion to this position has already made a big impression upon our organization. All welcomed his personal recommendation that we hire you, and we look forward to you joining our office. If I can be of any help with your upcoming move to London, please let me know.

John McCrell, 68. (Chemical toilet cleaner, North) – Taylor Shepard
Louis Pipe, 46. (Cat food tester, London) – Stick Shepard
Mavis Bath, 51 (Crime scene cleaner, South) – Pritch Kinney

Doug Reed, 39 (Undertaker, East) – Roosela Snow

Peggy May, 43 (Crocodile feeder, West) – Maggie Pincus

Sincerely,
T Smith
Regional Director of Orphan Services.

All four of the children stood staring at the letter in silence. Taylor broke first, grabbing the paper and scrunching it into a ball inside her fist.

"We had a deal!" she yelled, striding away as the others gave chase.

As they left, something moved in the hallway shadows as the four children passed by blindly. The shape waited, watching them as they moved quickly away, then the hooded figure stepped out into the dim light and pulled something out of a pocket. There was a sharp beep as the black square in the pale hand came to life.

"So?" said a voice.

"I'm not sure. What should I do? Do I kill her or not?" said a cold voice from inside the hood.

There was a pause.

"No, she may still be of use," it said finally. "For now, just follow her."

"And if it turns out that we don't need her? What then?" said the hood.

"Then you can kill her," said the box casually.

The hooded figure smiled as the black box went cold. It waited a second, enjoying the thought of killing again. Then, it put the box back into a pocket and walked quickly after the children.

Back in the dorm, the four children sat miserably on their beds, trying to think of anything to stop them from being broken up. At first they had thought they might be able to persuade Miss Devlin to change her mind, but upon arriving back in the dorm they had found her in a defiant mood.

"I don't care about our deal!" she'd snapped after Taylor had barged into her office. "That was just something I needed done. A little favor to get me what I wanted. And now I have what I want, so I'm off to a nice easy job in London! And you can get as upset as you like about being split up because it doesn't bother me in the slightest. It wasn't even my idea! You can thank Minister Marsh for that! It turns out that he hates you all even more than I do! So get used to it! In two days this heap of an old woman will be closing down and you'll all be off to wherever it is he told me to send you! With any luck, you'll never get to see each other ever again, and neither will I!"

Taylor kicked the bed in anger, fuming at the memory, while the others sat quietly around her. Maggie put her head in her hands, trying to make sense of it all. Everything in her life seemed to be crashing in on her and the only thing stopping her from going crazy was being with these three internals. Yet now they were being taken from her too.

And why? They had delivered the package, they had given it to the virus, they had survived the fight between her stepmother and Chipper. They had done everything they had been asked to do, but none of it had helped. And there was still the creeping thought that it was all too much of a coincidence. There was something there, something she wasn't seeing, some reason that all of this was happening to them. But the more she thought about it, the more only one thing made sense. It was her. This was all happening because of her.

Mildred picked up the book of photos and began to look at it for the tenth time that day. Malcolm smiled up at her as he always did, his smile lighting up the world. A ladybird landed casually on the corner of the page and Mildred brushed it away, annoyed at its intrusion. There seemed to be so many insects coming into the house these days. It was almost as though they knew something she didn't.

Turning the page, Mildred saw that one of her favorite photos had come loose from its holding, its corner peeling upward like a white tongue. Inside its curl was a young Mildred holding Malcolm's hand tightly. Annoyed at the thought of losing this special memory, she pushed at the corner with her old fingers, only to feel it stick to her thumb. Without thinking, she pulled back, wrenching the photo free as it flipped onto its back. Reaching for it, she went to put it back in place when suddenly she froze. There, inside the book that she knew so well, was something she had never seen before. Something so precious that she couldn't believe it had been there all this time. For there, on the back of the photo, was a note from Malcolm.

Malcolm, I was looking at our wedding album again tonight. This is where you'd laugh and call me silly because you know I do it all the time. But tonight was different. The photo of us on the church steps had come unstuck, and when I tried to stick it back down it came loose, and that's when I found it. On the back of the photo...your note...the one you'd left for me.

23

Irritable Bowels

The next morning brought little to help their problem. The long beetle ride to school had been made worse by Charlie Comp 17, deciding to choose today as the day he would take a long overdue shower, leaving the kids soaking wet and late when they finally arrived for the day. They were surprised to find the rest of the class standing in line by the front door after they snuck in.

"Oh good," said Professor Rose, ignoring their lateness, "A full class for a special day. I was just telling everyone else about our surprise field trip!"

A murmur of excitement rose through the room as the four late arrivals wrung their wet clothes.

"Okay!" continued the professor. "Today we are lucky enough to have been allowed a special trip into the bowels of a body. Now, you all know that it's a dangerous area where we're usually forbidden to go, but we're lucky enough to have been given permission to visit a body that is soon to be closed. They've agreed to shut the whole system down while we tour so we'll be quite safe. It won't be the nicest smell later on for those who live there, but this is truly a once in a lifetime educational experience, so I think they'll understand!"

The four children looked at each other and groaned.

"That's right, Sticky boy," whispered Ridge over Stick's shoulder, "We're going to your house. Let's see what the dumps look like in an old dump."

Stick turned, full of the evening's anger, only to see Ridge turn his back as he laughed at his own joke with Backus and Belvin.

"Come on." Pritch sighed, pulling him to the end of the line that was forming. "Let's get this over with."

If they thought the first beetle ride of the day had been bad, they were soon learning that the second one was far worse, courtesy of a broken heater and Backus and Belvin in the seats behind them.

Stick grimaced as he felt yet another ball of skin bounce off the back of his head, before forcing himself to stare out of the window. Far below, Mildred was fast asleep, her mouth wide open, only the slight rising of her chest letting the world know that she hadn't already been closed. Around her, ants and spiders busied themselves with deliveries for the closing ceremony, while above them a fly darted up and down as it delivered sandwiches to the workers below. It was just about to land next to a delivery moth when it suddenly shot upward as if terrified. Swooping in behind, it was quickly replaced by several large wasps flying in a perfect line formation that peeled away one by one to land on the flowery duvet below. With a quick shiver, the sides of each wasp opened, spilling out hundreds of tiny figures dressed in white that quickly formed a broken circle around Mildred's sleeping figure. The wasps zoomed away through the kitchen.

Above them, Stick looked down with a bored face as the other children in the beetle fought to see what was happening below. He had overheard Miss Devlin talking on the SBC that morning about the arrival of the Leukocyte security forces. With the growing list of important people who were coming to Mildred's closing party it had come as no surprise.

Security seemed to be growing everyday, and Stick thumbed at the ID pass that he had grown accustomed to using at all her entrances.

Seemingly unnerved by the new arrivals, the beetle landed with a hard thud before maneuvering itself next to the door under Mildred's toenail. Stepping inside, the students stared in awe at the muscular security man who checked their names against a list, as another growled at them to keep moving. Trudging forward, they soon found themselves outside the door to the orphanage.

"This place is horrible!" said Ridge loudly as they passed by, "What sort of person would live in a place like this? Only losers would live here!"

Stick grimaced as Maggie pushed him forward.

"Well Ridge," said the professor unaware that four of her students lived here, "It's true that this is no longer a place that anyone in their right mind would choose to live. See the layers of fat that line the walls and the weak blood flow that cuts off the heat? It's quite disgusting. But that's what happens when bodies get old. They need upkeep. And without the proper care, they become like this...quite horrible."

Waving a hand at the walls, she smiled happily as Ridge asked her to describe all the other things that no longer worked in an old body like this. Several minutes later, the class arrived at a door marked 'BOWELS' as the professor finished her description of all the things that were wrong with Mildred. The four children looked up at the sign, happy for anything that would make the stories stop, when suddenly their day got worse.

"Hello children!" said Ira Marsh, throwing open the door with excitement, "Welcome!"

The four children stared in horror at the self-serving smile, shining from the center of the orange face, as Pritch gripped Taylor's arm in case she tried to attack.

Behind them, Professor Rose pushed blindly forward as she made her way toward their host with an outstretched hand.

"Minister Marsh," she said nervously, "I don't know how to thank you for this opportunity. When I received your SBC call last night that you could arrange this for us…well I almost didn't know what to say! The bowels have so many restricted areas. For the students to have the opportunity to visit some of those areas…well it's truly an educational gift!"

Marsh flicked back his long blonde hair and broadened his smile even more.

"Not at all, the pleasure is all mine," he said, his eyes flicking onto the four children. "Come along. Time is being wasted. Let us get started, shall we?"

Following him down the hallway, the four children found themselves keeping as far away from him as they could. Up ahead, a line had formed and they joined it, waiting to be handed an earwax candle and a small nose whistle in case of emergencies.

"What the hell do you think he's up to?" whispered Stick as he scooped up a candle, "he's never done a selfless thing in his life. It's got to be something to do with us, don't you think?"

Up ahead, Ira Marsh glanced back before continuing to talk loudly to the group about how lucky they were to have him, a former Minister for Waste, giving them a tour. He said they should really tell their parents about how much they appreciated what he was doing for them.

"I don't like this," whispered Taylor, shaking her head, "keep an eye out."

Several wary minutes passed, and soon they found themselves standing in front of a dark hole that sat beneath a large red sign that read 'DANGER. NO ENTRY. DANGER.'

Professor Rose turned to the students to tell them to stay together when Minister Marsh began talking.

"Now, children, I have a little adventure for you today! It's quite safe. The system is shut down so everything in there is absolutely harmless. Nobody is going to get eaten by a sludgie or anything!" he said with a wink. "Now, I just need you all to find a partner. There, there, quick as you can."

At the back of the line Maggie felt Taylor grab her arm as she pushed Stick next to Pritch.

"Everyone got a partner? Wonderful! So here's what you are going to do. You're all going to go off in pairs. Do not worry. I've arranged for some enzymes to give each of you a tour. Wonderful little fellas, they work down in the bowels all the time. They know the place inside, outside, upside, and down!"

Ten tiny green figures scurried out of the darkness to form a tight line behind the minister. Each of them carried a large hammer and a forced grin that sat beneath a single unblinking eye.

"Err. Minister," said Professor Rose, "are you sure that's safe? Wouldn't it be better to keep the children all together?"

Ira spun around, and Maggie thought she saw the slightest look of anger on his face.

"Not at all!" he said, placing his hand on her arm. "The enzymes will keep them all quite safe. And it will be so much more fun this way. Besides, I've arranged for you and I to have a lunch served on my private dragonfly. Give us a chance to get out of this old bag and get some fresh air...so we can get to know each other better!"

Professor Rose paused, before giving a small giggle.

"Wonderful!" Minister Marsh grinned. "Let's get them started, shall we?"

One by one, he pushed the pairs into the darkness as an enzyme skipped ahead of each one. When there were only two pairs left, he paused as a thoughtful look crossed his face.

"No, I think this might work better," he said pulling Maggie forward to stand next to Stick. "There, that makes much more sense to me. Now, go, enjoy your tour. Don't forget to be back within the hour though. The machine has to be turned back on by then, and you really don't want to be down there when that happens!"

Before she could think, Maggie felt his large hand pushing her forward as the small enzyme darted in front of them. She looked back and saw Taylor glare at the minister before she, too, disappeared out of sight. Ahead, the enzyme walked quickly, occasionally pointing out strange rocks in the ceiling or steaming yellow pools as he led them down into the darkness. On and on they trudged, and soon the soft walls began to drip a thick goo that pulled at their clothes as the ceiling became lower and lower. Then, they were suddenly free of the small corridor as Stick lit his earwax candle, revealing a rippling, dark ceiling that arched high over their heads, its walls slowly rising and falling as though something large was breathing on its surface. Happy to be able to stand upright again, Maggie breathed in deeply, only to regret it as the taste of something rotten filled her mouth.

"This is the ascending colon," said the enzyme in a bored voice, "it's where we put all the waste for the bacteria to eat. Once they've had their fill, we move everything onto the next section."

Memories of all the pictures of bacteria Maggie had seen at school flooded through her.

"Err…aren't bacteria dangerous?" she asked nervously.

"Usually, yes, but we're fine as long as the system is off. And besides, these ones are under our control. Some bacteria can actually be quite useful if you train them. Like these," he said with a sweep of his small hand.

He turned on the light attached to his helmet, sweeping its brightness across the ceiling. With the darkness removed, Maggie and Stick could see that the shadowy ripples were actually sleeping creatures that lay stuck to the brown roof. Each one was large with a slimy brown body that breathed slowly beneath a small white head; their bulbous eyes barely closed beneath tightly stretched lids. In the center of each head, a sharp beak opened and closed rhythmically seeming to count the minutes as they slept.

"Those are sludgies!" said Stick, panicked. "Are you mad? Those are huge! They're big enough to eat us!"

"Alright, son. Calm yourself," said the enzyme with little caring, "like I said, we're fine as long as the system is off. Look at them! They're fast asleep! The only thing that would wake them is a delivery of waste, and that's not going to happen. If it did, well, then we'd be in trouble. They eat everything they can fit inside them and then some. And they aren't picky, they'll eat whatever is in front of them, including children. They'll eat all day if you let them. No, it's best they stay up there. Later on, we'll turn on the machines and

then when they've eaten we'll put them back up there to sleep. Then whatever they haven't eaten gets moved onto the next chamber."

"How do you put them to sleep?" asked Maggie, feeling like they would wake up any second.

"Oh, that's the easy part," said the enzyme casually, waving at a rack of white tubes that leaned against the wall behind them, "all you have to do is use one of those granuls. See what you do is…oh, hang on…that's my SBC radio. I have to get this, it's the minister. I'll be right back."

Suddenly he was gone, his voice disappearing into a small black box as he turned off his light and walked through the doorway from which they had come. Maggie and Stick watched him go as his voice faded into nothing. Above them, one of the sludgies squirmed and Maggie instinctively grabbed hold of Stick.

"Don't worry, he'll be back in a minute," said Stick, trying to sound as though he believed it.

Both of them stared at the ceiling and waited for the enzyme as they listened to the sound of the sludgies' large beaks clicking dreamily in their sleep. Minutes seemed to drain away, and Maggie remembered the warning to be out of there before the hour was up. The earwax candle in Stick's hand began to drip on the floor beneath them and he slid it over into Maggie's palm as he began to fumble in his backpack. Pulling out a toothie, he looked at her with a relieved smile.

"Just in case," he said, his eyes never leaving the ceiling.

Maggie felt the precious light running between her fingers. Time was passing fast and she felt for the small nose whistle in her pocket, the enzyme still nowhere to be seen.

"Maybe we should try to find a way out?" said Maggie.

The candlelight shadowed Stick's face, betraying his fear.

"I don't think we stand a chance of finding our way back. Those tiny corridors are like a maze back there."

Maggie nodded, wishing she'd paid more attention to all the turns the enzyme had taken them on to get here. Suddenly, the heat in Maggie's hand changed to pain as the last of the wax dripped away, leaving behind the burning wick. Juggling it, she stared at it, willing it to stay alive, but it was no good. Seconds later, the flame shrank until it formed a tiny red glow that quickly dissolved into the darkness that surrounded them. Next to her, Maggie heard a dull thud as Stick desperately tried to break the toothie, before something started rolling away.

"I dropped it!" said Stick.

Maggie felt him leave her side as he scrambled on the floor.

"Hurry up!" said Maggie urgently.

"I'm trying!" said Stick angrily.

But Maggie didn't hear him. Her head was filled with the dull hum that had begun to ripple beneath her feet. Above her, the clicking was multiplying as the humming became steadily louder. Then, everything seemed to fall silent as something opened behind her. Suddenly, she felt her socks fill with a warm wetness as the chamber flooded. Then there were splashes, like boulders being dropped into a lake, as something dropped from the ceiling.

"Stick!" shouted Maggie, desperate against the clicking that now surrounded them. But there was no answer. Stick couldn't speak. The snapping that had begun to circle them had stolen his voice.

Someone had started the machine. The sludgies were awake. It was feeding time.

Mildred said thank-you to the nurse as she took away her empty tray. After a brief smile she too was soon gone, rushing out the door as she hurried out of the house, her mind already with her next patient. Beneath the blanket, something rumbled as Mildred's wrinkled hand rubbed at her stomach, feeling her lunch talk to her. She had eaten too much. She never ate that much anymore. These days she rarely ate anything at all. But how could she resist? It had looked so good. Her favorite. Turkey with mashed potatoes and gravy. Just like she used to make for Malcolm.

Malcolm, I ate well tonight. It's the first time I've eaten since...since I found your note. I haven't had much appetite since I read it, but tonight I was hungry. Maybe it was just because it was your favorite—turkey with mashed potatoes and gravy, just like I used to make for you. Maybe it's a sign.

24

Bad Blood

Maggie turned in a circle searching for something, anything, in the darkness. The flood around her ankles was rising and she felt something lumpy dip inside her shoe as the smell of turkey gravy filled the room.

"STICK...STICK!"

The clicking of beaks around her became ferocious, pounding in her ears.

"STICK...PLEASE!"

There was no reply, just the non-stop clicking that rippled in the flood around her. Something snapped against her leg as a beak pulled at the lump of gravy, which seemed to be glued to her sock.

'CRACK!'

Stick appeared as the bright light of the toothie surrounded him. He splashed toward her, and Maggie watched as he kicked out at the clicking mouth that was attacking her sock. The sludgie angrily snapped back, desperate to finish what it had started.

"COME ON!" shouted Stick, pulling at Maggie, "WE NEED TO GET TO THOSE GRANULS!"

Maggie followed blindly, feeling the slimy brown water splash up into her face as she ran. Around them the toothie spread its bright light, revealing a sea of sludgies that were angrily diving up and down in the slimy water around them, searching for something to eat. Maggie slipped against a brown tail and fell to one knee as one of the sludgies reared its head, snapping angrily. Frozen against what was about to happen, she watched helplessly as the snapping beak loomed over her, before the light of the toothie smashed hard into its side sending it reeling backward into the brown lake. Maggie looked up into Stick's panicked face as he pulled her upright and ordered her to run.

The rain of sludgies grew—more and more splashed down around them, pushing Maggie deeper into a panic. Desperate to avoid the brown bodies slithering around her knees she sprinted forward. The rack of white tubes that the enzyme had promised would help came into the light.

"What do we do with them?" said Maggie, collapsing into the rack.

"I don't know. I was hoping you did," replied Stick, swinging his bag at the head of yet another sludgie attack.

Maggie looked at him; the thought that this might be the end consumed her. Panicked, she grabbed one of the tubes, desperate for its help, only to find its smooth surface free of any buttons to make it work. The clicking was becoming unbearably loud now as Maggie tried to stay clam, desperate to think of a way out. Next to her, Stick had given up trying to make the granul work and was swinging it wildly at the sludgies. They had formed a circle around them as their clicking ate its way inside their ears.

In desperation, Maggie pressed one hand over one ear and the tube over the other as she tried to block out the noise, determined to think. Instantly the clicking was gone, replaced by a loud slurp as the granul sucked itself across her face until it covered one eye. Maggie staggered backward, shocked, knocking more of the white tubes off the rack as she pulled at the granul that was now firmly attached to her head.

Suddenly the darkness was gone, and the world was consumed by a green light with a small red circle at its center. In front of her, a lime-green Stick was still fighting wildly as one of the sludgies raised itself up, unseen behind him, preparing to bring its open mouth down on top of him. Instinctively, Maggie screwed up her eyes, not wanting to see what was about to happen, when a bright beam shot out of the end of the tube. Opening her eyes, she saw the sludgie behind Stick was now frozen, its body covered in crackling green electricity. Then, just as quickly, it shot upward like a puppet before sticking itself to the ceiling, its eyes closed as if it had been asleep for hours.

"Oh! That's how they work!" said Stick, turning to see the white tube that had absorbed half of Maggie's face. "So you blink and it triggers, right?"

Without realizing, Maggie blinked again, releasing another bolt of light, as one more sludgie shot back up to the ceiling. Stick turned his tube and pushed his face into it. Soon the flashes of light were firing everywhere as they both filled the ceiling with sleeping sludgies.

"Come on," said Stick, pulling Maggie toward the small doorway, "I think we're going to have to find our own way out after all!"

Happily, Maggie ducked into the small corridor and heard a satisfying 'plop' as she pulled the granul from her face. Behind her, Stick shot a last beam of light into the main chamber as he squeezed in through the door and slid it closed behind them. He dropped his granul and crawled next to her, where they both formed an exhausted heap, heaving relieved gulps of air. Finally Stick moved, leaving Maggie sitting there as he propped himself up on one knee and rummaged in his pocket. He pulled out the emergency nose whistle and blew hard on it, only to fill his face with anger as it failed to make a noise.

"Why, you little…." snarled Stick, throwing the useless whistle to one side; something caught his eye.

Farther down the hallway, the enzyme was leaning against a wall and drinking from a small bottle as he talked into his SBC radio, oblivious to the two children behind him. Stick crawled quietly over and tapped him on the shoulder. The enzyme spun around, a look of confusion filling his single wide eye.

"But…how…you were supposed to…." he stammered.

Stick glared at him, and Maggie looked at them both not knowing what to do. A crackle broke the silence as Ira Marsh's voice came over the SBC radio.

411

"Creek? Creek, are you there still? Is it done?" he said, calling for the enzyme who could only stare in shock at the two children.

Stick reached over and grabbed the SBC from his trembling hand.

"Ira...this is Stick...we're here...both of us... don't worry. We'll be back in a minute. Creek's bringing us back to see you now!"

Back at the entrance, Professor Rose threw her arms around Maggie and Stick and squeezed them tight. Tears stained her makeup, and Maggie felt her relief pour over them.

"Oh, children. I was so worried. The machine came on and you weren't back. I thought the worst!"

Stick wriggled free as Maggie stared at Minister Marsh through the folds in the professor's sleeve. Unlike the professor, he showed no signs of relief, his face full of barely hidden anger. Stick stormed over and dropped the SBC radio at his feet, his eyes burning into him. Ira Marsh glared back at him before turning and walking away. Stick stood trembling with anger, and watched him go, until Maggie came over and touched his shoulder.

"I don't understand. Why would he do that to us? We nearly died in there. I know he doesn't like us but the worst we've ever done to him is play a few pranks! Nothing worth trying to kill us," said Stick.

Maggie looked at his confused face, unsure of what to say when she felt Professor Rose's hand on her arm.

"Look, you two can go if you like. Minister Marsh told me you all live here. It's been a long day and it's not worth you flying all the way back to school just to fly back here again. Go relax. Pritch and Taylor should already be up there. Minister Marsh sent them up there when they finished their tour."

Stick turned silently away as Maggie said thank-you. Suddenly Stick spun back around.

"Did you say Minister Marsh sent them back to the orphanage?"

"Yes…that's right," said Professor Rose in a confused voice.

"But you didn't see them come out?"

"No. Minister Marsh was kind enough to watch the door after our lunch. One of the enzymes gave me a brief tour. I've always wanted to see the inside of the waste system. I studied it in university and this was too good an opportunity to miss. Didn't you think it was absolutely fascinating?"

But there was no reply. Stick and Maggie were already sprinting away. They needed to get back to the orphanage fast.

"Where are they?" said Stick, bursting into Miss Devlin's office.

Miss Devlin turned slowly to look down her nose at him. All around her, boxes were stuffed to the brim as though she was preparing to leave nothing but the children behind her.

"I presume you mean Pritch and Taylor?" she finally sneered.

"Yes!"

Miss Devlin turned and took a glowing ball from the shelf, before wrapping it slowly in an old piece of skin.

"They've run away," she said coldly. "They came back about half an hour ago. Told me that since they weren't going to be placed together they were leaving."

Stick and Maggie stared at her in disbelief.

"I tried to stop them, but they were adamant… and what could I do to? You can't blame them for wanting out of this dump. Why shouldn't they leave?

It's not as though they'll ever achieve anything. Better off out, I say. I was surprised they didn't want to wait for you, but they said they didn't care. But don't you worry. I've already submitted a report to the authorities explaining what happened. I'm sure they'll have someone looking for them very soon. Perhaps they'll even find them...eventually."

Maggie stared blankly at the box marked 'official papers' which sat at the bottom of a large stack.

Stick stared at her in disbelief; Maggie saw tears forming in his eyes.

"Thank-you, Miss Devlin," said Maggie, faking politeness as she pulled Stick out of the office. "We should go pack, too. Big day tomorrow."

The door closed silently behind them as Miss Devlin watched them leave.

Back in the dorm, Maggie flipped up the secret hatch and pushed Stick down inside.

"I just don't get it?" he mumbled, "Pritch and Taylor wouldn't have left without us, would they? I mean, we argue but she's still my sister. Devlin's lying! But if she's lying, does that mean they didn't come back? And if they didn't come back, where are they? And why was old Marsh so ready to kill us?"

Maggie slipped in after him and pulled the flap closed behind them. In the darkness, there was a crack as she broke the last of the toothies hidden inside the door.

"I think it's time for me to tell you the truth," she said pushing him forward.

Malcolm, my stomach has been hurting today. Something's not right in there....

25

Cleaning the Wound

Stick stared at her wide-eyed. Maggie stared back, wondering if he would ever blink again. The secret den suddenly felt very small as silence crowded the air around them, leaving them both unsure of what to say.

"That's why I think they wanted to kill us," she said finally, "I don't know for sure, but I think that Ira and Devlin have made some sort of deal with the internals…I mean the bad ones, the ones that are trying to get to me. That's why we had to deliver that box to my old house. They made a deal to help them, and in return they got new jobs. They'd have done anything to get out of Mildred, and I think they found a way…by using me. I think the rest of you were just in the way."

"So, you're saying…you are a…soul?"

Maggie stared at him and nodded. For a second, Stick's hand moved, as if he were about to reach out and touch a ghost, then he stopped himself.

"And all that stuff about a secret war and internals tricking souls into staying in the mind is true?"

Maggie nodded again. Stick gave her a look like he was waiting for her to tell him that it was all a joke.

"It's true," said Maggie softly, "My father had some sort of gift…like a special power that meant he could control bodies without using any internals. They think I have it, too. I don't though…at least I don't think I do. I'm sorry. This is all my fault. If I'd never come here none of this would be happening to you…to all of you. I should have left. I promise you, I would of if I'd thought for a second that they would try to hurt you, or the others, I just thought they'd only be after me."

Stick stared hard at her, and Maggie hung her head, unable to deal with the thought of just how much he hated her right now.

"So, how do we fix it?" he said suddenly.

Maggie looked up, thinking she had misheard.

"You're not angry?" she said hopefully.

"Of course I'm not!" said Stick. "Look, in case you haven't noticed, things weren't exactly going great for all of us before you got here. Mildred's been going downhill for a long time and that's not your fault. The only thing you've done is try to help me…all of us. And I don't blame you for not telling me you're a soul. If it wasn't for what happened today I don't know if I'd have believed you even if you had said something. But now it makes sense. How you knew nothing about living inside a body? Besides its not like we're at war. We're not, are we? Just because your friends are? I mean because I'm like…the enemy?"

Maggie jumped forward as the pressure of keeping in her secret escaped into one giant hug. Stick stood frozen, unsure what to do before giving an embarrassed cough.

"Yes…well," he mumbled as Maggie leaned back, smiling, "but we've still got to find out what happened to Pritch and Taylor. After that we can talk about all of this soul stuff."

Maggie stared at him, feeling too relieved to think. He wasn't mad at her. She'd thought he would turn against her, hate her, but he hadn't. He hadn't let her down. He never let her down. Just like her dad. Just like family.

419

Stick coughed and paced the room, leaving footprints in Mildred's soft fat as he tried to think.

"What would Taylor do?" he whispered to himself over and over.

Maggie watched him walk back and forth when a thought jumped into her head.

"Ira...he must know where they are! He was talking to the enzyme today on the SBC radio to make sure he knew what was happening to us. Wouldn't he have been doing the same for Pritch and Taylor? Unless, they didn't make it out?"

"Na!" said Stick decisively, "Taylor's too smart for his traps. She's always been way cleverer than me. If we got out, then so did she. If they're not here, then someone's got them, and you're right...Ira must know where they are. We've got to find him and make him tell us. But how do we do that?"

"Mildred's closing!" said Maggie excitedly as Stick shot her a look of confusion.

"He'll be there! You've seen the list. There are way too many powerful people coming for him not to make an appearance. He won't be able to stay away. And we're going to be there, too! The passes Miss Devlin gives us every day should get us into the main cavity and everything! There's no way we won't able to get to him!"

"And when we do, we'll make him tell us where they are!" continued Stick, "If he won't…well, then we'll scream and shout and tell the whole hall how he took Pritch and Taylor. Even if we can't prove it, there's no way they'll let him keep his new job with that hanging over him. He'll have to tell us."

Maggie stared at him, feeling more hope than she'd felt in a long time.

"Come on, let's go get ready!" she said.

The next morning, Maggie and Stick awoke early. Both had slept little that night, and the thoughts that had kept them awake were still running through their heads as they pulled themselves out of bed and into the cold. Deciding to make an early start, Stick went to get their daily passes from Miss Devlin as Maggie dressed quickly in the clothes she had prepared the night before.

Pulling on her sweater, she emerged to find Stick standing in front of her pale-faced.

"The passes," he said, offering up handfuls of tiny pieces of paper. "She ripped them up and left them on her desk. Her office is empty. She must have left during the night."

Maggie stared at the ruined passes that were their only way to get to Minister Marsh.

"What do we do now?" she said, feeling helpless.

Stick stared down at them, his face filling with a sudden rage.

"Well, we're not giving up. Come on!" he said firmly.

Striding over to Taylor's bed, he stuffed the portable memorizer, two small SBC radios, and a handful of toothies in his backpack. Then he turned and grabbed Maggie's arm, pulling her toward the end of the dorm. As Maggie walked past the beds, she saw the darkened shapes of three girls etched on the wall next to Roosela's empty bed. Without thinking, she went to read the names written beneath each one when a growl from the shadows stopped her in her tracks.

"Are you mental?" said Stick, pulling her back with a shake of his head, "Don't you remember what she has under there?"

As Maggie turned away, she heard the growls slowly disappear as she followed Stick between the seemingly endless lines of beds that framed the dormitory. Soon her legs were tiring and she gave a relieved sigh; Stick finally waved for her to stop as they reached the end of the long room.

"Here," he said, standing by the last bed. Unlike the other beds in the dormitory this one was free of dust, its peeling paint clearly revealing the letters 'S P T R' scratched into its frame.

"This was where we tried to make our first base," he said with a smile, "didn't work of course. It meant having to walk past Roosela, and she quickly worked out what we were up to and told Devlin. But I think it should still be good for what we need."

Dipping under the bed, Maggie watched as Stick peeled back a large flap of skin that had been laid carefully over the pink flesh below. Pulling gently, he felt the small scabs that had formed, sealing its edges like lumpy glue, forcing him to pull harder until they finally popped against his strength, revealing a dark tunnel below.

Trying not to show her nerves, Maggie watched as he snapped a toothie in half before jumping inside. Sliding in behind him, she stayed close, wishing she were the one holding the light, as they crawled upward through the soft tunnel. Soon Maggie felt her legs begin to tire once more as the ceiling narrowed, forcing them both to continue forward on their bellies.

"Mildred has put on weight since I was last here," groaned Stick, squeezing around a corner. "Not much farther."

Up ahead, a light was shining dimly and Maggie dragged herself forward, hoping he was telling the truth. Finally, with one last heave, she emerged from the tunnel to find herself on a small ledge that made her gasp at the drop below. Far beneath them was the main chamber, its floor covered in neat rows of chairs facing the stage that had been built for Mildred's closing ceremony. The tiny figures of the guests dotted the floor in front of it, and one by one they made the way to their seats, unaware of the two children hidden high above by the huge memorizer screen that was showing pictures of the famous faces below.

"Good, we're not too late to find him," said Stick, pulling out a small shard of glass. Holding it up to his eye, he scoured the growing crowd below as Maggie squinted in vain at the tops of tiny heads.

"Don't you have some sort of soul magic eye superpower you can use?" said Stick with a snort, "here, try this. It's a piece of old iris, it'll help you to see."

Maggie gave him a fake scowl. Behind it a sensation of relief ran through her, happy that he wasn't treating her differently now that he knew who she was. Holding the shard of glass up to her eye, she squinted as a picture formed on its surface. No longer were the heads tiny, each one suddenly huge on the top of the glass. Slowly she moved it backward, shrinking the picture until she could see each face one by one.

"There!" she said suddenly, pointing at two tiny heads in the distance.

Far below, Ira Marsh and Miss Devlin were standing at the entrance to the main room, flashing fake smiles at anyone who would notice them. Suddenly, a smartly dressed man, surrounded by security, entered the room as Ira rushed in front of him and shook his hand before anyone could stop him.

"That's the prime minister," said Stick, leaning into Maggie. "Look at Ira. Still sucking up to anyone who'll listen!"

Below, the prime minister gave him a polite smile before moving off toward the stage. Ira looked smugly at his back. Then with a nod to Miss Devlin, they both moved across the hall, maneuvering between the other guests, as they headed toward a door marked 'EXIT.'

"Are they leaving?" said Stick urgently. "Why are they leaving? Quick. We have to get down there and stop them."

Maggie watched as Stick peeled back another loose piece of the wall. Working swiftly, he soon revealed another stretch of dark tunnel that he quickly dived into.

"After Mildred got fat I started building lots of tunnels. I never finished this one. I ran into one of the main bloodlines and had to stop. But I'm thinking we might be able to open it up a little and get inside. Then we can just swim down to the main hall. It's the quickest way."

Maggie's brow furrowed. She didn't think that much about life inside a body could still shock her, but the idea of swimming inside the tiny tubes that pulsed warm blood around Mildred sent a ripple of fear through her.

"Stick, I don't think that's a great idea. Isn't there another way down there?"

Stick stopped, refusing to answer her.

"Shhhhhhhhhhhh!" he hissed, raising his finger.

Maggie glared at his backside.

"Don't shhhh me! It's a dumb idea, alright?"

"SHHHHHHHHHHH!"

Maggie felt her anger about to burst, when she heard it. Somewhere up ahead, there were voices. Voices she recognized. Squeezing past Stick, she scrambled ahead, eager to see if she had heard correctly. The yellow walls of fat were particularly tight now, but without caring, Maggie pushed herself against their squidgy lining before emerging into a small square room, no bigger than her bed. Here, the fat in one wall had been cut, as though sharp nails had scratched long lines into it, revealing four shafts of light. Maggie pressed her face against one of them; Stick scrambled in after her and did the same.

The room on the other side was small with a boney ceiling and yellow walls. In one corner, pressed behind a large scab, stood a pile of wet fat while next to it two figures slouched back to back, their heads hung low. Maggie shifted to get a better view when one of them bobbed upward.

"Taylor!" said Stick loudly, before Maggie punched him, drawing an apologetic look.

Both of them stared as the second head lifted and flopped onto Taylor's shoulder, revealing Pritch's tired face. Between them, long slivers of grey hair had been tightly bound around their wrists, like thick wire that held them together.

The urge to scoop out the walls and free them was nearly overwhelming when Maggie heard the voice again. Slowly, it entered the room, and this time they could both see the man who was talking, his face shielded by his dark hood. Behind him, a large black creature followed, its tail slithering smoothly behind. It strode back and forth across the room.

"Marburg," said the voice. "Just be patient. Everything is going according to plan."

"Don't tell me to me patient," snarled the bacteria through pointed teeth, "I've waited long enough for this day. Ever since the kids gave me this key all I've done is wait, and I'm bored of it! It's not in my nature! I want to get up there and kill that heart! Just thinking about it is making my skin itch!"

A long forked tongue curled out and licked at tight black lips.

"Easy, Marburg," said the voice again, "we have to wait. As soon as you shut down the heart, all the exit doors will lock and we need the main chamber to be full when that happens. There will only be enough air in there to keep them alive for a little while, and with no air production they'll all be dead within the hour. Just wait until the prime minister begins his speech. The hall will be full, and hundreds of those self-inflated internals will die! The nurse has been instructed to block all the doors and windows to the old woman's room, so there's no way any rescue crews are getting into Mildred Potts, 80. The internals will only be able to watch their deaths on their memorizers, powerless to do anything to help their prime minister and his pathetic followers. That is your moment! That's when you show yourself! That's when you claim their deaths! Can you imagine how terrified they'll be when they think that you alone did all this? And that you disappeared using a key that wasn't supposed to exist...a key that gives you access to every single body out there! You'll be a legend, Marburg! Ebola... Rabies...Smallpox...Dengue...they'll all wish they could be you. The internals will watch some of their most protected people die before their very eyes, and it will all be because of you! And they'll know...if you can do this then you can do it again...and again... whenever you want. None of them will ever feel safe again!"

Marburg stared at the wall as his mind played with the idea of his glorious future.

"Yes," he said finally, a long line of green slime slipping between his smiling teeth. "I'll show them who is in charge around here. They'll cower before me!"

The voice turned, its face still hidden beneath the hood.

"Don't forget that when that day comes...and it will come...don't forget who is really in charge here, Marburg. You can have every internal in the world fearing you. You can keep that for yourself. But no matter what the internals think, it will be me who is in charge. Just as Arac predicted. It will always be me. I'll stay in the shadows and you can have all the glory you crave. Just as long as you never forget that you are here to follow me...and that's how it will always be."

Marburg spun around, his tail slapping hard into Taylor. "Yes, of course. You are in charge, Janus."

Janus turned and pulled back his hood, confirming Maggie's worst fears. Thoughts of the morning Pethora had rescued her from him flooded back. The blame he had placed on her for her father's death. His sleeping shape at the desk. The fear that had filled her as they had sneaked past him, terrified that any second he might awaken and carry out his plan to kill Maggie. All of it came rushing back as she stared at him, standing right there on the other side of the wall.

Pressing her hand against her stomach, she tried to stop the flips that had suddenly taken it over. The Janus she knew lived in a young body, his hair blond and spikey, but now she saw him for who he really was, the grey hairs betraying his old age. Only his eyes still seemed to resemble the Janus she remembered, the light within them burning bright with a look that Maggie always feared.

"What about the girls?" said Marburg eventually.

Janus paused to scratch his nose, before waving a careless hand in the virus' direction.

"Leave them here. I know you want to kill them, but there will be plenty of death for you to enjoy soon enough. Besides, they're not going anywhere. I'll have someone fetch them just in case they are needed, but I can't be bothered dragging them around anymore. It's bad enough that idiot Ira messed up and only got two of them. Now I have to go and find the other one myself. Never trust an internal to do a job properly."

Marburg fixed his disappointed eyes on the two bound girls.

"Let's hope you aren't forgotten, maybe I'll be back to check!" he hissed at them as he followed Janus out of the room.

Behind the wall, Maggie balled up her fists fighting the urge to pound them into the torn flesh. Her father would never have wanted this. He only ever wanted to help the souls live in peace with the internals, not kill them. Janus was wrong to say this was what her father wanted. He would never have ordered this. How dare he lie! And why was Ira working with him? Wasn't he working with the internals? The ones who had killed her father?

Suddenly, Stick dropped his bag and ripped at the wall. The thin slits of fat tore easily under his angry strength, and soon there was a hole big enough for them to climb through. They both sprinted across the room.

"Taylor, Pritch, wake up. Now, please! We have to go!" he urged, pulling at the strands of grey hair that bound their wrists.

Pritch eased her head upward as Taylor snapped to life.

"Is that your breath? You really need to brush your teeth once in a while," she said with a smile.

Stick stared back with a grin that he rarely showed her.

"What's going on?" said Pritch sleepily.

Maggie helped them up as Stick returned to the hole and rummaged in his bag. There was a sudden crackle as the memorizer glowed to life.

"What are you doing? This is no time for memories!" said Maggie, "we have to stop that virus before he kills everyone."

Pritch stared at her, confused, as Taylor seemed to be lost in thought.

"I know we have to stop him!" said Stick, "that's why I'm trying to see if all the guests are here. They said nothing would happen until they had all arrived."

Crowding the small screen, Maggie, Stick, and Pritch watched impatiently as the screen on the memorizer slowly sharpened into a picture of the main cavity. Taylor rubbed at the red marks on her wrists. Many of the guests had already taken their seats, and only a few empty places remained as everyone stared at the large monitor overhead. The faint sound of someone commentating drifted from the memorizer; its picture changed to show what everyone was looking at.

"Hey!" said Pritch suddenly, "look! They're showing the day Malcolm asked Mildred to marry him. That's our favorite."

Taylor leaned in to see. The huge screen flickered over the heads of the guests, when suddenly it changed to a video of Malcolm lying on his deathbed, Mildred by his side.

"Hang on. That's new; they never showed that bit before. Is that a new memory? I thought we'd seen them all?"

Malcolm whispered something into Mildred's ear, making her cry, as the commentator began furiously apologizing for technical difficulties. Below, the audience stared glumly up, surprised to be watching such a sad memory at a celebration, as an internal at the back of the hall worked furiously to try to change the memory back.

"I've definitely never seen that memory before. She can't be remembering more, can she? Not now?" said Pritch.

A frustrated Maggie stabbed at the memorizer's 'off' button. "We haven't got time for this. Look, they are all here! We have to stop Marburg!"

Stick pushed the memorizer back into his bag, and pulled it over his shoulder.

"What are we supposed to do?" said Pritch, looking confused, "How are we supposed to stop a virus like that? Shouldn't we go get help? We can't stop it. This isn't a job for us, we're just kids. We need to get the anti-bodies."

Stick glanced at Maggie, wondering if he should tell them her secret. She was far from just any kid.

"Pritch is right," said Maggie suddenly, "but we have to try. You two get down to the main chamber and warn everyone. Tell them to get out of Mildred while they can. Stick and I will go after Marburg and Janus. If we hear anything, we'll call you on these."

Spinning Stick around, she grabbed one of the small SBC radios from his backpack and pushed it into Pritch's hand. Taylor looked at her coldly for a second, as though unsure if this was something she wanted to do.

"Okay," she said finally, "we'll call you when we get down there."

Stick bobbed his head around the entry door, then he pointed to the hole in the wall.

"Go left and keep crawling down. Don't try and swim down the bloodstream, it's a terrible idea. Just keep going forward. You'll come out in the janitor's closet behind the stage. Tell them that Mildred's heart is about to stop and to get out now. And tell them...tell them Mildred might not be ready to die after all."

Maggie forced a confused smile as Pritch and Taylor climbed up into the hole.

"Good luck."

"You, too. Both of you," said Taylor, glancing at her brother.

Malcolm, the bad dreams are back. I know you wouldn't say it's a bad dream, but you aren't the one who has to wake up crying. Last night's dream was about the night you died. When you pulled me in and told me that you loved me for the last time. Then you told me that you wanted me to be happy. That you wanted me to keep going...for you. The same thing you told me in your note. I don't like that memory. Not now, when I feel that I'm so close to the end...when I know that it's too late.

26

A Lethal Injection

Stick raised his hand, insisting that they rest.

The climb to the heart was usually easy for him, but behind Maggie's relentless pace he had soon found himself breathlessly struggling to keep up.

"Are you sure you don't have special powers?" he said wheezing.

Maggie grabbed his arm and pulled him onward. The thought of Janus's betrayal of her father filled her mind, flooding her with energy.

"Come on!" she said, "Taylor just called me on the radio. She said she saw Ira and Devlin leaving on a fruit fly. They must be about to start their plan. Any second now they might shut down Mildred's heart and lock all the doors. We're running out of time!"

Up ahead, a large archway with the words HEART - RESTRICTED stood before them, the large door that usually filled its entry lying uselessly next to it on the floor. On top of it, the figures of four dead anti-body security guards lay lifeless, their peaceful faces speckled with black. As if they had gone to sleep and simply forgotten to breathe.

Knowing it was too late to help them, Maggie vaulted over the broken door; Stick followed closely behind. Once inside, they were consumed by a darkness that forced them both to a sudden halt. Up ahead, a small glowing red light dared them to keep going. Knowing there was no other way, they both stared through the darkness at the pink walls that oozed a yellowing liquid, the scars of a recent battle.

Stick swung the bag from his back and pulled out the memorizer. Turning it around, he waited for it to glow into life, the dull light from its screen just enough to guide them forward. Glancing back, Maggie saw the prime minister and Thaddeus Miles walking across the stage, the audience applauding furiously as the two men made their way to a white podium at the front.

"We have to hurry!" she whispered.

Rounding the hallway, they felt the pounding of Mildred's huge heart rippling up through their feet. Then it was before them, towering overhead like a monster that swelled to life, its walls shining with a pink slime glowing between the patches of fat that checkered the once perfect surface. At its top sat a large pink bulb that was steadily glowing brighter, as though something inside it was being born, when suddenly the light crackled. It released a blade of white that shot down the middle of the heart, lighting up the room as it was received by another bulb at the base.

It was here that Marburg stood, his alien shape suddenly silhouetted by the burst of electricity that slowly faded into nothing before him.

Maggie stood hidden in the doorway. The race to get here had been fueled with thoughts of revenge, but now that they had arrived she realized she had no clue what to do. Worse still, Janus was gone. Whatever she did now would not stop him, leaving him free to continue spreading his lies about her father.

"Ladies and Gentlemen of the internal world," said a distant voice from the memorizer, "we are here today to say goodbye to Mildred Potts, 80. A body that has been so much more than just a body. She has been a home, a place of work, a place of fun, a place of shelter, a place of kindness."

Maggie felt herself lost in the words as her thoughts turned to the day she met Mildred. Poor, broken Mildred. Her home. Their home.

"I have an idea!" said Stick, snapping her back, "you distract him while I sneak around and hit him on the head with the memorizer. That should stop him. At least until Pritch and Taylor can warn everyone."

Maggie looked at him blankly, searching her mind for an alternative.

"Okay," she finally said, pulling on her shirt, "but go quickly, I don't know how long I'll be able to keep him talking."

Stepping out from the shadows, she felt her insides tremble, as Marburg stood motionless, his eyes feasting on the heart before him. Out of the corner of her eye, Maggie saw Stick ducking through the shadows that circled the room's edge; a long black nail ran down the length of the guardrail, separating Marburg from Mildred's heart.

"Marburg," said Maggie timidly.

Marburg stood motionless, still staring at the heart as another bolt of electricity shot in front of him.

"MARBURG!" said Maggie firmly.

The long black tail twitched, before sliding to one side like a curtain as Marburg slowly turned. His eyes glowed red with a fury that sent a chill through the small girl who stood before him.

"Hello, child! How lovely to see you again," he sneered.

Maggie took a step forward and tried to stare back at him, before her fear pulled her eyes down to her feet.

"Marburg, please don't do this, please," she said meekly.

His black shape glided over until he was so close that his rotting breath filled her lungs.

"So, Maggie, did you find your powers yet? Or are you a nothing like they say? Of course you are, otherwise why haven't you stopped me already? I hear you've become rather sweet on this old lady? That you've made friends with the internals? So I presume that's why you're here, to stop me killing them?"

Maggie's fear mixed with confusion. How did he know these things?

Over his shoulder, she saw Stick moving silently behind him. The plan was working. She had to keep him talking.

"Marburg, I don't know what Janus told you, but this is not what my father would want you to do. He wouldn't want you to kill internals. He wasn't like that!"

Marburg threw back his head and released a laugh that filled the huge room with its crackle.

"You really think he wouldn't want me to do this? To kill them? The same man who created the paralysis elixir? The very potion that allows souls without powers to control the internals in their body. How do you think they do it, Maggie? Have you been inside a body controlled by the paralysis elixir? Do you know what it does to the internals? How it controls them, makes them into slaves? Can you imagine what it's like to be in constant pain and not be able to make a sound? To only watch as you follow orders, unable to stop yourself? And you think your father, the man who made it possible, would care what happens to these internals?"

Maggie wanted to scream, to tell him that he was lying, but something inside told her to listen. The bottles that filled her father's office. Her never being allowed into any of the bodies controlled by the others in the house. Thaddeus Miles talking about the pain of being controlled. It all made sense. But that would mean her father had lied to her. No! It wasn't true. It couldn't be true.

Anger curled her insides as a blade of fury shot up her spine, swelling her tiny shape, as she suddenly felt huge against Marburg's lying red eyes. Curious about this new passion, he leaned in closer when, without warning, the floor burst upward releasing a furious cannon of blood. Powerless against its force, Marburg felt himself thrown high as he crashed against the boney ceiling, the blood pounding against him, pinning him like a rag doll. Then, just as quickly as it was gone, the river of blood fell back into the hole as Marburg crashed in a twisted heap on the floor next to it. Maggie took a deep breath. Marburg was motionless. His limbs lay awkwardly broken at his sides, and as she walked over to him she felt the blood that surrounded him pool beneath her feet. The urge to vomit began to overwhelm her as she stared down at his dead body. Suddenly, the red eyes clicked opened as his rising head stared back. Pulling himself upright, he slowly clicked his body back into shape, bone by bone, until all his loose limbs snapped into their homes.

"Why, Maggie," he sneered between brown lips, "it seems they were wrong about your powers, but it takes a lot more than that to kill me."

The footsteps behind him came rapidly as Stick emerged from the shadows, holding the memorizer over his head. His scream bounced off the walls as he ran, and before Marburg could react, Stick was behind him, crashing the memorizer down onto his curved skull as it found its target, before bouncing to one side. Stick closed his eyes against the blow before opening them, expecting to see Marburg crumble to the floor. But the black shape hadn't moved. He was still standing, motionless, like a statue that was trying to understand what had just happened. Then, Marburg slowly curled the corner of his mouth into a smile and laughed.

Stick stood frozen in shock with his teeth clamped firmly over his lip. The red eyes met his, and for a moment they stood staring at each other. Then, Marburg slowly curled out a long fingernail and raised it to Stick's chest. The touch was almost silent, only the sound of a tiny pop revealing that any contact had been made. Then, Stick looked over at Maggie as the light drained from his eyes. She stared back at him, wanting time to stop, desperate to halt what she knew was about to happen. But it was too late. Stick fell to the floor.

Marburg looked down at him as though he was an annoying obstacle, before stepping over his body. Maggie ran forward and fell to her knees as the draining pool of blood circled around her. Pulling Stick forward, she willed him to be alive, wanting desperately to be wrong, but the slightest touch told her that it was too late. The warmth of his skin was already draining away as a web of black began to spread beneath its dead surface.

"STICK!" screamed Maggie, "STICK!"

Stick's dying eyes looked up at her as a single tear of blood ran down his cheek. Maggie's mind spun, searching for anything that could help, but there were only blank spaces where she needed answers that would save her best friend. Why didn't she know what to do? Helplessness flooded over her as she sat there, waiting.

Marburg reached the barrier at the base of the heart and walked around it, dismissing several warning signs that stood between him and the huge bulb. Another shot of electricity glowed on its surface, and for a second he stood motionless as though he had changed his mind. Then, he raised his hand, this time unfurling all four claws, and took aim. Driving hard he stabbed the black fingers deep inside its flesh as another bolt of electricity struck home, throwing him backward. Prepared for it, he pushed back against the blow with his tail as, once more, he thrust forward sending his hand even farther inside.

For a second, Mildred's heart continued to throb as though Marburg's exertions had been for nothing. Then, it released a shiver and skipped a beat before seeming to correct itself. Then it skipped again…and again. The blackness of the virus' skin spread upward, coloring the pink surface beneath its web. Then, Marburg forced himself deeper inside as his elbow felt the warmth of Mildred's dying heart, and he threw back his head and released a scream of delight.

A last bolt of electricity tried to shoot its way home, but was lost in the blackness that consumed everything. Then, it stopped. No more flashes of light came. The job was done. Mildred's heart was no longer beating. She was dead.

Oblivious to it all, Maggie held Stick tight, willing him to be all right. He looked up at her behind blood filled eyes. With a great effort, he coughed as though he was trying to speak. Maggie leaned close to him, trying to hear what he was saying.

"Save Taylor…Pritch…." he wheezed.

Maggie looked down at him and nodded as her tears fell onto his face. Then his eyes were suddenly cold. The life in them had left. He was dead.

Marburg strolled casually over as Maggie sat in shocked silence. The key that the children had delivered to him hung loosely on a chain around his neck, and as he bent down he touched it softly as though it were a medal for all his good work. Then, after glancing at Stick, he looked at Maggie without bothering to hide how little he cared about the dead boy in her arms.

"Oh well," he said casually, "He was as good as dead anyway. Now that I've shut down this old bag's heart, there will only be enough air to last an hour. Maybe even less. I might have even done him a favor, making it quick, not like those poor fools down there."

Maggie looked over at the memorizer that still glowed faintly in a pool of blood beside her. A large crack had spread down the middle of the screen, and behind it she could see the main chamber, its floor covered in upturned chairs. All around the crack, panic was born as the internals crowded under signs that read 'EXIT' and they pounded uselessly on the doors.

"See? See how pitiful they are? Now that I've stopped the heart, all of this body's exits are sealed. There's no escape for them now. Well, not without one of these," he said, tapping at the key around his bony neck, "They're trapped in here, and yet still they choose to act like that? They should accept their fate. They aren't important and they shouldn't act as though they are. Their choice has been made for them. They should be grateful that they are going to die. Now you on the other hand, you still have a choice. You undoubtedly have powers. The question is, will you choose to use them? Do you save yourself, or do you die here…with your friends?"

Marburg ran the back of a long finger down the side of Stick's dead face until Maggie slapped his hand away.

"Goodbye, Maggie Pincus," he said, rising up onto his black feet. "Maybe we'll see each other again. Maybe we won't. I don't really care."

Maggie held Stick tight as the black shape disappeared behind her. The pain of her father's death flooded her insides once again, returning to the home it knew so well. It was all too much for her. She wasn't strong enough to handle this. It hurt too much. Distant screams were coming from the memorizer as panic began to take up precious space in the sealed chamber. Through her tears, Maggie looked over at the broken screen to see two solitary figures standing in the center of the chamber, both staring up at the screen that showed Malcolm's frozen face above them. As if they alone had made peace with what was about to happen. As though they knew it was already too late.

Stick's final words filled Maggie's mind, pushing back her self-pity.

"Save Taylor...Pritch."

She couldn't stay here. She didn't want to leave but she knew that she had to. She didn't know how, but she had to try and save them. She had to. Something inside her told her that she would find a way. She had to go. Slowly she lowered Stick's body to floor and pressed her head against his. Then, with more strength than she thought she had, she scooped up the memorizer and ran toward the staircase; Stick lay motionless behind her.

She had to get to Mildred.

Malcolm, I'm so tired. I just want this to end... flies everywhere...but I don't care anymore. I just want this to end. I want to see you.

27

Unresponsive

As she reached the top step, Maggie willed her tired legs to keep moving. Every second felt like a minute and she cursed herself for not being faster when so many lives depended on her. The door to the mind hung limply on one hinge, and she sprinted inside its entrance as the heat hit her like a wall. For a second, she hesitated, gathering the nerve to walk into the fiery globe that hung in the middle of the room. All around her the burning sensation screamed at her to go back, but she had to keep going. She needed to see Mildred. If it wasn't too late.

"Hello, Maggie."

Maggie froze as the cloaked figure stepped in front of her. Fear spilled through her insides and tickled her throat as she tried to think. Then it was gone, replaced by anger, as she remembered what Janus had said. How he had lied to Marburg about her father.

Slowly, the cloaked figure raised a hand to pull back its hood. Maggie's mind spun with all the things she so desperately wanted to say to him. The man who had betrayed her father.

"I've missed you so much!"

As the hood dropped back, all of Maggie's thoughts dissolved. The perfect face of Pethora was smiling down at her before rushing forward, pulling her into a familiar hug.

"How? It's…I can't stop!" stammered Maggie, reluctantly pulling away.

Pethora's perfume hung between them, pressing Maggie's memory into happier times that she had shared with this soul. A soul who had saved her life.

"Wait here," stammered Maggie, "I mean, don't go…I mean, go. It's not safe here. Janus has a plan. Everyone in Mildred is going to die. You have to leave. I don't know how. All the doors are locked. I don't know how to open them. I have to try and get to

Mildred…to make her want to live again. Then the doors will open!"

Pethora stared down at her with the same smile that always made Maggie feel safe. As though something good was about to happen.

"It's okay," said Pethora brightly, "I'm here to take you away. Just like I promised I would. You don't have to worry. I know how to get you out of here."

Maggie stared up at her.

"You do? That's incredible. I have to tell Taylor and Pritch! They can tell everyone else. The SBC radio —I still have it! But I still need to get to Mildred… Stick…."

Rummaging through her bag, Maggie looked for the SBC radio when her eyes met Pethora's. Her perfect blue eyes stared back at her, blinking heavily as though something was wrong. Maggie felt the pain of saying Stick's name.

"Taylor and Pritch, they'll be fine," said Pethora, pulling her into another hug, "and you. You will be fine, too. You've just come off the tracks a little. Forgotten what all of this is about. I just need to get you home so you can remember who you are—and what it is we're fighting for."

Maggie pushed herself away, trying to understand, when she saw her SBC radio in Pethora's hand. Following her gaze, Pethora looked down at the small black box as Maggie watched her, helpless to stop what was about to happen. Then it was gone, Pethora threw it effortlessly behind her where it touched the fiery wave of heat around Mildred's mind, before disappearing. Only a last few drops of melted plastic lingered before they, too, evaporated on the floor below.

"You need to remember who you are, Maggie. The internals are our enemy. We are at war here. This…." she said with a sweep of her perfectly manicured hand, "This is just part of that war. Today is a good day for us. Can't you see why this has to happen? Don't you remember what the internals did to us? What your father taught you?"

Maggie took another step back. Everything was turning upside down. Stick was dead. Pethora wanted her to let all the internals die. Nothing made sense.

"You said you'd come for me once you'd found my body," she said finally.

Pethora let out an unfamiliar laugh.

"That old thing? You don't need that body. With your powers and the elixir you can have any body you want! Why would you want that one back? We didn't even bother keeping it!"

Maggie stood in silence.

"Don't you understand?" continued Pethora, "We didn't put you here to be safe. We put you here so that we could test your powers. That's why you're in this antique! We had to see for ourselves if you could be of any use to us. Your father didn't think you had any powers, but he was wrong. You have powers and you can help us win this war. You can free souls! This was all a test, and you passed with flying colors!"

Pethora smiled as though she was revealing an amazing gift. Maggie only felt the seconds dripping away. Sensing something was wrong, Pethora spread herself wide blocking Maggie's path.

"So this test…to see if I had powers? What if I hadn't passed, what then?" said Maggie, trying to think of what to do, "and what about everything today. All the internals that are going to die…is that part of the test? Is it all because of me?"

Pethora's smile widened. "Well, not just you, Maggie. I mean, we never knew that all of this would happen when we put you in here, but let's just call it a lucky bonus!"

A feeling of revolt ran through Maggie as she looked at Pethora. Suddenly, she didn't seem so beautiful anymore. All at once, the heat from Mildred's mind invaded the space between them, and Pethora's smile disappeared.

"Look, Maggie," she said coldly, "there are a lot of things happening here that you don't understand yet. Things that I will explain later. But, for now, can we just get out of here before this old woman shuts down for good?"

Maggie stared up into Pethora's perfect face. "No."

Pethora blinked in shock, as though she didn't understand the word, and for a second she hesitated, biting her lip as though she was trying to keep something inside.

"Oh, Maggie, you've just been here too long. You've started thinking of the internals as your friends. But they are not. They are here to serve us. They are beneath us, but they insist on thinking otherwise. Our job is to teach them their place. Don't you see that? They are like naughty children and we are their parents. They need to be punished, they need us to give them structure so that they can grow to fulfill their potential—to serve us."

Maggie glared at her. Stepping forward, she went to push past her, only to feel Pethora push her backward with surprising strength. Maggie hit the wall behind her hard as Pethora's flawless hands drove into her shoulders, pinning her firmly, as strands of shining blonde hair fell free, her faultless face twisting in anger.

"YOU WILL DO AS I SAY!" she roared, "I'M IN CHARGE HERE, NOT YOU! MAKE NO MISTAKE! THIS USELESS OLD WOMAN IS DEAD AND THE INTERNALS INSIDE HER ARE NEXT. WE ARE LEAVING NOW! SO DO AS I SAY…OR ELSE!"

Maggie pushed with all her strength, but it was useless. It was as though Pethora was made of iron.

"Please, don't do this. I'll come with you. But first let me talk to Mildred. You said it yourself. Killing the internals was never part of the plan, it was just a lucky bonus. So why not let me try to make her want to live? I promise I'll come back. If you don't believe me, then come with me."

Pethora's eyebrows curled upward as if Maggie had just insulted her.

"No two souls can be in the mind at the same time! How stupid do you think I am? It would be certain death to try to walk through that wall of fire if there was already another soul in there!"

Maggie stared, confused.

"But, I swear I've done it before! Let me go in and talk to her. If it doesn't work then I'll try to connect to her body myself. I want to save them. Stick told me to help them. I need to do this. Please, let me do this. Then I'll do whatever you want."

The anger in Pethora's face washed away, and her grip softened.

"Oh, Maggie. You have so much to learn," she said, her voice soft once more, "you can't connect with her. It's too late. Don't you remember? What happens to a body we're in control of happens to us, too. This old woman's heart has stopped. If you connect with her, then you'll be just as dead as she is. It would be suicide. I'm sorry. My answer is no. You are too important to us now. So come on, let's go. Now!"

Pethora stepped back as Maggie nodded her head in surrender. The heat was rising and the cool of the doorway beckoned in welcome, as they both turned to leave. Pethora pulled back her hair as they walked, twisting the loose strands expertly back into place, before slipping it inside her cloak. But as she raised her hood, Maggie saw her chance. Ducking low, she spun quickly, bolting back toward the fiery wall with all the energy she had left. Pethora whipped at the space behind her. With all her might, Maggie ran until she was just steps away from Mildred's mind. The heat stung her face, and again her thoughts screamed at her to stop. Instinctively, she raised her hands before the wall of fire when a weight hit her from behind like a rock, buckling her knees. For a second, Maggie felt herself falling, before her legs found the strength to straighten. Above her, Pethora was screaming wildly as her fingers scratched at Maggie's neck, demanding her to stop. The weight was too much to bear. As she took another step, she stumbled again as Pethora's legs tangled themselves inside hers. Once more, the heat on her skin screamed at her to stop, but again she pushed back, forcing herself to try to reach the other side of the wall.

"STOP!" shrieked Pethora.

With everything she had left, Maggie threw herself forward. For an instant, they both hung in the air, each of them flying toward the circle of fire, until Pethora's screams suddenly turned to pain. Twisting upward, Maggie saw her attacker's perfect hands begin to burn as they hit the fiery barrier. Time seemed to freeze as their eyes locked. Pethora's stare howled at

Maggie as she touched the white wall, before her skin instantly began to bubble as the wall that ate hungrily at her face threw her backward. Then, just as quickly she was gone, forced backward by the brain wave as Maggie slipped inside, leaving the fire behind her.

The pain of hitting the ground was gratefully received as Maggie felt the cold floor against her palms. Rolling onto her back, she tried to gather her mind away from what had just happened as her body tingled with urgency. She squinted and told herself to focus, before opening her eyes to see the glowing cord that hung from the center of the ceiling. Trailing it downward, she looked for Mildred, only to see it hanging empty.

"Malcolm," whimpered a voice.

Maggie climbed to her feet, relieved to see Mildred sat in the corner, sobbing into her hands.

"Malcolm," she whispered again, "I'm so sorry, Malcolm."

Maggie knelt next to her, feeling overwhelmed at what she needed to persuade Mildred to do.

"Mildred," she said gently, touching her arm.

Mildred looked up. Tears dripped over her quivering lip, behind the grey strands of hair that framed her puffy blue eyes. Maggie stared into them, hoping that she would recognize her, but saw only sadness.

"I failed him!" she sobbed. "He wanted me to live a good life and I wasted it!"

Maggie looked down at her. Her insides told her to tell her that it would all be okay, but her thoughts screamed that there was no time. She had to do this quickly.

"Mildred! You can't give up! You have to try again!" she said, grasping her shoulders, "you can reconnect. You can keep living. It's your body! It does what you tell it to! It shut down because of Marburg, but you can fight that. I know you can. You can make it work again. It listens to you. You can do this!"

"No…no…no…NO!" screamed Mildred, "It's too late. Everything has shut down. I don't know what's happening. I don't know how this works. I don't understand. I just know that this is it…this is the end."

In desperation, Maggie grabbed her backpack and pulled out the broken memorizer. On the screen, the picture slowly faded to life as Malcolm's face appeared on the ceiling of the main chamber. Beneath him, the bodies of the internals littered the floor as they struggled for air. Mildred wiped at her tears, wanting to see her husband clearly, when suddenly his face changed from its frozen state, and he began to whisper.

"I love you, you have to keep living, whatever it takes I only want you to be happy. Whatever it takes, you need to do it for me."

Mildred stared as fresh tears dripped onto the dead face behind the screen.

"This memory appeared today for the first time. I know you've been thinking of it, it's been playing over and over," said Maggie gently, "I know you're scared, but this is what he wanted. You can't keep this inside anymore; you can't pretend it didn't happen. He wanted you to be happy. He wanted you to live! It's not too late. You have to try."

Mildred ran her hand down the side of Malcolm's face on the memorizer. A small smile appeared, and suddenly her tears stopped, as he looked directly up at her.

"I love you," repeated Malcolm.

A sudden hope filled Maggie as his words seemed to sink into Mildred.

"I love you, too," said Mildred.

Raising her hand, she reached up to touch the face of her dead husband behind the glass, when suddenly she stopped, her hand falling like a great weight to the floor.

"But I can't do this, I'm sorry, I just can't," she said.

Suddenly, Malcolm was spinning away as Mildred grasped the memorizer and threw it against the wall. His voice filled the room one last time as the cracked screen gave way and smashed into pieces against the white wall, before dropping into silence on the floor below.

"Whatever it takes…."

Maggie looked at Mildred, realizing it was over. Once more, the confused blue eyes were staring back at her, broken. Then, the tears were there once more, pouring out, as Mildred rolled onto her side.

"I can't…I just can't," she whimpered.

Maggie stood frozen. She had failed. There was only one thing left to try. She had to try to connect to Mildred's body herself, even if it was suicide. A voice inside her told her to run, that she could still escape with Pethora and Janus, but she pushed it aside. She couldn't leave. She had to try. She had to keep her promise to Stick.

At her feet, Mildred was sobbing now, crying uncontrollably into her wrinkled hands, as Maggie willed herself to be angry with her. She thought of all those who would die, all the internals in the main chamber below who were running out of air. How they would die because she was too weak to try to live. But, as she looked at Mildred, she knew it wasn't true. This wasn't her fault. This was the work of Marburg, and Janus, and Pethora…and her. They had done it all to test her. She had to try.

With shaking hands, she turned and crossed to the glowing cord that hung from the ceiling. Inside it, tiny rods of light dangled limply as they waited to dig their way deep inside her head. Fear at what she was about to do overwhelmed her. This was the last chance and she had to try. Grasping the cord with two hands, she plunged it downward until she felt the tiny rods of light bite at her skin. Suddenly, a pain filled her chest, curling her toes into tight balls inside her shoes, and she felt herself falling backward into a dark hole. Above, she could see the room spinning away as the pain increased. Flailing her arms, she tried desperately to grab anything that would save her, but the darkness offered no help. The room was nearly gone now, its light just a star above that was quickly disappearing. Then it, too, dissolved. All was black. There was nothing.

Malcolm...why, Malcolm...why? You know I'm not strong enough. You were the strong one. Why can't you just let me join you? Why must you keep reminding me that I've failed you? I'm not strong enough. I keep telling you that I can't do this without you, but you keep telling me I have to. Why?

28

Infected

'BANG! BANG! BANG!'

Maggie sucked in a breath, and her eyes flicked open. The light hurt, but the tingling pain in her head demanded that she keep them open. Confusion choked her as she tried to make sense of the tiny TV, and the small mantle piece covered in shrunken photos, and a single birthday card floating below her feet. Everything seemed familiar, and yet, she couldn't place any of it. A buzzing fly shot by, startling her, before the demand to close her eyes came again, forcing her to fight as she strained against it. Something was telling her that she had to stay here.

'BANG!'

She was in Mildred's living room! The pictures, the TV, she was used to seeing them all when she was tiny, but now they were the small things. She was the one towering over them!

'BANG!'

She was inside Mildred! She was Mildred Potts, 80!

'BANG!'

Her joy quickly disappeared as she remembered why she was here. She had to save them. She had to make Mildred work again. But the banging called her.

'BANG!'

There it was again, from behind the door in the kitchen. Someone was thumping on the door. There were voices, too. Someone was shouting, calling her name.

"MILDRED! MILDRED POTTS! CAN YOU HEAR ME? SOMEONE CALLED US. THEY SAID YOU NEED HELP, BUT WE NEED YOU TO OPEN THE DOOR, MILDRED. WE CAN'T MOVE IT!"

Maggie turned to look into the kitchen, but found herself frozen. Nothing would move. Once more, she tried, but again, Mildred's head refused to turn. The pain in her chest returned as her mind filled with panic. She had to move. She had to get help. Desperately, she formed a picture of herself pushing the huge head with her tiny hands, turning it like a gigantic boulder as a tingle of electricity filled her spine.

'Move, move, MOVE!' her mind screamed.

Suddenly, the mantelpiece disappeared as the doorway to the kitchen filled her view. Now, she could see the blue light of a distant ambulance flashing between thick boards that had been nailed over the window. Next to it, the door was shaking as someone pounded on it from the other side, desperately trying to move the unseen chair that was jammed under the door handle.

'BANG!'

"MILDRED! I NEED YOU TO OPEN THE DOOR!"

'BANG! BANG!'

Suddenly, Maggie's confusion was gone, she knew what she had to do. She had to get to whoever was out there. They could save her. Save Mildred. Save everyone.

Once more, she willed Mildred to move with all her strength and was rewarded with just a wiggle of her toes. Again she tried, but everything was too heavy. She was the muscles now, tiny Maggie, powering the whole body with her mind, like an ant trying to push a bus up a hill. Angrily, she willed her to move once more as a rush of energy ran through her. One of Mildred's legs moved out from under the covers. Quickly, she demanded her other leg to move. A rush of triumph filled her as both feet swung over the side of the bed. The effort was exhausting, but finally she managed to sit up, ready to take a breath before attempting to walk to the door. A sudden pain grasped her neck. There was no air. Again she tried to take a breath, only to feel her throat tighten as it sucked uselessly at the huge lungs below. Looking down, Maggie saw Mildred's limp chest refusing to work. Panic filled her, and she lifted a wrinkled hand and grasped at her nightshirt while Mildred's old nails clawed at her throat, begging for precious air. Suddenly the blackness returned, slowly dissolving everything she could see.

'BANG!'

'NO!' she screamed silently to herself.

"MILDRED! YOU NEED TO OPEN THE DOOR, MILDRED!"

'DO IT NOW! NOW!' she silently demanded.

Something hit her between her eyes; a burning sensation bounded through Mildred's body. A sudden strength filled her, and she pushed herself upward and staggered forward toward the door. The blackness was still creeping into her sight, but between its hollows she saw her goal floating in its center. She had to open the door.

"MILDRED!"

She had to get to them. She had to. But now the strength was leaving just as quickly as it had come, pouring out of her like an upturned bucket. The blackness was winning. She wasn't going to make it. Somewhere in the distance she could hear the banging on the door and she searched her vision trying to find it. There it was! The door…but it was too far away. She was too weak. Thoughts of the internals inside her dying, Stick's body, Pritch and Taylor gasping for air, Malcolm's last words, everything filled her. She wasn't going to make it.

Anger overtook her again as the thought of Janus and Pethora choked her mind. This was all her fault. All the lies that she had been told, she had believed them all, and now her friends were going to die.

A scream filled the room, and Maggie realized it was coming from Mildred's mouth. Her mouth.

"MILDRED? MILDRED, IS THAT YOU?" said the voice behind the door.

All the pain bursted out of Maggie as a rush of electricity exploded in her chest. Every sense inside her crackled, and she felt Mildred's body throw itself toward the back door with all her strength. In the center of the blackness, she saw a wrinkled hand reaching desperately for the chair that was blocking her only hope. Forward, she flew as the electricity burned through her chest, demanding that she reach it. Then, she was there, her finger touching the wooden leg, making it move. She grasped at it, knowing that she had to push it farther. Then, perhaps…perhaps they could save her.

With all the strength she had left, Maggie willed the old body forward, watching as the boney old finger bent backwards as it tried to hold on. But it was no good, the chair didn't move. Now, she was falling away, away from her last hope. She tried to scream, but nothing came. There was only the sound of a hard slap as Maggie watched Mildred's hand fall uselessly onto the kitchen's cold tiles.

"MILDRED?"

But Mildred could not reply. Maggie could not reply. She could only look up at the chair that remained firmly jammed under the door handle, locking everyone out. Then, that, too, was gone, swallowed by the blackness that returned to consume everything. It had won. She had failed. Mildred Potts, 80 and Maggie Pincus were going to die.

Taylor and Pritch lay next to each other in the main chamber, looking up at the memorizer. Moments before, Malcolm's last words had fallen silent and the screen faded to black. Beneath it, the bodies of hundreds of internals lay gasping on the floor, all of them too weak to move without the precious air they needed so badly. With the last of her energy, Taylor rolled onto her side and looked at Pritch. Both of them lay motionless as Taylor tried uselessly to read her friend's private thoughts. Then, Pritch reached out to hold her hand. Grasping it tightly, Taylor smiled and rolled onto her back. Then, they both closed their eyes and waited.

Marburg stood on the kitchen counter, three cloaked figures standing next to him, as they all looked down at the giant old body that had just crashed to floor in the valley below. A smile crept across his black face as he studied his masterpiece. One of the cloaks turned as though about to say something, only to be silenced by another's raised hand. Quiet had been demanded, and without a word they all turned and walked toward the wasp that sat buzzing behind them. It was time to celebrate.

Mildred lay silently in the dark of her mind. The air was cold and everything had gone black. Her mind told her to look for an escape, but something else told her to wait. It wouldn't be long now. From out of the darkness she heard a pop, and then, suddenly, there was bright light that hung in the air, calling to her. Silhouetted against it, stood a shadowy figure, its small body swaying from side to side. Then, it was gone, falling out of sight into the shadows below. Now, there was just the light. The bright light that called her name. She needed to listen. She needed to go into the light. It was time for her to leave this place.

Malcolm, it's dark and cold. I think I'm dying. There's a light...a bright light. It's calling me. There's someone there. I can't see their face. Is it you? Is that you waving to me? I can't tell. They've fallen. There's just the light now, calling me, but something feels different. The pain is gone. I understand now. I understand why. I'm ready, but it's too late.

29

Awakening

The lights above the sign flickered, flashing the words 'HEART-RESTRICTED' for only the empty hallway to see. Inside, the walls were becoming cold as wet drips formed, creating tiny streams that ran down the black heart, hanging limp like a deflated balloon. Beneath it, Stick's skinny body lay motionless like a forgotten toy; his blank eyes stared up at nothing.

Then, it came.

At first, the fizzing disappeared as quickly as it had come. Then it returned, only this time it was louder than before. Without warning, it was joined by a crackling that swept down the walls, filling the roof with sparkling electricity. More followed, fighting for space, until the electricity danced angrily with itself. The crackling was deafening now, then a torrent of electricity burst inward, dwarfing what had been there just before. Hungry for space, the flood of light filled the chamber, sweeping Stick's body upward as it flipped him over and over. His dead hands flapped uselessly against his face. Spinning through the air, his body was driven against Mildred's dead heart, unable to resist, as he was held firmly in its center by the electricity that swarmed him like thousands of tiny fingers.

Now, the white hands seemed to call for help as more electricity danced towards him, their crackling nails stabbing at the heart's black walls. A burning smell arose as the fingers worked hard, skillfully picking at the black shell as they peeled it like a boiled egg. Soon, its job was done as the last of the blackness fell away, leaving a raw pink ball that hung limp, the tiny figure of Stick still pressed into its side. Seeming to sense that its work was done, the electricity left, pouring out of the doorway until it was gone as quickly as it had arrived. Without the tiny hands to hold him, Stick's body fell hard to the floor, slumping awkwardly. It was surrounded by the gentle fizzing of the last of the pools of blood drying into crust. Then, there was silence.

Everything seemed to have been washed clean and, yet, still death remained. Then something flickered. Stick's eyes went wide and stared. Above him, the huge surface of the pink heart wall was trembling as though it was about to fall. Then, he saw it, the pink bulb at its top. It was glowing.

The light called to Mildred, pulling her forward. Slowly, she got to her feet as though hypnotized, and walked toward it, powerless against its call. Stepping closer, she could see tiny images emerge from its shine, pictures of her life that talked to her, telling her to come home. A feeling of peace overwhelmed her as they drew her in, each one making her happier than the last as they played out memories of happier times. The face of Malcolm danced close to hers before disappearing to be replaced by other familiar faces. Her mother, her father, her sisters, her brother, her friends. They were all here talking to her. Everything screamed at her to go forward and join them, when her foot hit something and she looked down to see the body of a young girl she recognized lying motionless below. Instantly, everything came rushing back. This was the girl who had told her that Malcolm wanted her to live, how it wasn't too late…how there was still time.

Without thinking, she bent and scooped the body up in her arms before turning away from the light. Walking toward the wall, she watched without surprise as it split wide, as though under some silent command, as she carried Maggie away from the heat outside to lay her down in the cool hallway just beyond. With a pause, she looked down at Maggie's frozen face before sweeping back a strand of brown hair that was curled across her cheek.

"I'm going to try," said Mildred gently, "I understand now. I understand it all. I hope I'm not too late, but I'm going to try."

Then she was gone, back into the mind, as the wall of white heat slowly closed behind her. It was time to go into the light.

The wasp's bulbous eyes glared angrily at itself as it passed the huge mirror that filled the windows of their tiny insect. Silence filled the air as two of the cloaked figures sat motionless, while behind them, another sat crying into the hands she pressed inside the dark hood. Marburg stared out of the window, easily ignoring the pain next to him. Below, the gigantic shape of Mildred Potts, 80, lay motionless, causing his grin to widen. One of the hooded figures pulled the wasp upward, and it landed softly on the pink wallpaper before crawling behind the frame of the mirror and into the small hole that was their exit. In the dark interior, Marburg's smile remained as the image of Mildred's dead body played over in his mind, making him only happier. It was a scene he was sure he would remember always. A scene that would live in internal history forever. A history that would be remembered as his making.

Mildred Potts's lifeless body lay on the floor; the banging that had filled the room was now silent. Far above, an insect buzzed loudly then, it too, was gone, fading quickly into nothing as it made its escape. A last cry of 'MILDRED...CAN YOU HEAR ME?' boomed behind the door, before the silence returned, leaving her body to lie cold on the floor below. Outside, the two giant figures in bright yellow jackets bent down to pick up their bags, before turning to leave. Walking down the small overgrown lawn behind the house, neither of them spoke while they both wondered if they had failed or just wasted their time.

    'CRASH!'

Both of them stopped in their tracks, before turning to run back to the door. One of them went to shout a warning, but before the words could escape he felt the door handle turn easily in his grasp. Excitement filled him, and he pushed it open to see the same scene that had obsessed Marburg only seconds before. An old lady, her cold unseeing eyes staring at her outstretched arm. But something had changed. A small something that would have made Marburg stare in horror. For no longer was Mildred's hand lying coldly on the tiled floor, now it was wrapped tightly around the leg of a fallen chair. The chair that, only moments before, had been blocking the door.

"Get the box," said one of the men as he pressed his fingers against Mildred's neck, "I can't find a pulse."

I did it…I did it, Malcolm.

The light was bright, too bright, and she squinted, pushing it out of her head. Through the blur, she could just make out the outline of flowers and balloons at the end of her bed, before the light stabbed into her brain once more. Instinctively, she raised a hand to cover her eyes, desperate to understand what was happening, when a familiar voice stopped her in her tracks.

"Welcome back, Maggie Pincus."

Looking out between her fingers, Maggie saw the bald head of Thaddeus Miles through tired eyes. Slowly, she lowered her hands as she tried to work out where she was.

"You're in hospital," he said as though reading her mind, "you're quite safe. Nothing to worry about... for now."

Maggie tried to stare at him, but the light was making her head hurt and as she reached up, she felt the bandage that was wrapped tightly around it.

"You've had quite a nasty accident there. It seems you were found unconscious outside the mind with lots of cuts on your head. No one's quite sure where you got them from. I mean, I think I know, but then no one really wants to listen to anything I have to say right now. It seems that there's already too many questions being asked to add any of mine into the mix. In fact, that's why the prime minister asked me to be here when you woke up. He's the one who sent you all these flowers by the way, he's very keen to be nice to you, it seems that he wants to make sure that you're in agreement with what happened last week. That Mildred Potts, 80 was a confused old lady who blocked all the doors in her house and then accidentally shut down when her heart malfunctioned. Fortunately, she was able to let in the ambulance men who successfully re-started her heart, saving all the internals trapped inside her. That is what happened, isn't it? I mean, we both know that the last thing the prime minister wants right now is for the Internal National News to start digging into what really happened to Mildred."

Maggie nodded slowly. The pain in her head stabbed again, and she blinked it down, trying to make sense of everything that she was hearing. For some reason, they wanted nothing to do with the truth of how Marburg had been the one stop Mildred's heart, but something inside told her not to fight the lie. That this was for the best.

"So, what's going to happen to Mildred now?" she said finally.

"Well, that's where the good news begins. It seems that your beloved Mildred Potts, 80…sorry… *our* beloved Mildred Potts, 80, has been given a reprieve. After everyone saw her come back to life, the last thing the prime minister wants to do is to try and close her again. So, she's to be given a full refit. As we speak, they are scooping out all of her fat deposits, bringing in new nerves, repairing her bones, and hiring new muscles. They've even decided to re-open the orphanage, which means that you no longer have to leave, and you and your friends will be getting lots of new children joining you. It seems that the future is suddenly bright for our Mildred. Even she seems to be playing along. For some unknown reason she seems to be rather happy with everything nowadays. Almost as if someone had talked to her and made her see things… differently."

Maggie looked down, trying to hide her smile, as she avoided his eyes.

"Of course there's bad news, too, there's always bad news. You see, all of this has helped me to remember where I know you from," he said in a gentle whisper, leaning over her bed.

For what felt an eternity, he stared at her, and Maggie tried to work out what to say.

"Of course, no one wants to hear my theory on who you are. It seems that the timing is far too 'inconvenient' right now with this scandal going on. They'd just prefer that you, and I, both keep our mouths closed about this forever. So, that's what we're going to do. I'll stay in charge and you'll live here with your little friends. But, just between you and I, you should know that I'll be watching you, Maggie Pincus. I know that there's something very different about you, and I know that you know it, too. If you really are who I think you are, then I've been looking for you for a very long time. And I'll be around to make sure that your future is very different to the one that's been predicted."

Maggie stared back at him as hard as she could, until another stab of pain pierced her thoughts. Ignoring her pain, Thaddeus Miles turned and picked up his jacket from the back of the chair, before walking toward the door.

"I'll be sure to let the prime minister know how you're doing," he said brightly, without looking back, "In the meantime, enjoy your three little friends. They've been waiting outside for days. I'm glad you're feeling better, Maggie Pincus."

Maggie watched him go as she tried to make sense of everything he had said. After all that had happened, she thought they must have realized who she truly was, at the very least she had expected to be in trouble. She had done lots of things that an internal wasn't supposed to do after all, but now it seemed as though she might have escaped without anyone blaming her for any of it. Doubtless, Minister Miles was mad at her, but what did she care? Stick was gone, so nothing really mattered. Sure she was happy that

Mildred was going to live, and it was good news that she could still live here while she worked out what to do next. But it didn't change anything. Stick was dead and it was her fault. And what was he talking about, 'three little friends?' Did he not know what had happened?

"MAGGIE!" The door flew open.

Maggie stared wide-eyed as she tried to make sense of what she was seeing.

"STICK!" she finally screamed, jumping out of bed and pulling him into a hug, "Is it really you?"

Stick returned the hug; his cheeks began to flush red.

"Ah, look at him blush like a little girl!" said another voice behind him.

Maggie turned to see two others standing next to her.

"PRITCH...TAYLOR!" she screamed.

She grabbed them both, squeezing them into the hug as Stick gave a nervous choke, which Maggie ignored. At that moment, she didn't care about anything but this. She could only hold them tight as she said their names over and over as their arms wrapped around her.

"Come along now!" said a thin voice behind them, "I said before, just one visitor at a time! You three have been sneaking in here all week and it's not good at all. She'll be out of here before you know it, but for now I must insist that two of you leave!"

Maggie opened one eye and looked at the perfectly round woman in the red uniform who stood glaring at them.

"Sorry, nurse," said Pritch happily, "me and Taylor promised we'd go show the new kids at the orphanage around, so we really should be going anyway. But don't worry. We promise not to sneak in here later for another visit!"

The nurse glared at the two girls as they left, before busying herself with peeling back two flaps of skin, revealing a large window.

"Ten minutes, and that's it!" she said, leaving Stick and Maggie alone.

Silence filled the air as Maggie got out of bed and slowly walked over to the window, trying to decide what to say next. So much had happened and she still wasn't sure what to make of it all, or what she could tell Stick. Outside, she saw the gigantic world of a hospital room. It, too, was filled with flowers that circled the room, barely leaving space for the tall machine that flashed quietly in the corner as it monitored the grey haired patient who sat in the bed next to it.

"She's been up and walking already," said Stick, pulling open another window, "She's even had visitors. Turns out she's got two sisters and a brother. First thing she did after she woke up was to call them. She keeps talking about making up for lost time, and I don't think that smile has left her face since everything happened. She's like a whole new woman."

Maggie stared out at Mildred Potts, 80, while sitting in her hospital bed. Her face looked different, so full of life, and a rush of pride ran through Maggie as she realized that Mildred had finally found the strength to do what Malcolm had always wanted. She was living again.

"Have I really been here for a week?" she said finally.

"Yeah," said Stick with a grin, "and you're not going to believe everything that's happened while you've been asleep either! I was in the bed next to you for a while, but they let me out a few days ago. We've been taking it in turns sitting with you ever since. It's not been easy, not with old moody nurse Globin chasing us out all the time."

Maggie smiled. The memory of him dead in her arms filled her, before a rush of happiness swept it away as she watched him pick at one of the huge slices of grape from the bowl next to her bed.

"I have so much to tell you," he said absentmindedly, chewing, "first of all, Mildred isn't getting closed down! We can stay! And you won't even recognize the dorm anymore. It's like a hotel! Old Devlin's still there. Turns out she'd spent so much time lying about how sad she was to leave us that when they decided not to close Mildred, the prime minister himself told her that she could have her job back! But, get this, now she has to be nice to us! She's terrified that we'll tell anyone what we know, so she actually has to do her job properly. I've had breakfast in bed twice this week and she's promised to get us all tickets to DizzysKneeLand this summer! They've got a rollercoaster that goes all the way up to the top of his head, and spins you round ten times, before you get back down to his feet. I swear it'll make you throw up! It's going to be awesome!"

Maggie's smile broadened as she listened to Stick. She was thinking about Mildred, remembering the old woman who had carried her out of the mind when she had lost contact with her body. Mildred, who

486

had told her she was going back to reconnect with her body. Mildred had done what she couldn't. She had found help. Mildred had saved them all.

"I haven't told anyone who you really are," said Stick suddenly, snapping Maggie back. "Not even Pritch or Taylor. And we've all sworn to keep it a secret about Marburg, too. Thaddeus told us that we had to, otherwise they might start asking what really happened that day, and if that happened then they might just have to split us up after all."

Maggie walked back over to her bed, and Stick sat down next to her. His smile had suddenly disappeared and he stared at his feet. Maggie reached out to touch his hand but stopped as he gave a nervous cough.

"Thank-you, Maggie," he said hesitantly, "I know that it was you who saved me. I know because I was already awake when they started Mildred's heart again. I watched the electric shock, that the ambulance men put in her, fill her heart to get it started again, and I remember that there was another shock before that. One that brought me back to life. I remember it all, and I know it was you. They'd have never been able to start her heart again if it was still full of poison, and you did something that killed all of the stuff Marburg put in it

—the same stuff he put in me. I know it was you, and I know that it means you do have special powers, after all—like Marburg said you did. All the stuff that happened…the zit exploding out of nowhere at school…me beating Ridge at the hormone battle…it was you…you were helping me along, but I promise I'll never say a word. I just want to say thank-you, you know, because you saved my life."

He held Maggie's hand, and his smile returned.

"You don't have to say thank-you. I think I did some things…felt some things. I don't understand, I guess they are powers, but I really don't know how to use them, so can we just forget them? Please, I just want things to be normal. I'd rather pretend that they just don't exist. Please don't say thank-you. I did something, but I really don't know how I did it."

"So, what are you going to do now?" said Stick eventually, "I mean, are you thinking of going back… to being a soul? I won't say anything if you are. I mean, I hope you stay, but if it's what you…."

"Of course I'm staying, you big idiot!" she said before he could finish, "You guys are more family to me than those others will ever be. This is where I live now. Mildred Potts, 80 is home!"

Stick beamed. "Okay, but if I'm going to keep your secret, then I'll have to call you nobo…like a lot!

"And I'm going to have to call you dork…like even more!" Maggie smiled.

Malcolm, you knew all along. When I thought I couldn't do it, you knew. You knew that I could. Now I see it, too. I thought that I couldn't do this without you, but now I know. I'm not alone. That's why you sent the girl—to make me see that you'll always be with me. I hope she'll be okay. I did the best I could to help her. I will do this, Malcolm…for us. I got out of bed today. I don't even remember the last time I got out of bed. There's a playground outside my window, it's surrounded by trees. I forgot how beautiful the outside could be. Thank-you, Malcolm. I won't let you down. I'll do what you asked, I'll be happy…I promise.

30

Scar Tissue

Mildred walked barefoot through the grass. The sun felt warm on her face and she laughed heartily as she approached her sister, who was pulling a face at Mildred's bright pink outfit.

"What?" laughed Mildred as she knelt to unroll her mat, "The man in the store said it made me look twenty years younger!"

High above, perched on the edge of a bright green leaf, four tiny figures sat watching the yoga lesson beginning below. The warm sun spread between them. Looking down, they all watched with silent pride as Mildred stretched out both her arms wide, while balancing on one leg, drawing impressed looks from the younger members of the class.

"How does she do that?" said Pritch in amazement.

Two months had passed since the day Mildred had nearly died, and they all were still amazed at how much life had changed. As promised, Mildred had undergone a full refurbishment, including a new gym, swimming pool, and movie theater. Even the food was better now, and Rita and Rita's kitchen was always crowded with guests, despite the special supply of booger bangers that they kept on the boil, at all times, just for Stick. Miss Devlin, too, was keeping her promise, and if you could ignore her strained smile you would only see an orphanage that had become a fine home to over 200 happy children. Best of all, Mildred herself seemed happy after all these years. No longer did she sit in her living room staring at the TV. Now her days were spent outdoors, filled with laughter and friends, oblivious to the thousands of internals who spent their days on her shoulder enjoying life above their homes.

"Do you think she'll stay like this forever?" asked Stick.

Pritch casually bounced her foot against the green leaf's edge as Taylor pulled out a bag of candy, before offering it to the others.

"I certainly hope so," said Maggie, picking a green gummy hair, "This is good."

"Yep, well as good as it is, I can't hang around here all day," said Taylor through a mouthful of bubbly gums, "I promised to help teach some of the younger kids to swim in ten minutes."

Jumping to her feet, she watched as a gigantic butterfly landed perfectly on the leaf's edge just inches away from her.

"Wait for me!" said Maggie, chasing after her. "I've got somewhere to be, too."

Back inside Mildred Potts, 80, Maggie waited, patiently, for the hallway to be empty before ducking under the secret flap of skin in the ear canal that was a short cut to her mind. Since the day Mildred had nearly died, Thaddeus Miles had ordered the whole area restricted but it hadn't taken long for Stick to show her how to make a secret tunnel that allowed her to get past his barriers.

Once inside, she ducked beneath the 'DANGER' sign that covered the doorway before walking in to feel the heat of Mildred's mind tingle against her skin. Pressing her hand against the fleshy wall, she waited, feeling for the movement that would tell her that Mildred was lying flat at the end of her yoga lesson.

Something inside her told her that this was the right moment, and without pause, she walked directly into the fiery wall as it disappeared behind her.

"Mildred?" said Maggie softly.

Slowly the figure in front of her turned. The white cord that hung from the ceiling slowly detached from her head.

"Maggie! I'm so glad you came!" she said, pulling her in for a hug, "I'm so sorry, I haven't got long. I get to lie down and meditate at the end of yoga for five minutes. Really I just take a nap, but it's just long enough for me to detach and see you without the internals getting suspicious!"

"That's okay," said Maggie. "I'm just happy to see you. How are you?"

Mildred smiled. "I'm good—thanks to you!"

"Oh stop!" said Maggie, smiling back at her, "I didn't do anything. If you hadn't started all your machines up, we'd have all been dead. I should be the one thanking you!"

Mildred laughed deeply. They had been seeing each other regularly for weeks now but every conversation seemed to start this way, before quickly turning to talk about what was happening in their lives.

"What did you say these were called again?" said Mildred through a mouthful of something grey.

"Candy liver chunks," said Maggie, pulling one out of her pocket for herself.

"Boy! This does not taste like liver on the outside!" said Mildred, licking her fingers, "If all liver tasted like this, kids out there would be begging to eat it!"

Maggie laughed. She wanted to stay here all day with her friend, but something was telling her it was time to go.

"I think the yoga teacher just told you all to sit up," said Maggie.

"How do you do that?" said Mildred, getting to her feet, "It's spooky!"

"I have no clue!" Maggie laughed, "Anything I can bring you next time? Black and White Bladder Beans, Vanilla Diaphragm Balls, Sugar Sternum Sticks?"

"Those would all be great!" said Mildred as she hovered the white tube over her head. "How about you? Anywhere you want me to take you this week? My brother keeps inviting me to visit him. How do you and the others fancy a few days by the coast?"

Maggie smiled before turning to leave.

"Whatever makes you happy is fine with me," she said over her shoulder, "see you in a few days."

Mildred smiled as she pulled down on the tube. Maggie stepped through the wall.

It was time for them both to get on with life.

Malcolm, I understand now. I'm not alone. I was never alone. I don't know why I was chosen to outlive you, and I don't think I'll ever get used to it, but I see now that there is still a life out there for me...a life with friends and family. It'll never be as good as the one I had with you, but it can still be a good life...and I choose to live it.

Deep in the shadows, on a tiny leaf, two cloaked figures stood watching as Maggie Pincus boarded the butterfly, leaving her three friends behind. Quickly, the brightly colored wings fluttered to life as they lifted into the warm air, before beginning a scattered path down toward the old giant, dressed all in pink, below. Silently, it landed on her shoulder as she turned to look at it, her smile widening as the sun reflected off its wings. Gently, she offered it her finger, hoping that it would crawl aboard, as it graciously accepted the short cut to its final destination.

Mildred reached forward in a stretch as the butterfly shuffled impatiently on top of her nail. Others in the class looked over now, all of them smiling, their eyes unable to see the two tiny figures emerge from beneath the butterfly and scurry toward the entry below Mildred's nail.

High above, the two cloaked figures looked down, their tiny eyes seeing what the giants could not.

"I don't know if I hate her or adore her right now!"

Pethora looked up from inside her hood as a pained look appeared in her eyes. The shining blonde hair still hung freely, but her face was changed. No longer was she the beauty that she adored being. Now half of her face was wrinkled beneath burned skin, a remnant of the day she had fallen into Mildred's mind wave as she tried to stop Maggie.

"It's true," said Pethora, her withered lips cracking behind her words, "she is…gifted."

"She is beyond gifted!" growled the dark hood next to her, "She removed the Marburg virus from a heart! Do you know what sort of power you have to have over a body to do something like that? She even brought an internal back to life. She is beyond incredible!"

Pethora dabbed at a line of drool that fell from her damaged face. Her anger at hearing him flatter Maggie was almost too much to bear, and she spat the last of her spittle on the floor before staring up at him with eyes full of fury.

"Oh, do get over yourself, Pethora!" he said dismissively, "It's just a face. So, now you're ugly. Get used to it. How you look is irrelevant. We are at war here!"

Pethora stared down at her feet, feeling the shame of his words.

"What really matters now is that girl down there," he said, stabbing a thick finger at the tiny figure far below. "She may have wandered and forgotten who she is, but she is part of the prophecy. I just need to put her with the other two and she'll see sense. Once they are together, once they realize how powerful they are, it will all become clear. This is happening, Pethora, just as I knew it would. We may have just lost the battle, but we are about to crush the war."

From inside the cloak, two hands emerged to scoop back the hood, removing the dark from the face within. Free of the shadows, his bald head seemed to shine beneath the stubbly flecks of silver that circled his ears and face, while his blue eyes shone bright with excitement. The same blue eyes that he had given to Maggie.

"Yes, Arac. Of course, you're right. I'm sorry, I'm being selfish," said Pethora meekly.

But Arac heard nothing. He was crouched at the edge of the leaf, staring down at the tiny Maggie who was about to disappear beneath Mildred's nail.

"You are my daughter," he said to her, "and, soon, you are going to win this war—for me!"

Book 1: The End

Made in the USA
Middletown, DE
24 September 2019